The Affair

Books by Morton Hunt

THE NATURAL HISTORY OF LOVE
HER INFINITE VARIETY: The American Woman as
    Lover, Mate and Rival
MENTAL HOSPITAL
THE TALKING CURE
    (*with Rena Corman and Louis R. Ormont*)
THE INLAND SEA
THE THINKING ANIMAL: A Report on the Rational and
    Emotional Life of Modern Man
THE WORLD OF THE FORMERLY MARRIED
THE AFFAIR: A Portrait of Extra-Marital Love
    in Contemporary America

The Affair

A Portrait of Extra-Marital Love
in Contemporary America

by MORTON HUNT

An NAL Book
THE WORLD PUBLISHING COMPANY
New York / *Cleveland*

First Printing—1969
Published by The New American Library, Inc.
in association with The World Publishing Company,
2231 West 110th Street, Cleveland, Ohio 44102

Library of Congress Catalog Card Number: 73-96924
Printed in the United States of America

WORLD PUBLISHING
TIMES MIRROR

To Eveline

contents

chapter 3   TEMPTATION

chapter 4   CONSUMMATION

chapter 5   FLOURISHING

chapter 6   DECAYING

chapter 7   AFTERMATH

Contents

author's note

Marital infidelity in all its forms—ranging from the occasional secret daydream through the chronic "one-night stand" to the once-in-a-life-time *grand amour*—is a subject of considerable interest to nearly all adult Americans; indeed, many find it the most engrossing of all contemporary concerns. The historians of some future civilization may think us frivolous or foolish for having been absorbed by this matter at a time when thousands of nuclear weapons were poised on launching pads around the world, when the planet's air and water were being fouled by our own effluvia, and when the growing loss of both external and internal controls over violence seemed to portend the disintegration of our society. But we are not the historians of some future civilization; we are the hapless citizens of today, the inhabitants of a world so impersonal, so disconnected, so unconcerned about our individual needs that we assign immense value to our love relationships, seeking in them all that is lacking elsewhere in modern life. Unfortunately, married love is rarely able to provide more than a part of what we hunger for; accordingly, extra-marital love is not a trivial matter, but one of considerable importance to us.

Yet despite its importance, there is astonishingly little writing about it except in the form of fiction and drama—neither of which can be uncritically taken as a guide to reality, since each is more apt to interpret life than to transcribe it. As for non-fiction writing on the subject, there are only a few statistical studies, some reporting of case material by therapists, a handful of confessional autobiographies (mostly by sex-symbol film stars), and a good deal of exhortation by ministers. The actual experiences of unfaithful men and women—their very words and deeds, their guilt and joy, their poetry and perspiration—have gone almost unrecorded, even though they are as fascinating as anything in fiction and a far more reliable source of information about the meaning of infidelity in modern life.

The present book will, I hope, go part way toward filling this gap. In it I have tried to describe the major types of extra-marital affair in contemporary America as I learned about them from people I interviewed or to whom I sent questionnaires. From their stories, it became clear to me that different kinds of affairs interact with different kinds of marriages in patterned ways—some extremely damaging to the marriages, others relatively innocuous, and still others distinctly beneficial. But although I have offered such generalizations as seem valid and illuminating to me, this is not primarily a work of advocacy or doctrine; my major aim has been to record and re-create a series of significant extra-marital experiences, and to make it possible for the reader to share the lives of other people and vicariously feel what they felt. At different times during my research I was titillated, amused, troubled, overjoyed, or deeply distressed by the things I heard, but throughout I was fascinated and in the end I was informed. I hope the same will be true of my readers.

I have not attempted to be encyclopedic. This is a portrait of the extra-marital affair in American society today, with the emphasis on the patterns of behavior of the white middle class; lower-class, and especially Negro lower-class, concepts of sexuality, love, and marriage differ considerably from those of the white middle class and deserve to be described in a separate book. I have, moreover, either excluded or mentioned only in passing certain kinds of extra-marital behavior too remote from the central theme of this book to warrant treatment here—homosexual or incestuous affairs, sexual experiences with prostitutes, and forms of extra-conjugal sex which have no relation to the affair, such as rape and masturbation.

But within these limits, the book presents the fruits of research on a national scale. I describe my research methods in some detail in the Notes on Sources; briefly, however, my information comes from the following:

—Ninety-one tape-recorded depth interviews running from one to fifteen hours of total interview time; the subjects were men and women in all parts of the country, nearly all of whom had had or were still having extra-marital affairs (the remainder consisted of "wronged" mates, or unmarried lovers of persons having such affairs);

—A small number of diaries—most of them brief, one very extensive—kept by various interviewees; a dozen collections of letters exchanged by extra-marital lovers; and sundry tape-recorded comments and observations by friends, acquaintances, ex-mates, ministers, doctors, and others involved with some of the key interviewees;

—Nearly forty interviews and much correspondence with psychologists, psychiatrists, sociologists, marriage counselors, and other persons with special knowledge of the subject;

—Three hundred and sixty completed replies from respondents all over the country to a questionnaire designed and administered on my behalf by a social-science research team at an eastern university;

—The previously published data and findings of other persons; I reviewed some hundreds of items, the most useful of which are listed in the Bibliography.

Of all these sources, by far the most enlightening and vivid were my ninety-one depth interviews. In polls and opinion surveys, including my own, samples consist of many hundreds of persons; this provides statistical validity, as far as the answers go—which isn't very far, since the kinds of questions that lend themselves to exact scoring on a large scale rarely yield insight or the feeling of actual experience. To live in imagination within other people's flesh, and to learn what their extra-marital experiences had meant to them, I had to concentrate upon small-sample investigation-in-depth rather than large-sample experience-in-breadth. Not that my sample seemed small to me; by the time I had heard ninety-one life stories, I felt I had lived as long as the Wandering Jew, and was as ready to rest.

The large-scale statistical studies, moreover, can be misleading to the unwary. The Kinsey data, for example, show how many men in each age group are unfaithful, and what per cent of their "outlet" is achieved outside of marriage. But these figures were compiled by equating every orgasm with every other orgasm; the one-hour chance copulation with a stranger far from home is treated as equivalent to the love-making of two people who experience exaltation with each other that they have never known with their mates. Extra-marital acts can range from the casual to the involved, the bestial to the inspirational, the sybaritic to the guilt-ridden, but the statistics on incidence, average frequency and duration, and the like, do not make such distinctions. Yet one has only to listen attentively and non-judgmentally, as I have tried to do, for these meaningful distinctions to become evident.

But what is the crucial factor that underlies these distinctions? According to what principle can one distinguish among the various types of affairs so as to make sense of their disparate causes, meanings, and effects? After testing a dozen hypotheses on my material, I concluded that the most significant factor seemed to be the *degree of involvement*—the extent of intimacy, ego identification, sharing of goals, and so on—between the lovers, and also between each one and his or her mate. It is along this major dimension, therefore, that I have classified my material. Four major case histories appear intermittently throughout this book; two represent variations of the high-involvement affair and two represent variations of the medium- or low-involvement affair, while the marriages of the various participants run the gamut. But even four archetypal histories, however carefully selected, could not tell the whole story; bits and pieces of some sixty other stories therefore appear throughout these pages in the effort to do justice to the richness and diversity of the human experiences I have been made privy to.

All the men and women who told me their stories did so in the knowledge that I was writing this study, but with my assurance that I would carefully preserve their anonymity. Every significant deed, speech, and emotion in this book is drawn from real life; I have, however, scrupulously hidden the identities of the persons involved by altering their names and various other external characteristics, while preserving the psychological and social dynamics involved. Any resemblance to real persons is strictly intentional; any identification with real persons is, I trust, impossible.

Many of those I interviewed wanted to know whether my purpose was to condemn affairs as immature, selfish, neurotic, and destructive, or to argue for freer and more permissive attitudes toward infidelity as the salvation of modern monogamy. These represent the first two of the three possible moral attitudes toward infidelity described by Bishop James A. Pike in *You and the New Morality*. The three he names are: *code ethics,* with its precise and invariable rules ("Thou shalt not commit adultery"); *non-normative contemporary ethics,* ("Anything goes" or "Do what you like as long as you don't hurt anyone"); and *situation ethics,* in which the balance of right or wrong, good or bad, in any voluntary act depends on the total set of circumstances and the probable effects of the act. The latter is my position. The evidence, I believe, clearly shows that in some circumstances an extra-marital affair severely damages the marriage, the participants, and even such innocent bystanders as the children; in other circumstances it does none of these things, and is of no consequence; and in still other circumstances it benefits the marriage by ameliorating discontent, or shatters the marriage but benefits the individual by awakening him to his own emotional needs and capabilities. I therefore believe that each extra-marital act ought to be judged as morally evil, morally neutral, or morally good, according to the totality of the circumstances and the effects on all concerned.

This is not a simple ethic, but it is the one that seems valid to me. But it is not a view I adopted beforehand; it is the conclusion I drew from what I had observed. I invite my readers to lay aside their own presuppositions and look with me at the hidden reality all around us; when they have done so, let each agree or disagree with me as he chooses.

—MORTON HUNT

New York
February, 1969

Humani nil a me alienum puto.
(Nothing human is foreign to me.)

—TERENCE

chapter 1: ONE TERM, MANY MEANINGS

i the affair: a sampler

Men like to ask themselves vast abstract questions to which no single answer is ever adequate. Queries such as "What is matter?", "What is life?", or "What is love?" yield much philosophizing but little enlightenment; they are too broad to permit more than vague generalizations by way of reply. But every such question can be subdivided into smaller, more specific questions, and these are more nearly answerable in concrete and meaningful terms. Physicists no longer strive to say what matter is; it has proven much more productive to say how matter behaves at various energy levels. Biologists no longer seek a general definition of "life," finding it more fruitful to explore the specific ways in which living things, from virus to man, interact with their environments and duplicate themselves. Similarly, behavioral scientists no longer try to say what love is, but rather what it consists of and how it functions in given cultures and between persons of given psychological types.

So, too, with the question, "What is an extra-marital affair in present-day America?" Although in other times and places the extra-marital affair might have had one dominating pattern and one generally agreed-upon meaning—a proof of *machismo* in one society, the expression of idealistic love in another, and so on—in our own society there are several distinctly different kinds of extra-marital affair, each with its own reasons for being, each with specific effects upon the individuals involved and upon their marriages.

On one day last winter, for instance, the following scenes all took place within a few hours of each other:

—In the late afternoon, at the paper goods section of a supermarket in Denver, a man in his early forties and a somewhat younger woman stop their carts side by side and study the products on the shelves while talking to each other softly. She has the healthy ingenuous look of a Scandinavian country girl; he is tall and bulky, well-dressed but somewhat rumpled. When anyone comes by, they busy themselves with napkins and paper towels, but in moments of semi-privacy they talk about his present project (he is a building contractor), her children (she has three), her latest efforts to get back to part-time work (she was an interior designer ten years ago), how restless he was last night because he wanted her and has not slept with her for ten days, and how she adores the look on his face when he says things like that.

They have been lovers for three years. In her marriage she has never known anything like the easy communication, the total absorption in each other, that she knows with him; he, in his marriage and three previous affairs, was never passionate and truly loving, as he has been with her almost from the beginning. Her marriage is painless, vacant, and businesslike; his has long been quietly hostile and virtually asexual. He and she progressed from initial joy to subsequent guilt and the agonies of seeking justification, and then to a period of searching for an ultimate answer. Her father is, however, a prominent conservative minister, and she could not face the prospect of scandalizing and alienating him by divorce; the contractor, meanwhile, has held off starting his own struggle for a divorce until she does. They reached this impasse almost two years ago and gave up discussing the subject in order not to be broken apart by it. They spend one afternoon a week in bed together at the apartment of a bachelor friend of his, and sometimes manage a summer evening at another friend's mountain lodge not far away; nearly every day they talk on the phone while her children are in school, and two or three times a week they arrange to see each other for a few minutes in the supermarket, the library, a large book-store, or the lobby of a hospital, in order to hold hands, to look at each other, and to talk about everyday things. So it has been for a long while; the frozen surface of their marriages is all sham, but beneath it, unseen, their love flows on and is the reality of their lives.

—In a Cleveland hotel a well-tailored, lamp-tanned man of thirty-five or so sits on his bed, staring out the window; it is getting dark outside, and a long empty evening lies ahead. He pores through a small green leather address book and then dials a number. "Julie, honey!" he says in radiant genial tones, and waits for a surprised, happy reply. A look of puzzlement comes over his face. "Why, sweetheart," he says, "it's Ellis. I wrote you I'd be here some time this week—didn't you get my card? . . . Do I gather you can't talk freely now? Can I ask questions and you just say yes or no? Good. You've got someone else there—another travelling friend. No? . . . A relative, then. No? . . . You haven't gone and got married —you *have?* . . . Hey, darling, that's wonderful! Couldn't happen to a nicer gal. Congratulations! . . . Okay, I'll cut out now before I get you in trouble. So long—and good luck." He hangs up and curses softly. Three strikes and out—not one working contact left in Cleveland, and four days to kill here. Better get going, he tells himself; he smooths the sides of his hair, adjusts his tie, and heads off for a downtown bar to look for a replacement.

A manufacturer's representative, he covers a six-state area, spending a quarter of his time at home with his wife, the other three quarters on the road with, as he tells his male friends, "my twenty-five to thirty other wives." He is a dutiful, if very limited, husband to them: About once a week every one of his current female friends gets a brief card or note from him and thinks herself something special in his life; each sees him and sleeps with him about once every couple of months and finds him a warm and enthusiastic lover. The only exception is his legal wife; she gets little from him but complaints about her housekeeping and her budget, and although he sleeps with her, their love-making is wordless, perfunctory, and swift. For years she wondered why he changed so soon after marriage from the warm and considerate lover she had known; she could find no answers, and gave up seeking them long ago. Now and then she accuses him of being interested in some other woman, but he either laughs at her scornfully or flies into a righteous rage. She once studied his address book when she had a chance, but found no women's names in it; it never occurred to her that he uses a code, and that over a hundred names in it, accumulated through the years, represent women he has had affairs with in a decade of marriage.

—A station wagon parks in front of a shabby rooming-house in a working-class neighborhood of Camden, New Jersey; a young woman, prim and plain-featured but voluptuous of figure, gets out, looks around the dark street nervously, and hurries inside. She climbs to the fourth floor and knocks on a door. A husky black-haired man, his shirt open halfway to the waist, lets her in and locks the door; smiling, but without a word, he takes her coat off and slowly draws her into his embrace. She pulls off her glasses and throws them on a chair; they clutch at each other and writhe, uttering small pleased sounds as though tasting something good. In another moment he picks her up, laughing, and dumps her on the narrow bed. For the next half hour their conversation consists chiefly of monosyllabic sounds, laughter, and appreciative murmurs; the only words they speak are of ultimate simplicity— "You're something!", "Oh yes!", and "Now, *now!*" Later, when they are calm, they lie together silent and half asleep, and after a while start all over again.

As she is leaving, it occurs to her that in nearly two hours she has exchanged no more than a few dozen words with him. Driving home, she thinks about this with mingled shame and pride: She, the wife of a departmental chairman of history at an ivy-league college and herself a Ph.D. candidate in English literature, she, a contemporary bluestocking, has discovered in herself the capacity—and an addict's craving—for simple, animal sex. Joe, an Italian-born long-distance truck-driver with a wife and three children six hundred miles away, gets to town about once every ten days and spends a couple of hours with her in wild, wordless coupling; each time, before meeting him, she looks forward to it with almost unendurable eagerness, but when she tries to imagine spending a whole day or even a weekend with him, she recoils at the thought: What would they say to each other, what would they *do*, when they were too fatigued to continue? Even after five months of the relationship, she is still quite astonished that one so shy, cerebral, and idealistic as she should be able to enjoy this man as a pure stud—and to be, as he assures her she is, "a great lay."

—In the evening, a man and woman, both in their early thirties, sit in a car parked by a beach near Bridgeport, Connecticut. They look out over the still, dim stretch of water; they hold hands, sigh, gaze at each other—two pale ovals, darkly smudged with eyes, mouths, nostrils; they whisper endearments and cover each other's faces with gentle kisses. They speak of their longing for each other, their feelings of loyalty toward their families, their surprise at being in this situation. They speak of the thing that brought them together —the play, being done by a local drama group, in which they both have leading roles; they discuss the scenes they are to rehearse tonight, delighting in each other's comments and finding each other sensitive and thoughtful. He looks at his watch; they have had an hour together and must hurry to the rehearsal.

In the three months since they fell in love, this is all that has happened between them except in imagination. He was raised a Congregationalist in Connecticut, she a Catholic in Boston, both in staid and moralistic homes. Although each suffers spells of excruciating desire for the other (the worst times being when they are lying beside their mates in the dark, trying to fall asleep), and they have talked a great deal about how and when to consummate their love, they remain immobilized by fear, guilt, and the thought that thus far they have done nothing "wrong." At least, so it was until recently, but three times during the last month he was unable to make love to his wife when he tried to; deeply alarmed, he went to his doctor for a check-up and a long talk, and learned that he was physically healthy but suffering the psychological effects of infidelity. He has begun to think that he ought to confess everything to his wife, hoping that she will do or say something that will make his decisions for him and "clear the way"—but to what, he does not even know.

—In the privacy of his library, in his suburban home outside Chicago, a graying but youthful businessman takes out and re-reads a letter that arrived at his office today; it is safe to do so, for his wife never disturbs him when he is at work. The letter, from a young divorcee who lives a third of the way across the country, reads, in part:

. . . . You know, my darling, that I am writing this not because I want to, but because I have to. I don't think I'll ever get over what happened just before Christmas, when I came home from our stay together with such deep, swelling, tender feelings to face absolute nothingness. Ed, dear, I need to love someone very much; I'm filled with ideas, thoughts, discussions, emotions, and without someone to give them to I'll just shrivel up. But I can't share and give everything that I have via the Post Office, the phone company, and two or three weekends with you per year. We have to put it on a different basis. Whenever you're here on business, or I'm there to see my family, let's meet and have fun—and let it go at that. I have to, for my own sanity.

He cradles his head in his hands for a few moments, then puts a sheet of paper in the portable typewriter and replies:

. . . . I said to you the first evening we met, and many times since then, that I have no rights in our relationship. I've told you honestly that I'm well-married, and mean to stay that way. But now I realize that there is *no* relationship at all unless we *both* have rights. Mine include the right to care, and the right to want you to care. I can't accept it any other way. And I think: It is so rare in this world for two people to affect each other as we do. The touch of my hand on your arm when we were walking down Randolph Street and the way you knew all that I meant at that moment. The little looks of special understanding we gave each other the night we went to the theater. The way we talk to each other in a shorthand nobody else could understand. And now you want to continue our relationship but strip it of its emotion and content, leaving me nothing. No, that's not true; there would still be sex, which with you is marvelous—but that's not enough. I must have rights, even if we are a thousand miles apart. Don't make us lose this very rare and special thing we have, even though we keep it at the cost of loneliness and pain.

ii an ambiguous term

The foregoing examples give some idea how wide a range of meanings and experiences the term "extra-marital affair" covers in American life. But it is not easy to specify the absolute limits of that range: The term means different things to different people, some applying it to behavior that others do not think warrants the name.

I asked my questionnaire respondents, for instance, whether the following situation constituted an extra-marital affair: "A married person has sexual relations with someone he or she picked up in a bar"; half the men and women who had never been unfaithful thought it did, but only about a third of the unfaithful agreed. Differences in definition also appear between the sexes: A third to a half more men than women classify as an extra-marital affair a situation in which two married strangers meet at a party, swiftly develop emotional rapport, and have sexual relations that same night. Apparently, women are more apt to define an "affair" as a relationship involving depth of feeling, and would regard quick, spontaneous extra-marital sex as "cheating," "running around," or "stepping out." Even the seemingly unambiguous term "infidelity" is not uniformly defined. A number of men I interviewed felt there was no "real" infidelity involved in having sexual relations with a call girl while away from home on business; to them infidelity means caring for another woman, seeing a lot of her, and spending part of the family income on her.

Such ambiguities may account in part for the lack of expert consensus on the frequency of extra-marital affairs in America or even as to the most common form of affair. Some sociologists assert that the casual sexual encounter is the most typical extra-marital experience, while others think the most typical is the deeper and longer-lasting involvement. But in few of their surveys have they even tried to inquire about the respondent's actual extra-marital experience because of the supposed difficulty of getting answers on so sensitive a subject; instead, they have solicited the respondent's attitude toward infidelity and his estimate of the amount of extra-marital activity around him. The answers to these queries cannot yield a reliable picture of the incidence or meaning of infidelity today, for they are guesswork, at best, and subject to the errors of ignorance and the distortions of wishful thinking.

Other data come from the collected experience of marriage counselors and psychotherapists; these are no better, being distorted by the professional attitudes of the counselors and therapists and even more so by the self-selected nature of their patients. A few years ago the Family Service Association of America, on behalf of *The Ladies' Home Journal*, sent each of its 300 member agencies a questionnaire asking, among other things, for an estimate of the percentage of the agency's clients whose marital problems were connected with infidelity. The answers ranged from less than one per cent in a large city in Florida to almost 100 per cent in a city in Oregon. This certainly cannot mean that adultery is a hundred times as common in Oregon as in Florida; but whatever it does mean, it makes it clear that estimates of adultery based on voluntary clients or patients are virtually worthless.

To date there is still only one major source of sound statistical information on extra-marital sexual activity in the United States—the first and second volumes written by Alfred Kinsey and his associates, of the Institute for Sex Research at Indiana University. Despite the limitations of Kinsey's methodology and sampling procedures—his sample, critics have said, is overweighted with the too-willing; it is more a group of the self-selected than the randomly selected—these reports do say how many men and women in a very large, more-or-less national, sample have ever experienced sexual relations outside their marriages. In brief the findings are these: In each five-year age group of married men, somewhere around a third (27 per cent to 37 per cent) had at least some—that is, at least one —extra-marital experience, while the cumulative figure—the total percentage of men who had extra-marital experience at any time during their married lives—was a good deal larger. As the authors wrote, in their celebrated estimate, "On the basis of these active data, and allowing for the cover-up that has been involved, it is probably safe to suggest that about half of all the married males have intercourse with women other than their wives, at some time while they are married." For women, in each five-year age group between the ages of 26 and 50, somewhere between one in six and one in ten had at least some extra-marital experience; the cumulative incidence was calculated at about one in four, although it is possible, according to the authors, that the true figures might be still higher due to cover-up.

These are the best, and almost the only credible, figures available. But since *Sexual Behavior in the Human Male* was published in 1948 and *Sexual Behavior in the Human Female* in 1953, I returned to the same source to ask what the figures might be today. Dr. Paul Gebhard, successor to Kinsey and present director of the Institute, said that he and his staff, on the basis of their recent work and their general impressions, feel there has been a continuation of previous trends. To quote Dr. Gebhard: "If I were to make an educated guess as to the cumulative incidence figures for 1968, they'd be about 60 per cent for males and 35 to 40 per cent for females. This is change, but not revolution. The idea that there has been a sexual revolution in the past decade or two comes from the fact that we have so rapidly become permissive about what you can say and print. That isn't the same as actual change in behavior; still, all this talk *is* going to change the overt behavior of the next generation." But how much it will do so, and whether men, women, and marriage will prosper or suffer from the changes, is not scientifically predictable; perhaps, though, we will feel entitled to make some reasonable guesses about the future after we have looked at the present more closely.

---

iii an ambivalent people

The ambiguity of the term "extra-marital affair" is part of the general American ambivalence toward such relationships. Despite the immense change in what it is permissible to say and to print, the United States still has a dominant sexual code which disapproves of premarital sex and condemns common-law marriage, illegitimacy, abortion, sexual variations and deviations of most sorts, and, of course, adultery. We hear a great deal today about those growing minorities that openly flaunt the code—the undergraduates who openly sleep together and even room together, the show-business celebrities who freely speak of their love affairs, the homosexuals who publicly indicate their bent through clothing, speech, and the companions they are seen with. What is much more significant, there continues to exist a vast underground of good middle-class citizens who overtly accept the code but in fact secretly disagree with, and violate, one or more parts of it.

In *The Significant Americans*, a study of the sexual mores of upper-middle-class people, sociologist John F. Cuber and his coauthor, Peggy B. Harroff, term the traditional code a "colossal unreality" based on "collective pretense" and on the systematic misrepresentation, by most people, of what they think and do sexually. They are not alone in this finding: Virginia Satir, a leading family therapist and co-founder of the Esalen Institute at Big Sur, told the 1967 convention of the American Psychological Association that "almost any study of sexual practices of married people done today reports that many marital partners do not live completely monogamously. . . . The myth is monogamy. The fact is frequently polygamy."

There are widespread indications of this schism between code and reality. Christian and particularly Calvinist tradition continues to make adultery a punishable offense in the criminal codes of 45 of the 50 states; maximum penalties range from a $10 fine in Maryland to a five-year jail term, plus substantial fines, in Maine, Vermont, South Dakota, and Oklahoma—yet these laws are almost never enforced except when, as very rarely happens, some aggrieved third party introduces a complaint on which the state must act. Prior to 1967 the only ground for divorce in New York was adultery, and accordingly the State granted some 7,000 to 8,000 divorces annually on this ground (the law has since been liberalized), but even though all the defendants were shown in divorce court to have done something that constituted a criminal act, the County District Attorneys prosecuted none of them. Legislators, however, continue to reflect the hypocrisy of their constituents: During New York's penal code revision of 1965, it was proposed that the unenforced and outmoded criminal statute against adultery be removed, but the legislators rejected the suggestion by a three-to-one vote. Even in Illinois, a state which has modernized some of its sex statutes, adultery continues to be a crime if "open and notorious"; in other words, it is criminal if made public knowledge, but non-criminal if kept quiet.

Whatever disapproval most Americans exhibit toward infidelity, their fascination with it is evidenced by the ubiquitousness of the subject in movies, television, novels, and drama; significantly, in these media it is often presented as an exciting and beautiful experience, and even in the movies is no longer required invariably to end in disaster. A story like Elia Kazan's *The Arrangement*, in which adulterous lovers eventually find happiness together in marriage, might have pleased the bohemians and radicals of thirty or forty years ago, but could hardly have been a national best-seller. Yet when the kind of people who read and enjoy this novel today are asked to state how they feel about adultery—even by professional pollsters guaranteeing them anonymity—they tend to give lip service to the traditional code. Are they deliberately lying? Probably not; more likely, they are of two minds about it all, and can find justifications or excuses for it in some cases (including their own, if they have been unfaithful), while condemning it on principle.

A large majority of the respondents to my own questionnaire said they always or usually disapprove of adultery; those who had had affairs themselves were somewhat more tolerant, although even in this group over half were generally disapproving. Other and larger attitude surveys have shown the same thing. As recently as 1958, sociologist Harold Christensen reported that only six to twelve per cent of a sample of midwestern college students thought adultery ever justifiable for men; the figures may have grown in the past eleven years, but not much, if we may judge by other sex-attitude surveys. A national poll conducted for *McCall's* magazine in 1966 showed somewhat larger percentages tolerant of adultery where home life was miserable, the marriage sexless, and the like, but a large majority still condemned it under almost all circumstances. Half of all the *McCall's* respondents, in fact, said they had *never* felt any sympathy with, or tendency to condone, the extra-marital affairs even of friends or acquaintances. Where then, we must ask ourselves, do all those avid movie-goers and TV-watchers, never tired of infidelity as a theme, come from? One can only suppose that what people say they feel about the matter, or even what they think they feel, is only part of what they actually feel.

The most common American attitude toward extra-marital affairs is somewhat like the American attitude toward paying one's income tax: Many people cheat—some a little, some a lot; most who don't would like to, but are afraid; neither the actual nor the would-be cheaters admit the truth or defend their views except to a few confidants; and practically all of them teach their children the accepted traditional code though they neither believe in it themselves nor expect that their children will do so when they have grown up.

This is what the disjunction between code and reality looks like, when one penetrates the facade:

—On a Saturday night, in a meagerly furnished apartment in a large Southern city, a young man and woman sit in stony silence watching television. They had been separated and now are attempting a reconciliation, largely because they have a one-year-old son; it is not going well, however, and despite the effort to live with him again, she is still secretly seeing a man she had had a relationship with during the separation and avoiding her husband's sexual advances whenever possible. Toward midnight they go to bed; he makes a feeble try, she pleads weariness, and he turns his back on her in anger and eventually falls asleep without another word. She lies awake, watching the hands of the luminous clock on the night table. At about 1:30 A.M. a car drives up and stops almost under their window; she recognizes the sound, and swiftly slips out of bed, throws on a coat, and hurries downstairs. The man at the wheel drives off to Lovers' Lane, where the two of them feverishly make love in the cramped back seat. At 4 A.M. she slides herself back between the sheets of the bed, sleeps until the clock goes off at 7:30, and then rises, dresses, and makes breakfast. At 9:30 A.M. she is sitting in front of a classroom full of eight-year-old children at the Methodist church, and beginning the lesson on the meaning of communion.

—In a well-to-do suburb of Philadelphia, a slender, somewhat overdressed and over-coiffed woman of thirty-eight speaks of some new facts she has learned about life since her separation from her husband: "You could ask all these married couples around here and they'd lie in their teeth denying that anything happens except for a little fooling around at parties. But I learned the truth when my husband and I broke up. The first couple of months, about ten of my friends' husbands called me with one excuse or another—some didn't even bother with an excuse—and wanted to take me to dinner, or openly told me what they were after. It shook me up— I didn't know what to believe in any more. Since then, I've noticed things I never used to notice—I've seen Frank's car parked at the Marriott Motel in the afternoon, and Joe Goodbody's car a half block from Lynn's house one night when Lynn's husband was on an out-of-town trip. God! Sometimes I feel so bitter and cynical. I lived in the middle of this for years and never knew what was going on; it was all a lie around me."

—A salesman who represents several small manufacturers tells how he began his infidelities at thirty, after nine years of happy marriage: "It never occurred to me to fool around; I didn't know any different, and none of my friends in our town were doing anything, as far as I knew. Then I started in for myself as a free-lance sales representative in New York, and I saw for the first time how things really were. Everybody was screwing anything they could, whenever they had the chance. People I was doing business with would come to town and expect me to fix them up, or they'd want me to go cruising the bars with them and help them find something. I learned about human nature; I saw it the way you don't see it until you're behind the scenes. And it seemed like everybody was having fun and not getting hurt. So I was *ready.* One night I was having a drink with one of the out-of-town manufacturers I represented, and he sent a note over to two girls in the far corner, and first thing you know we were with them, and it was great fun. Later, I took mine home in a cab and put an arm around her, and the next thing I knew I was making it with her three or four times a week, and really living it up. It was tremendous. I never wanted any of that originally—all I wanted was to be a small-town boy and love my wife."

—In Washington, D.C., a forty-four-year-old woman sums up

the effects of the dozen affairs she has had during her very happy‹ marriage to a man she has never thought of leaving, and who is unaware of her way of life: "When I compare my life to the lives of women I know who haven't had affairs, I feel I'm happier than most of them and my marriage is better than most of theirs. Not that I would ever dare admit it, or urge anyone else to do the same thing. Besides, to tell you the truth, I don't even approve of affairs, on the whole. I feel that most people can't handle them and still have a good solid marriage. But I can, and I don't regret a single one."

—A late-night disc jockey on a southwestern radio station, plump, boyish, and thirty-seven: "One day my wife told me she was going to have dinner and spend the night with some friends who live forty miles away; the maid would sleep in and take care of the kids. So I went to see this girl I was making it with, and because my wife wasn't home and I didn't have to get back any special time that night, I forgot to wake up until early the next morning. When I did, I thought, 'Oh God, if Deirdre gets home first, she'll see that I haven't been there and the fat will be in the fire.' So even though this eager girl is lying next to me naked and waiting, I'm dialing the phone, sweating and trembling and praying I reach Deirdre at her friends' house before she starts home. But when I get the number at last, her friends sound puzzled and say she isn't there and hasn't been, and they hadn't been expecting her.

"So then I knew. I'd wondered for weeks whether she might not be having an affair with my best friend, and now I knew. I left that naked girl right where she was, and threw on my clothes and rushed out to beat Deirdre home and establish my own innocence while confronting her with her lies and her cheating. I was boiling with rage. I drove home like a maniac and she wasn't there, so I mussed up the bed, talked to the maid and the kids for a minute, and then cleared out. In the afternoon she called me at the studio and I told her not to tell me any lies because I knew she hadn't been where she was supposed to have been; I sounded like a hellfire-and-brimstone preacher when I said it. She was quiet for a while and then just said, 'I guess there's nothing to say,' and hung up. Before dark, she and the kids had moved to her parents' house; I came home to an empty house that night and walked around looking at everything and seeing my whole life in ruins. She had been cheating on me with one of my closest friends and didn't even want to be forgiven! That night I woke up with what felt like an immense stone crushing my chest and I grabbed the phone; half an hour later I was in the hospital under an oxygen tent. The attack kept me flat on my back for three weeks. By the time I got out, she had seen a divorce lawyer—she didn't want to come back and didn't give a damn what I thought or felt about it. She actually married that bastard after a while."

*   *   *

It may well be that within a generation or so, the schism between code and reality will greatly narrow and the ambivalence felt by so many Americans about the matter will diminish. The theoretical liberalism of one generation is often absorbed into the feelings of the next one, and what had been permissible only in thought becomes so in action. Yet revolutions, sexual as well as political, change the outward appearance and structure of things more quickly than they do the deeply internalized emotions and habits that constitute much of the stuff of each culture. Fifty years of socialism in Russia have transformed the economy and the power structure of that nation, but most Western observers find the Russians still rather puritanical, submissive, dogged, and given to alternating between moodiness and gaiety. Similarly, the so-called sexual revolution in America will produce certain outward changes —particularly in the direction of greater tolerance of whatever other people do—but much smaller changes in how most people feel about their own behavior; the ambivalence is deep-seated in our character. Significantly, the considerable increase in premarital sexual freedom has not radically altered the basically monogamous nature of the male-female relationship: Young men and women today expect and require fidelity of each other in their premarital love affairs, and infidelity among them remains, by and large, concealed and guilt-producing. Although it does seem likely that there will be some increase in the incidence and openness of extra-marital activity in the next few decades, most Americans will probably continue to keep their unfaithful longings and acts secret, and to profess personal allegiance to the ideal of fidelity.

---

iv a tale of two traditions

American ambivalence about the extra-marital affair is the result not only of the clash between code and reality, but of a mixed cultural heritage which has given us two distinctly different conceptions of marriage and, concomitantly, two distinctly different conceptions of the extra-marital affair, its raison d'être, its hazards, its rewards, and its outcome.

One of these traditions, in existence for a thousand years, views the extra-marital affair not only with tolerance, as a forgivable moral lapse, but positively, as a valuable and even essential part of the full life. This is not as odd or rare a notion as it may sound; on the contrary, what looks both odd and rare in historical and cross-cultural perspective is lifelong fidelity to a single marital partner. Reviewing the data available for 185 societies studied by anthropologists, Professors Clellan S. Ford and Frank A. Beach of Yale University reported that the pattern of lifelong monogamy, with fidelity a requisite, is a virtual anomaly: Only 16 per cent of the 185 had formal restrictions to a single mate, and of those, less than one third wholly disapproved of both premarital and extra-marital liaisons. Actual approval, rather than mere toleration, of extra-marital liaisons of specified types existed in 39 per cent of the societies. Nearly always, women were more restricted in such matters than men, both because they were men's property and because men wanted to be certain their sons were their own; even so, according to Kinsey, 10 per cent of known societies have freely allowed women extra-marital sex and 40 per cent have allowed it to them on special occasions such as seasonal orgiastic festivals or even their own wedding nights (defloration by someone other than the groom—sometimes in the form of the "droit du seigneur"—was formerly widespread in European cultures), or with special persons such as brothers-in-law or honored guests.

It should not come as a surprise, therefore, to realize that our European inheritance brings us not only the rigid Judeo-Christian condemnation of extra-marital relationships but a contrary tradition as well. Greek, Roman, Teutonic, and Celtic strains were stirred into the mix long ago and subordinated to, but never eradicated by, the Christian sexual code. Adultery, celebrated by Ovid as a stimulating and life-enriching game, vanished from the open places for a millennium only to reappear, idealized and ennobled by the troubadours and courtiers of medieval France. *L'amour courtois*, or courtly love, was only pagan love somewhat made over —baptized in Christian values, washed nearly clean of sexuality, but definitely extra-marital in nature; indeed, according to the code of *l'amour courtois*, love is impossible within marriage and can exist only outside it. The lustier side of paganism eventually reappeared as time passed, and was slowly rejoined to courtly love; by the Renaissance, the synthesis of love and sexuality—still directed towards someone other than one's wife or husband—was popular not only with the courtly but was beginning to win favor among the wealthy mercantile class.

But the Reformation and the rise of the bourgeoisie changed things considerably, especially in northern Europe. The Calvinistic middle class, too righteous and too hard-working to spend their energies and their money on illicit love affairs, trimmed and adapted romantic love until it could fit within marriage: The early English Puritans, and most notably John Milton, wrote about marriage with a degree of romanticism and sensuousness that does not at all fit the textbook notion of Puritanism. The poetry, the idealism, the tenderness, the high valuation of womanhood, the dedication of lovers to each other, the belief in the ennobling influence of love, all were borrowed from courtly love and made part of the concept of marriage rather than of extra-marital liaisons.

Thereafter the two traditions—the pagan-courtly and the puritan-bourgeois—tended to crystallize. In the northern European puritan-bourgeois tradition, marriage came to be viewed romantically and idealistically as the most intense, most meaningful of human relationships and the only one in which sex, love, and parenthood were socially and morally acceptable. Any outside emotional or sexual involvement was seen as directly competitive with some part of this synthesis, disruptive of it, and therefore evil. This view gained further hold when divorce became feasible (at least for the moneyed classes) in Protestant countries; the extra-marital affair became a pathogenic invader that could digest the inner substance of the marriage, kill it, and triumphantly grow into a new marriage. So viewed, the affair could not be tolerated or permitted to co-exist with marriage; the two were mortal enemies. The most common way of handling the enmity between them was to tell one's self that it was literally impossible to be unfaithful if one truly loved one's spouse; conversely, any infidelity came to be seen as self-evident proof that one did not, could not, love one's spouse. (In the *McCall's* survey, 70 per cent of the respondents subscribe to this doctrine.) For people who hold this view, affairs are unavoidably productive of guilt and conflict, must be kept secret, and tend to remain either purely physical encounters without any emotional content or to grow into deeply emotional relationships that can easily disrupt or destroy marriage.

In contrast is the pagan-courtly tradition found mostly in southern European countries, though it extends throughout France. Marriage was, and remained, a practical, functional arrangement having to do with property, children, necessities, and creature comforts. It included sex, of course, both to produce children and to obtain simple relief, though not ecstasy (as the French say, *Faute de mieux, on couche avec sa femme*—If there's nothing better, a man sleeps with his wife), but emotional and romantic involvement, and intense or exuberant sexuality, were sought and found outside in extra-marital love affairs. The idealism and seriousness of the late-medieval inventors of romantic love wore thin over the centuries, but their gestures and manners endured; in a mock-serious form combining sexuality with specialized and limited emotionality, the pagan-courtly tradition proved eminently suited to the needs of the blasé aristocracy—and even, with dilutions and simplifications, those of the rest of southern European society.

For at all social levels in the Catholic countries, marriage was and still is virtually indissoluble, practical, and functional; and since romantic love was never amalgamated with it, and had quite distinct purposes, the affair never became a competitor of, or threat to, the home. A husband's infidelity, if discovered, might be grounds for screaming, scratching, and smashing of crockery, but not for an embittered visit to a lawyer or priest. The role and status of wife are distinct from those of the mistress; the latter does not intrude upon the former or endanger her rights. As a result, secrecy is not crucial (although one must have a decent respect for appearances) and guilt remains minimal, the unfaithful person actually feeling pride in his status as a lover. Since love and sexual pleasure are not harnessed to family life, they can be taken seriously in a light-hearted way, which is to say, taken lightly with utter seriousness. The affair is a delightful and important part of life—but not important enough to warrant risking one's career, social position, or comfort; its joys are real but replaceable, its agonies genuine but easily overcome by another love. All told, such an affair is not the competitor to marriage, but its supplement.*

In America's colonial years, particularly in New England, the puritan-bourgeois pattern was dominant: The harsh laws against adultery, with their fines, whippings, the forced wearing of the scarlet "A" or even the branding on the forehead, are familiar from history and fiction. These laws did not extinguish adultery; they did, however, continue and strengthen the tradition that it was ugly, vile, deserving of harsh treatment, and exceedingly dangerous. But elsewhere in the country, and even in New England when immigrants arrived there from other backgrounds, the pagan-courtly tradition entered American life. It has remained underground, never being openly accepted except in a few special

---

*There were and still are major differences between the lower-class pattern of infidelity and the pagan-courtly pattern I have been describing. Lower-class men are more inclined to seek casual and totally uninvolved sexual episodes outside of marriage than are upper-class or middle-class men, and less inclined to play the complicated role of extra-marital lover. Moreover, lower-class men still rigidly cling to their old primitive code, according to which extra-marital sex on their part is a minor infraction, but on the wife's part is unforgivable and harshly punishable. In Sicily and Greece, even today, a husband who kills an errant wife is subject to lesser penalties than one who commits any other type of homicide. Times, however, are changing: such killings are dwindling in number, and in Italy the Penal Code provision granting such homicide special leniency is now under legislative attack.

communities or upper-class enclaves, yet for a century or so it has been one of the models Americans use when trying to fashion a way of life that meets their individual needs. The many people who cannot tolerate, or who feel confined by, the intimacy and emotional interdependence of romantic marriage find the southern European pattern more comfortable; it sets limits to the interaction of husband and wife, and seeks supplemental but measured doses of intimacy and love outside of marriage. Although this pattern has always been publicly disapproved of and has been forced to remain underground, it too well fits the emotional needs of many adults to go unused and unappreciated.

Our cultural heritage is thus schizoid. It offers us an approved model of marriage which, for all its values and its beauty, is suited to the needs and emotional abilities of only some—perhaps a minority—of us; it simultaneously offers us a deviant, disapproved model which, for all its disadvantages, is suited to the needs and emotional abilities of the rest—perhaps even a majority—of us.

In some ways, the approved model seems better able to make good some shortcomings of modern society: In our fragmented and anomic culture, romantic and faithful marriage partners are an island of emotional security for each other. Yet it also seems ill-adapted to other conditions of modern life. We now live longer and marry earlier than formerly, but to love only one person emotionally and sexually over a forty- or fifty-year span, and to keep that love intense, revivifying, and physically gratifying all that time is, for most people, very difficult if not impossible. Many people, for the sake of their children, forbid themselves any act that could endanger their marriages, and convince themselves that they are quite happy, but some authorities have come to doubt that the majority of men and women are really happiest when monogamous and faithful. It may be that many of those who do remain faithful to a single partner throughout life pay dearly in terms of frustration, resentment of their mates, dessication of their emotions, and the limitation of their potential for rich and rewarding lives.

The disapproved model seems better suited to the emotional capacities and requirements of many people, particularly men. It offers renewal, excitement, and the continuance of experiences of personal rediscovery; it avoids the demands and challenges of intimacy; it is an answer to the boredom of lifelong monogamy; it solves the problem of the ever-present temptations of modern society by yielding to them. But again, those who choose this alternative may have to pay for it: Infidelity is expensive and time-consuming, it conflicts with the home-based habits of middle-class society, it is socially and professionally hazardous, it may be psychologically traumatic to one's self, wife, and children if discovered —and even if not discovered. And while the long span of life today is likely to make fidelity a bore, infidelity becomes a less feasible answer with each decade of life. Unfortunately and unfairly, this is truer for women than for men: The middle-aged woman, competing with younger rivals, is at a very severe disadvantage in our youth-oriented culture. Ben Franklin's famous letter notwithstanding, young men—and older ones too—are not much inclined to prefer the gratitude of the older woman to the texture and shape of the younger one.*

Both alternatives, it is apparent, have their special advantages, yet both are imperfectly satisfactory for a number of reasons. But this dilemma should come as no surprise: It is the very essence of the human condition that we want many things that cannot all be had at the same time. Life continually requires us to choose between alternatives, each of which offers us something but costs us something; no matter which one we take, we cannot help regretting that we had to give up the other. The grasshopper played and sang, but died young of cold and hunger; the ant got through the winter nicely, but never knew the meaning of joy.

---

*Writing to a young friend, perhaps with tongue in cheek, Franklin gave eight reasons why an old mistress was preferable to a young one, the eighth and clinching one being, "They are so grateful!"

chapter 2: DESIRE

i its prevalence

Man's thoughts, even more than his actions, belie the notion that he is by nature a monogamous animal. Nearly all husbands and wives, even the well-mated, the righteous, and the hard-working, sooner or later find themselves not only desiring extra-marital relationships, but committing infidelities in their minds—adventures fantasied deliberately, voluptuously, and at some length. When such thoughts first spontaneously arise, they are likely to be rudely dismissed, but they return repeatedly, each time being banished with more difficulty; eventually they are invited, welcomed, and enjoyed—but at a considerable cost in guilt and even in alterations in the daydreamer's outlook.

But why? Nothing really happens. Yet something does, after all, for such fantasies often yield pleasure and a temporary easing of the hunger from which they arise. Although in the teenager or the unattached person this might create no problem, in the married person the obtaining of secret pleasure with an imagined lover feels like an act of disloyalty. And perhaps even more: People suffering severe sexual frustration or emotional deprivation in their marriages may find such fantasies whetting the appetite rather than temporarily appeasing it, and breaking down their defenses against actual infidelity.

NEAL GORHAM

Neal Gorham (as I shall call him), whom we will meet again and again in the following chapters, is unique, as is every man, yet he is much like other men; his experiences are at once individual and yet fairly common, specific yet typical. Gorham, now thirty-eight, looks placid, well-fed, and uncomplicated; he is chunky and of medium height, dresses well but conservatively, has neatly parted straight blond hair, a square open face, and the thick, carelessly molded features of his farmer ancestors. But we are misled by his looks. He is a sensitive and gifted man, a poet *manqué* who yielded to the need to make money and became an advertising writer in a small New York agency, but who, in his spare time, still sweats over poems of contemporary despair, has completed a blank verse drama about Calvin, and hopes someday to be able to leave advertising for something that would make him feel more worthy. None of his poetry has been published, nor has his play been produced, but every week certain newspapers and minor magazines print his poetic evocations of Caribbean holidays or of evenings made magical by the use of the right men's cologne.

Neal has long been rather proud of his departures from orthodoxy. Raised a Presbyterian, he became an agnostic during his college years; reared in a comfortable Long Island suburb, educated at Yale, and now a resident of Darien, Connecticut, he has for years been a left-liberal Democrat, and an avid reader of *I. F. Stone's Weekly* and, more recently, *Ramparts* and *The New York Review of Books.* But six years ago he was dismayed by the appearance in himself of yet another deviation—one he neither sought nor welcomed. On page 5 of a diary that he began in April, 1966, and kept locked away in the desk at his office on Lexington Avenue, he talks to himself about it: *When did it all start? Not the first time I kissed*

*Mary, not the first time I desired her, not the first time I saw her.
It started three years ago, when Those Thoughts sprouted overnight,
like a wet-weather plague of brown mushrooms on the green lawn
of my mind. That was the first betrayal in ten years of marriage; that
was when it began.*

Shy and inhibited in his teens, he had had few sexual experiences and no real romances until his junior year at Yale; then he
met Laurie Van Zandt, fell in love with her, and thereafter never
went near another girl. He and Laurie were married while he was
in the Navy, and though he was away from her for long months at
a time, he never went prowling in search of another woman; in fact
he never even permitted himself to envision the unfaithful act.
After years of marriage, if confronted on the beach by a tempting
body, he still refused to let himself speculate as to what it would
be like to test that unknown flesh. When Laurie took Robin and
Billy for a six-week summer visit to her parents in Virginia, and
desire tormented him in the night, he tossed and sighed, imagining
scenes of voluptuous abandonment, but his fancied partner was
always his wife.

But suddenly and unexpectedly there came the first of the
daydreams of other women. *I should have been warned; I should
have sensed the shape of the future and taken heed; but I did not.*
The first episode was unforgettable. He had had dinner with two
clients, Jack Gillespie (an account executive) and Gillespie's date,
Norah. Gorham had never met Norah before; she looked a little
like Sandy Dennis, girlish and fragile, buoyant and yet secretive. He
found her utterly lovely, and kept glancing at her when no one else
noticed; she, alone, did notice, and seemed to look back at him time
and again with some special recognition, some obscure message in
her eyes. Gorham was nervous; he had never experienced this
before, not even in his college years, and went home after dinner
greatly stirred but filled with anxiety. He made no effort to reach
her, and never even saw her again, but the night he met her, *I lay
in bed and was unfaithful to Laurie even while her warm plump
behind was tucked up against my belly. It went like this: Gillespie
and I have another business meeting some night; he's late, and
Norah comes into the restaurant looking for us; I signal her and she
sits down beside me. I offer her a drink; we make small talk, are ill*

at ease. A long silence; then I say softly, looking down at my hands,
"We seem to be uneasy with each other." She: "I feel it too. What
is it?" Another long silence, a long look; we know what it is. At that
moment Gillespie walks in and from then on all is brisk and busi-
nesslike, but her eyes and mine meet again and again. Two days
later my phone rings; it is she, upset; she needs to talk to me. I tell
her I had badly wanted to call her but had not dared. We meet for
lunch, are almost inarticulate with emotion; we ask each other what
to do with this unsought thing between us. I: "Tristan and Iseult
drank the potion and had no choice, and neither do we." I pay the
check; silent, trance-like, we go to a hotel; I register, we go upstairs
without a word, and then, good God! the tenderness, the ferocity,
the insistent explorations by lips and fingers; the surging and sigh-
ing; the weariness and happiness—and then the guilt, the search for
the Meaning of It All. End of my script. O vile beast, to lie in bed
pressing against my wife and mentally screwing another woman!
He put his arms about Laurie, kissed her neck and cheek in an
upsurge of pity and love, then stopped lest the sudden tears in his
eyes fall upon her face and waken her to discover that something
was dreadfully wrong. *Yet a week later I did it again with Norah,*
a week after that with another woman, and still later with others.
And I never realized, poor fool, that Laurie and I had been drifting
into trouble for years and that this was the fever symptom. I lay
dreaming and let us get ever sicker until the disease was past all
curing.

* * *

There are some, of course, who neither feel the polygamous
urge nor find themselves committing imaginary infidelities: they
include the very few who remain thoroughly happy and satisfied in
their marriages, and the much larger number who are so ruled by
conscience that not only detailed fantasies but even desire itself are
barred from consciousness. Such people, however, are in the
minority; the majority of American husbands and wives do,
whether only occasionally or very frequently, feel such yearnings
and envision scenes of sex or romance involving themselves and
people other than their mates.

A hundred thousand priests, psychotherapists, and marriage

counselors could be witness to this statement, for they hear about it every day. The major piece of published evidence, however, is from a survey made thirty years ago by the psychologist Lewis Terman. Using the questionnaire method to study marriage patterns, he found that nearly three quarters of middle-class American husbands and over one quarter of their wives admitted feeling a desire for extra-marital intercourse anywhere from occasionally to almost all the time. A decade later Kinsey, using a somewhat different approach, got comparable results. But since freedom to talk and think about sex has increased almost exponentially since Terman and Kinsey gathered their data, it is certain that the figures are higher today—particularly for women, who have until very recently been under far stronger prohibitions than men.

The fantasies generated by these desires are as varied in style and content as are the individuals who confect them. Neal Gorham's are only one type; others range from the brief and fragmentary to the extended and detailed, from the purely sexual to the wholly romantic, depending on the strength of the individual's polygamous desires and of his conscience. Some people indulge in bouts of fantasy rarely and spontaneously; others schedule such reveries daily as part of their regular planned activities. Some focus their attention on the emotional side of the imaginary encounter, avoiding scenes of actual sexual consummation; others imagine only the physical acts and ignore any preliminary or subsequent story line. Some construct ideal extra-marital companions for their fantasies; others build their daydreams around actual persons they know and desire. The following examples illustrate some of these variations:

—A research physicist in Texas was puzzled and troubled when, after four years of a good marriage, he gradually became inexplicably unhappy. "There was a kind of gnawing dissatisfaction that I couldn't put my finger on. She was managing things well, the kids were doing fine, I was making decent money for the first time. I couldn't understand my own mood." Now, two years after divorce, he sees that his interests had broadened while his wife's had not and that, at the same time, he had moved away from his Fundamentalist background and begun to place high value on sexual and romantic expression while she had remained devout, inhibited, and antipathetic to both sex and emotionality. "As my discontent grew, I began to wonder what it would be like with another kind of woman. I somehow fell into the habit of having long daydreaming sessions while driving to and from work. I would look forward to it as if I were really meeting someone I loved; sometimes I'd even make an excuse to go to bed early so I could be alone with my thoughts again. I'd create a creature unlike my wife, with all the qualities I hungered for, and once I had made her up I would have a number of adventures with her over a period of many days; then finally I'd drop her and make up a new one. I'd meet each new one casually in the office; then slowly it would become romantic, and we would meet and do things together—climb mountains, go skiing, take boat trips, watch the sunset, have a fine dinner, kiss each other tenderly, lie in each other's arms. For some reason I hardly ever visualized actual love-making, although that was supposed to be part of it. The strangest thing was that I didn't think of all this as adultery. It was as if it were sanctioned and could exist in addition to my being married."

—An engineer, now forty-six, says that he has daydreamed extensively about sex ever since his teens, when such scenes accompanied his masturbating. Marriage interrupted his fantasy life, but after half a dozen years or so he found himself occasionally replaying some of the old mental movies or devising new ones along the same old lines, though without masturbating. "When I was a kid, it was a matter of hunger. In recent years, it's been a matter of the tedium and the everydayness of married life. But the fantasies have been much the same. I always think of some very voluptuous girl (she has to have great big ones—that's essential) and I think about the many things I'd like to do to her and have her do to me. But it isn't just sex I daydream about. I always was a romantic, and even though I'm very fond of my wife, I still sometimes let myself dream that I'll meet this gorgeous and very intelligent girl and have crazy sex with her, and that slowly it will grow into a tremendous love that will last the rest of my life. It seems as if I can't help having such thoughts now and then, even though I'm middle-aged and bald and long married."

—A slim, blond youth of twenty-two, belatedly completing his undergraduate work at a midwestern university, has been married for two years to a local television personality; her activities and her success, such as it is, have created tension between them and given him a sense of inferiority. For many months he has consoled himself by coming home from school in the afternoon, when she is at work, and going to bed for a couple of hours, ostensibly for a nap; in actual fact, he surrenders himself to daydreams of success as an architect, his career involving trips to Chicago, Kansas City, and Des Moines—all of them being cities in which girls he knew in high school now live. He calls them up, and each, though married, is able to meet him privately for dinner to talk over old times; each ends up in his hotel room, making impassioned love to him but never doing anything to break up his marriage. "Over a period of a year I've gone through the whole roster of girls I knew in high school and had every one, in my daydreams. It sounds sick, I guess, but I need it."

—During her second pregnancy, the wife of a Boston businessman became infatuated with her obstetrician, a handsome but rather arrogant man twenty years her senior. She planned her conversations with him for a week in advance, brought him flowers or trinkets, acted openly flirtatious and worshipful, and played back to herself afterwards, again and again, his every word and action. "I was like a high-school girl with a crush on the football hero," she says. "It didn't have anything to do with my marriage—that wasn't much good, but it never had been, anyway." Some time after the birth of her child, she fell prey to a minor but stubborn ovarian infection and had to see him every week to be examined and treated. During the examinations she felt almost faint, and one time told him that she had a crush on him; he responded in a dignified and appreciative way, but nothing more, which only made her adore him more intensely. When she heard, later, that he had just been remarried, she was so jealous and furious that she never went back to him.

—In a suburb of Akron, a pretty housewife in her early thirties, happily married but fretful about her fading beauty, flirted a few times with a neighbor, a former athlete who was inarticulate but superbly physical. Finally, at a party, they kissed once or twice in the kitchen. She felt excited and elated, and that night, in bed, thinking about his powerful arms and his strong body pressed against her, she made a strange discovery: When her husband started making love to her, she could close her eyes and visualize the neighbor, pretending that it was his lips and hands on her body, his rigid organ driving inside her. "From then on for some months," she recalls, "it made sex very much more stimulating. It surprised me—I never thought I could or would do such a things."

---

ii its sources

Students of human nature as dissimilar as Freud and Kinsey agree that mankind is biologically polygamous; monogamy is an artifact of upbringing and social regulation rather than part of instinctual human nature. In American society, however, people are so thoroughly indoctrinated with the opposite idea that it is difficult for many of them to accept their desires for extra-marital relationships as natural; even if they have no intention of carrying them out, they look for circumstances that will justify the appearance of the desires and thus minimize the guilt they feel.

The justifications they find are familiar enough: the sexual coldness or failing appeal of their mates; the excessive absorption of their mates in business, child-rearing, or community activities; long separations due to business or illness; emotional conflicts of all sorts (nagging, power struggles, belittling, domination); exasperating habits, boring talk, silence—in short, everything from the unavoidable tedium of life to the severest kinds of mistreatment one spouse can inflict on the other.

In part, these alleged reasons are only rationalizations; they comfort the daydreamer for the time being, and when his minor ennui or vagrant itch has disappeared, he recognizes that he was being unfair and dismisses the justifications—until the next time. But in larger part there is truth in the justifications, even if they are exaggerated. Indeed, the more a person fantasies extra-marital affairs, the more likely it is that he has cause to; clinical evidence about daydreaming does show a direct relationship between the amount of time a person spends daydreaming about a given satisfaction and the extent to which he is being deprived of it. Dr. Jerome Singer of the City University of New York found, for instance, that daydreaming about food or money is far more frequent among the socio-economically deprived and financially insecure than among the well-off, and in my own interviews I found extramarital fantasies to be far more frequent among sexually deprived and emotionally insecure husbands and wives than among the merely bored.

Recent experiments have shown that volunteers who are deprived of dreams by being awakened each time their eye-movements indicate the onset of dreaming soon become hostile, irritable, and even deeply disturbed; apparently, certain kinds of dreams are a necessary psychic release, and though they do not cure or eliminate conflicts and sources of tension within, they perform an essential function by temporarily discharging dangerous accumulations of psychic pressure. And this seems to be one of the functions of the daydream as well. Fantasy is not a cure for life's shortcomings, but it can be a mild analgesic, a substitute satisfaction—and even, in cases of severe deprivation, a stimulant to corrective action. Occasional fits of fantasied infidelity usually indicate nothing more than the normal human desire for variety, which they partly satisfy; continual obsessive fantasies of infidelity are more likely to indicate severe frustration and marital discontent, which they cannot alleviate but which they may prepare the daydreamer to relieve by means of actual extra-marital relationships.

This is not to say that the severely deprived daydreamer is always an innocent victim; often the very person who turns inward for comfort and sustenance is as much to blame for the deprivations he or she suffers as is the mate. The man who feels that his wife is unresponsive and partially frigid may so have dominated her that she sees him as a father-figure, and this seals off her sexual feeling for him; still, he experiences the result as rejection and coldness on her part. The woman who feels lonely and ignored because her husband is wholly absorbed in business may have driven him to it by being a complainer, a nag, or a self-centered bore, but even though his compulsion to work excessively long hours is her fault, she experiences it as a deliberate withholding of love.

PEGGY FARRELL

An example of the not entirely innocent victim driven at first to extra-marital fantasies (and later to actions) by major marital discontent largely of her own making is Peggy Farrell, another person we will encounter from time to time throughout this book. Now thirty-one and divorced, she lives with her ten-year-old son in a middle-income garden-apartment development in Brighton, about five miles from downtown Rochester. Her ex-husband has moved to another state and defaulted on alimony payments, but last summer she completed social-work training, and has been employed since then as a staff social worker at a large hospital. She hopes to take advanced training someday and become a marriage counselor.

At first glance, Peggy hardly seems like the sort who would ever have turned to fantasy for consolation. Short and bouncy, snub-nosed and pert, she wears her sweaters a little too tight, her evening eyelashes a little too long, her black curly hair a little too short; her manner is teasing, cheerfully tart, and sometimes deliberately vulgar. At a party or in a cocktail lounge, men sniff the air and head toward her like dogs toward a bitch in heat, yet most women like her, perhaps because she offsets her sex appeal by being wryly self-deprecating. She speaks in a bantering, slangy manner, yet makes it plain that she considers her life rather a mess, and that if she laughs at any mortal thing, 'tis that she may not weep. This is how she tells her story:

"My parents were second-generation Irish, and I was raised a 'good Catholic.' You know what that means? It means hung up sexually and full of knots. But I don't know which was the worse influence—the Church or my parents. I had a lousy childhood; my parents fought all the time, and I was the prize they fought over. It made me a spoiled brat.

"I left the Church in my sophomore year in college, probably as a form of revolt against my folks. But it wasn't enough for me, so I found a way to hurt them even worse: I fell in love with a fellow-student—wait, now; are you *ready?*—a jet-black Negro from the Deep South! *That* really did them in!" She giggles, then shakes her head almost sadly in wonderment at herself. "Then I discovered

that he was married and had kids down South." She strikes a
mock-tragic pose, hand to forehead. "Oh, *woe* is *me!* How can I
torment Mother if I can't marry the guy? So I dropped him and
grabbed Andy on the rebound. Andy was a lapsed Catholic, divorced, bearded, alcoholic, out of work, and still on parole for a
marijuana conviction, so he was practically as good for torturing my
parents as my black. Great! So at age twenty I got pregnant by him,
dropped out of college and married him—and lived unhappily ever
after."

Turning serious, she admits that the marriage began well
enough, and that for a few months she was "quite blissful, playing
house and trying to be the young wife of *House Beautiful.*" Then
somehow things went abruptly sour, although she cannot recall any
specific incident that was responsible. "It probably wasn't any one
thing, anyway. All I know is that after several months a very
strange, frightening feeling came over me, as if the ground was
slowly caving in beneath me and I couldn't move to get away, or
as if I was dead all over but still conscious. I don't know why.
Maybe it was because I'd made my revolt and there wasn't any
lasting joy in it. Or maybe it was because Andy had reformed, and
where was the fun in being married to him, if he was all straightened
out? He went dry with AA help, got a job—he's an accountant—
and said he was through pretending to be a swinger. What he really
liked was to stay home and watch TV or work with his tools. I
couldn't stand the dullness of it all, and the brat in me came out.
I have a nasty mouth and sometimes I would needle him; I would
tear him apart while he just sat there quietly, until finally he'd turn
purple and belt me one. For some goofy reason, that would almost
make me feel good."

The oppressiveness of the marriage relationship seemed to her
to stem in part from a sexual limitation of her own which she speaks
of with a characteristic mixture of flipness and self-mockery. "In
bed, it was Dullsville all the way—I never had an orgasm with him.
Before we were married, it seemed fun, despite that fact; afterward
it was just wham, bam, thank you, ma'am, and off he'd go to sleep.
What a bore! . . . Oh hell, that isn't fair. It wasn't all his fault. I might
as well admit it—I'm frigid. I never had an orgasm in any of my half
dozen affairs before marriage, and I've never had one since. I just

love men and I *adore* sex, but the one present I'd like for Christmas is an orgasm."

Except when she was fighting with Andy, she liked him (she says they were really rather good friends), but she felt acutely bored and depressed, especially during the confining time of pregnancy and early motherhood. Even worse than the boredom was her sense of insignificance. During her childhood, she had been wooed by both parents as part of their struggle with each other; whenever there was temporary peace between them, she would feel ignored and valueless. In her teens she had discovered that by twitching her round little bottom, making eyes, and verbally teasing boys or men, she could make them pursue her, and that this always gave her an exhilarating feeling of personal worth. "I guess I never got over it. Even if I hadn't picked the wrong guy, for all the wrong reasons, I would have missed it more and more as time went by. As it was, I began thinking about other men right after the time I had that first sinking feeling about my marriage. Not that I wanted to get rid of Andy—dull or not, our marriage was a pretty comfortable arrangement—but I was drowning in my own misery, and when I would think back over the flirting and petting of my teens and the affairs that began when I was seventeen, I'd remember how great that all made me feel, and I'd tell myself I just *had* to recapture that feeling somehow. How? Only one way—by playing around outside my marriage. I know perfectly well that the Church and society say that's 'wrong'—but it's even more wrong to feel as miserable as I was feeling.

"So I began to look at every man in the neighborhood—the clerks in the stores, the deliverymen, the mailman, the neighbors in our development—and I would try to imagine how I'd start up with each of them, and what it would be like. But I never gave them any signs, and none of them ever gave me any. No wonder—I was a mess! I had a skin condition that came on after the baby was born, and I had forty, count them, *forty* pounds of extra fat. At the age of twenty-one, I was a middle-aged heap of blubber. One day when I just couldn't stand myself any more, I went to the doctor and got started on a strict program of dieting and drugs to clear up my skin and to lose weight. I looked at it as a training program to get myself ready for outside campaigning. It was hard work, and it was slow, but as the months passed I began to lose weight, my skin cleared up bit by bit, and I even started experimenting at home with hair colorings. and the sewing machine. The better-looking I got, the more impatient I was for my future to arrive. I'd look at my body in the mirror and do things with my own hands, pretending they belonged to one of the men I'd been thinking about, and it was almost too much to bear."

* * *

But it does not require marital discontent and emotional depri- vation to stir up disturbing and provocative fantasies of infidelity; it takes only our own polygamous instincts, particularly when ex- acerbated by the passage of time. Those whose marriages are satis- factory, and even those whose marriages are genuinely happy, are not immune. We grow slowly tired of the things we have, even though they first delighted and fulfilled us, and want other things that will delight and fulfill us in the original way. "Ah! *Vanitas Vanitatum!*" wrote Thackeray. "Which of us is happy in this world? Which of us has his desire? or, having it, is satisfied?" We cease to notice or to be pleased by the painting that has hung on our wall for a decade; we grow accustomed and dulled to the love we won long ago. The face that was endlessly absorbing, the touch that was electrifying, the personality that was fascinating, eventu- ally become merely comfortable, like the morning's scrambled eggs and coffee. For a while this may seem tolerable, but as the years dwindle in which one might yet recapture the lost intensity, a certain desperation appears. *Will there be no more than this? Am I to grow old and die, never knowing the rest of it?* mourns the woman before her mirror, discovering another fine line at the cor- ner of her mouth. And the graying, slightly overweight man on his way to work, seeing a lovely girl pass by with whom he feels for an instant that he could burn brightly again, chides himself, *I should not think such things . . . but how am I to live out the rest of my life, never knowing that feeling again?*

It may have an even more fundamental cause than our adult awareness of time, sameness, and human imperfection; it may be built into our primitive animal nerve structure. Male rats, monkeys, and bulls all have been observed to copulate repeatedly, when restricted to one partner, until they are exhausted and stop—yet if new females are offered to them at this point, the worn-out males are remarkably restored, and begin copulating with the new partners with nearly all the verve and excitement they originally had. Reviewing such experiments along with the anthropological evidence, Kinsey and his colleagues concluded that the polygamous urge is built into the mammalian nerve structure, and that man is no exception. The male human being would, in fact, always behave polygamously were it not for social restraint; as for the female, her somewhat weaker polygamous inclination is a matter of social conditioning rather than of instinctual nature. Ford and Beach provide evidence on that point: In their summary of the sexual patterns in 185 societies, they point out that wherever there is no double standard in sexual matters, and extra-marital liaisons are permitted, women are as eager and ready for variety as men.

The desire for newness and variety is apparently deeply rooted in us all; fidelity to a single sexual partner is not an innate universal human need, but a contrived and culturally conditioned one. We are by nature polygamous, by upbringing monogamous, and therefore perennially at war with ourselves. And this is why so many of the married—even the happily married—sometimes dream of other loves to refresh their dulled palates, to recall the taste and glow of new love, and to partially allay the harassing desire that comes over us with the years to know another and more exquisite love before it is too late.

EDWIN GOTTESMAN

Edwin Gottesman, another of the several people we will see more of throughout this book, exemplifies the point. Gottesman, born and raised in the Bronx and now a businessman in Washington, D.C., has done very well for a man of forty who started with nothing and whose father, a Polish-Jewish carpenter, never finished high school, never acquired American ways, and still speaks with a strong accent. Gottesman, his wife, and his two children live in a handsome ten-room colonial house, complete with swimming pool and a dozen original oils by contemporary artists, on two acres of wooded land in Bethesda, Maryland. Their neighbors and friends include a number of highly successful businessmen and professionals, and Gottesman's own worth is close to a million, most of it in shopping centers he helped develop and which he owns in part. He is a shrewd, hard-driving investor whose special skills include the ability to find land suitable for supermarket or shopping center development, and to pull together syndicates of participants in such a way that his own cash commitment is minimal but his potential rewards are great.

Gottesman is one of those short, pudgy, business-fixated men to whom the look of youth does not adhere; they appear and act middle-aged from their early thirties onwards. Somewhat round-shouldered, he has a small potbelly, his flesh is pale and formless as though he had never played an outdoor game in his life, and his faded brown hair has begun to thin noticeably. The impression he gives of middle age is heightened by a habit of which he is unaware: When he was a child in the Bronx, an anti-Semitic gang beat him up badly, deafening him in the left ear, and whenever he is listening to someone in a noisy place, he is apt to cup his hand behind the other ear and strain to hear. For all that, there is a dynamic and vital quality about him when he is at work; when he is pacing up and down in his office snapping out dictation to a secretary, or bargaining hard and wittily with a prospective seller or purchaser, there is an intensity and manliness about him that can be quite compelling.

To get where he is, Gottesman had to work with tenacity and single-mindedness. He put himself through college, earning a degree in economics in four years while holding down a full-time job. "I worked by day in a brokerage house, went to school at night and all summer, and studied until I couldn't see straight. I lived on four hours of sleep for months at a time. After my Bachelor's, I went into the stock market for myself, and took afternoon courses until I got a degree in business administration. By then, I could afford a car, and on weekends I would drive down into Jersey and Delaware looking for good buys in land, or if the weather was rotten I'd spend the time studying reports on the market. I worked, worked, worked all the time; I never played. I was always trying to better myself, I was trying to become a man of substance."

Too busy to have much of a social life, he rarely went out and seemed little interested in girls until, at twenty-two, he met Betsy

Weiss in an afternoon course in Social Problems. Betsy was one of those attractive, aloof girls who seem oblivious of the men around them—particularly of someone like Edwin, who clearly came from a poorer and more recently arrived family. Actually, Betsy was a shy and lonely girl, and although at first she was a bit contemptuous of the earnest, zealous Edwin, after a while she found herself impressed by his swift, incisive mind and piqued by his lack of interest in her. And emboldened by it—for it was she who took the initiative. She meant merely to tease him, but wound up having hamburgers and coffee with him; she meant to have one date with him, but went on seeing him regularly; she meant to go out with him only until summer, but ended up marrying him two years later because he and she had become a comfortable necessity to each other. Gottesman explains: "I can't say we were ever wildly in love. We went together a long while and felt good about each other, so we got married. It wasn't earth-shaking; it just seemed like the natural thing to do."

Like the courtship, the marriage was comfortable and companionable; neither partner had any complaints, or at least none they gave voice to. Within relatively few years, especially after moving to the Washington area, Edwin was doing very well financially, and although in business he was a hard bargainer and generally tight-fisted, at home he was generous; for her part, Betsy had the good taste and the imagination to use his money well to make a gracious life for them. What with two children, a lovely home, his absorption in business life and hers in race relations (she was active both in the Anti-Defamation League and the N.A.A.C.P.), their life together was good; their days and years drifted by like leaves floating on the surface of a gently flowing stream.

But sometimes, when Edwin and Betsy saw a movie or play in which people were deeply in love, he felt vaguely embarrassed that he and she had never had such feelings. Now and then he wanted to seize Betsy and embrace her passionately, but he felt he would look absurd; she would probably laugh, pat him on the cheek, and ask what had come over him. One summer night he wanted to make love in the moonlight on the second-floor porch, but even though no one could have seen them, she said she'd feel self-conscious; besides there might be bugs outside. Yet she almost never refused him sex when he wanted her, and nearly always had orgasm, and for some years Gottesman thought that his sex life and his marriage were about as good as anyone could hope for.

Then his real-estate transactions began to bring him into frequent contact with a group of half a dozen investors and developers in Philadelphia. They had known one another intimately for years, and spoke freely to each other of their personal lives; Gottesman was astonished to find that all six of them, although married, either had occasional pick-up affairs while away from home or steady "girl friends" in the city. At first he was shocked, then fascinated, and eventually jealous. "I couldn't help wanting what they seemed to have—secret meetings with beautiful women, really uninhibited sex, the feeling of being daring and young and successful with women. Betsy was a wonderful wife, but our marriage was very much like a good business partnership. I was only thirty-six, but sometimes I found myself thinking that my chance had come and gone, and that I would never experience all the rest of it. I had so much to be grateful for, but I felt I was missing something important and that time was passing me by."

He began having fantasies—but curiously stunted ones. Setting out on a business trip, he would start thinking that this time something might happen. He would meet a beautiful woman on the plane, or in a restaurant or hotel; some minor incident would give him reason to speak to her, and though she would be chilly to him at first, after a little talk she would sense that inside this thick-waisted, slightly balding businessman there was a passionate and hungry soul. They would talk for hours in a cocktail lounge, say beautiful things to each other, explain their lives, their hopes; finally, late at night—but here the fantasy always faded out. "I wanted to imagine all of it in detail," he says, "but somehow I never could picture the sexual part. My mind would switch away to other things. I could daydream only the preliminaries." Perhaps he could not make himself believe that any beautiful woman would ever look at him with the glowing face of desire; yet time and again—particularly after hearing other men talking about such things—he would spend the night with restless visions, yearning for something impossible, cursing his looks and his lack of confidence, lamenting his loss of youth. In the morning he would rise, weary, angry and impatient, and shake off the thoughts as a dog shakes off water, telling himself that other men probably lied about how much they enjoyed themselves and that he was undoubtedly leading a more satisfying life than those who were driven to seek outside solace. Somewhat comforted, he would temporarily put the whole thing out of mind and hurry off to work.

iii its control

Control of extra-marital desires can be exerted from within, in the form of an internalized sense of right and wrong, or from without, in the form of social penalties for violating the code. In Christian cultures, the social penalties have sometimes been severe, sometimes mild, but in either case the inner controls have usually been the more important. For within the Christian conscience there is imbedded the stern doctrine that not only must one not commit adultery, but must not even *desire* anyone other than his mate. Christ himself stated the uncompromising concept in the Sermon on the Mount:

> Ye have heard that it was said by them of old time, Thou shalt not commit adultery:
> But I say unto you, That whosoever looketh on a woman to lust after her hath committed adultery with her already in his heart.

A moral commandment so strict, and so at variance with basic human nature, can be obeyed only by means of mental mechanisms which hide desire from the conscious mind. The devout Christian may deny or repress his desire, burying it in the unconscious and refusing to admit that it exists at all; he may use unconscious avoidance, staying away (ostensibly for other reasons) from persons, places, books, art, and drama that might arouse and stir up the kind of thoughts he fears; through the process known as reaction formation he may convince himself that those persons or activities that appeal most to him are wicked, disgusting, or unhealthy; he may sublimate his unfulfilled desire by transforming the libidinal drive into an intense dedication to work.

By the use of any of these or a dozen other well-known defense mechanisms, some people are able to convince themselves that they are as faithful in their hearts as in their bodies. But it is an illusory and a dangerous fidelity. In the opinion of most psychiatrists and psychologists, such mental mechanisms solve one problem only at the cost of creating others. As Doctors Albert Ellis and Robert Harper write in their book *Creative Marriage*, "Suppressing, consciously, non-marital sex urges may be perfectly compatible with emotional health and happiness, particularly if the suppressing individual is obtaining at least a moderate amount of sex satisfaction in his or her marriage. Repressing, unconsciously, non-monogamous desires and one's feelings of shame about having such desires usually leads to serious emotional difficulty."

The difficulty may assume any one of a number of disguises, but the affected individual almost always fails to recognize what the source of the problem is, and remains unable to deal with it effectively. He or she may feel bitterly resentful of the spouse, fall into severe marital conflicts and struggles, develop sexual anesthesia within the marriage, suffer from psychosomatic ailments, depression, and the loss of work ability, or do things that are plainly self-destructive. More dramatically—and fairly frequently—the pent-up desire erupts in the form of an abrupt, surprising, almost involuntary plunge into overt infidelity with little or no control over its consequences. A capsule history will illustrate the point:

—In Philadelphia, a heavy-set graying hardware dealer, now forty-three, was a faithful husband until two years ago. Puritanically brought up, he was a virgin when he married at twenty-one. His wife's relative frigidity was a great disappointment, but he attributed it to his own personal deficiencies and did not permit himself to imagine other and better experiences. "I never spun stories to myself about other women for two reasons. One, you don't *do* that sort of thing—you marry a woman, she's your wife, you stay true to her in body and in soul even if there are no kids to worry about, as was our case. Two, what good-looking woman would ever look twice at a fat, gray-haired hardware dealer from Philadelphia?" Two years ago his personal secretary left to have a child and he hired a young divorcee as a replacement. For half a year he saw her every working day and even occasionally took her to lunch without permitting himself to think about any other kind of relationship with her. One day, looking at a batch of letters she had just typed up, he was surprised by the number of errors she had made. "I asked what had happened. She said, 'Mr. Garson, it's getting so that when I'm around you I can hardly concentrate on anything.' Whee-e-e-ew! I started to shake; I could hardly draw my breath. Twenty-four hours later we were in bed. It was fantastic, a volcano, a tornado. It was a complete surprise—I hadn't had the least goddamned idea how it could be. I broke into tears after I came. I wanted to marry her as soon as possible. We made love every night for a week; then I went and told my wife everything in a great emotional scene, and moved out that same night."

It is not likely that at any time in the past a majority of people have ever been able to deny the existence of the polygamous urge as thoroughly as this man did for twenty years of his life. Certainly, only a minority do so today; as we have seen, the evidence indicates that nearly all married men and at least a majority of married women are conscious of extra-marital desires from time to time, if not more often. Most of them, when the desire comes upon them, do not feel obliged to choke it back, but allow themselves to luxuriate in fantasies of adulterous pleasure; many of these people, however, continue to exercise other types of control in order to allay their fear that indulging in fantasy might lead them to become unfaithful in reality. A number of people, for instance, among those interviewed by Professor Cuber and Mrs. Harroff for *The Significant Americans*, claimed that they were emotionally ready for an extra-marital affair but simply had not been able to find a suitable partner—a fastidiousness which is an excellent defense against temptation. Another device, more common with men than women, is to exaggerate the danger of rejection or of failure to measure up to the outside partner's expectations. A forty-year-old man describes how his fears kept him faithful until a few years ago:

—"For years, I kidded around with girls in the office and at parties, but never for one minute expected to have sex outside my marriage. It went against my upbringing, but more than that, I was afraid. I'd never been a big success with women before I married, and after being married awhile I forgot what little I knew about how to go about it. I had no idea whether any woman but my wife would welcome an approach by me, and I thought that if I ever took the first little step and got turned down, I'd be absolutely crushed. But even if I didn't get turned down, I might prove to be a lousy lover with someone new—and *that's* a paralyzing thought. One time I was scheduled to go to a professional convention with a girl in my office, and she said to me with a deliberately innocent look on her face, 'When we get out there, you and I are going to fuck each other silly.' I managed to smile and say, 'You bet,' or something brilliant like that. She was fairly attractive, and after the initial shock wore off I began to get pretty excited—but I also felt very jittery about it. The closer it got to the date of the trip, the more nervous I felt, and a few days before we were to go, I told my boss that there had been a death in the family and asked him to send someone else in my place. I told myself I had done the 'right' thing by not being unfaithful to my wife—but the truth is that I was too scared to try it."

But he was deceiving himself. His sense of inadequacy as a male had limited his premarital sexual activity but not kept him from it completely; it only became an insuperable obstacle in the case of extra-marital behavior, which would have been a far more serious violation of his moral standards. His fear of failure—like certain kinds of paralysis—was both a symptom of inner conflict and a form of protection against its effects, a point which Dr. Ernest van den Haag, a psychoanalyst and lecturer in psychology at the New School for Social Research, puts succinctly: "It is perfectly possible to be faithful out of neurotic motives."

The general view of psychologists and psychiatrists, especially those of Freudian orientation, is that healthy control of one's extra-marital desires is based on full awareness of those desires plus a realistic appraisal of all that is involved in gratifying them: the risk of harm to one's mate and to one's children, the ruination of one's marriage, disgrace in the public eye, and all the rest. For most people, this is too demanding a method of restraint; if they do exercise inner control, it is usually in the easier (if less truly adult) form of unthinking obedience to the dictates of conscience and fear of their own overpowering guilt feelings. Gerhard Neubeck and

Vera M. Schletzer of the University of Minnesota studied a number of couples who had been married about a decade and found that those people who had been unfaithful generally had consciences of low strength; the strong-conscienced people, even if unhappily married, tended to stick to daydreaming. Kinsey's data on the inhibiting power of religion are similarly illuminating: Among Protestant women in their early thirties, only seven per cent of the religiously active were unfaithful as compared to twenty-eight per cent of the inactive. (The contrast between religiously active and inactive men was much less marked.) The brand of religion was not important; the data show only trivial differences in the rates for the various faiths, the devout within each group being very largely faithful to their partners, the inactive being far more likely to have extra-marital experience.

Nearly all observers agree, however, that the inner controls have lost much of their power in recent years. A majority of Americans still believe in God, but if He is not quite dead, He speaks to them rarely, and then only in a feeble whisper. The same is true of the internalized guidelines implanted by parents and culture. The result, as we saw in the previous chapter, is widespread ambivalence —overt disapproval of infidelity combined with surreptitious fascination by it or even acceptance of it. The internal controls still exist —are still even powerful, in many people—but for a growing number of others they are no longer effective deterrents; they may delay matters, they may create a considerable amount of guilt, but by themselves they are sufficient to prevent only a minority of contemporary Americans from seeking to satisfy the polygamous urge.

What does hold many of them back are the external controls —the penalties which others stand ready to impose on the discovered violator of the code. One person, in particular—the spouse— is as effective an enforcer of fidelity as ever. Many men and women who would like to have extra-marital experiences, and who do not regard it as a particularly evil thing to do, are deterred by their fear of what their mates could, and probably would, do to them if they found out. The wronged husband or wife has great leverage: He or she can mistreat the errant partner with impunity, demand all sorts of reparations, and, as an ultimate punishment, threaten divorce. Even if the marriage is not a happy one, the last is a dismal prospect:

The break-up of the home and the division of property, the separation from one's children (in the man's case), the disruption of friendships and familiar patterns of daily life, the disgrace one suffers in the eyes of friends, the harsh financial terms the adulterer is almost always forced to agree to—all these continue to act as powerful restraints of extra-marital behavior.

Other external controls, however, have lost a good deal of their effectiveness in the past generation. The law does not prosecute the adulterer, and business, the church, and society are not nearly as likely to punish him severely as they once were. He does still run some risk of blighting his career prospects, of being unobtrusively eased out of positions of community leadership, and of being ostracized by certain of his friends and acquaintances, but penalties of this sort are most likely to be applied in small and close-knit communities where nearly everyone knows what is going on and where many feel an obligation to show their disapproval even if they feel none.

This may explain why, in my questionnaire sample, only a tenth of the people living in towns of under 5,000 population said they had had affairs, as compared to a quarter of those who lived in cities of 500,000 or more. Novels as dissimilar as *Peyton Place* and *Couples* have made much of the sexual goings-on in small towns, but since big cities have higher rates of all other sorts of deviancy—divorce, alcoholism, suicide, overt homosexuality—the infidelity rate undoubtedly follows suit. Small towns are not actually hotbeds of adultery; it is merely that whatever goes on in them is known about, talked about, and made much of. In the big city, where deviant behavior can better be hidden, or where people can pretend not to know about it, much more happens, is ignored, and goes unpunished.

---

iv its realization

Given the right conditions, the desire for extra-marital relations overcomes the controls. But what are the right conditions?

There is, of course, no single or simple answer; each extra-marital affair is the resultant of a complex interplay of forces either making for or diminishing desire versus others either strengthening or weakening the controls. An emotionally normal, relatively happy man, in a conventional community, might never become unfaithful despite opportune encounters with attractive and willing partners. The same man, if his marriage fell into disrepair or if he had a career setback, might grasp those opportunities—but even with special incentives and willing partners he might still remain faithful if he moved to a community where the pressures to conform were stronger. Or perhaps he might be so freed from external controls by a permissive community and a permissive wife as to act upon even a low-level urge; yet even in a permissive community and marriage he might not, if he were particularly timid or religious, or if he lacked opportunities.

The victory of desire over controls can therefor occur effortlessly or come about through violent struggle; the desires themselves can be ordinary and healthy, or exaggerated and pathological; and the factors that weaken the controls can range from the normal to the malignant. The traditional code made no such distinctions; infidelity was categorically evil. Curiously enough, Freudian psychology—so often blamed for unleashing lascivious desires—has carried on the Judeo-Christian tradition, translating unswerving moral condemnation into an equally unswerving presumption of pathology. Until very recently, nearly all American psychoanalysts, psychotherapists, marriage counselors, and social workers regarded extra-marital activity as invariably symptomatic of diagnostic entities such as "immaturity," "narcissism," "character disorder," "fragmentary superego," "ever-present anxiety," and "infantile love-needs." A few quotations will illustrate the prevailing outlook among Freudian-oriented professionals:

Infidelity, like alcoholism or drug addiction, is an expression of a deep basic disorder of character.
FRANK CAPRIO, M.D., *Marital Infidelity*

Infidelity is often a neurotic and sometimes psychotic pursuit of exactly the man or woman one imagines one needs. . . . It is primarily a return to behavior characteristic of adolescence or earlier.

LEON SAUL, M.D., *Fidelity and Infidelity*

Infidelity may be *statistically normal* but it is also *psychologically unhealthy*. . . . It is a sign of emotional health to be faithful to your husband or wife.

HYMAN SPOTNITZ, M.D., and
LUCY FREEMAN, *The Wandering Husband*

The evidence for this view consists, first of all, of case histories: frigid women seeking arousal, impotent men hoping to become potent, pathologically jealous husbands and wives who convict their innocent mates of infidelity and so make it happen, men who forever need to prove their manliness and women their appeal, browbeaten wives and castrated husbands who can feel like whole persons only outside their marriages, twenty-year-olds embroiled in childish fights who take revenge on each other by cheating.

Yet offering such examples does not prove that all infidelity emanates from psychological illness. To extend what one sees in unfaithful patients to all the rest of the unfaithful is like making observations in a geriatric ward of a mental hospital and concluding that all old people are mad. The psychotherapists may be right about the infidelity they do see, but the vast mass of the unfaithful do not seek treatment and it is unjustifiable to assume that they are identical with those who do.

Consider, for instance, the matter of unhappy marriage. Many patients in therapy explain their infidelities as a reaction to marriages that are stifling, contentious, or loveless, or to the nagging, suspiciousness, domination, or sexual coldness of their mates; the therapist, however, wants to discover why the patient chose such a mate in the first place, or why he endured the misbehavior without finding any better remedy than furtive outside solace, his assumption being that such a choice and such enduring of a bad relationship could come only from neurosis. And it is true that when one looks beneath the surface of the complaints, the assumption often proves correct. Here, for instance, is the surface:

—"She was always belittling and criticizing me; she made me feel stupid and ridiculous. One time I was refinishing a table and sanding the underside carefully because I like things to be perfect and truly beautiful, and she nagged me something awful and called me a fool for wasting my time on something no one would ever see. She pestered and belittled me about everything, and after four or five years I couldn't bear to even touch her at night. About that time, I began to feel very strong desires for other women I met. After a while, it grew so strong that I had to do something about it—and with the first one, the dam broke."

Beneath this surface, there was neurotic motivation rather than mere misfortune, for the speaker, after seeking comfort in a score of affairs and finding it only very briefly in each, finally entered therapy and slowly discovered that he had chosen to marry a powerful and punishing woman very much like his own mother —and hence had neither been able to fight back nor to divorce her. After two years of therapy, a divorce, and a stretch of bachelorhood, he was able to marry again—this time choosing a woman of a wholly different sort.

Nonetheless, the very same kinds of complaints are offered by many people who have no pathology, and who never visit therapists. Behavioral scientists who sample and test married persons on a broad scale get a quite different perspective on the matter from that of the psychotherapists. Sociologists who have studied unhappy or broken marriages find that neurotic choice or neurotic interaction are at fault in only a minority of them; Jessie Bernard, for instance, found that well over half the cases in a large study she made consisted of essentially normal people who had merely chosen poorly because they had been too young or inexperienced to know their own needs at the time. Similarly, Cuber and Harroff found that although many of the unfaithful spouses they interviewed had disappointing or frustrating marriages, most of these people were psychologically normal.

Among the people I interviewed, many who had sought relief from unhappy marriage in extra-marital affairs had later been divorced and subsequently made successful second marriages—without benefit of therapy. Yet these people often spoke of their first marriages in tones identical with those of the neurotic complainants. One cannot, therefore, call all such complaints, and all such infidelity, neurotic. Indeed, I get the impression that quite a few people who ascribe their infidelities to unhappy marriage or disagreeable mates do so without much real grievance because such complaints come closest to being acceptable to friends and confidants.

Sexual deprivation or frustration, though often a part of the unhappy-marriage syndrome, is also many times mentioned separately as the only reason the individual ventured outside of marriage. The mate and the marriage are characterized as generally satisfactory except for this defect—which the unfaithful person was forced to remedy as best he could. The analytically oriented therapist or marriage counselor takes this complaint, too, to be a symptom of neurosis in the very person who makes it, for here, again, he asks the questions: Why did he or she choose an unresponsive mate, what did he or she do that destroyed the mate's responsive capacity? And true enough, some of my interview subjects who specified sexual deprivation or frustration did reveal a neurotic basis within themselves for the problem. One young woman, for instance, already once divorced, explains why she was unfaithful to her second husband within a matter of months after their wedding:

—"He and I got along so well in other ways, when we were going together, that I didn't worry about his one big problem. It was this: He was fine at the preliminaries of sex, but usually ran into trouble when he tried to carry through. Even when he succeeded, it was never any great shakes. I figured that after we were married, he'd relax and get over it bit by bit, but he didn't. In fact, things got worse right from the start. Most of the time he just couldn't manage to get it up. Nothing I did helped—and I tried everything. About the only thing that ever worked was for him to lie there and masturbate until he was hard—sometimes it took him half an hour —and then turn to me and get it over with as fast as he could. I was crawling the walls. I had to get some help for myself or blow up."

This young woman, with a passionate disposition and plenty of experience—she had had a score of affairs between marriages— should have known better; she was deceived by her own need for a passive and inadequate man she could attempt to work miracles with. Unfortunately, she proved to be no miracle-worker, and the marriage broke up less than a year after she started having affairs.

In contrast, many of those whose justification for infidelity is sexual frustration had neither made a neurotic choice of mate nor created the frustrating situation; they had simply chosen marriage partners before they were experienced enough to know what they were getting, or without any testing of the sexual relationship.

—"I was a virgin when I married seven years ago. Does that seem odd, these days? Well, that's the way I was brought up—I was a good little convent girl, and I didn't know a *thing*. After we married, I believed everything he told me—I believed him that once a month was about normal, that it shouldn't take long, and that most women didn't have orgasms. I was the most frustrated bundle of nerves you ever heard of, and I didn't even know what my trouble was until I happened to look at a marriage manual in the library and began to discover what it was all about. At first I simply couldn't believe my eyes, but after a while I did believe them—and then I couldn't *stand* my own frustration."

Similarly, there are many other situations in which infidelity is presumed by the orthodox Freudian to be a symptom of neurosis, but can also be a sign of a healthy struggle to repair an ego damaged by conditions the individual could not have anticipated. Nearly half of the men and women I interviewed indicated that the need for self-esteem was a major motivation behind their infidelity. Some of their statements could be interpreted as the complaints of neurotics, but others seem more like the expressions of people struggling to keep or recapture emotional health. Two examples of the latter:

—"As a teen-age boy, I had terrible acne. I was very shy and never tried to make out with girls. When I finally got over it, I went and married a girl who had no more experience than I—and who turned out to be unable to have an orgasm except when I stimulated her manually. That does a *lot* for a man's confidence and good opinion of himself, doesn't it? She's willing enough and all that, but after five or six years of it, I had to find out if I was a real man or just a finger."

—"After his first affair came out in the open, he decided to give me a rundown on all the others he'd had that I hadn't known about. They'd all been with friends of ours, most of them better-looking than I. I was sick—I felt absolutely undesirable. After living with that thought for a couple of years, I couldn't stand it any longer; I had to prove to myself that I wasn't so terrible. It was a calculated thing, on my part. I deliberately chose the time and the place—and the man I thought would do the most for me."

In much the same way, other factors contributing to infidelity are thought of by therapists as aspects of neurotic behavior, but can also be aspects of normal behavior. Revenge, mentioned as a leading reason by about one out of twenty of my interviewees, occurs in both contexts; so does the use of alcohol, which was mentioned by roughly the same number of people; and so does long absence from the spouse, which was mentioned by about one out of eight.

Even within the ranks of the therapists, some of the younger and less orthodox men are beginning to argue that although all affairs are symptomatic, sometimes they constitute a symptom not of illness but of health. According to Dr. Louis R. Ormont, a group psychoanalyst in New York, the emerging analytic view is that every monogamous marriage is bound to thwart the individual's natural sexual and emotional drives somewhat; within reasonable bounds, this is tolerable, but when a marriage thwarts the drives extensively and offers too few rewards in return, the healthy individual may well seek satisfaction of his needs extra-maritally. The therapist may still consider that the marriage needs treatment, but not that the unfaithful person was acting neurotically.

Love, of course, is the most celebrated of the important needs for which people go outside the borders of marriage. Indeed, in fiction and drama it is the grand classic cause of infidelity. It takes the innocents unawares, overpowers them as completely as any magical potion or arrow shot by Cupid, and causes them, helpless and hence virtually guiltless, to become unfaithful to their mates.

But the picture is something less than accurate. First of all, love is actually rather uncommon as a cause of infidelity: Among my interview subjects, only one out of every ten men and one out of every five women spoke of it as having been the primary factor in bringing about their first affairs. Second, in some cases violent romantic infatuation is thoroughly neurotic in character: The loved one is hopelessly unsuitable, or cruel, or a source of intolerable guilt feelings (being, perhaps, a sibling's or dearest friend's spouse). Finally, even when a reasonably healthy person is emotionally frustrated within marriage, love for an outsider rarely comes suddenly, violently, and irresistibly; more often, it grows slowly, and the individual becomes aware of it and voluntarily continues the association, knowing that it is bound to become an affair:

—"He was a friend of my uncle's, and during that long awful winter, when my husband was away and the baby was so sick, he was wonderfully helpful, kind, and manly—everything my husband wasn't. Over the months, I began to care for him, and he for me, and it grew very strong in us long before we became lovers. When we did, it seemed only natural."

Others say that love was a major aspect of their first affair, but not at the outset; they became unfaithful in response to other, less complex needs, and afterwards found love growing within them:

—"They sat me next to him at the dinner table. I was hypnotized by him, and he knew it and played up to it. I knew that he had a wife far away, and he knew that I had a husband just as far away—and that I was thinking of getting a separation. The tension built up in us all evening; I had never felt anything like that before. I had always been such a good little girl, even if unhappy, but I knew that if he asked me to go to his hotel room, I'd do it without a moment's hesitation. I had to be with him physically; that was all I knew. I was wild about him—but in love with him?—no, I came to love him much later on, when I got to know him."

Thus, even in the normal individual with normal controls, severely frustrated drives can produce infidelity. But this does not explain the extra-marital behavior of the considerable number of people who are emotionally normal and contentedly married, who suffer from no serious frustrations in marriage, and who are not living in unusually permissive surroundings. Over half of the unfaithful men and nearly a third of the unfaithful women I interviewed said that their marriages were either happy (or at least not unhappy) at the time they began their first affairs, and among my questionnaire respondents the comparable figures for both men and women were even higher. Cuber and Harroff found much the same thing; a number of the unfaithful people they interviewed seemed in no way driven, but said they were merely adding to life's enjoyment.

Robert Whitehurst, a sociologist at Indiana University, has gathered evidence to show that certain perfectly normal experiences in the lives of middle-class American businessmen wear away at their inner resistance to infidelity, and that some of them eventually become unfaithful to their wives without the thrust of special needs or of pathological conditions. Among the factors making for this change are the passage of time, with its diminishing of communication and intensity in marriage; exposure to the "fringe ethics" of the business world and the consequent loss of youthful idealism; and business achievement and its increased exposure to opportunities for extra-marital adventures. The end result is that for many middle-class Americans, and especially for successful middle-aged men, "extra-marital involvements . . . can be considered an extension of fairly normal (meaning non-pathological) behavior . . . without strong guilt feelings, without underlying intrapsychic complications, or other commonly described neurotic symptoms."

The passage of time, of course, affects not only Dr. Whitehurst's cases but everyone. Kinsey offered the most detailed data available on this point. Looking at those people in his first two studies who are of the same general social and educational level as the people in this book, we find that men are more likely to be unfaithful with each passing year up to middle age, only fourteen per cent being so during their early twenties but more than twice that many by the upper thirties and lower forties. The pattern for college-educated women is virtually the same, though the percentages are smaller all along the line. Apparently it is not only rats, bulls, and monkeys who are prey to tedium and who welcome a new stimulus. Men—and women, too, despite their stronger inhibitions—are susceptible to the appeal of novelty and change after long years of sameness, particularly in their thirties and forties when tedium is compounded by a harassing sense of the brevity of life and youthfulness.

Indeed, it is the simple, natural, regrettable experience of boredom—sexual, emotional, or both—that is by far the most frequent cause of infidelity in normal people who for years controlled their extra-marital desires. Not that they tell this to their friends and confidants; for the most part, they offer them any and all of those more acceptable justifications we have been examining. But among my interviewees, well over half of the men admitted that one kind of boredom or another was the major reason for their first affairs;

so did an even larger number of women, almost two thirds of whom blamed the emotional boredom of marriage. (Among those who had had more than one affair, the figures were even higher.) They said things like this:

—"I love my wife—I wouldn't want to live with anyone else —but after fifteen years of the same thing . . . Jesus, when there's no thrill left in it, you have to get out and have a little change of pace."

—"I used to say there wasn't enough communication between my husband and myself, but that wasn't really the trouble. We'd said nearly everything worth saying long ago. When I found myself communicating with another man, it was because we were new to each other."

—"For all those years, my wife never refused me and almost always had some kind of orgasm. But she never *relished* it, she never said appreciative things, she never saw the silliness there can be in it, or the beauty, either. That's the way it was in the rest of our life, too—everything cut and dried, no excitement, no playfulness, no sense of wonder. We were a damned good working team —and it slowly got to where I felt I had to experience something else, or I'd be taking it out on her."

—"His family was warm, stable, and traditional, and this appealed to me because my parents had been divorced. But although I liked the security of marriage to him, I gradually became terribly restless. He's solid and good, but very flat in his emotions. For a while, I thought he was deliberately holding out in his feelings and I almost hated him for it, but I came to see that that's just the way he is. He's the only man I've ever wanted to be married to, but things got so stagnant that I couldn't endure it."

Finally, there are a number of middle-class Americans whose inner controls are so weak as to be virtually nonexistent, and who, given suitable opportunities, will effortlessly and inevitably be unfaithful even without the thrust of intense boredom. Some of them might be classifiable as having personality disorders or developmental defects, but far more of them are psychologically normal and have merely incorporated in the unconscious the values of the pagan-courtly tradition rather than those of the puritan-bourgeois tradition. These people, then, are neither unfaithful out of neurotic motives, nor out of frustrations and deprivations within marriage; they are simply polygamous persons in a monogamous culture.

LEWIS AMORY

Some of these points can be exemplified in the person of Dr. Lewis Amory, of whom we will see more in later pages as we follow the course of his current extra-marital affair. Amory, a forty-six-year-old cardiologist, is in his professional prime, and for the past seven or eight years has ranked as one of the better men in his specialty in the Chicago area. He lives with his wife and two daughters in a handsome Georgian home in Lake Forest, where large lawns, lush shrubbery, quiet side roads, and gentlemen's agreements insulate well-to-do white Protestants from traffic, slums, poverty, Negroes, and Jews. Amory regards himself, however, as a liberal; he occasionally lunches with Negro and Jewish doctors (though none are in his country club) and it pleases him occasionally to strike a faintly radical stance before his more conservative friends on such matters as marijuana, avant-garde art, and folk-rock music.

For this is part of staying young, and he finds that extremely important. Despite his heavy office schedule and his rounds at the Michael Reese Hospital, he takes time off to visit the Chicago Athletic Club at least twice a week for handball, steam, and massage. He is a trim and well-built man nearly six feet tall, with a broad, ruddy face, jutting chin, and sandy hair cut brush-fashion; his hairy, muscular hands and forearms look reassuringly strong to his patients, and his erect posture and grace of movement communicate a sense of health. Like many a very physical person, however, he is relatively uncommunicative; his manner is laconic and guarded, and he often replies to patients' questions or friends' remarks with only a faint smile or noncommittal murmur.

Amory comes from an impeccable, though not affluent, background; his father, a moderately successful insurance agent, was an Episcopalian, Republican, and active Rotarian. The elder Amory was also a man of the world, and young Amory, as a teenager, sometimes overheard his father and his father's friends, in the country club locker room, coarsely and good-humoredly talking about sexual adventures outside of marriage. Amory spent two summers, during his undergraduate years, as a swimming coach at a resort hotel in the East, and saw and heard enough there to make him blasé and worldly; even at that age he knew the difference between the facade of American morals and the reality behind it, and was not disturbed.

At Harvard he was a reasonably hardworking pre-med student, but found time for the swimming team and for a good deal of dating around—Radcliffe and Wellesley girls for important events, secretaries and "townies" for more down-to-earth evenings. He went to bed with one or another of the locals about once a week from his sophomore year on, and was rather amused that sex seemed to pose emotional and practical difficulties for so many of his classmates who were forever talking about it. He was drafted in 1943, in his senior year, and spent most of the next three years as a hospital aide at various air bases in the South and then in East Anglia; wherever he was, he always managed to find a passable local girl friend, but never was deluded into thinking any of them more than a temporary convenience.

In early 1946 he returned to Harvard, finished his senior year, and entered Harvard Medical School. Here he was again a fairly diligent student, but always carefully allotted time for his sex life and for dates with college girls. In his second year he met Arlene Richardson, a Radcliffe junior who had everything he wanted in a wife. She was willowy and blonde, cool and poised, competent on horseback and on the tennis court, intelligent but not competitive. She was a more serious Episcopalian than he—Amory had been inactive ever since his confirmation—and felt strongly about not having intercourse until she was married or, at least, engaged. Amory dated her about once a week, and did not press the issue; meanwhile he kept sleeping with a long-haired habitué of a bohemian coffee shop in Cambridge and with a nurse. This seemed to him a reasonable way to solve his problem, and harmless as long as Arlene knew nothing about it. A friend of his once expressed surprise that it didn't bother his conscience; Amory merely shrugged, and thought that his friend sounded like a ninny.

After a year, he and Arlene regarded themselves as in love, and were formally engaged; rather gingerly, they got around to sleeping together, and he began to see less of the other girls and eventually stopped altogether. They were married in June, 1949, right after her graduation, and shortly moved into a tiny apartment in Brookline for his senior year at medical school. In an off-handed and detached tone, he explains how he felt at that time about his marriage and about fidelity:

"We had a lot in common, we looked right together, we got along well. It was a very successful marriage, right from the start, despite some problems and tense periods in the first year or two, mostly due to money. Also, despite taking precautions, she got pregnant four months after we were married, and that made my final year pretty hectic. I was often tense and tired, but I never blew up; I just got quiet and tight, and didn't feel like talking to her. But that didn't last too long, and it certainly wasn't why I first went outside the bounds of marriage.

"Why did I? No special reason except that I felt like it. I knew perfectly well what the Church had to say about fidelity, and what Arlene expected, but I never actually gave the matter a second thought. If I *had* thought about it, I would have figured that I was a man like other men, and that I would probably start cheating sooner or later. How could it be otherwise? It's life."

Amory cannot recall having had fantasies of extra-marital activity before his first affair: "I don't remember any period when I felt deprived, or dwelt on thoughts of sleeping with someone else, or felt compelled to go out and look for a little action. It just seemed to happen by itself." He pauses, looks thoughtful, finally shrugs and makes a confession: "I suppose I always had a wandering eye—I would flirt with the nurses even right after we were married. And if I never had any fantasies about any of them, that's probably because I wasn't holding back; when I finally wanted to do something with one of them, I went ahead and did it. That was relatively soon after I was married—a little over a year, I think. It wasn't anything important. Just a flurry with a nurse, because I needed some sex—Arlene was near the end of her first pregnancy—and also because I had a hankering for a little change. I hadn't been with any woman but Arlene in a year and a half, and that's a long while. Also, sexually she never was the greatest—our sex life has always been all right, but not what you'd call exciting; she's a quiet type, not very intense in her feelings. So I thought it would be fun to get laid somewhere else, and it was, but it didn't mean anything more than that."

He felt no guilt about that first infidelity, and sees no reason why he should have. "I didn't love the nurse; I loved Arlene. Nothing changed just because I rolled around with someone else for half an hour. I was only doing what men always do. Why do we have to lie to ourselves about our nature? A friend of mine was terribly upset when he began feeling itchy pretty soon after getting married. He asked me, 'How long after a man is married does he start to look around and want something else?' I asked how long he'd been married and he said 'Six months.' I said, 'Don't worry about it. That's about par for the course.' So I didn't feel guilty— my only concern was that I didn't want to get caught and hurt anyone.

"I saw the nurse about once a week for two or three months and then it petered out. For a few months I didn't bother with anyone else—an intern doesn't have much time for such things, anyway—but then I stumbled into a good thing with the wife of an accident case who had to stay in multiple casts for a couple of months. After her there was another blank period, and then came a second nurse. With each of these girls it was strictly fun and games, no strings, just once a week or so for a couple hours. I had damned little time, anyway, during my internship and residency, and no money or freedom to get around. When we moved to Chicago and I went into private practice, things changed. I could take a little more time, I began to have some money to spend, I met people and got around. But I never ran wild, I never overdid it. All I wanted was one at a time, for a little excitement and friendship and some good sex, about once a week."

He seemed to have had two reasons for limiting things this way. One, his patients were more important to him than anyone had ever been in his life up to this point; he lavished time on the worst cases, read the cardiology literature religiously, and attended meetings and symposia whenever he could. Second, he deliberately kept his affairs tepid in order not to disturb his marriage. "Any time I saw a woman getting genuinely involved in me, or found myself thinking about her too much, I'd arrange things so that I was too busy to see her for a while, or I'd 'forget' a date with her, or something of the sort. I always *liked* the women I went out with and enjoyed seeing them, but I didn't want more than that, and never had anything with any of them that would have made me consider, for one moment, breaking up my home, leaving my wife and children, and abandoning my way of life.

"My relationship with Arlene has been rather good, I'd say, even if not very close because of my being so busy and away from home so much. It certainly isn't a total relationship; partly that's because I've had other women in my life, and partly because Arlene seems to be interested only in the children, the house, and her country-club activities. But I like having some open space in the marriage anyhow. When we were first married, I would work in the university library two or three nights a week rather than at home just to have a little privacy. After I went into private practice, I preserved some freedom for myself by telling her that twice a week I would spend the evening in town having a workout at the club and a few hours of cards with the boys. Even when I didn't feel like it, I'd stay in town for the evening in order to keep my franchise, so that when I had something else in mind, I'd have my story ready."

But his careful planning and his connections with a whole series of women have not been the result of any gnawing dissatisfaction with his marriage—at least, none that comes to his mind. "Naturally, we would have a fight now and then or a spell of not talking to each other, but it has been a good marriage. I suppose a psychoanalyst would say there has to be something wrong with it or I wouldn't have been doing these other things all along, but I don't agree. I'm not convinced that men can ever find everything they want in one woman or that monogamy is a normal state. I have never tried to justify to myself or to any woman what I do by saying that there's something wrong at home. I'm quite satisfied with my home life, but the outside relationships have always added something—they've kept me feeling young, eager, interested in life. I guess I could be faithful if I wanted to, but life would be far duller, and I wouldn't make as good a husband or father because I wouldn't be as happy a man.

"Arlene has never found out about all this, or made any complaints about our marriage. I'm not home much, but she's busy with her own things, and though we don't have a lot of sex, what we have is okay and both of us enjoy it. But I haven't let her get keyed up to where she'd want a lot of sex, because then I might not have the drive for my outside relationships. Perhaps that sounds selfish of me, but she doesn't act deprived. It's much the same in other areas of our married life: If I got into the habit of telling her most of what I think and feel, it would be hard for me to keep the rest under control. There's so much I do and experience in my present relationship with Terry that I'd be very apt to slip up and reveal some of it, if I talked a lot at home. Better that I remain a private sort of person. A man has to preserve his right to think and do things that he doesn't account for to his wife."

chapter 3: TEMPTATION

i lead us into temptation

Fiction and fantasy often use the meeting with the fascinating stranger as the prelude to the first affair, but in actual fact, as most people realize, the first affair is far more likely to involve a partner already close at hand and well-known. One third of my questionnaire respondents and interviewees had their first (or only) affairs with persons who had been close friends before becoming their lovers, and another quarter to a third with persons they were reasonably well-acquainted with. This is only partly a question of convenience. To go outside one's usual rounds, consciously and deliberately seeking temptation, would seem morally far worse than to have temptation thrust upon one by Fate in the form of someone who is almost unavoidable. The temptation that first overpowers conscience, fear, and other defenses is likely to be both convenient and unsought.

Even so, the tempted ones are co-conspirators with Fate.

Though passive, they are receptive; they know or sense the presence of danger but linger, fascinated and fearful, half-hoping that they will be helplessly carried along to the desired goal.

—A former model, now raising two children and running a home, enjoys the half-jocular flattery her closest friend's husband offers her (he always compliments her on her superb body and laments, in mock-serious fashion, that he has never had the chance to explore it). Once, their tongues freed by liquor at a party, he and she tell each other about the faults of their marriages. By chance they run into each other a week later while taking their children to a Saturday afternoon movie; they sit next to each other, and when their arms accidently touch on the armrest, they do not move them apart for a moment or two. He stops by one afternoon to give her prints of some pictures he had taken at the party, and asks if she'd like to go sailing with him one day next week; she knows, of course, that his wife hates sailing and never goes. She is alarmed, but reminds herself that he is her best friend's husband and that he has never made any improper move; she accepts. Years later, in psychotherapy, she admits to herself that she expected and wanted what happened that day on the boat.

—In a small midwestern college, the chairman of the drama department and a young woman from the music department work together deftly and harmoniously at a rehearsal of the student production of *The King and I.* After the students leave at 10:30 P.M., they sit and talk in his ascetic, paper-cluttered office, and drink bitter reheated coffee from the electric percolator. At first they discuss the show; somehow, though, they drift off into talk about themselves, their interests, their hopes, their marriages. This happens five or six nights; then, during Christmas vacation, each is acutely aware of not seeing the other and recognizes what has been happening. At the first post-vacation rehearsal, each sees in the other's face an open admission. After the rehearsal, they drive to a park, kiss frantically, discuss whether they should break off at once or become lovers, arrive at no decision, and agree to meet the next night to discuss it further.

Our choice of a lover, like that of the beast of the field, owes a great deal to propinquity; while thinking ourselves in the grip of some special and unduplicated passion, we find our ideal in something conveniently near at hand. As the leprechaun in *Finian's Rainbow* sings, "When I'm not facing the face I fancy, I fancy the face I face." But few are willing to admit this. What they feel seems the result of something far grander than nearness and willingness; it appears to them that they are being manipulated by a power greater than themselves.

NEAL GORHAM AND MARY BUCHANAN

In the fall of 1965 Neal's firm lost the Caribbean hotel account that had provided over half his work. The agency being small, this was a serious loss, but by January there was a new account in the shop—a large book publisher—and Neal, who had written the presentation, was assigned to it as both account executive and writer. This threw him at once into close and almost daily contact with the book company's advertising manager, Mary Buchanan. *First met her with her boss, Calvin Prestwick, sales manager: he a heavy wheezing mass, she a lean graceful whippet; he stolid, damp of hand, face-mopping, aging, she freckled and red-haired, gamine, young; he impervious to humor (or merely disapproving), she playful, nimble-witted, good at verbal ping-pong. I was startled to learn after first meeting that she was his wife; wondered how happy she was with him.* This first conference was concerned with the advertising campaign for the spring list. Time was critically short, especially for ads for the monthlies, and Neal decided to rely on personal conferences with the book company's staff for much of his information about the spring titles. Calvin Prestwick sat in on the first of these meetings, but said little; when Neal and Mary threw in jokes and absurdities unexpectedly, he chuckled dutifully, but more often looked blank or begged them to be serious.

After two hours, a number of major decisions had been made and the work to be done had been roughly outlined. Neal suggested that because of the late date they ought to put in several long sessions of collaborative work—including evenings, if necessary—to get the crucial items out of the way. Prestwick agreed, but said that he himself wouldn't be present; Mary handled the details of advertising and, in any case, he was about to leave on a three-week trip to visit the major book-stores and jobbers. *Hard work, those first sessions, but exciting and full of accomplishment; great relief from Caribbean sands and men's cologne. The second time—or was it the third?—we decided to continue on into the evening; over to Danny's Hideaway for dinner; there we still talked business, but all around us were dating couples, and when I lit her cigarette and ordered Martinis for the two of us, I felt as if we, too, were on a date. Strange, familiar, long-forgotten mood; pang of regret for other times, other places; agreeably wicked feeling of playing hookie from the present. Wondered how she saw me—as an advertising writer or as a man? Felt silly for thinking such things. Wondered, too, how she and Prestwick got along in bed together. Repellent image: his large loose body lying heavily on her taut fine-boned one, squashing her breasts. By the end of dinner, our talk had drifted far from book advertising; I was warming my Courvoisier in the goblet and sipping appreciatively when she said, very softly, "You're quite a sensuous person, aren't you?" A flare of light, a thumping in my chest, my face growing hot . . . Be careful; this is not one of your daydreams. But then later she asked why I was staring at her hands; was she gesticulating too much?—and I, suddenly bold, said something about how beautiful they were. She blushed. Pleased with myself and a little excited; had never openly flirted with any woman since meeting Laurie. A dangerous business?—no; I love Laurie, would never be capable of cheating; no danger. . . .*

But he had not let himself see how things had changed in his marriage to Laurie, one-time beauty and bit-part actress now beginning to fade and thicken; belatedly seeking a new self in college but not finding it; disillusioned with the professional theater long ago but now resentful of Neal because she "gave it up for his sake"; once interested in everything he did, now bored by his advertising writing and faintly patronizing about his unpublished play and poetry; once eager to join their bodies at night, now quietly unwilling or at best acquiescent and apathetic; once easily aroused by his touch, now usually unmoved and, even when excited, rarely able to yield herself enough to achieve satisfaction. To all of which Neal had adapted himself in one way or another: by his adoring and indulgent absorption in eight-year-old Robin and six-year-old Billy; by escaping to books or the typewriter for long hours in the study over the garage; by using the warmth and ease of alcohol to loosen the clutch of anger upon his stomach when Laurie was being cold or cutting. He had not let himself see how vulnerable he was; but *it was the next evening that Mary touched me and later spoke that fateful sentence. Or was it the time after that? Four months have passed; I should have captured it then; now it is like something drawn in sand and blurred by the breeze. We had gone back to the board room after dinner to work on the juvenile list; the building was chilly and she suggested we work in their Tudor City apartment, five blocks away, where all was warm and quiet (step-son Freddy away at prep school, Prestwick on the road). I joshed her (a trifle nervously) about what her staff would think if they knew. "They think it already," she said, smiling just a little. Felt excited, shaky; thought myself absurd. Worked in her dinette, papers spread all over, hands often close. Phoned home; while I was dialing, she, passing behind me on the way to freshen my drink, rested her slim fingers on my neck for an instant and said, "It's good to have you here." Stab of desire in me; wanted to turn, pull her toward me, press my face to her bosom; instead I just smiled, touched her hand with mine. Later, having finished our work, we talked about ourselves for an hour; and I realized that with her I felt unaccountably manly, witty, and brilliant. And then it happened: As I was leaving, she looked at me oddly and said, "I'm afraid this is beginning to bother me," and swiftly closed the door between us.*

Mary Buchanan: 5′5″, 118 pounds, slim-waisted, small and firm of bosom, trim of ankle; bright brown eyes and lopsided grin in round, lightly freckled face under a fluff of reddish-brown hair. Born in Binghamton, N.Y. in 1932, thirty-four when Neal met her; A.B., Barnard, 1952; father a freight-yard switcher; raised a Catholic, became relatively inactive during college, still attends mass on holidays, although barred from sacraments because of her marital history: married at twenty-two, divorced (no children) at twenty-six; married her boss, Calvin Prestwick, at thirty, three and a half years before meeting Neal Gorham. "I went with Cal for a year before we got married, and the last few months of that year I all but lived with him and his son, Freddy [Cal had insisted on custody as the price of giving his first wife a divorce]. I was great with Freddy, and Cal could see me as a good mother, while I saw Cal as a kindly, strong, fatherly lover—just what I wanted, after four years of marriage to an emotional adolescent and three years of dating slick, egotistical New York bachelors who were on the make but were scared to death of feelings. After getting along beautifully for a year, Cal and I got married, and about the same time, he promoted me to advertising manager. Which thing did us in I don't know, but we were never the same after that. I was so damned much better at the book business than he that it was embarrassing; he benefitted by my work, but it seemed to him that I was always cutting him down. And after we were married, I found out he wasn't a big strong Daddy at all, but a weak, petulant boy, wanting me to take charge of everything—but angry as hell when I did so. A year or so of warfare, and then truce. Our sexual relationship, which had been okay but not great, withered away because my sexual feelings for him faded out, and because even when he wanted it, he hardly ever demanded it. Other than sexually, we got along well enough—we could always talk about a thousand things, and at work I tried hard not to outshine him when anyone was looking. We had a civilized, reasonable relationship for a couple of years, and I thought it would last the rest of our lives.

"Then along came Neal Gorham. He was the first man I'd ever met who bested me intellectually without even trying, and did it lightly and amiably; it made me feel weak inside. And he didn't even know it—he didn't have any idea how appealing he was as a person. Or physically, either, and that only made him all the more so. I was astonished to find myself distinctly stirred up the first or second time we worked together. When I lost my sexual feeling for Cal, I lost sexual desire altogether; it was so total that I wondered if there hadn't been some physical change in me. I thought the desire would never come back, but I didn't care. The only time I'd do it was when Cal would grow mad at my turning him down all the time, and I'd think, 'Oh boy, he may walk out on me.' Then I'd perform beautifully and play him as if he were a puppet on a string; I knew exactly how to give him enough to keep him in line, without having any feelings myself. I was using sex as a weapon—as most women do.

"But I never used it as a weapon with Neal, at least not in the beginning. I didn't want an affair; I didn't want to stir up my hopes or my hungers after having learned to live without them. But the feeling kept growing in me, and I couldn't ignore it. I thought to myself, 'Damn him, damn him! I'm frightened, I'm *feeling* again, I'm *alive* inside.' I could read him like a book—passionate but inhibited, burning to have me but scared to death and unable to make a move. I knew he never would unless I cued him. I don't know what I had in mind—I didn't think it through, I just did what I felt like doing. One night, after all sorts of verbal skirmishing, I had an irresistible impulse: As he was going out the door I said, 'This is starting to bother me,' and shut the door on him fast—but not before I saw the look on his face and knew that I had pushed the right button."

* * *

The seemingly innocent persons who have temptation thrust upon them by Fate are thus usually not so innocent after all; knowingly or half-knowingly, they have connived at their own seduction. Even where the temptation seems to have been purely accidental, the outside observer can see unconscious volition at work in the unfaithful in the form of a refusal to avoid or remove one's self from a high-risk milieu or situation. The faithful husband who goes on a convention trip with a group of men he knows to have a taste for pick-ups or call girls has voluntarily put himself in the line of fire; he is to blame if he gets hit. The husband and wife who intend to be faithful, but make themselves part of a social circle in which, it is rumored, there are mate-swapping and sexual parties, are willfully increasing the chances of "accidentally" being faced with temptation too great to resist. The Serpent was not wholly to blame; had Eve walked away, she would not have heard his beguiling words

---

ii moth and flame

Even in their first infidelities, many people—perhaps even a majority—do not wait passively for temptation to overtake them; they actively cultivate the possible temptations around them, or deliberately seek out special situations which they know will give them the chance to play an active part.

Party flirtation is probably the most common way of actively confronting temptation. When middle-class couples who know each other fairly well get together, particularly at a large party where the liquor is flowing freely, there is often a certain amount of half-jocular but definitely seductive skirmishing across the marital borders. Such flirtation does not necessarily signify the intent to have an extra-marital affair; it may be an end in itself, an agreeable game that yields its own satisfactions. A man dancing with a friend's wife may find himself sharply aware of the texture of her skin, the size of her waist, the pressure of her bosom against his chest, all of them different from the skin, waist, and bosom he knows so well that he has ceased being aware of them. He holds his partner a little closer, whispers some appreciative word in her ear; when she responds with a pleased murmur, he feels like the creature he once was, or wanted to be—an attractive, somewhat mysterious, and slightly dangerous male, rather than a weary commuter, husband, father, and handyman. His wife, chatting with half a dozen people elsewhere, is agreeably aware that one of the men in the group is discreetly looking at her with a special, private, approving manner; she feels warmed by it, laughs a little more gaily, speaks with new animation, lets her eyes once or twice meet his for a second, feels beautiful.

Besides pleasing and reassuring the individual, flirtation can arouse man and wife from torpor, giving each a renewed awareness of the other; properly used, writes psychoanalyst Edrita Fried in *The Ego in Love and Sexuality*, it can be a constructive force in keeping marriage vital. But even failing this, it can provide valuable relief from constraint: Dr. Paul Gebhard of the Institute for Sex Research feels that flirtation, including "party gropery"—the brief surreptitious petting that often goes on in gardens, on balconies, and in kitchens—is analogous to the orgiastic festivals in which married people, in preliterate societies, were permitted a brief period of release from the confinement of marriage—a holiday from which they returned relieved and renewed in spirit.

But our society has no clear-cut rules governing the use and limits of flirtation, and we are therefore often unsure whether a given act is playful or serious, safe or dangerous. The man or woman who is merely playing may be alarmed to discover that his or her playmate is very much in earnest. A woman may act responsive to a man's touch while dancing, but when he then suggests that they meet for cocktails next week, she is offended and indignant. He feels like a fool, and worse than that, fears that his wife will hear about it, for the secret is in unfriendly hands; he may be damned for a sinner without having enjoyed any sins.

Even more disconcertingly, a man or woman who meant only to play a game may experience unexpected reactions that carry him or her, willy-nilly, beyond the point of no return:

—A twenty-eight-year-old accountant in a large western city: "My wife and I spent a lot of time with the Wickers that winter, sometimes bowling, sometimes just drinking beer and talking. Francie Wicker and I would make eye-passes at each other, and occasionally touch hands for a moment under the table. It was dumb of us but very exciting, and we never got caught. I didn't mean it to go anywhere, but she managed to mention once or twice what time Arnold left for work—he was on a night shift at the aircraft plant —and after mulling it over for a while, and feeling pretty nervous about it, I finally slipped her the word that I'd drop by and have a beer with her some time. When I did, we sat far apart and talked for a long while; it was very strained between us. But I could tell how she felt, and she could tell how I felt, and finally I went and sat beside her and put my arms around her and said, 'We're really in trouble, aren't we?' She didn't say anything; she just nodded."

Because of the ambiguities and the risks involved in party flirtation, men and women in search of temptation sometimes prefer to look for it outside their own social circle, in settings where an indication of interest, or seductive behavior in another person, is less ambiguous or where, at least, the risks of embarrassment and revelation are minimized. In business offices, cocktail lounges, planes, trains, and the like, the flirtatious manner is not so often merely a game of the moment; and even when it is, mistaking it for something more serious is less likely to be harmful.

Yet even in a relatively unambiguous and safe situation, the neophyte may not clearly recognize his own intention; he may at first, or for a long while, refuse to acknowledge his purpose in pursuing a temptation well outside the confines and the regulating forces of his own social circle. Such was the case with Edwin Gottesman.

EDWIN GOTTESMAN AND JENNIFER SCOTT

In the fall of 1965 Edwin Gottesman visited Philadelphia frequently, in connection with a project for a new shopping center near West Chester, a town just west of the city. In trying to assemble a tract of land from several different owners, he chose to have three small real-estate agents front for him and his syndicate, so as to keep prices from soaring to unreasonable levels. Late one October afternoon, he visited one of the real-estate agents at his shabby street-floor office in Upper Darby. In the outer room, a secretary who was typing told Gottesman that Mr. Hartman was expecting him and that he could go right on in. Gottesman queried Hartman about the status of several of the needed parcels, and rather forcefully told him that he was moving too slowly on them. Hartman squirmed and apologized, blaming the weather, his rheumatism, and the secretary outside, Jennifer Scott, who was inept but whom he hesitated to fire; depressed by the recent break-up of her engagement, and deeply in debt for an operation, she had been talking of selling herself to some rich old man, or else of committing suicide. Gottesman was shocked; he swung around and looked through the glass panel at the girl, whom he had scarcely noticed on his way in. She was tall and slender—almost skinny—and had black shoulder-length hair, loose-hanging and rather untidy; her skin was pale and her face long and almost classic, though cheapened by excessive eye make-up and heavy false lashes. She seemed to be, at the most, in her early twenties, but sat round-shouldered, either from weariness or dejection.

Gottesman felt sorry for her and wondered how different she might be if someone were kind to her and took her in hand. He and Hartman discussed their business for nearly an hour, at which point Gottesman, feeling he had been rather hard on the man, suggested they have drinks and dinner together while finishing up the last details. As they emerged from the office, Jennifer Scott was putting on her coat and closing up. Gottesman thought she looked lonely,

sad, and in need of a decent dinner, and impulsively invited her to
join them; surprised and a little hesitant, she accepted.

"At the time I thought of her as nothing but a charity case. Or
let's say I *thought* that's how I thought of her. But at dinner we
wound up our business fast, and I got to talking very freely and
proudly about my house and my children and my art collection; I
could see she was impressed by me, and I played up to her because
I liked the way it made me feel. Afterwards, Hartman went his own
way, and since she lived in downtown Philadelphia and I was going
by cab to my hotel, I took her along and dropped her off at the front
door of her building. By that time, I found her rather pretty—much
more so than I realized at first. I still thought of her only as a nice
kid with lots of problems; it didn't occur to me to see her as
anything more, and certainly not as anything for myself. But when
I phoned Hartman the next morning with a couple of additional
ideas, she recognized my voice at once and was warm and friendly,
almost personal, on the phone, and it made me feel very good, very
set up. I talked to Hartman, but all I could think of was that I should
have asked her to dinner tonight—I could phone Betsy and tell her
I wouldn't be able to get back until tomorrow morning. As soon as
Hartman hung up, I dialed back to talk to her—and hung up again.
'What kind of *narrishkeit* is this,' I asked myself, 'me, a married
man with a wonderful wife and two fine children—what business
have I got inviting a tough-luck girl fifteen years younger than me
to dinner?' Three times I dialed, three times I hung up. I walked
over and looked at myself in the mirror in my room. 'You fool,' I
said, 'stop the nonsense!' But then I said, 'No, not a fool—a *cow-
ard.*' And that did it: I phoned again, and asked her to dinner."

She accepted eagerly and agreed to meet him at Arthur's Steak
House on Walnut Street. Waiting for her at the bar, he felt excited
and a trifle wicked. He glanced at himself in the mirror, thinking
that freshly shaved, and in a clean white shirt and a two-hundred-
dollar custom-tailored suit, he wasn't bad-looking, after all; he told
himself that he should remember to smile more often. She arrived,
cheerful and lively; she wore a gaudy op-art dress from a bargain
counter, but Gottesman thought it looked wonderful on her. Their
conversation was a trifle awkward at first, but then they fell into a
game of telling each other how dreadful their childhoods had been,

each trying to top the other, until they went off into a gale of laughter. Jennifer had grown up in bleak working-class neighborhoods in Camden and Philadelphia; her father, a lathe operator and auto mechanic, fought with her mother continually and left her several times before finally divorcing her and moving to Long Island. The four children had been farmed out to relatives, brought back home, and farmed out again; Jennifer had run away twice and been brought back by the police. She dropped out of high school in her senior year and disappeared into downtown Philadelphia, where she lived with a semi-communal houseful of artists and models for a couple of months; then she went back to stay with her mother and finish high school. Since then, she had lived downtown alone and worked at various secretarial jobs without liking any of them; she aspired to be an artists' and photographers' model, but thus far had had little luck getting such work.

Evidently, she had had a number of involvements with men, though Edwin couldn't tell how many had included sex. "But I didn't care. I wasn't concerned. To tell the truth, I don't even know what it was that drove me to keep on seeing her. At home, I'd be playing with the kids in the living-room, or talking to Betsy at dinner-time, or we'd all be having breakfast around the dinette table, and I'd think, 'It's stupid to waste my time and money taking some ignorant low-class girl to dinner. What do I *need* it for? And what if Betsy ever found out—what could I say about it?'

"But I had to come to Philadelphia about once a week that fall and winter, and every time I planned a trip up there, I found myself calling Jennifer and taking her out. The truth is, I got a thrill out of it. And it didn't seem stupid when I was doing it. She was good company and we always talked a lot; she was interested in my business deals and loved to hear all about them, and I enjoyed telling her. We went to nightclubs a few times, and to a movie or two, and one Saturday afternoon I even took her into a few art galleries and tried to open her eyes to things. Usually I'm very stingy with my time, but something about her made me feel differently. I was able to give her things—good dinners, good talk, little presents, a taste of the bigger world—and meanwhile she made me feel younger and more interesting than I had ever felt in my life. And even romantic. One night we were walking in the falling snow, in Rittenhouse Square, and she took my hand and put our two hands in my pocket; I felt marvelous, I felt *handsome.* And that night she waited at the front door of her crummy little apartment for me to kiss her goodnight, and from then on I always did. But I never got any hint of anything more, and I was afraid to try. Besides, the business of lying to my wife and keeping secrets about these little dates with Jennifer was all I could manage; I wasn't ready for more."

Nevertheless, the lack of sexual intimacy began to trouble him after a while. Not that he felt any great desire for Jennifer; he didn't, and in any case he was having regular and quite adequate sexual relations with Betsy. Fearing that Jennifer might not find him physically appealing and that any overt approach might ruin their relationship, he did nothing—and the longer this went on, the harder it was for him to imagine himself breaking the pattern.

After he had known her about three months, he was offered an important role in a syndicate created to buy a large piece of land in Puerto Rico and build a hotel on it; he decided to spend a three-day weekend there working on the matter. While telling Jennifer about it, he asked her on the spur of the moment whether she'd go there with him; she broke into a dazzling smile, said without a second's hesitation that she'd love it, and affectionately took his hand and kissed it. Edwin's heart began pounding, and he hardly knew what to say or how to act, but she took the lead; she played with his hand all during dinner, twining her fingers in his, and that night in her barren little living-room she opened her mouth to his tongue for the first time and ran her hands slowly up and down his back. He fumbled for her breasts, but she took his hands gently and whispered, "Let's wait till we get there. It'll be so much more special."

He wandered blindly back to his hotel, asking himself what in God's name he thought he was doing—and knowing that nothing would stop him from doing it. He lay awake for hours, picturing the two of them, a tangle of pale limbs and dark hair, lying on a moonlit bed in a room overlooking the ocean; at last he fell asleep, only to dream of the same thing. In the morning, though weary, he was buoyant and happy with his secret; after breakfast, emerging into the winter sunlight, he walked jauntily down the street, wondering whether any of the people hurrying past him on their way to work were as alive and as cheerfully immoral as he.

*   *   *

Edwin had hardly known his own degree of readiness; he might never have faced temptation, had it not arrived accidentally. But some people know their own minds better than he, and consciously go out hunting for temptation rather than relying on chance to present them with it. One favorite place in which to look for it is the cocktail lounge; not all of them, to be sure, are frequented by people hunting casual sex partners, but in large cities many a better lounge does serve as a respectable social setting in which extra-marital social contacts can be made. A recent study by two sociologists reports that over seventy per cent of the men in one high-caliber cocktail lounge in a West Coast city were married, successful, stable persons looking for nothing more than a little excitement and sexual variety. The women in the lounge, all unmarried, were younger than the men and much less successful; they too, however, were not seeking marital prospects but only companionable, casual, sexual liaisons with married, sophisticated men.

When the novice first enters such a setting, he is apt to feel uncomfortable; he lacks the feel of things, is unsure just how to talk or act, cannot tell whether the women he sees around him are decent or are "hookers," does not know how he looks to them. He may be so unsure of himself that he goes time and again without asking any of the women for dates and almost without talking to them. He comforts himself by thinking that he is either virtuous or choosy. But when the balance of things tips the other way and he does make a date with one of them, he promptly discards his old self-appraisal and thinks of himself as either daring or charming. A thirty-nine-year-old consulting chemist, married to his first and only girl friend since his late teens, explains how it felt when he finally crossed the line:

—"For years I'd been hearing other men talk about their affairs and thinking I was missing something, but no matter where I travelled or how many women I saw on planes or in hotels, I never had the nerve to do or say anything. Sometimes when I was with a whole group of people, I might kid around with some woman, but it was never for real; I played it safe by being funny." In Seattle on a consulting job, he was talking to a beautiful woman at a company reception at the Olympic Hotel; he wanted to ask her to dinner but lacked the nerve. An hour later he saw her in the hotel dining-room with another man. He was furious at himself, and went to the cocktail lounge after dinner, determined to do better than he had. Service was slow; he couldn't seem to get waited on at his table, and went to the bar, where he stood next to two girls and a man who had drinks in front of them. I said, for a joke, 'You people must have special pull with the bartender.' They smiled, and I started chatting with them. The extra girl was lively and nice-looking, and friendly enough, but I couldn't get up the courage to ask her to spend the evening with me. After a while the other girl said to the two of them, 'It's too noisy—let's get out of here.' I didn't say anything, and she said to me, 'Come on. Make it a foursome.' That did it; I went along as the nice-looking one's date, and in a little while I was doing fine—I clowned around with her, but I also talked seriously, I danced with her better than I ever did with my wife, I found myself flirting like somebody I didn't even know. I couldn't believe it; it wasn't the cautious, stick-in-the-mud me at all." About 1 A.M. he drove the girl home; he was uncertain whether to call it quits or not, but she asked him to come up for just one quick nightcap. He had no idea whether this was what she really meant or whether it was a euphemism; he hesitated to do anything that might bring a rebuff, and was ready to leave after ten minutes. But she led him, drink in hand, out onto her little terrace to look at the mountains, and when they sat down on the settee, she placed herself quite close to him; then he knew, and put an arm around her.

PEGGY FARRELL, ET AL.

Like this man, Peggy Farrell had made up her mind to go in search of temptation but started out hesitantly, acquiring confidence through experience; in all forms of deviant behavior, the first transgression is the most difficult one. It took more than a year for her to lose her excess forty pounds; by then, she was also free of the skin disorder brought on by her hormone imbalance. She had settled on a short boyish hair-style that emphasized her sprightly features and contrasted with her slightly plump, very curvy body. Her mood had long since changed from one of depression to one of excitement and nervous expectancy. "I was good and ready to see what might happen, but I was also pretty jumpy about it. I'd been imagining affairs for a couple of years, but I wasn't sure I'd know what to say or how to act. And I wasn't sure that anyone would really want me—I was still thinking fat even though I was looking thin. But there wasn't anything moral about my hesitation; I had turned my back on the rules long ago. Anyway, an affair wouldn't hurt my marriage. Nothing would. Except when I was picking fights with Andy, we got along all right, but we didn't seem to have much more to say to each other than a couple of roomers in the same boarding-house. Besides, I thought an affair might even help, by making me easier to live with."

Her anxiety kept her from doing more for several months than testing out a few flirtatious looks now and then, and since her opportunities seemed limited to store clerks and to bridge opponents, she got nowhere. Then, in the late spring, a friend of hers invited the Farrells to a large party; privately she told Peggy it would be a swinging affair, with a number of men who were always on the make. "Andy wanted to go to a big party about as much as he wanted to go to an execution. But I had come bouncing in to show him a new dress I had made for the party, so he said, 'Why don't you go without me? I'll stay home and we'll save the price of the sitter.' I thought, 'Wonderful! Great!' But I played it cool so he wouldn't see how I felt. When the time came, off I went, looking damned good and just whirling with excitement."

Nonetheless, she told herself that she meant only to look things over. "I wore my wedding ring—I was still green, and didn't have the guts to take it off—and I promised myself I was only going to put one toe in the pool, to see if the water was chilly." For a while, she drifted around aimlessly at the party talking to other women and studying the men from a safe distance. One man's looks and manners appealed to her. "His name was Tim Conner; he was lean and trim, and had brilliant blue eyes, and although his hair was quite gray he was only in his thirties. A very good-looking but shy fellow. When I saw him, he was in the kitchen talking with some other people; his wife was out on the patio, where there was dancing

—another break! He and I started stealing looks at each other. I was cold sober, and he was half-crocked, but I felt as free and giddy as if I were half-crocked, too. After a while he and I maneuvered off into a corner of the dining-room by ourselves, and he said, 'What's happening?' I said, in a shaky voice but looking straight at him, 'I don't know. What *is* happening?' Then both of us were embarrassed and silent for a minute—and then both started laughing at ourselves and each other. We got a couple of fresh drinks, and went and sat in a corner away from everybody else, and talked about a thousand things, trying to find out all about each other, and hoped nobody was noticing us."

She cannot recall exactly what they talked about that first time —it didn't really matter—but she does remember the intense exhilaration of having something going on at last. Toward the end of the evening, when people were beginning to leave, Tim faltered, then screwed up his courage and asked her if they would ever see each other again. "Well, there it was! Flirting at a party is one thing, but agreeing to meet somebody privately, even if just for a drink, is something else altogether. But by then I was ready for it, so I said, 'That's up to you,' which was saying yes. He looked relieved, as if he had been afraid of a rebuff; then he said, 'Well, I'll phone you sometime soon.' 'Oh God,' I thought, 'I hope he means it, let him really do it! I *need* to have something going on, something besides chit-chat with my next-door neighbor, and pablum and nose-wiping and laundry and dishes.' I didn't dare believe he really would call, but he did, the following Tuesday, and we had a long talk. He was all torn up, worrying that it was wrong, so I said, 'What's wrong with just talking? There's no need to get upset about something that hasn't happened and mightn't ever.' That's a good way to handle a man like that; it puts him on the offensive. So we made a date to meet one afternoon, when I could get away easily—my next-door neighbor and I swapped baby-sitting for each other. There's no place much—and no safe place—in Brighton, so we met in town at the bar in the Sheraton Hotel, where a lot of singles meet pretty freely. We drank and talked and looked into each other's eyes for an hour. I loved it; I felt like myself again. From then on, every day seemed to have some meaning: It was the day he'd be calling me, or it was only one more day till we'd meet at the Sheraton again, or whatever. I ignored Andy more and more, but at least I wasn't picking fights with him. I was definitely easier to get along with than I had been for a long while."

If that were enough, the moth would never get burned by the flame; but it was not enough, at least not for Peggy. When the little trysts continued for over a month without any indication on Tim's part that he had further plans, Peggy's initial delight quickly waned. "I started to feel cheated and frustrated. All he wanted was to be romantically in love, but once I got used to what we were doing, I was ready for the rest of it, and I felt that if he cared as much as he said he did, he'd want the rest of it, too. I wasn't about to let it stay where it was—and I told him so. You should have seen his face! He looked like he was going to pass out."

* * *

A small number of men and women go in search of temptation not only without guilt, like Peggy Farrell, but with the aid and encouragement of their spouses; this makes the temptation all but tantamount to the yielding, since both the inner and outer defenses have been so largely dismantled. Some husbands and wives who are bored or unhappy with each other, and who have been titillated by discussions or articles dealing with experimental marital arrangements, employ the "conjugal vacation" or "summer divorce," an arrangement in which each partner goes off on vacation alone with implicit—or even explicit—freedom to behave like an unattached person and to have a bit of a fling. For seasoned adulterers this might present no problem; for husbands and wives who have not yet been unfaithful, the conjugal vacation is a difficult way to start. Even though it offers sanction to both spouses, neither one knows just how successful he or she will be, how to go about looking for partners, or what to say about his or her marital status and motives. Even worse, perhaps, is the inevitable competitiveness: When husband and wife meet again, each is bound to be curious about the other's experiences and to feel either smug or jealous if there are any differences in achievement.

The conjugal vacation, though socially deviant, seems to be expressive of normal boredom more often than of serious pathology. But according to a few accounts in psychological journals

and to several of my interviewees, extra-marital affairs are sometimes virtually thrust upon an unwilling or unaware spouse by the
other, and this usually represents serious pathology on the part of
the conniving one. Impotent or homosexual men sometimes drop
hints to their wives or even openly urge then to have outside affairs;
frigid or homosexual women sometimes tell their husbands to feel
free to enjoy sex with other partners.

Sometimes the offer is made not in words, but in the form of
a temptation. One man brought a good friend of his home for dinner
time and again, but always got drunk and sleepy and took himself
off to bed right after dinner, urging his wife and friend to stay up
and talk as long as they liked. One woman invited an attractive
female friend of hers, who lived in another city, to be their house
guest for a week; in the middle of the visit she went off on a
suddenly remembered two-day business trip, leaving friend and
husband alone together. Yet even where so many of the restraints
against the act are removed, those to whom temptation is so freely
tendered do not always accept the offer; most women and some
men are unable to enjoy the mere frolic or diversion, and want
nothing less than a total loving experience. The one kind of temptation to which they might yield is precisely the one kind their com-
plaisant mates would not think of offering them.

iii brinkmanship

Unlike Peggy Farrell, a fair number of novices at infidelity stop
short on the brink of sexual activity, and remain there for an indefinite time without discomfort or frustration. While allowing themselves considerable emotional involvement, they limit the physical
aspect of the relationship to the porch-settee or back-seat fumbling
they knew in their teens, and believe this to be not "really" unfaithful. They seem to pattern their extra-marital relationships after old
Doris Day movies or radio soap-opera, vintage 1950, the intimacies
they allow themselves consisting of long, yearning phone calls,
impassioned letters, and secret meetings for lunch or cocktails in

obscure country inns or dark hideaways in town, where a booth well toward the back can be a world apart.

And in those bittersweet, stolen hours, what talk they lavish upon each other, what amphorae of rare words they unstopper and pour forth! And what is it that they talk about? Hardly the films of Buñuel, or radiocarbon dating, or Black Power; not minimal art, organ transplants, or the decline of big cities; but their childhoods, their marriages, their favorite things, their feelings about each other. "The reason lovers never weary of being together," wrote the acerb Duc de La Rochefoucauld, "is that they are always talking about themselves." But also about each other: Both, in telling about themselves, sense how the other must feel in response; both, in listening, feel as the other wants them to feel. And in this microcosm of mutuality they possess infinite space; they feel as though they are experiencing "real" and "important" things for the first time in years.

Yet the conversation comes back again and again to the one most obvious topic of all—the missing link in their relationship. They speak, sometimes obliquely, sometimes directly, of their attitudes toward love-making, of their wish to possess each other fully, of their reasons for not doing so. There is no end to their yearning, their regret, their self-denial; but all these painful feelings are paradoxically gratifying. The man may reason, plead, cajole, and finally fall silent; so much the better, for the woman can then reach across the table to him, beg him to understand, to give her time—time not to learn to want him ("Oh, I do—you must *know* that"), but to handle her own conflicts. And with this, he feels that she has, in a sense, yielded; he is exhilarated, proud, and able to be patient, while she, having emotionally given herself, is intoxicated with it all, and yet can go home without having the actual deed on her conscience. So they linger until it is late; then they arise and leave their comfortable niche outside of time and place, going out into the brightness and reality of day like children emerging from the wonderland of a Saturday afternoon movie, dazed and astonished to find the everyday world still there.

Some women find most of what they need in these limited forms of contact. The emotional quickening, the awareness of desire in one's self, the unreal flawless love that exists in stolen hours of talk and hand-holding—these things can assuage the loneliness they feel in a poor marriage, make them feel desirable and loving again, give them a precious secret to exult in whenever they need to. Surprisingly enough, some men are also content with unconsummated involvements that have romantic and emotional values. An attractive middle-aged artist describes this phenomenon in himself:

—"I like to be in love with somebody—doesn't everyone? I like to create a mood, to generate feelings by using all the props and gestures of romance: flowers, thoughtful little gifts, drinks at out-of-the-way places. I can manage to be intensely intimate with a woman across a coffee-table while simply talking. When I feel that she and I are both opening up and becoming aware of each other—and that both of us know it—it's almost as pleasurable as going to bed with her. Sometimes more."

Others are gratified not so much by the romantic content as by the symbolic sexual victory. A forty-five-year-old businessman puts it this way:

—"There's more thrill for me in the game than in the prize. When you get a girl to admit she'd like to go to bed with you, but she's afraid to because you're married, that's enough. That makes me feel as pleased with myself as actually getting her into bed."

The people who play at extra-marital love in this way may remain on the brink for weeks, months, or even years until, bored or fearful, they drop the relationship or, becoming bolder or more needful, complete it. I am not sure how common this is, there being no major survey on the matter, but Kinsey, though he offered no data on non-physical involvements, gave some on physically limited ones: One out of every six married women, he found, had done some petting outside of marriage but never had extra-marital coitus. (He failed to gather comparable data for men.) If one allows for all those whose extra-marital involvements advance no further than necking, the figure would surely be much larger.

Here is how brinkmanship felt to one young man, whose experience is typical:

—"I saw her every time I came to the city on business, and for a long while I was sort of a big brother to her. Then it got to be a dating thing, and after a while we began to neck. One night, very late, she told me I could stay overnight in the extra room because her roommates were away. I fell into bed in my underwear and she came in and sat on the edge of the bed. We were both feeling very mellow, and I said, 'Will you come to bed and just hold me for a while?' I meant it, too, and she could tell. She turned off the light, shucked her dress, and slid into bed with me. I held her but didn't touch her all that night, and for weeks did the same thing whenever I stayed over. I was married, a father, and a good upstanding citizen, and I told myself that I was just playing, and not doing anything really wrong. Stupid as it may sound, I thought that all of this—even my being sort of infatuated with her—was more or less all right, but that having actual sex with her would be making a statement about my marriage, would be admitting that it was dying or dead."

In this and similar cases, the deterrents with which we are already familiar were at work. This man had had a strong moral upbringing, had been quite inexperienced before marriage, and felt rather unsure of himself with women; most important of all, he subscribed to the puritan-romantic ideal of marriage, and therefore felt that a consummated affair would be not a mere diversion or supplement to marriage, but a mortal threat to it.

NEAL GORHAM AND MARY BUCHANAN

Neal Gorham, too, sensed the danger to his formerly total marriage and hesitated on the brink; Mary Buchanan, though she had touched things off with Neal, herself had twice sought to make such a marriage and twice failed, and therefore belatedly felt alarm, fearing that an affair would shatter her patchwork relationship with Cal.

The night she had said to Neal, "This is beginning to bother me," he drove home in a stupor (he had come in by car that day, the late trains back being few and slow); his eyes saw the signs and the other cars on the Thruway and the Connecticut Turnpike, but his mind saw only scenes of love-making with Mary. The visions made his legs twitch involuntarily; he recalled once seeing a male dog twitch in the same way, upon scenting a bitch in heat, and he laughed at himself derisively and yet with an odd self-affection.

Halfway home to Darien it occurred to him that perhaps she had meant him to act, and he thought of turning back, but the mere idea brought on such a surge of prickling anxiety that he dismissed the notion and continued on home.

Laurie was in bed with the lights out, but woke momentarily and murmured a sleepy hello. He dallied in the bathroom, hoping she would be asleep again before he came out; she was, and he eased himself into bed. *Tried to hold my mind down; it was whirling, lifting, soaring. After a long while, drifted off toward sleep, at which point suddenly felt as if I were falling into nothingness and awoke with a terrible start; lay awake long, heart thumping, sweat trickling down. Grew calm, drifted off again—and again the sense of falling, the unseen hand gripping my heart; leaped up in bed as if to save my life. Told self it was a clear sign: must go no further with Mary; and so fell asleep.*

But in the morning the vapors dissolved, and all he could think of was Mary, her parting words, and his fantasies. He felt near to bursting with his knowledge; it made him energetic and ebullient, but he took pains not to show it, since Laurie was accustomed to see him taciturn and sluggish in the morning. *Phoned Mary from the office without even taking off my coat, spilling out warm words —and astonished to hear her begin to cry. I: "Mary, darling, why are you crying?" She: "I shouldn't have said that last night. I knew what I was doing, and it was wrong. I have no right to endanger my marriage and yours. We mustn't talk of this any more, we mustn't see each other alone. I've ruined a wonderful friendship." I, galvanized, replied with a torrent of words, pleading, reassuring, adoring. Amazed to hear myself; had no idea I could be like that. Said we mustn't run away from it; we'd be haunted by the thought forever; we must at least meet for lunch and be open and honest about our feelings, even if we agreed to do nothing more.* She agreed, and at lunch her tight, pinched look slowly yielded; after a while they were holding hands under the table, whispering words of love, telling each other how careful they would be not to let this affect their marriages (it would be something extra, something over and above marriage). But how not to let it do harm? She said she thought they ought not sleep together, at least not until they could handle their feelings; he, looking spartan but feeling unexpectedly relieved, agreed.

Mary: "I was scared to death. After two marital disillusionments, I no longer believed there was such a thing as a good marriage, or at least not the kind I'd dreamed of. I had decided to settle for a lot less, but I did want to keep what I had. I felt that if I slept with Neal, it would stir up feelings so strong they would be bound to tear my marriage apart. I'd be crazy to chance it. The thing with Neal had been a marvelous flirtation; then I'd begun to want more than that, and had said what I did that night to make it happen. But one minute after the door closed, I was cursing myself and feeling childish and stupid. What kind of game did I think I was playing? Neither Neal nor I would be any good at light-hearted infidelity, but anything deeper would only mess up both our lives. I rehearsed a little speech calling it all off, but when I heard the sound in his voice the next morning I lost my resolve. Yet I was terrified that it would get out of hand. I hoped that if we kept it a small glowing ember of romance and affection, and didn't let it blaze up into sex, it would be all right."

They met the following night for dinner, radiant and happy; deceived by their truce into thinking themselves safe. They had no idea what they were eating; all that mattered was to be with each other and gaze into each other's eyes. As they were leaving, Neal said firmly that they were going to her apartment; he added that he knew what they had agreed, and would respect it, but that he and she had to be in each other's arms for a little while. She nodded, mutely. In her apartment they sat on the couch and kissed, self-conscious and awkward at first, but soon eager and fervent.

They went no further that night. For the next few days they lived with thoughts of each other, often drifting through the hours somnambulant and remote, yet performing great chunks of work in short intense bursts. They spoke on the phone in hushed tones, bought little presents for each other, and felt themselves immeasurably luckier than the people all around them. Three days later they met again. In her apartment, holding her close, he put his hand on her breast and caressed her with a gentle insistence she could not refuse; at first she asked him in a whisper not to, but then sighed and yielded to her feelings. Fully dressed, they lay on the sofa in each other's arms for an hour, close and yet making no effort to be closer. *How strange, two people in their mid-thirties acting like teenagers—or don't even teenagers act like this any longer? Home to sleeping Laurie, with an aching groin. Showered to be sure no telltale perfume on me, slid into bed, at which point felt immense affection for Laurie and vowed never to let my new love hurt her. Held her sleeping body close, kissed her back, ran hands over her (am I a monster, to do this right after being with Mary?); eased my hand between her thighs and toyed gently, slowly, until she sighed, awoke, and rolled over to accept me. Felt great tenderness and passion for her—and then found that she was doing it mechanically, patiently, to get me finished and to sleep. Asked her afterwards, half-sadly, half-angrily, "Don't you ever want me the way I want you? Don't you ever hunger for me that way?" Long silence; then: "I don't know. . . . Not really, I guess. . . . I'm sorry."*

Mary: "For a while, we behaved like two kids. A couple of times we even took off our outer clothing and lay in bed together in our underwear, quaking with desire. Neal would have gone further if I'd said the word, but I kept reminding him and myself that we might not be able to control our feelings. But the last night before Cal was due home, we were in bed and I was clinging to him and thinking how incredibly good it was to feel so much desire and to know I wasn't really frigid, and all at once I said to myself, 'Oh hell, I don't care. It's bound to be worth it, and I'm only going to have one life.' So I took off my bra and panties and said—God! it sounds so corny!—I said, 'Take me!' He wrestled out of his shorts at once, and in a moment there we were. For about five seconds it was wonderful and then, in the twinkling of an eye, in one instant, I dried up. Just dried up! It hurt me so that I couldn't bear to have him move. I didn't have an iota of desire left—just despair and disgust with myself, and rage at my rotten Catholic conscience. But Neal was marvelous: He kissed me a hundred times and told me it was all right, he said he understood that I was still afraid and guilty, and felt sure it would pass—but we really did have to take our time and limit ourselves; he knew we'd be lovers in the full sense sooner or later, and there was no hurry." *Strong sure words. Pleased me to be able to say them, even though I knew I was, in part, shamming —because, though immensely disappointed, I also felt strangely relieved that I hadn't yet been unfaithful. (Legally I had; there had been two or three strokes, and one is enough; but there had been no orgasm.) Glad I would have more time to encompass all this before the moment of commitment: that curious little exercise in which a bit of one person's flesh is fitted into a convenient place in another's and briefly jiggled to and fro until a dollop of fluid is squirted from one into the other. A trifling event, when seen in perspective—which is just how neither she nor I will ever be able to see it.*

* * *

How long does it take most husbands and wives, in their first affairs, to proceed from the beginning to that trifling event? I know of no statistics other than those I myself gathered in my questionnaire; the sample is small, but the results are at least suggestive.

In their first (or only) affairs, just over one fifth of the men had intercourse within one day of beginning the relationship, and one seventh did so within the first week. Another seventh took between a week and a month, and about one third, probably experiencing conflicts similar to those we have just observed, took somewhere between one and six months. The remainder—another seventh of the group—took anywhere up to years, and one man never did consummate the relationship.

Women were a little slower. Almost none had sex during the first day or even within the first week of the relationship. Nearly a third took between a week and a month, and another third took from one to six months. The rest—just under a third—took anywhere from half a year to several years, and two women never had intercourse at all in what they considered their first affairs. In subsequent affairs, both sexes were somewhat quicker to complete the relationship.

Though I could not extract comparable statistics from the interview material, I did get from it some definite impressions as to what affects the duration of brinkmanship. Long-delayed consummation usually involves one or more of these factors: little or no premarital experience, no previous extra-marital relationships, strong inhibitions due to religion or familial influences, marriage that is or once was romantic and involved. Per contra, swift consummation usually is linked with one or more of these: ample premarital experience, previous extra-marital relationships, relative freedom from religious or personal inhibitions, marriage that is cool or conflicted and relatively uninvolved.

LEWIS AMORY AND THERESA SCHROEDER

Lewis Amory's present affair, though it has lasted longer and been somewhat deeper than his previous ones, exemplifies many of these points.

On a bitterly cold, windy February day four years ago, Mrs. Theresa Schroeder arrived at Dr. Amory's office on Michigan Avenue in downtown Chicago. The nurse took down relevant data: 36 years old, 5' 2½ ", 108 pounds (snugly and agreeably distributed, though the nurse did not note that); referred by Dr. James Thorne, an opthalmologist whose office assistant she was. Complaint: recurrent spells of tachycardia.

The caseload was light this morning; several patients had cancelled because of the cold weather. The nurse ushered Mrs. Schroeder into Lewis Amory's office and introduced her to him; he liked the look of her at once, and was pleased that he had extra time that day to spend with her. She was not beautiful, having the broad face and somewhat flat features of her mother's Bavarian ancestors, but she had a wide warm smile, bright gay eyes, and a breezy manner —characteristics Lewis liked in other women precisely because his wife lacked them. He carefully elicited her medical history, and then said that he needed to know more about her personal life, tachycardia often being caused by emotional stresses. She told him that she had been divorced four years ago, had two sons, aged fourteen and ten, worked as Thorne's office assistant (she had taken practical nurse training right after high school), and had been dating three men during the past year, one of whom, a chronic bachelor, kept deciding to marry her and then changing his mind.

Amory took her into an adjoining room and gave her a thorough examination, after which he handed her over to his nurse for an ECG. When she was dressed again, the nurse brought her back to his office for a conference. He told her he could find no organic basis for her attacks of rapid heartbeat and believed them to be the result of emotional stress, as he had suspected in the beginning. He discussed with her the problems of her kind of life —the responsibilities of a divorced mother, her financial burdens, and the emotional strains involved in her various dating relationships, especially with the on-again-off-again bachelor. Her recollection of the visit:

"I liked him the moment I saw him. He's strong, quiet, and manly—just the opposite of the high-strung idiot who couldn't make up his mind to marry me. After the examination, he talked to me for a long while about my life. It seemed perfectly natural and comfortable, although I didn't know at the time that this was most unusual for him—Lewis doesn't talk freely to anyone new, and not even to most people he has known for a while. As a matter of fact, that first time he actually said a few little things about his own life: I was speaking of my worries about my younger boy's behavior, and he told me two or three stories about his own daughters to reassure me. I found myself intrigued by him as a man and not just as a doctor. I wondered if he was still married, or had been divorced or widowed; I couldn't tell because even though he spoke about his daughters, he never mentioned a wife. I had a feeling he liked me as a person and was treating me a little differently from his other patients.

"Finally he wrote out a prescription for a tranquillizer and told me that I had to simplify my personal life somewhat, and that if these things didn't take care of the condition, he might want me to try a little psychotherapy. I got up to leave, and he came with me and walked me out through the waiting room to the elevator outside. He said, 'Are you ever in this part of town at the end of the afternoon?' and I said yes, sometimes on Tuesdays and Thursdays, when Dr. Thorne went to the clinic. He said, 'Well, next time you're near here, give me a ring and let me buy you a Martini.' I said, 'Boy, I could use one right now!' Then I felt silly, because it must have sounded like I was coming on strong, but all I meant was that I was relieved to have the examination over with and to find out that my heart was all right. He said he couldn't now, and the elevator came at that moment, so I said goodbye and got in. I thought he was the most exciting man I'd met in years, and I hoped he really liked me as much as he seemed to."

Lewis: "There was a real spark between us. I had almost always stayed away from patients; it's risky, and Terry was especially risky because she'd been sent me by her own employer, a physician, but I didn't want to let her go without putting out a feeler, or I might never see her again. It made me nervous to do so—I delayed so long that I barely had time to ask her to have a drink with me someday when the elevator arrived—but from the look on her face and her reply, I felt sure she'd call me. A few days later she did. She said she was going to be in my neighborhood at half-past four or so, and had I really meant that about buying her a Martini? I said of course I had, but I couldn't make it until six, and she said that would be fine. That was a giveaway, but I don't think she realized it.

"We met at a quiet little bar on Ohio Street, not far from my office, and talked our way through three or four rounds of drinks. Both of us got pretty well loosened up; in fact, I practically told her my whole life story—something I almost never do, but with her I felt like it. She felt the same way—she's a talker, anyway—and told me all about herself. I had liked her general appearance when she walked into my office, and in the examining room I'd had a chance to find out that everything was in very good shape; in the bar, as we got to know each other better, I found myself very much attracted to her in every other way. I had a strong hunch that we could be a very good thing together, if it didn't hang her up that I was married. So I brought my marriage into it by telling her that there was something happening between her and myself that never happened at home; she seemed to like that, and didn't appear to be cooled off by the news that I was married.

"I called my answering service and the hospital, and everything was all right, so I asked her to have dinner with me; she phoned her older boy and told him to heat up some TV dinners for himself and his brother. Then I phoned Arlene and said something about an ethics committee meeting that would make me very late; I might even sleep at the club. I wanted to be ready for anything, even though I wasn't counting on it. . . . Guilt feelings? Hardly. I'd been doing it for fifteen years. Besides, it didn't hurt Arlene in any way as long as she didn't know."

Terry: "When I called him for that first date, I had no real reason to be in his neighborhood that afternoon. I think he guessed that, but I didn't care. And from the moment we met in the bar, it felt good to me; it felt like he was right for me. We drank and talked and drank and talked, until we both were very high and had told each other an awful lot about ourselves. Then we were both starving, so we drove over to Morton's Restaurant—and kept right on talking, all the way through dinner. Somewhere along the way he told me a little about his marriage; he gave me the idea that it wasn't the greatest and that he stayed away many evenings, but he didn't pretend for a minute that he was on the brink of divorce. He was very straight about it. Well, I had never gone out with a married man and always thought it a bad business, but this seemed different and special, and I decided right then and there not to run away from it, but to take a chance and to find out.

"I guess we must have covered just about everything from beans to sex that night—including some pretty intimate details about the latter. I'd been around a good deal in the last four years, and slept with about a dozen fellows, but I didn't usually talk sex with a new man right off or he'd get the idea I was a pushover. But this time it all seemed okay. I phoned home again at about ten o'clock and told Bill and Jamie to go to sleep without waiting up for me. I was feeling crazy about this guy already, and wondering what would happen later on in the evening. It almost never hits me that fast, but I was letting go.

"Then it was way past eleven, and as he was paying the check he said to me, 'I'm not driving home tonight; it's too late. I'm staying at the Shore Drive Motel. It's only a minute away; come on over and just say goodnight, and then I'll run you home.' I don't know when he made his room reservation; maybe when phoning the hospital or his wife. I knew what was going to happen after all that talk about sex, but I said, 'Why not?' and went along with him, as calm as anything. I don't know why I did it. The second or third night, okay, but the first night? Oh, wow! What a mistake; he's never gotten over the idea that I was too easy. He took that room, he asked me to come over—but what he really wanted was for me to put up a struggle and make him wait until the next time."

Lewis: "When I phoned Arlene to say I might not be home, I also called the motel and made a reservation just in case. But I was surprised that Terry came along without a bit of resistance. She hadn't seemed all that easy; I hadn't taken her to be loose. I wasn't sure what would happen—I figured probably a bit of necking or petting, and a pretty firm no about anything more, for the time being. But when we got to my room and I started kissing her and all that, suddenly, to my amazement, we were both shucking our clothes without another word and diving into bed. To this day I don't quite know how it happened."

iv the drop-outs

From the Kinsey study of women plus my own interview and questionnaire data, I would hazard the guess that about a quarter of all middle-class American wives, and somewhere between a tenth and an eighth of their husbands, have had some kind of extra-marital experience that stopped short of intercourse. A fair number of these people—a quarter or more—consider that in doing so, they have been unfaithful to their spouses. In an age said to be thoroughly hedonistic, it is remarkable that so many people go so far only to stop short and go no further—and even more remarkable that many, nevertheless, feel they have committed an infidelity.

Have they, or have they not? The judge, the biologist, and the minister would offer differing criteria as to what constitutes infidelity, but the most important in terms of the effects upon people's lives is the psychologist's criterion of "subjective reality." Even if what people think has happened is a grossly distorted perception of the events, their interpretation of those events is the reality to which they react; in the well-known dictum of the sociologist W. I. Thomas, "If men define situations as real, they are real in their consequences." Flirtation, party gropery, clandestine meetings, long hours of physical preliminaries are objective facts—but what affects the participants is the interpretation they put upon them. Those who go no further and who feel they have remained faithful may suffer little guilt and no change in their feelings towards their mates; those who stop short and yet consider themselves unfaithful may suffer considerable guilt and severe disturbance of the marital relationship.

In some cases, the failure to physically complete the affair may even have a greater effect upon the individual, long afterwards, than would consummation. Precisely because the lovers never experience each other fully, they may continue to idealize each other and the act of love, imagining perfections in each other and fulfillments in the act quite beyond those of reality; they thereby remain enslaved by the affair long after it has ended.

A case in point is that of a young couple, deeply infatuated with each other but both strongly moral, who never went beyond kissing and mild petting in the several months that their affair lasted. (We saw them earlier, sitting in a parked car at the beach at night, before going to a rehearsal of the local drama group in which they had met.) Although they were tormented by desire, they never gave way to it, and although they thought themselves much in love, they never asked their mates for divorce. How deep their feelings actually were is questionable, for when word of their meetings leaked back to their mates, they confessed everything and promptly gave each other up.

But a full year later they are both still deeply troubled by the dream of love. The man, in fact, has had to enter psychotherapy in an effort to shake off the deep despair and sense of pointlessness that have dominated him since the end of the affair. The woman, though not quite as depressed, describes her painful continuing state of mind in a letter which reads, in part:

> My outlook on life was completely changed by what happened. The affair made me aware of my own need to think and to communicate with someone I am deeply in love with. Before, I was asleep; ever since, I have been awake—and living with a sense of incompleteness. Yet I do not regret what happened. I would rather *know*, and not have what I want, than live out my life without ever having known. But it's so difficult. For a whole year I haven't been able to tell my husband I love him, not even in bed. . . . There was a time when I looked forward to my future with him when the children would be older and on their own; now I try not to think of that future. We don't quarrel, and he loves me in his own way, but I don't know how to survive within this marriage.

Evidently, for certain kinds of people, even an unconsummated affair can have significant consequences and be a powerful force in one's emotional evolution. It may be a liberating and enlarging experience or produce constricting guilt and depression. It may yield temporary relief from frustration and boredom or exacer-

bate marital discontents to the breaking-point. It may leave a trea-
sured memory of something good or a smoldering discontent that
eventually burns down the house of marriage.

chapter 4: CONSUMMATION

i the great divide

People whose allegiance is to the puritan-romantic ideal of marriage, and who prefer totality and intimacy in a love relationship, are likely to regard the first extra-marital sex act with a mixture of terror and fascination; for them it is a consummation of almost sacramental—or heretical—character that will profoundly and irreversibly change them, even if no one else ever knows about it. In contrast, people whose allegiance is to the pagan-courtly ideal, and who prefer their love relationships to be limited in scope and in depth, take the consummation in stride; for them it is a kind of initiation into adult privilege—a scary, exciting, and delightful thing to do, but one which does no harm as long as it is skillfully managed and kept suitably hidden from view.

The puritan-romantics, with whom we shall concern ourselves

first, read and think about infidelity for years, earnestly and uneasily discuss it with their friends, indulge in fantasies and feel guilty for doing so, progress with considerable anxiety to flirtation, emotional involvement, and the preliminaries, and arrive at last at the very doorway of their desire—yet even then cannot believe that they will ever really cross the threshold. For whatever they have done thus far, it is minor compared to the final physical connection, an act to which they ascribe an almost mystical significance.

But back of that mystical significance are down-to-earth factors. People for whom the consummation assumes immense emotional and moral importance are likely to be church-goers or, at least, the children of parents with "strict" ideas. Many of them, as we saw earlier, live in areas or communities where infidelity is sternly frowned upon and where the unfaithful are liable to social ostracism. For some of them, an important inhibiting factor is low self-esteem, or unsureness of their own sexual adequacy; they fear they might be rejected or, if accepted, might prove inept and unsatisfactory. Many, perhaps most, have always had, or thought they had, a deeply involved marriage, and fear that even a single extramarital sexual experience would touch off a process inevitably destructive of that marriage.

Where any of these factors prevail, the individual is likely to delay taking the step until pressures have grown great and experience of the world has eroded early idealism. Half the men I interviewed did not have their first affairs until they had been married at least six years, and a quarter of the men did not begin until after ten years. Women did not delay quite so long; those who became unfaithful tended to do so while they still had their youthful looks.

According to cultural mythology, these same people—conscience-directed, romantic, faithful—first fall deeply in love, then are overcome by urgent physical desire, and so break the marriage vow; according to the cynic, they first feel the physical pull, then persuade themselves that they are deeply in love, and having thus ennobled the urge, commit the deed. In all likelihood, most cases fall in between these extremes: In people of this character type, sexual arousal and caring tend to go together; one creates the other, the other increases the first.

NEAL GORHAM AND MARY BUCHANAN

Even at their very first meeting, when they and Calvin Prestwick had discussed the advertising campaign for the spring books, Neal and Mary had not only liked each other as personalities but found each other physically appealing. For both of them, indeed, the two things were all but inseparable: As they worked together and began to care for each other, the physical pull became disturbingly strong, and from the moment they touched and kissed, their feelings intensified rapidly. Both of them, therefore, were deeply apprehensive about the consummation of their affair, knowing it would produce major emotional changes in them. Mary's sudden dryness in the middle of their first attempt at sex was an involuntary flight not just from the sex act but from total emotional commitment.

In the several days after that abortive attempt, Neal tried in vain to check the intensity of his feelings by the deliberate exercise of cynicism, *asking myself whether it was a hungry soul that accounted for this love, or merely a congested groin. Wondered whether, if I had laid a few women each year since getting married, Mary would still seem unique and totally right for me. Then angrily told myself that this love was real, was what I had dreamed of for years, what I had feared to die without knowing. Laurie and I once had it in part; but between Mary and me there was not part but all. Whether playful or serious, relaxing or working, cerebral or physical, we were key and lock, melody and harmony; or, as in Plato's conceit, the lost halves of each other, at last reunited. . . . Then sneered at these high-flown sentiments. More likely, I was like a wild beast at rutting season, else how explain what I did the night Mary and I failed to complete our love?* He had driven home in an intoxicated mood, overcharged and yet relieved by the postponement, frustrated and yet in high-strung good humor. Laurie was sitting up in bed and reading, and to his own surprise he was glad to see her; he wanted company. She made a pot of hot chocolate and brought it into the bedroom, but before settling down on the bed with him to drink it, she went into the bathroom and reappeared with her hair down and smelling faintly of a light cologne. Neal noticed, understood, and felt both excitement and guilt. *Could never have believed*

*it of myself—straight from the arms of my love, and instantly,
gladly, unfaithful with my wife! Never hesitated, but rejoiced in the
chance; was sharply aware—and fascinated by my awareness—of
the differences between her and Mary: her mouth tighter, slower to
yield; her breasts larger, looser; her body more ample and generous,
but lacking in eagerness and vibrancy. Yet because of this fresh
awareness, it was extraordinarily exciting. And Laurie even succeeded that night, catching up in one frantic effort during my dying
spasms. But how could I enjoy it so much—and yet want Mary all
the more? Had a most unoriginal thought: Perhaps a man need not
love only one woman and in only one way. Laurie the wife, old
friend, home base; Mary the lost half of me, grand passion, dream
of love come true. Perhaps I could love both, each in a special way;
perhaps that was the simple, obvious, and overlooked answer.*

Bemused by all this, he drifted through the next two or three
days, now witty and alive, now quiet and remote. His secretary
tried to avoid him and hoped that whatever it was would pass soon;
Robin and Billy tried to capture his attentions by plying him with
questions and even presenting him with a dead field-mouse they
had found, but they dispiritedly·went away together when they won
only a forced smile and a vague reply; even Laurie asked him what
was wrong, but accepted his explanation that he was concerned
about the firm's somewhat shrunken billings, and was trying to
dream up an idea or two for a presentation to a potential new client.

Mary, too, had a few difficult days, and for comparable reasons. "Cal came home and I made a special effort to be friendly, but
I couldn't bear the thought of his making love to me. I pleaded a
migraine the first night; he didn't say much, but he looked hurt and
angry. It was a lousy excuse, too, because I'd been talking to him
about his trip up to a few minutes before. But even the talking had
been hard for me—I wasn't interested in what he'd been doing, and
all I wanted to think about was Neal and me, how close we'd been,
how I had copped out—and how much I wanted to make love to
him completely. In the next few days Neal and I had a couple of
long talks on the phone, but the big question—*When?*—hung over
us all the time. Meanwhile, I got myself half-crocked one night and
let Cal climb in my bed; I know a trick or two that gets it over with
fast, and I pulled them on him.

"Then on Friday morning of that week Neal called, very excited. Mid-year vacation was about to start, and Laurie had suddenly decided to take the children to visit their grandparents in Virginia for a week. Neal said she'd be leaving early Saturday morning, and I should come up by noon time the latest. I said, 'What can I tell Cal? And won't your neighbors see me come? And where . . . I mean . . . Neal!—in your own house? Your own bedroom?' First he was reassuring, then pleading, then stiff and angry; finally he said he guessed it was a bad idea, *all* of it. I said he should give me some time, and he said, in a frosty tone of voice, 'Take all the time you want,' and hung up.

"That night I got quietly drunk at home. Cal didn't say anything. I pretended to be reading, but I stared at the same page for half an hour and never saw a word. At ten o'clock the phone rang. It was my mother, calling long distance; she had bad news—Ellen Barnett, my oldest friend, had committed suicide. Mother told me the grisly details: Ellen had slashed her wrists, and her husband had practically waded in her blood to get to her. Even though we hadn't been all that close in recent years, something tore loose in me. We'd played together, grown up together, both had careers and divorces and second marriages—and she had just thrown away all her chances of loving and being happy, while I had mine at hand. I don't think her death was the crucial thing in my decision, but it felt like it that night; if nothing else, it settled the question of *when*. I came out and told Cal what it was all about, exaggerating my misery— I had a plan—and then I said I had to talk to Mother again, and closed the bedroom door and phoned Neal at home. If Laurie had answered, I would have hung up, but Neal did. I said, 'If you still want me, I'll be there tomorrow.' He seemed stunned, but then he said, 'Yes, of course I want you, you *know* how much I want you. Come, but call first, to be sure everything's okay.'

"I took a tranquillizer and went to bed; I cried, half in earnest and half acting. Poor Cal wanted to be helpful but didn't know what to do. In the morning I said I had to be by myself—I was going to take the car and drive way out into the countryside, and I'd call him during the day, but maybe he ought to plan to have dinner at the Players' Club after his usual Saturday afternoon bridge game in case I didn't make it back in time. He didn't ask any questions—not even how come I wanted to drive, when I usually hate driving, especially in winter. I thought, 'You poor dope. I try not to make love to you after you've been away three weeks, I get drunk at night, I tell you I'm going driving all day because an old friend committed suicide, and you don't ask questions, you don't tell me not to, you don't even suspect anything. You've got it coming to you.' I guess I sound like a terrible bitch. Well, I was—a bitch in heat."

On the way, she stopped at a gas station and called Neal; Laurie and the children had already left, and he was in a fever of impatience. He gave her instructions, and told her to pull right into the garage; the house, well away from town, was reasonably isolated on its own acre and a half of ground, but it would be best to have her car out of sight. Waiting for her, he paced the house, peered out of the windows toward the rain-lashed road visible through the wet black trees, looked at himself in the mirror, sat down with a paper, flung it aside, and prowled the house again, *unable to believe what was happening, what might now come to pass: that thing I thought I would never do, and after which I will never be the same. It was nearly noon; where on earth was she? Killed time by building a fire in the living-room fireplace, then making up a batch of whisky sours and two sandwiches; heard car door slam in the garage—heart in my chest struggled for an instant—ran to garage, saw her pale, drawn, frightened face; pushed the button and lowered garage door, then embraced her. Both of us stiff and nervous. Told her I had drinks and lunch ready; she relaxed, realizing there was time.*

But after one drink in front of the fire they were kissing each other feverishly and lunch was forgotten. He took her by the hand and led her into the bedroom, where they abandoned their clothes on the floor and fell into bed and each other's arms—at which point it occurred to him that he had not locked the doors; what if one of the children was taken ill and Laurie turned back? He explained, got out of bed, and hurried around, naked and absurd, putting the chains on the doors; then back to bed, where he clung to her for a moment, growing warm again, and began to devour her, to feast upon her, to drink her in with grateful murmurs. *Meant to be slow and careful with her, but the moment I found her to be slippery and open, I did not wait: up and over, between her legs, and put myself into her—within her!—she gasping, glad. Strange, how I was view-*

ing us from a distance, seeing us doing it, thinking: This is the moment from which things will date; this is even now being woven into thousands of invisible connections in each of our brains, a network of memory in which we are forever caught; we will never be the same again.

There was no trouble this time. Mary, though unused to his pattern of movement, was intensely excited and responsive, *clutching, kissing and biting me; writhing, straining, moaning; and at last uttering a series of sharp, almost tormented cries that slowly died away, all these being things I had never seen or heard. I might have lived and died, never knowing a woman could be like that in response to me. I was so fascinated that I did not even reach my peak when all this was happening in her. Stopped, uncertain what to do. Her face was wet with tears, she was showering kisses on me and whispering words of love and thanks; and all this suddenly made it start at my toes, even while I was motionless, and rise up through me; then, wildly and joyfully, I drove myself into her with strange hoarse outcries as my being leaped forth and became hers. . . . We lay and stared into each other's eyes, speechless, for a long while. I said I had never known, never suspected, how it could be; she told me I was a superb lover, had brought her back to life, had made her burn brighter than ever before.* They lay close, sweating, unwilling to move apart. (Laurie, he thought, would have hurried to the shower.) From then on, the day was all laughter, talk, touching, and exploring; kissing and mouthing each other's bodies (so simple and natural, those same acts Laurie felt squeamish about); then the spark rekindling the flame, the ending of it practically an agony of pleasure this time; and still later everything yet again as if there were no limit to their capacity. Late in the afternoon, when at last they ravenously wolfed down the luncheon sandwiches, they compared impressions and were not quite sure whether they had made love three or four times in five hours; the discussion made them giggle like naughty children, *and I said: "Mary, I love you, Mary, I adore you; now it has begun." And we both grew silent and thoughtful for a moment.*

Mary: "I kept asking him that afternoon, 'What's happening to us?' I had never felt desire again and again like that; it thrilled me but it also frightened me. I felt as though I were losing control, as though something were taking over; I felt I would do anything for him—break up my marriage, give up my career; what did any of it matter?

"After we finished the sandwiches, I phoned home; Cal was there. I had hoped he would be down at the club, playing bridge. I said I was way up in Dutchess County, somewhere beyond Rhinebeck, and had been sitting in the rain, on a mountain overlook, just thinking. Now I was going to get something to eat and would be home by nine or ten o'clock. He sounded rather cranky, but I felt relieved that I'd been able to carry it off without any real difficulty.

"Neal and I took a shower together and got dressed; we agreed to call it quits for the day because we were both tender, so he rebuilt the fire and we sat in the living-room for hours, talking and holding hands, and drinking some more. At nine o'clock I got up to leave, but I had an irresistible urge—I stood before the fire and slowly took off my clothes, without a word. His face! We made love right there, on the rug before the fire—what a cliché! I paid for it later; my backside was sore for three days from the hardness of the floor. Another shower, a touch of make-up, a little work on my hair, a last long goodbye, and off I went, exhausted but terribly happy.

"I got home near midnight. Cal was propped up in bed, reading a manuscript, and in an icy mood. He asked how I was and I said, 'Much better'; he said 'Good,' and went back to his reading. I think he was suspicious but didn't dare admit it even to himself. I flung off my things and fell into bed, thinking, I don't know where this will take me, but I'm alive and in love, and it's never been like this before. I was relieved when Cal turned out the light; I could let myself smile in the dark."

* * *

People like Neal and Mary approach the Great Divide of extra-marital sex with strong conflict, desiring but fearing it, filled with longing but harassed by guilt. Neal and Mary, powerfully motivated by their love and by their first failure to complete the act, were able to resolve the conflict, master their fears, and rationalize their guilt out of sight; as a result, the experience was intensely emotional, hypersexual, and deeply satisfying. But for many others who are unable to resolve their conflicts, the first experience may be deeply distressing and even devoid of sexual pleasure; nonetheless, it represents to them a crossing of that Great Divide and the beginning of another life:

—A gentle, sensitive woman, all but ignored by her husband (a department-store buyer who travelled continually), slowly grew close to the family lawyer; a tender, idealistic love developed between them, but remained platonic for many months because he recognized her unreadiness for anything more. She had been strictly brought up, had never known sex outside of marriage, and had never found it arousing or satisfying; she would have been quite content to have the affair remain platonic forever. But after nearly a year, when she and he were picnicking by a remote mountain stream, he calmly and gently began undressing her for the first time, and although she was very frightened, she passively allowed him to continue, and to make love to her. "I suppose I must have wanted him to, because I didn't stop him, but I was astounded and horrified to see it actually taking place. I couldn't believe I was letting it happen. Of course I didn't have an orgasm; I didn't even *feel* anything. Afterwards I cried, off and on, for a couple of hours. I felt I had wrecked my marriage by this transgression and destroyed the beautiful and innocent relationship between us. At the same time, I adored him more than ever, and he himself seemed pretty pleased about it all and not particularly upset by my crying. I didn't intend for us ever to do it again, but of course we did, and it slowly got better and better until finally I knew what it was really about. But I was a long way from it that first time."

Where it is the man whose guilt-feelings are unresolved, the first experience may be a total failure; unlike the woman, he may be unable to complete the act. But despite the alarm and despair this occasions, such men usually persist in trying again and again with the same person until they overpower their own guilt-feelings; for them, the first completed act may have an even greater symbolic and emotional meaning than it did for Neal Gorham.

In others, though guilt is present, it plays a less crucial part than does low self-esteem; the latter is what makes the first sexual act particularly alarming and ominous. The poor opinion of one's sexual self may have existed since adolescence; a good marriage could have improved it, but a mediocre or poor one would only have confirmed it (indeed, a poor one could even have shaken a reasonably self-confident person). For such people, the first sexual act outside of marriage is approached with great anxiety; yet once completed—even if clumsily or in a situation lacking emotional content—the mere fact of sexual success does give it immense importance and make it seem a crucial event:

—A young stock-broker had been ill at ease with women ever since his acne-troubled teens and (as we already heard him say) had grave doubts about his own masculinity because his wife could be satisfied only if he stimulated her manually. Over a period of half a dozen years the desire to prove himself grew tormenting, but it was his fear of rejection or failure that immobilized him rather than his feeling that it would be wrong. He did, however, gradually nerve himself up to a few flirtatious acts; then a friend's secretary called to thank him for a successful stock tip he had given her, and sounded so friendly and inviting that he asked her to have a drink with him. After the drink, she suggested, on some flimsy pretext, that they stop by her apartment. "She wasn't very attractive—she was too heavy, for one thing—but I knew that I *had* to try myself out sooner or later, and maybe this was it. At that point, I had almost forgotten about any feeling that it was wrong, but I was afraid to make a move. Afraid of *what?*—just *afraid!* But she made it simple for me: She actually started the necking, and one thing led to another. But before I went ahead with it I asked if she was safe, and she laughed and said yes, she already had her diaphragm in—so obviously she'd been expecting and wanting this with me. It wasn't the greatest. In fact, the ironical thing was that she has an even worse hang-up than my wife—she told me afterwards that she can't come, that she hasn't ever come in her life. But even so, I felt proud of myself; *I had made it!* And she liked me, and seemed very pleased about the whole thing. So it was a beginning, and I figured I wouldn't be half as unsure of myself the next time."

There is a good reason why guilt feelings and fear of one's personal and sexual inadequacy so often go hand in hand: They are both the products of an upbringing in which the parents are strict, demanding, and dedicated to traditional puritan-romantic values. The children so raised often turn out to be forever dissatisfied with their own achievements, and hence low or at least uncertain in self-esteem. This includes their opinion of themselves as sexual creatures, where the problem is compounded by the fact that, believing sex without love to be dirty and degrading, they do fairly little experimenting in their teens and early adulthood, and enter marriage unsure of their own sexual ability and their needs in a partner. Finally, they are strongly imbued with a belief in the value of fidelity and a total relationship; extra-marital involvements, even if trivial and purely sexual, seem to them a serious violation of loyalty and a potent threat to married love.

All this is markedly true of people in their thirties and older; but those in their twenties are little different, despite the much-touted sexual revolution. It is still true, and will be so a long while, that the very people who believe in intimate and faithful marriage will often be somewhat unsure of their own sexual appeal and secretly desirous of broader sexual experience than they have had; for them the first extra-marital sex act will continue to represent a major and irrevocable step, often changing their feelings about themselves, their marriages, and their goals in life.

---

ii nothing to it

But many middle-class Americans, on approaching a first extra-marital experience, do not regard it as a particularly momentous or significant event. The millions of adherents of the undercover pagan-courtly tradition view infidelity not as a grievous wrong or the outcome of great suffering, but as an all-too-human weakness and the outcome of a perfectly normal desire for variety and newness. Accordingly, they approach the first infidelity without going through a long and arduous inner struggle, and find it exciting rather than frightening, challenging rather than guilt-inducing.

Who are these people? In contrast to the kind we have just been looking at, they are more likely to be only superficially religious, or the children of parents with easy-going moral attitudes. Many of them live in big cities or in sophisticated suburbs in which infidelity is not severely condemned and the unfaithful are not socially ostracized. They are more apt to be reasonably self-confident, and any doubts they have about their own acceptability or sexual adequacy are not serious enough to immobilize them. Many of them do not want or cannot manage a high degree of involvement with their mates, and cannot see why a little discreet extramarital sex should have any effect on their marriages.

Where any or several of these factors prevail, the individual is likely to take the step fairly early in the course of marriage. Over a third of the unfaithful men and women I interviewed began their first affairs within the first two years of marriage, and a quarter of the men and a sixth of the women did so within the first year.

Our culture promulgates a myth of romantic love in which, as in the archetypal story of Tristan and Iseult, infidelity is the result of overwhelmingly powerful love, involves an agonizing violation of deepest loyalties, and inevitably has disastrous consequences. In unromantic truth, millions of unfaithful Americans feel no strong passions either before or after the act, suffer little or not at all from feelings of disloyalty, and experience no disastrous consequences of their actions. And even though they may offer excuses for their infidelities, the flat and casual tones in which they tell about them and the playful mood in which they seem to have undertaken their first affairs are in striking contrast to those of the people we have just observed.

—A tall, boyish-looking newspaper space-salesman, now thirty, very much likes to go out at night to noisy and convivial places—bars, parties, basketball games—while his wife much prefers to stay at home reading or puttering around the house. The difference between them appeared almost as soon as they were married; after only eight months he concluded that he and she were incompatible and that he had made a mistake which, both of them being Catholic, he could not rectify. At that point he began going out by himself, despite her protests. At first he went to games or met friends at bars, but after two months he flirted with an unmarried girl at the office Christmas party and saw her home to her parents' house by bus, where he ardently kissed her goodnight in the vestibule. "It was easy. She was looking up at me in a way that showed she expected me to kiss her. Things got pretty hot in a couple of minutes, but her folks were home, so I didn't go in. She

said she wished I had my car, and I said she could bet I would the
next time. I felt very elated by the prospect. I didn't feel very much
conflict about it even though I was a church-goer. A couple of
weeks later I picked her up in my car after she'd been bowling. We
drove to a quiet spot by the river, and messed around for a while
and got pretty excited. Finally we crawled into the back seat and
made it there. You never saw such steamy windows. It was tremendously exciting. . . . Guilt? No, I was pleased to find that I felt no
guilt, no remorse. But I stopped going to Confession from then on
because I knew I was going to keep on seeing that girl. . . . Love?
Well, mentally she was more stimulating, and sexually much more
exciting, than my wife, and I felt she was drawing me out of that
deadly home situation, which was a good thing. So I had a lot of
feeling for her, but I didn't love her. Actually, I'm not sure I've ever
loved anybody."

—A young divorcee (whom we heard from earlier) fell in love
with a man who was only partially potent with her. Expecting that
he would improve after marriage, she broke off with her two other
boyfriends and married him, but his condition worsened rapidly;
soon he had to masturbate at length to get ready for intercourse,
and then had to complete the act as fast as possible in order not to
lose his erection. She found herself growing tense, irritable, and in
need of satisfaction. "After a couple of months of very limited
success on his part, I was bitchy and all keyed up. I couldn't stand
a lot of things about him—he's not very careful about his clothes,
he doesn't wash enough, he's weak and indecisive—but I don't
think anything would have bothered me much if the sex had been
getting better. One day I got a wedding present from George [one
of her two ex-boyfriends] with a note saying he hoped my husband
would appreciate me as much as he had, and I wrote back saying
he probably would, in his way, though it wasn't George's way. I
tried to put it so he would get the idea, and he did. He phoned and
we made a date to meet at a coffee shop. I didn't have any qualms
about doing so; I was feeling desperate, and I couldn't wait until my
husband made it—in fact, I was beginning to think maybe he never
would. So George and I met, and went to a motel and spent the
afternoon making love. It was sensational. He was married, by the
way, and he'd been having trouble too—his wife was very cold. We

were a pair of wildcats that afternoon. George and I have been taking care of each other's needs for the last three months and it's great for both of us. And it's great that we like each other but aren't in love—there are no complications."

In both these cases, the protagonists viewed the first infidelity without alarm, did not consider it as a landmark in their lives, liked but did not love their extra-marital partners, and were seeking not self-esteem or a truly loving relationship but fun and satisfaction. For people with such an outlook, infidelity is an agreeable and perhaps important supplement to marriage; even if the marriage is cool or flawed, it can be quite stable under these conditions. But many of the people who enter easily into their first extra-marital affair and who make casual affairs a way of life consider themselves happily married and have no complaint about their spouses; they merely regard extra-marital relationships as a normal and reasonable enrichment of life.

LEWIS AMORY AND THERESA SCHROEDER

This has been the case with Dr. Lewis Amory, the Chicago cardiologist, since the beginning of his marriage. Neither as a recently married young intern nor as a long-married successful specialist in his forties did Lewis ever feel actively discontented with or frustrated by his marriage; he simply never thought of it, or of any marriage, as being fully satisfying. From his first extra-marital affair to the present one with Terry Schroeder (number 20), no woman in his life has seemed to him, even momentarily, worth divorcing Arlene. But his loyalty to her has little to do with love; it is, rather, based largely on propriety. Arlene looks and behaves right, entertains well, is a good mother, and is linked to him by the sacrament of marriage performed in the Episcopal Church. She is an integral part of his private domain, the boundaries of which encompass his medical practice, spacious home, well-groomed lawns and plantings, country club, church, wife-daughters-maid-dog-parakeet, and mistress.

Even when they were living on his intern's pittance (plus a handout from his father) in a fourth-floor walk-up in Brookline, his feelings about Arlene were much the same: Marriage was the good and proper thing, Arlene was the good and proper girl—but a little diversion on the outside neither altered his feelings about her nor signified disloyalty.

So effortless and free from deep significance was his first extramarital relationship eighteen years ago that he has to make an effort to remember it. "The first, I think, was the nurse with the big ones. Yes, that's right; it was just after I started interning at Mass. General. I hadn't slept with any woman but Arlene in a year and a half, so I was probably ready, but also I was kind of horny because she was eight months pregnant and I wasn't even sleeping with her any more. I met this nurse in the coffee-shop during lunch hour; I couldn't believe that her bosom was as large as it seemed, and I started talking to her. I could tell she liked me, so after a while I asked her to meet me for a drink after duty hours the next day. She did, and we hit it off at once. I was pretty sure how it would go— if you've had some experience, you can tell. She and another R.N. shared a little apartment a few blocks from the hospital. I asked about the other girl's schedule, and found she was on duty, so I invited myself back to the apartment. . . . No, I didn't feel any conflicts about what I was about to do. It had nothing to do with Arlene, any more than my sleeping with other girls did while Arlene and I were going steady.

"Anyway, the nurse and I went up to her place and made love. It was great. They *were* as big as they seemed, and she was a lot more passionate than Arlene. Afterwards I felt very cheerful and in good spirits; I had a feeling of accomplishment, the way I do after presenting a paper to a group of cardiologists, or playing a better-than-usual game of handball. I saw her about once a week for the next couple of months; then it petered out because, except for the sex, she was boring."

All Lewis's recollections of the women he has known are similarly low-keyed and vague; he can recall a case of myocardial infarction or of aortic stenosis of fifteen years ago in far more detail and with much greater emotional vividness than his first night with the nurse or most of her successors. His first sexual experience with Theresa Schroeder—the divorcee with tachycardia, which he diagnosed as a reaction to the emotional and financial uncertainties of

her life—was something very different: It remains sharply etched
in his memory not just because it happened only four years ago, but
because it was so unsatisfactory compared to most of the others,
and hence surprising and bewildering to him. "For some strange
reason I didn't really expect anything to happen that first night. She
certainly was attractive enough, and I certainly was interested in
her. Maybe *that* was it, maybe I liked her so much that I didn't want
her to be an easy thing like the others. I was astonished that we
were taking our clothes off, and disappointed that she was proving
to be a pushover. I suppose I have an old-fashioned view of women:
There are two kinds—the kind you marry and the kind you play
with. And that night I was mixed up in my feelings. As a result, it
wasn't very good; in fact, it was terrible. *I* was terrible. Yet I was
in good shape and hadn't been having any difficulty elsewhere. I felt
very much upset, even after I finally managed it with her."

Terry: "Later on I was surprised to find out just how much he
had been around, because that first night he was like a beginner.
He's a real Victorian son-of-a-gun, with a lot of the old double
standard. He had never had any sexual problem with other women,
but there was something real going on between us and apparently
he didn't actually want me to go to his room or sleep with him that
night. He made a pass at me automatically and expected me to say
no, but I didn't. So *he* put up the resistance. I mean, everything was
fine until we got into bed—and then it was almost hopeless. I was
crazy about the guy and wanted him, but after an hour of our
getting nowhere my ego was taking an awful beating. I was wondering what the heck was wrong with me, what did he find repulsive
about me; he kept saying 'I don't know what's wrong—too much
to drink, I guess'; and I kept telling him, 'It's all right, please stop
worrying.'

"After a long while, he finally succeeded. It was very quick,
and no good for me, but at least we had done it. We were both
exhausted and didn't have much to say, and somewhere around two
A.M. we got dressed and he drove me home. I felt awful. I hadn't
ever felt as good about anybody during a first date as I had about
him, but I figured I had disappointed him somehow. I wasn't sure
he'd ever call me again, and I thought I must be nuts, falling for a
married man who had told me he'd never break up his marriage for
anybody."

Lewis: "I had an odd reaction afterwards that I'd never had before—I felt cheap, and I felt that she was cheap, too. I had wanted her to be different from the others, and she wasn't. Also, I had kept back one important thing from her: I was still mixed up with another girl, a cocktail waitress, a very sexy and flashy type. I'd been helping this girl out (she had two kids, and was having a hard time), and I wanted to get out of the situation but I had to be sure she could make it on her own before I walked out. It bothered me that I had lied about that to Terry; maybe that was part of it. Whatever it was—and it was probably a little bit of everything— I felt let down and disgusted with myself and her. Even though the evening had been so great up to midnight, by the time I drove her home I decided I wouldn't see her again. I went back to the motel and went to bed, telling myself that it wasn't important and that she was just another girl, but I couldn't get to sleep until I admitted to myself that I did want to call her again, only not right away; I'd wait a while and let it simmer down, and then I'd have another try."

* * *

Lewis Amory's sexual and emotional life is a contemporary version of the pagan-courtly pattern, although he would be surprised to be told so; it has never occurred to him that his mode of behavior is a hand-me-down from Athenian gentlemen of the fourth century B.C., Roman nobles of the early Empire, and French courtiers of the Age of Gallantry. This ancient pattern suits him chiefly because it requires no great intimacy in any one relationship, but permits limited intimacies in several easily manageable relationships. The unprecedented difficulty of his first night with Terry may have resulted from the fact that when he found intimacy extremely appealing with a woman who was intelligent, warm, and thoroughly sexual, the combination threatened him with a larger relationship than he could accept.

For Lewis and for many others who enter easily into the world of infidelity, extra-marital affairs are a luxury; for another group of people who likewise find their first such experience relatively effortless, extra-marital affairs are an absolute necessity—not as a source of pleasures supplemental to those of marriage, but as proof of personal power and a reaffirmation of desirability. This is what they briefly get from each new conquest; without it, their marriages and their very lives seem insufferable. It is the act of conquest, and not the relationship with the person conquered, that they find rewarding; accordingly, their affairs are shallow, brief, and numerous to the point of looking like a pattern of compulsive promiscuity.

PEGGY FARRELL, ET AL.

Peggy Farrell, a bright and thoughtful young woman despite her brash and impertinent manner, has wondered a lot about her own motives in taking off weight, improving her skin and hair, and deliberately setting out to have extra-marital experiences. For a long while she told herself that the main reasons were the "dullness" of her married sex life and her need to find a man who could make her orgastic and give her a sense of real womanliness. Today she recognizes that this was at most a subsidiary motive, for although neither her first nor any subsequent extra-marital affair—she had about thirty or forty in a seven-year period—brought her orgasm, she enjoyed them all and discovered in them a raison d'être. In random infidelities, lasting only a matter of weeks or months (or even, in some instances, one night), she found a continual source of renewal, a sense of worth, and a repeated proof of her personal appeal.

This was why she had so quickly become impatient and frustrated with the cautious brinkmanship of Tim Conner, the technically faithful married man who kept spending romantic hours with her at the Sheraton Bar but never sought to go any further. Peggy was not so much sexually hungry for him as she was emotionally hungry for the conquest itself. As it happened, opportunity gave her the chance to push things to a consummation with Tim a week after her frank demand that they go beyond barroom talk. Tim and his wife happened to have a particularly bad quarrel; she packed a bag, took their little son, and decamped to her mother's for an indeterminate stay. Tim told Peggy about it on the phone and, after a certain amount of judicious hinting and prodding on her part, he finally asked her, nervously and hesitantly, to come and visit him at his house. She did so the next night. "On the way there I was jittery, thinking, 'Oh boy, this is it!' But I was in for a little surprise." Again the giggle; again the rueful shaking of the head. "It nearly set me back a year. He was so nervous that he was an utter idiot. He got me upstairs and on the bed, and we got our clothes partly off, but what with the roller skates and toys on the floor, and his wife's curlers and creams on the dresser, he felt like a miserable sinner and couldn't get a hard-on. He did things to me with his hands, and I told him it was marvelous and out of this world, but he was so upset about being limp that it turned me off and I didn't feel a thing. After a while I told him I had to get back home, and I cut out. On the way back I felt terribly depressed; I thought that maybe I just didn't have it, maybe I couldn't get a man excited any more. But then I got home and took another good look at myself and said, 'Forget it, you're all right; there are greener pastures somewhere else.' I had to start looking again, but now that I had been through that one I felt like a veteran. I was willing to try anywhere, any time—parties, bowling alleys, bridge tournaments, political clubs, anywhere I could meet men. Especially married men, because I knew from my experiences before marriage that most single men want to fuck and forget it, but most married men have to sugarcoat it and make themselves believe they're in love with you—and that's what I wanted. But there *has* to be sex, or it's just make-believe. So goodbye Tim! I was on my merry way.

"I didn't waste any time, either, because even with Tim I had found what I hoped would be true—that having something going on made me feel good all day long. So I began hunting with a will. I went to block parties, Unitarian mixers, bridge tournaments, even to bars—let me tell you, it wasn't easy at first to go into a bar alone and have all those eyes on me, and a couple of jokers from Oshkosh thinking I was a hooker and making smart-ass remarks to me. And guess where I found someone—in a political meeting! Is that ever a gas? I'd heard from a friend that there was a big meeting of the Republican Club for people in Brighton and nearby, and I told Andy I wanted to go. He looked at me like I had to be kidding, and he said he never knew I gave a damn about politics, so I threw a few Nixon-Kennedy issues at him real fast (I'm really quite smart, you know), and he said okay, okay, but would I mind if he stayed home? I'd been banking on that, so I said I didn't mind, but I nearly broke up saying it." She breaks into laughter, and then suddenly looks rueful. "Poor Andy—was there ever a man so cooperative in putting the horns on his own head?"

For a moment she is lost in melancholy; then she shakes off the mood and continues: "Well, I went to the meeting, and buzzed around and introduced myself to people right and left. Finally I saw a man I liked—a tall, slightly stooped man in his fifties—old enough to be really vulnerable to a girl of twenty-two, like me. I managed to sit next to him and talk to him during the meeting. He was a professor at the Eastman School of Music, a kind and lovely man, with such a nice face; a real sweetie. I could see that he was almost an innocent, and ripe for the plucking. I didn't care that he wasn't any Rock Hudson; he was a dear. By the end of the evening, I could tell he wanted to see me again but was afraid to say anything, so I myself asked him if we could meet some time. He actually blushed; he told me he was married, and I told him I'd figured as much and didn't care in the least."

A few days later he met her for lunch at the Chalet in downtown Rochester; it was safe enough, since his wife rarely came downtown, and would not be doing so that day. Peggy was circumspect in her behavior but bold in her speech: After a couple of drinks she confessed that she found her husband dull and therefore unattractive, while he, the professor, was brilliant and therefore devastating. A brilliant man, she added, could do anything he wanted to with almost any woman. The professor pulled off his glasses and stuck them in his pocket; leaning across the table and looking very pleased and almost confident, he said in a low tone that he found her incredibly attractive and exciting, and that she made him feel as he hadn't felt in many years. "I wish that we could be alone together some time," he whispered. "We can," she said.

A week later the Republican Club had a meeting in downtown Rochester; two people who said that was where they were going were at the Towpath Motel a few miles away on Route 31. All day long, at the thought that a distinguished and important man was going to make love to her, Peggy had been filled with that kind of giddy excitement a child has on the day of a party; at dinner, she had to struggle to hide her exuberance from Andy. With her pulse racing from pure excitement rather than nervousness, she met the professor in the parking lot of a nearby shopping center, got in his car, and rode off with him; fifteen minutes later they were in the motel room having a drink.

He was quite nervous: What was he, a gray-haired man with

a barrel-shaped wife, six children, a score of published papers in musicology, an old inactive ulcer, and a round little potbelly, doing here? She came over and sat at his feet, leaning her head on his knee; she let him fondle her neck and shoulders awhile, and then, gently and very slowly, she stroked his thigh, hearing his breathing become suitably labored. Finally, clumsy-fingered and embarrassed, he began to undress her, and with some help was able to get the two of them unclad and into bed, where his obvious wonderment at her young body filled her with pride.

"He wasn't a very sturdy person, physically, and being nervous, he wasn't all there at the beginning, but I wasn't going to let this one go the way of the last one, so I asked if he would grant me a wonderful favor and let *me* make love to *him* for a while—and I went down on him. I knew what I was doing—it fixed him up, and in a little while he was ready. He did all right, considering. He wasn't big or powerful, like Andy, and of course he didn't make me come, but I thought it was just terrific. It was different, it was someone new, it was another person who wanted me and who got all worked up on account of me. Afterwards he seemed pleased and surprised, and was very affectionate and kind. He asked me, the way men always do at first, if it had been good for me too, and I said it had almost taken my head off. That was a lie, but I *was* happy; I was thinking, 'Peggy, old girl, you've done it, you've got a live one now, you've got a reason to feel good when you wake up in the morning.' I went home that night feeling better about myself than I had in years." She smiles a lopsided quizzical smile. "I suppose that sounds sick—being pleased with myself because I had just managed to cheat on my husband. But that's the way it was. That was me."

* * *

Some people, despite strong consciences and puritan-romantic values, find the first infidelity rather easy due to special circumstances that temporarily lower their defenses and override their conflicts. The combination of alcohol and a particularly uninhibited social occasion will sometimes do so. Office Christmas parties, large New Year's Eve parties, and certain other festive occasions may generate a special permissiveness; one feels that at such a time almost anything goes. At such a party, and with the help of a liberal intake of liquor, a conscience-directed or timorous person may effortlessly proceed to do, in a closet, attic, or car, just what had always seemed utterly impossible. But while this has often been written about, it is not actually very common; only one fifth of my questionnaire respondents indicated that alcohol had been a factor in their first infidelities, and only one twentieth of my interviewees mentioned it in any significant way.

Another influence is the impact of a particularly persuasive veteran of infidelity—one who is not only seductive and exciting but sympathetic and reassuring. Such a guide may make the Great Divide look, for the time being, like a mere sand dune:

—A high-strung poetic young woman, married to a stolid, plodding business executive, was taut and smoldering with emotional hunger. At an artists' party, she met a painter notorious for his womanizing. She responded at once to his appearance and manner: "He was dark, dynamic, bohemian, unprincipled—the very embodiment of all my teen-age fantasies. He frightened me to death and I loved it. And he was *on* to me just like that—he knew at once just how green I was and how vulnerable. Although he was the guest of honor, he took me around and got everyone to talk to me, and made me feel very special and very important. Along with painting, he ran a little print shop, and I stopped in a few days later on the pretext of looking for some prints for our library. He understood instantly, and simply took me in his arms, saying, 'I am pleased that you came.' He made it seem *right* that I should come to him if I wanted him. He talked to me for a little while, and was fierce and gentle, crazy and reassuring, at the same time. He told me that he and his wife wanted each other to have the maximum of happiness, and therefore allowed each other total freedom. My head was spinning. Then he said very quietly but very firmly, 'Now let's go upstairs,' and locked the front door and put a sign in it saying 'Back in an hour.' I went without any hesitation; in fact, I was positively joyous. The agony came long after, but when it first happened all I felt was, 'Well, it's done, I knew some day I would have to do it, so thank God I did it with someone like this.' "

It also occasionally happens that a person who ordinarily would be all but incapable of infidelity meets someone so much better suited to him than his or her mate, and feels so total an attraction, that the first sexual act comes about with little hesitation or guilt:

—A thirty-five-year-old woman went back to college after both her children got beyond grade school. Her marriage, though dull, was stable enough—until she walked into the first class of a history professor she had heard a great deal about. (He, for his part, had been "ideally" married for fifteen years and had never been seriously tempted to have any outside liaison.) "I'd heard so much about him and his reputation as a scholar that I imagined him to be austere, cold, and elderly. I went to the first class, and when he walked in—tall, erect, vigorous, with those piercing blue eyes deep in his head—it hit me right away, it was total impact. And he knew it—he kept paying special attention to me even while he was talking. I went to see him a couple weeks later about my term paper, and in a little while he was asking me to lunch. After lunch he took me to his car and we drove down to the river—it was something neither of us would ordinarily have dreamed of doing, of course— and the instant he turned off the key he reached for me and kissed me. I came up gasping and said, 'But not here!'—meaning sex, of course, although he hadn't even *asked* me yet. We agreed to meet two days later and become lovers: There was no hesitation on either part, even though this was completely outside the way of life of each of us. He says that if anyone had told him before he met me that he could behave like that, he'd have thought him an utter fool."

*　*　*

In sharp contrast, quite without the justification of love the initial extra-marital act may be nearly free of guilt and fear under the special circumstances of mate-swapping. Most people find the thought of mate-swapping repugnant; it violates deeply ingrained feelings about decency and sexual privacy. Nonetheless, for those who are acutely bored by their marriages or are having sexual problems in them, but who are held back from extra-marital relations by conscience or by lack of self-confidence, it may prove quite functional: It minimizes guilt by making the act legitimate and freely condoned, and at the same time overcomes lack of confidence by guaranteeing each participant a willing partner. (For all that, and despite the attention given it in a few outspoken periodicals and in some novels, it seems rather rare.)

The situation may originate in a discussion in which one spouse jocularly sounds out the other, looking for signs of willingness or openness to suggestion; finding it, he or she talks more directly, and after a while the two agree to give it a try with some other like-minded pair or with a group they have heard about. Or they may discuss the subject only after some other couple, already initiated, suggests it to them in one way or another during a social evening. A department-store junior executive and his wife, both in their upper twenties, recall the ease with which they began extramarital sex through mate-swapping:

WIFE: We had been having trouble with our sex life. Before marriage it had been okay, but afterwards I couldn't respond to him; I don't know why. After a while we agreed to let each other roam around freely at parties, and flirt or neck with somebody else. We both got a kick out of it, I in particular, because I was looking for something to get me stirred up; I thought it might actually help our marriage.

HUSBAND: Each of us might meet somebody at a party and go off and play around a little, but neither of us would go home with somebody else and actually have sex with them. We did discuss it though, and we talked about the possibilities of mate-swapping. Neither of us was jealous of the other; we agreed that jealousy and possessiveness had messed up the marriages we know more than anything else.

W.: Then we got friendly with Danny and Vera Carpenter, a new couple we'd met—both of them very nice-looking—and they came over here one night for hamburgers and beer. We were playing records and dancing, and while we were dancing, I realized Danny was responding to me and all of a sudden I was responding to him so much that I couldn't believe it.

H.: I could see it happening in them. Vera and I were dancing at the same time, and seeing them getting excited made the two of us get terrifically excited too. And as strange as it sounds, I wanted them to have each other; it felt right and loving to want them to enjoy each other. I wanted my wife to have a good thing happen.

W.: I think maybe Danny and Vera, or at least Vera, had had a little experience of this kind before, because neither of them seemed at all anxious or surprised by what was happening, and although we were unsure what to do next, Vera gave us the signal.

H.: She simply pulled me off into the kitchen so the two of them could be alone, and she said something to them about how we wouldn't be back until they called us back, and not to hurry. And in the kitchen, without another word, we got very passionate with each other, and it didn't seem in the least strange for us to take a couple of towels out of the bathroom and throw them on the floor and make love right then and there. We felt sure they were doing it too, in the very next room, although the music was up too loud to hear anything. It not only didn't feel strange to think they were doing it, it felt beautiful. And it made it seem perfectly fine for us to be doing so; somehow it gave us a special charge.

W.: As soon as the two of them left the room, Danny and I fell all over each other. I knew it was okay to do so. And it was wonderful for me—it was the first good experience I'd had in a long while. Afterward, when we were dressed, we called out to them and they came back in the room, and we all sat around drinking and making little jokes and smiling at each other. I couldn't get over the fact that it had been so easy and so natural. Later, my husband said the very same thing to me.

iii revelations

The immediate emotional effects of the first extra-marital sexual experience are usually mixed. A very few people have only positive reactions to what they have just done, and a few others feel only negative ones; the great majority, however, experience both positive and negative feelings, either intermingled or in alternation. Let us look first at the positive side.

Judeo-Christian tradition has always been scornful of the rewards of adultery, deeming them nothing but evanescent physical sensations, gone the moment the act is completed. Even certain pagan moralists spoke in the same vein: Good, upright Plutarch said that it was folly to cause one's wife distress and to jeopardize conjugal love for what was only a "brief and trivial pleasure." But most of the unfaithful bear contrary witness: While they may exalt the brief and trivial pleasure itself, they often have much to say of other and more lasting rewards. Among the fairly common effects of the first infidelity is the discovery, by the unfaithful person, that he possesses certain desirable traits he had come to doubt that he possessed, or perhaps never even thought he possessed. A third of my questionnaire respondents frankly admitted to having feelings of pride as a result of their first affair, and a large majority said it made them feel happier, younger, or more self-confident, at least part of the time. The testimony of my interviewees is particularly emphatic on these points.

For some people, the ego-reward of the first infidelity is not the result of any specific proof of sexual ability or emotional capacity, but of the general reassurance that comes from personal conquest. This is why Lewis Amory could say of his first extra-marital experience that it gave him a "feeling of accomplishment," and why Peggy Farrell, though she did not find the missing orgasm in her first infidelity, could say that it left her "feeling better about myself than I had in years." Other people say similar things:

—"I'd been horribly discouraged about myself; if my husband didn't want me, I wasn't worth wanting. But this made everything look different. I could win a man after all; I was fine."

—"I proved to myself that even as a man of forty-five I could still attract a new love, and it gave me a great psychological lift."

—"She appreciated me, she valued me, she would do anything I asked; this made me feel like a man again for the first time in many years."

—"That first experience made me feel I was something special, a woman worth paying attention to, worth trying to win."

But for a large number of people, the increased sense of worth and the heightened self-esteem is tied in with specific discoveries about their own capacities, particularly in the sexual area. Some who had lost their belief in themselves sexually in the course of a malfunctioning marriage are relieved and joyous, as was Mary Buchanan, at finding their capacities restored. But an even stronger and more dramatic reaction occurs in people who had never explored their own potential or developed sexual self-esteem before marriage, or within it, and for whom the first experience of extramarital sex is illuminating—indeed, dazzling:

—"For years and years my wife would say 'It's too late' or 'I don't feel like it, tonight,' and when she did agree to it, she seemed uninterested and hardly ever got worked up. We would argue about it sometimes, and she would tell me that she was sorry but I just didn't excite her; it wasn't her fault. Yet here I was with another woman, and my voice, my hands, even the way I smelled, all seemed extremely exciting to her. I was amazed at the intensity of her reactions—and at my own ability to keep coming back and making it happen all over again. In the morning when I got up to look for a cigarette, I caught sight of myself in the mirror and smiled at myself and said, 'I'm proud of you. You're great, and you never knew it.' When I left, I walked down the street with my shoulders back, feeling ten feet tall."

Women are less prone to react quite so strongly, since for them, in our culture, sexual ability is not so closely identified with success as it is for men. Nevertheless, some of them speak like this about the sexual awakening that a first affair can produce:

—"I was twenty-seven and hadn't ever responded all the way. I *thought* I had a few times, but I wasn't really sure. Then this man burst into my life—he was a client of my husband's—and put on a real campaign to make me. I played along with it. He was a shady type, a playboy and a gambler, and nobody I would ever let myself love, but he excited me tremendously. When we finally went to bed, he was very different from my husband—sensuous and ferocious, but at the same time so free and natural about it that it felt clean. I got so wound up the first time that I was almost crying. An hour later he came back for more and was able to last a lot longer, and this time I felt something new happening—it was as if I were losing control and sliding, or being carried away on a current of some kind. And then—I couldn't believe it—it was happening, it *happened!* I started laughing and crying, crying and laughing, and I couldn't stop for maybe ten minutes or more. I kept thinking, 'I'm complete. I'm a normal woman after all,' and I said to him, 'Bless you, bless you, for what you have given me.' "

For other people, the ego-reward of the first extra-marital act is very largely the result of seeing one's self in a romantic role. Even in a very contented and satisfying marriage, there is a tendency to lay aside the fond extravagant gesture, to forego the impetuous and impractical deed, to let pleasant routine drive away spontaneity and excitement; for some people, therefore, the first extra-marital affair revives old moods and reactivates the long-unused arts of courtship. For others, it enables them to experience these moods and use these arts for the first time. The person to whom all this is new experiences the more powerful ego-reward; he falls in love with himself when he first falls in love with someone else, for it is then that he can see himself as the person he has always wanted to be.

EDWIN GOTTESMAN AND JENNIFER SCOTT

This is what happened to Edwin Gottesman. He insists that his marriage has always been very happy, although pleasant rather than passionate, regulated rather than romantic. Betsy is too cool, well-mannered, and proper to elicit from him the sort of behavior he had dreamed of but never attempted. Jennifer, though much inferior to Betsy in intelligence and education, no match for her in looks, and not even (as he found out) equal to her sexually, had the ability to get Edwin to do impulsive, carefree, and dashing things he never thought himself capable of. He looked askance at her bare and dirty feet and her brazenly heavy eye make-up, he was shocked by her brink-of-disaster finances, her impulsiveness, and her irresponsibility—and found it all irresistible. He lectured and scolded her, tried to make her mend her ways, and proceeded to emulate her.

Even from the beginning, his trip to Puerto Rico with her involved deceptions and near-escapes such as he had never thought he could carry off. He had sent Jennifer a ticket for the flight from Philadelphia to Dulles Airport, and told her to meet him in the passenger lounge of Pan American Airways. But that afternoon Betsy insisted on driving him there. In the car, at the last minute, Edwin pretended to remember an urgent business call and hurried back into the house alone; he phoned Pan Am and arranged to have Jennifer paged and advised to wait in the cocktail lounge instead.

At the airport, Betsy saw him safely checked in, and then left; the moment she was out of sight he rushed to the cocktail lounge and collected the somewhat bewildered Jennifer, who, when he explained, was all giggles and admiration. He felt like someone in a French movie, adroitly maneuvering between wife and mistress, and remaining calm, sophisticated, and debonair all the while.

Jennifer, in a holiday mood, was enraptured by the luxury of first-class, the drinks, and the sight of the wrinkled sea, far below, succumbing to afternoon shadow although six miles above it they were still bathed in sunlight. She was even more delighted when he told her that Sol, one of the principals in the prospective purchase, had a seventy-five-foot yacht under charter at the Club Nautico in San Juan Harbor, and that they would be Sol's guests in a stateroom on board the yacht. Sol was one of the men Edwin had often heard talking about his affairs; when he had learned that Edwin was bringing a girl to Puerto Rico, he had been as pleased as an evangelist with a convert, and insisted on playing host to them.

To Edwin and Jennifer, neither of whom had ever been on such a boat before, the yacht was an exotic pleasure-palace. It had a spotless teak deck, gleaming chromium fittings, a luxurious main saloon with wall-to-wall carpeting and oil paintings, four luxurious mahogany-panelled staterooms, and a four-man crew to answer all wants. After changing to sport clothes, they joined Sol and his girl-of-the-month on the open rear deck. Edwin, lying back in a chaise longue, the soft night air fanning his cheek, the rum punch making his head a little light, his girl (eye-catching in snug pants and a deep-cut blouse) holding his hand, was almost overcome by the wonder of it all, by the spectacle of a handsomer, younger, and wittier Edwin enjoying a life he had never imagined possible for him. Oddly enough, it all seemed absolutely right and natural.

After a very late but excellent dinner served by the steward in the dining room, they had a brandy on deck and then said their goodnights. Edwin felt no anxiety or hesitation at this point; what came next also seemed right and natural. "I felt no tremendous charge of sexual feeling, just a pleasant excitement and a wonderful relaxation about it. No worry, no awkwardness, no sense of strangeness—*that* was the strange thing. The sex was a completely normal part of the situation. It wasn't physically overwhelming, just a good time, but I found it very satisfying because it was so easy and free, and because it completed everything. I couldn't understand why I had been so slow to try it with her—or why I had expected it to be such a big thing. But I enjoyed it anyway because I had been waiting for it so long and because there we were, making love under perfect circumstances. Also because I felt very warm toward her, and it was marvelous to be bringing things like this trip into her life—and mine. Afterwards we sat up and had a couple of drinks—there was ice and liquor in the cabin—and ate fresh mangoes and licked our fingers, and kidded each other about whose fault it was that we had been so slow to get to bed with each other. I felt like a real man of the world.

"We did it again, later on, and again I was a little surprised. She wasn't nearly as good at it as Betsy, who is calm and reserved all day long but gets very excited and active in bed. But it made me feel marvelous anyhow; I was delighted by the *idea* of what I was doing more than by the *thing* itself. That night I was completely in tune with the world and with myself."

* * *

A third kind of revelation involves not only sexuality and romance but deep emotional response: in other words, the discovery (or rediscovery) of one's self as a lover in the total sense. Usually this revelation has germinated in the preliminary stages of the affair, but with the physical consummation it shoots skyward like the fabled beanstalk. Two brief comments by people so transfigured:

—"I'd been thinking for three years about leaving my husband, but I was unsure of myself—afraid to face the single life, afraid the whole thing was a silly schoolgirl melancholia on my part. One weekend with Hugh [her lover] was all it took to teach me the truth. Not that I had any hopes of marrying Hugh—he was too Catholic to ever get a divorce—but in that one weekend I learned so much about my own feelings, and my ability to relate to a man like Hugh on every level, that I thought of myself in a completely new way. I almost hugged myself—and I almost cried for the years I had wasted thinking there wasn't any more to be had and that it was all fairy-tales."

—"The first time with her was exciting and romantic—April rain, secret meeting, great sex all afternoon, all that—but it still wasn't much more than a typical clandestine sexual encounter. But a few days later I took her with me on a business trip, and the second day of it we were driving along the coastal highway with the top down. It was a perfect, crystal-clear day, the Pacific far below us seemed to reach out to infinity, and this lovely girl was at my side, warm and loving, so unlike my tense, brainy, competitive wife. She sat close to me and rested her hand lightly on my shoulder, and all at once it dawned on me that I was in love with her, that I was a completely different and better person with her, and that this was what life was all about. It was an almost mystical experience. I felt alive, genuinely alive—on a different plane."

The exhilaration, expansiveness, and sense of discovery of one's true potential (or rediscovery of a long-abandoned ideal self) occur frequently enough to merit serious study. How common and how lasting these seemingly therapeutic effects are, and how profoundly they alter the individual's life, have great bearing upon the meaning of infidelity in modern society. But they have been very largely ignored by behavioral scientists; in keeping with tradition, the bulk of psychological and sociological writing about extra-marital love looks only at those cases of infidelity which emanate from neurosis or marital dissatisfaction, or which have dismal psychological and social consequences. To be sure, Kinsey, Ellis, and Cuber have all pointed out that a good deal of American infidelity stems from normal motives and does not have damaging results, but even they stop short and do not explore in depth the ego-enhancing and growth-producing value of certain extra-marital experiences. Both these things, however, are manifest in the story of Neal Gorham and Mary Buchanan.

NEAL GORHAM AND MARY BUCHANAN

Mary was glad that Cal, feeling sullen and uncommunicative when she got back from her long day away (supposedly driving around alone in the country), had turned off the light as soon as she got into bed. "I wanted to be alone with my thoughts of the day's events; I wanted to relive every moment of the love-making, hear again everything Neal had said to me. I was afraid that if Cal looked at me closely, he'd see it in my face. He'd see that I was another person, a whole woman again, and not just an advertising gal with a *mariage de convenance* and a dried-up heart. I suppose I should have been asking myself what the hell I was going to do with all my new feelings, and how I could keep my life from coming apart, but I wasn't asking any questions. I was just luxuriating in it, loving the fact that I was full of sap again. In bed that night, and even after I got up the next morning, I could still feel warmth and a good sort of sensitivity inside me, and it seemed symbolic: All of me was awake again.

"I took pains to be nice to Cal on Sunday. I told him I had gotten over the shock of Ellen's suicide by now and he'd been wonderful to be so tolerant. He accepted that gratefully, and became quite cheerful. I was glad; I felt so wonderful that I wanted him to feel good, too. It wasn't his fault, but mine, that I had been willing to live such a nothing life the past two and a half years. 'You stupid broad!' I said to myself, 'You let everything in yourself get switched off. You were playing it safe, accepting a little death in order to have a little life. But now you're fully alive again, and luckier than you deserve to be.' "

Neal, after Mary had left the house that Saturday night, sat before the dying fire with a brandy, exhausted but in a state of intense self-perception. *Sacrilegious thought: This is what it is like to undergo a conversion, to be born again, to see the light. Had thought I knew my own character: well-mannered, well-controlled, well-meaning; cerebral rather than feeling, tentative rather than bold, constricted rather than exuberant—in all, a typical pallid Darien WASP (even if not rich enough by local standards). But that night, before the fire, all seemed different. Every nerve-ending was sensate, every feeling perceptible, every recollection of that day's freedom a repudiation of my former self.*

When he woke the next morning, remembrance flooded his mind as sunlight fills a room when a shade is raised; he was instantly astonished and overjoyed. All morning he hoped she would manage to call, even though they had agreed not to take any unnecessary chances. The impulse to phone her on some pretext came over him time and again during the morning but he fought it down; finally, unable to concentrate on the *Times* or a novel he had been reading, he called his close friends, the Gambles, in Rowayton, and, explaining that Laurie was away with the children, contrived to get himself invited for early cocktails and Sunday dinner. The whole time he was with them he felt an outlandish desire to tell them about the converted and reborn Neal Gorham; several times he almost dropped hints but had the sense to stop in time, knowing that they would be revolted rather than delighted. It was a bizarre and disconcerting experience to be a new man in the old world.

---

iv the morning-after syndrome

It was the anthropologist Ruth Benedict who, some years ago, first clearly made the distinction between two major ways in which societies control disapproved behavior: the "guilt cultures" by building internal barriers into the growing child in the form of conscience and self-control; the "shame cultures" by means of external barriers or social penalties such as loss of face, fines, or imprisonment. Our own society, she suggested, had long been primarily a guilt culture, but was even then (1946) in the process of changing over to a shame culture more like that of the Japanese or the ancient Greeks.

Despite the rapidity of social change in the past generation, the shift is still in progress; guilt and shame exist side by side as controlling mechanisms both in the culture and in many individuals. There are, however, some perceptible polarities: In the case of infidelity, low-involvement personalities and adherents of the pagan-courtly tradition tend to be deterred more by the fear of exposure and its practical consequences, while high-involvement personalities and adherents of the puritan-romantic tradition tend to be deterred more by conscience and guilt feelings. Many people, of course, occupy a middle ground; in them first one mechanism and then the other operates, or perhaps both operate together.

But what happens when the deterrents fail, the individual commits the forbidden act, and gets pleasure from it, but no pain? The findings of behaviorist psychology would lead us to expect that the power of the deterrents would wane, and indeed we see evidence of this all around us: The hardened criminal, the guerrilla fighter, the revolutionary, and the stock manipulator all do with ease things they found nearly impossible in their earlier years. But this desensitization does not come about immediately; indeed, right after the very first deviant act there may be a brief but intense flare-up of fear or guilt, or both. Very soon after the completion of the first act of infidelity, many people—including some who at first feel expansive and euphoric—experience a temporary backlash of strong distressing feelings; it is as though they had been on a glorious bender, and now are suffering a severe emotional hangover.

Some novice adulterers, to be sure, never experience anything of the sort. From my interviews and from indications in other sources, I estimate that anywhere from a quarter to a half of the newly unfaithful feel no intensification of fear or guilt after their initial extra-marital experiences; indeed, some who were apprehensive beforehand about the bad feelings they expected to have are pleased to find they have none. Most of these unaffected people are, like Peggy Farrell, low-involvement and weak-conscience types who were relatively guilt-free to begin with, and who find that even their fears of failure or of discovery were exaggerated.

But others who also are nearly guilt-free do experience an abrupt increase of fear, and for good cause. After the mists of passion have cleared, they perceive, for the first time, certain unconsidered risks in what they have just done:

—"I didn't feel any after-effects until a couple days later, when the phone rang and my wife answered and seemed very much puzzled by what the other person was saying. From what I overheard, I could guess what was happening. It was the girl I had made out with two days earlier. I had told her I was single, because that seemed more likely to get me someplace; I also had said I lived with my folks, because I thought that was safe. But she looked up the last name and was trying to find me; naturally, she figured it was okay to phone. I nearly wet my pants when I realized who it was. For the next couple of weeks, I would practically jump out of the chair every time that damned phone rang. I never knew when the lid might blow off. I swore that if only I got by with this one, I'd never lie to a girl again, or at least I'd do a better job of it."

Any one of a number of events may give rise to such attacks of fear: the arrival in the mail of hard-to-explain promotion literature from a motel just outside the city; the appearance of a tiny rash or vague sensation of discomfort somewhere in the private parts; a delay in the onset of the month's menstrual flow; the forgetful slip of the tongue or inconsistency in one's story which almost gives the whole thing away ("*What* motel on the boardwalk? When were *you* in Atlantic City?").

Another type of negative reaction based on realistic external factors rather than guilt is revulsion against shabbiness or tawdriness involved in the episode. It may have taken place in a grubby third-rate motel, it may have been awkward and hasty, it may have been emotionally flat and meaningless; these and comparable conditions may leave a foul after-taste. A sample narrative:

—A young woman of twenty-three was married to an immature graduate student who always "relieved himself in me one-two-three and rolled off; sometimes I wanted to scream, but I was afraid of him." At a party she spent an hour talking to a handsome and very charming photographer, and afterwards could not stop thinking about what sex would be like with him. "It was the first physical attraction I had felt for anyone since my marriage. I was so relieved to feel something again that it seemed to me I *had* to go to bed with him. I dropped by his studio and found him working with a model; I asked how long she'd be there, and he gave me a long look and then sent her away. We had a cup of tea; then, with hardly another word, we made love. We were on a dirty, lumpy old couch, I was staring up at a skylight, we had nothing to say to each other. Besides, I didn't know until then that simple sexual excitement doesn't work for me. Even though I had felt so aroused by him, there wasn't anything else between us and I found I couldn't respond. He had a fine time, as far as I could tell, but for me it was awful; afterwards I felt dirty and degraded. I said goodbye as soon as I decently could, and rushed home and stood under the shower for half an hour, trying to wash it off of me."

But hers was a minor reaction compared to those experienced by conscience-governed people. Many of them, shortly after the first infidelity, suffer physical or emotional ailments caused by guilt.

These include insomnia, hysterical crying, inability to eat, vomiting, diarrhea, migraine headaches, inability to concentrate, compulsive hand-washing, and general depression. Distressing as these disorders are, if the victim is consciously aware of the guilt that causes them he can counterattack them with anything from liquor or tranquillizers to religious confession or psychotherapy.

Unconscious guilt is considerably more serious. It may result in any of the above symptoms, but since the sufferer fails to recognize the source of his difficulties, he is far less likely to deal with them appropriately. This is particularly true of certain of the more subtle emotional disorders it can produce. Sometimes these troubles are the expression of an unconscious wish to inform one's mate of the truth, in order to obtain the release of confession. More often they are forms of self-punishment, taking the place of the punishment the individual feels society or his mate should inflict upon him. Obsessive and baseless fears of discovery may haunt the individual, remaining stubbornly unexorcised by rational examination of the facts. A man who was tormented by the idea that he might talk in his sleep and reveal his infidelity to his wife was unable to get a good night's rest for over a month, and became physically and psychically debilitated. A woman who was fearful of pregnancy despite having taken the triple precaution of diaphragm, foam, and rhythm developed a phantom pregnancy that lasted two months and drove her to the very borders of a psychotic episode. Other people become virtually paranoid about phone calls, the morning mail, any obscure remark or potential *double entendre* uttered by their mates. And among the most distressing, and relatively common, sequelae of the first extra-marital experiences are various sexual disfunctions. The following two cases are typical:

—"My husband wanted to make love to me that very same night. I felt nauseated, I felt whorish and filthy, thinking all the while that his penis was in me right where the other one had been. That was a dreadful thought and it made me completely unable to respond to him; I couldn't feel a thing. I worked hard to fake him out, but I was scared to death that he might realize something was different. It went on like that for weeks."

—"After being a non-stop lover for two days, I dragged myself home, worn-out and happy. But I was worried about what would happen if my wife was in the mood for sex. Luckily, she was still getting over a touch of cystitis and couldn't do anything. But a week later, when she was all better, I still had no desire. Not a flicker—and only a week earlier I was walking around with a hard-on half the time, and able to make love five times in two days. She hoisted her little signals—the special nightgown, the night-light by the bedside—so I had to try, but it wouldn't come up. It just lay there like the proverbial wet noodle. I panicked. I broke into a cold sweat. I felt as if I were choking or about to have a heart attack. Could it be that at forty-four I was finished? Were my sexual organs no good any more, was my life as a man over? For days I couldn't work, I couldn't sleep, I felt as if I'd be better off dead. The feeling eased off a bit after a week or two, but the trouble itself lasted almost three months and didn't go away until I had spent about a dozen sessions with a psychologist."

In some people, the morning-after syndrome leads to a precipitous flight from the adulterous relationship. Several of my interviewees spoke of the slow build-up of desire and intimacy culminating in a first experience of extra-marital sex—at which point one partner or the other temporarily withdrew or abruptly severed the relationship. Even when there is little danger of being discovered, and even when the experience is liberating, life-enriching, and seemingly not in conflict with the marriage, deeply hidden guilt feelings may create an inexplicable sense of impending doom —a fantasy of punishment created by the unconscious—to escape from which it is necessary to flee from all that is so enjoyable.

EDWIN GOTTESMAN AND JENNIFER SCOTT

The yacht on which Edwin and Jennifer were staying had a telephone; the boat was plugged in to its own line on the dock whenever it lay tied up. In the midst of that first marvelous evening on board, Edwin several times unaccountably felt that he ought to call home to see if everything was all right. He impatiently brushed aside the impulse, assuring himself there was nothing to worry about, but in the back of his mind a nagging disquiet remained. When Betsy had first heard about the trip, she had wanted to come along, leaving the children with the new maid; Edwin had floundered around, offering reasons why she shouldn't—the maid was too new to be trusted, Betsy's presence would interfere with the business transactions, he wouldn't be staying at a hotel but on some sort of cramped little boat, and so on. Now he had an eery feeling that something might be happening while he was away that only he could take care of, or that would not have happened had he cancelled the invitation to Jennifer and brought Betsy.

In the morning he yielded, and phoned from the main saloon while Jennifer was still asleep. Betsy sounded querulous, testy, and even a trifle suspicious (or so he thought); she asked how things were going and he fumbled his way through several lies about the business deal. When he hung up he felt even more uneasy than before making the call. During the day, he, Sol, and two other partners (who were staying at the Caribe Hilton), visited the beach-front acreage they were interested in, spoke to the lawyer who represented its owners, examined a draft of the purchase contract and a memo of mortgage terms, and worked out the terms of a counter-proposal. As long as these things were going on, Edwin felt fine, but in the late afternoon, when he returned to the yacht and lay sprawled in the sun on the afterdeck next to Jennifer, sipping a rum punch and listening to soft music on a stereo tape-recorder, apprehension crawled back upon him and kept him from recapturing the previous night's euphoria.

He, Sol, and the two girls were to dine at the Top of the First in Santurce and then go to a native nightclub. Before dinner they went to their cabins to dress, and after he and Jennifer had showered, he drew her to him, pulled off the bathtowel she had wrapped around herself, and proceeded to make love to her. While it lasted, he felt better, but scarcely a minute after they had finished, as though on cue the steward tapped gently on the door and said there was a call from Bethesda coming through for Mr. Gottesman in five minutes. Edwin got an instant headache. He hastily pulled on some clothes, answering Jennifer's questions in surly monosyllables, and hurried to the main saloon, where nervous perspiration soaked through his shirt while he waited. It was Betsy, of course; she seemed distraught, said she missed him, apologized for sounding cranky that morning, said she was feeling unaccountably weepy, and wondered if he had to be away another two whole days. "I got a very strange feeling that I'd better get home fast or something terrible was going to happen. But what? A fire? Burglars? An automobile accident? My father having a stroke? My children—my little *mensch,* Buddy, my little rosy-face, Sue—coming down with something terrible? Betsy having an affair with someone, or finding out about me and taking sleeping pills to end it all? Ridiculous ideas came and went in my mind; none of them made any sense, but I couldn't get rid of them. Someday, if I have the time, I should go to a shrink and find out about that and a lot of other things that are mysteries to me.

"Anyway, I could hardly eat dinner, I was a lump at the night-club, and I slept miserably that night. In the morning I got Sol out of bed and told him I would have to work out the rest of the details back in Washington because I had to get back at once. I was leaving within the hour, and had already made a plane reservation. I lied to Jennifer and told her there was only one available seat on the plane and she'd have to come back the next night on her original reservation. Sol said privately that I was being ridiculous, but he was a good sport about it. He said he'd take the girls over to the pool at the La Concha in the afternoon; he had a lot of friends there, and he'd have no trouble finding Jennifer an escort for the evening, and would get her to the airport the next night.

"She was disgusted with me. I overheard her saying to the other girl, 'What kind of fool am I to get mixed up with a man like this? He takes me away for a three-day stay, and the minute his wife calls he goes running home and leaves me on my own, fifteen hundred miles from home.' I gave her money for cabs and other expenses and kissed her goodbye on the cheek, and got out of there. I didn't think she'd ever want to see me again, and at that point I didn't care. I just wanted to get home."

*   *   *

Though Edwin thought what troubled him was anxiety about his family, alone and helpless while he was far away, his rout had in fact been caused by guilt feelings. At the unconscious level, his conscience was threatening him with punishment for having violated his own moral code; he merely projected the punishment outside himself onto persons he held dear. If his relationship to

Jennifer had been openly competitive with his relationship to Betsy, he would very likely have been consciously aware of his guilt feelings, but this was not yet the case.

NEAL GORHAM AND MARY BUCHANAN

To Neal Gorham, however, it was clear very early in his affair with Mary that his feelings for her directly challenged and imperiled his marriage and were, in part, an expression of his resentment towards Laurie; accordingly, when he suffered from an attack of morning-after symptoms, he was clearly aware of what was causing them.

The statement in his diary about being able to love both Laurie and Mary without either love's invading the other had been both wishful thinking and a hopeful denial of precisely what he feared and had begun to feel. The first full-scale attack of guilt came about a week after the ecstatic day of consummation. During that week, he and Mary talked on the phone long and intimately every day but scheduled no business meetings, thinking it safer at this point not to be together in front of other people. Mary managed, however, to spend most of one afternoon with him in a room at the Elysée Hotel and a whole evening with him in Darien (she told Cal she was having a reunion dinner with two college classmates in Scarsdale). Both meetings were rapturous; not even the *mise-en-scène* of a small hotel room, in the afternoon, could spoil their mood. ("*Amor vincit omnia*," said Neal—"any place, any deception, is transformed by love like ours." But he winced: It sounded grandiose and not quite true, even as he said it.)

Friday night he was alone at home. Laurie phoned to say she'd be leaving Virginia either just after lunch on Saturday, or early Sunday morning, depending on the weather. She wanted to know if he felt all right; she said he sounded weary or depressed. He protested his perfect health, but realized that he had been cool in his manner, perhaps even a little hostile. She had misinterpreted it, but he knew: *It was the first alarming indication of something happening to my feelings for Laurie. Was disquieted after I hung up. Poured long drink and sat in big chair, reminding myself how much I loved her. Got to thinking about her long drive home, the rainy weather, the sleep-inducing Jersey Turnpike. . . . What would happen*

*to me if she had an accident in which the children escaped unhurt
but she died? Almost wept thinking of it; plumbed the depths of my
grief; but of course it would permit Mary and me—God! Was the
whole fantasy a death-wish against Laurie? Unquestionably; I could
not deny it. (Doctor Grutman would have been pleased; I did learn
something from him six years ago, after all.) Too sickening a
thought to be endured; hated myself for it; paced through the house,
banged fist against door frame in passing (hurt my hand; sneered
at self for doing so); refused to believe it and yet knew it to be true.*

He drank too much, went weaving to bed, and leaped up in
cold-sober alarm five minutes later, having just remembered that he
had forgotten to check the house over minutely for bobby-pins,
lipstick-marked cigarette butts, and other clues. This took half an
hour; then he remembered the sheets and their unmistakable stigmata, pulled them out of the hamper and put them through the
washer and dryer, killing time in front of the television set; finally
he stuffed them back into the laundry hamper. *Got to bed at last
at 3 A.M., still shaken by the close call. Was obviously an apprentice,
didn't know the ropes. Frightening. (Three days earlier, had trem-
bled visibly while registering under false name at the Elysée; what
if the clerk had asked for identification? What could I have said?
What would he have done? God!) Fell asleep. And then had the
nightmare. Two people—Laurie and a man I couldn't see clearly—
were erecting some kind of octahedral structure taller than themselves out of large flat segments, like pieces of a stage set. They had
fitted almost all of them together, and only one was missing. Watching them, I was almost strangled with dread, and awoke, gasping,
heart racing. But why the terror? No Dr. Grutman handy, but I
thought about it long and freewheelingly, as in analysis, until it
came to me: Laurie and Cal are putting the pieces together, and
when they fit the last piece into place, it will all be clear—they will
know about Mary and me. All night and the next day had a knot
in my stomach that even two Equanils couldn't untie. Tried to read,
tried to write, both no good. Glad when it grew late enough for me
to shave, dress, and leave for the Simpsons, where there was a cock-
tail-and-buffet party. Evidently Laurie wasn't going to get home
until Sunday, which pleased me since it gave me one more day before
having to face her and my feelings. And this thought made me detest
myself anew.*

Mary, though she was not spared a similar attack, had a less severe one because of the nature of her marital relationship. "I hadn't minded lying to Cal in the early stages of the affair, not even that Saturday when I was supposed to be driving all over Dutchess County and weeping for Ellen. But once Neal and I became lovers, I started to feel lousy about deceiving him, because now the affair was real and had a future that had to be bad for Cal. I made up lies in order to meet Neal those next two times, but I found I didn't like myself in the role of liar and cheat. Also, I could see that Cal was puzzled but afraid to challenge me, and I knew that over the past several years I had made him that way; I can be tough and bitchy, and he had become weaker and more timid than he was when I first met him.

"What bothered me most of all was the realization—it came to me while I was driving back after the second time in Darien— that although I was hiding the affair from Cal, I was hoping he'd figure it out from the way I was acting, and do something rash— raise hell, throw things, hit me, walk out on me. I didn't want to be responsible for breaking up the marriage; I wanted *him* to be. But I also knew that even if I succeeded in bringing this about, Cal wouldn't be the guilty one, *I* would be. I decided that Neal and I had to be more careful; we mustn't take chances that were only disguised efforts to try to get caught. It wouldn't do any good to say *mea culpa* if I were the one who had to forgive myself, and couldn't."

chapter 5: FLOURISHING

i ways and means

For most middle-class Americans, the extra-marital affair is rarely
an uncomplicated romp or weekend peccadillo—nor, on the other
hand, a convenient and rewarding arrangement that can be main-
tained for many years. The flourishing of the affair, from its consummation to its decline and senescence, most often lies in between
these extremes. In my two samples, though the data for men and
for women differ somewhat and vary between the questionnaire
survey and the interview sample, they are generally comparable
and can be summed up as follows:

—Between one tenth and one quarter of first affairs last only
one day;

—Only a little over a tenth last more than one day but less than
a month;

—Close to half last more than a month but less than a year;

—About one quarter last two or more years, but only a few of these endure four years or more.

Affairs after the first one have a generally similar pattern of duration, except that even fewer of them last only a week or less.

These findings contradict both Kinsey's impression—which he did not support with statistics—that the weekend fling was the most common form of affair, and Cuber's feeling that the very long-term, or even lifelong, affair, was fairly frequent; both, however, were sampling populations rather different from mine, Kinsey dipping lower in the social scale, Cuber limiting himself to the upper-middle class. But my own data—and I know of no others—are unambiguous on this point: For middle-class Americans, most affairs endure on the order of several weeks to several years.

Kinsey also had the impression that most extra-marital activity occurs in sporadic concentrated bursts—during holidays, trips away from home, and the like—but again, my data and my interviews suggest otherwise; more than half of my informants said they saw their extra-marital partners at least once a week on a relatively regular basis.

But to do so over a period ranging from weeks to years involves a host of practical problems. Consider, first, communications. Although any pair of extra-marital lovers have managed to communicate, to some extent, during the earlier stages of the affair, after the consummation both their need to do so and their awareness of the risks are greatly increased. But there is little way to learn technique from others; the unfaithful have no identifiable subculture as do such special groups as the divorced or even marijuana-smokers, and nearly every unfaithful person is therefore on his own. Occasionally, of course, a few like-minded men or women will confide in each other, as was true in the case of Edwin Gottesman's business associates; sometimes fiction and drama do offer hints; and at least two recent non-fiction books, *Adultery for Adults* and *A Guide for the Married Man* (which also was a movie), present in humorous fashion a number of suggestions—many silly but some very practical—about the technical problems involved in infidelity. Nevertheless, most of the newly unfaithful have to work things out for themselves or acquire expertise from their partners—the latter situation easily leading to trouble in, perhaps, the following fashion:

She: But what if he's home when you call, and he answers the phone? You know that he comes and goes during the day.

He: I won't hang up—that's too suspicious. I'll say, "This is *Life* magazine calling. We have a special offer to new readers. . . ."

She: (*acidly*) You seem to know just what to do. You must have had a lot of experience.

He: I just made it up this second.

She: Oh, please! I don't *care* if you've had a lot of other affairs—

He: Yes, you do. I can tell. So what if I have?

She: Are you going to fight about it?

He: Who started it? Me or you?

She: Who started what?

He: Women are impossible, really impossible.

She: I'll bet you really know.

Even if both partners are novices, they are bound to recognize the need for a safe, agreed-upon time for telephone calls and for some signal or warning procedure in case anyone else is unexpectedly nearby. But most newcomers to infidelity feel deeply uncomfortable when talking about such matters. Even though they both know that lying and deception are inherent in infidelity, neither lover wants to be seen by the other as a liar or deceiver, and they fumble and squirm when first working out the details. These discomforts fade away after a while; people grow accustomed to their own deviations (if they go unpunished) and gradually work out rationalizations which make the erosion of their values feel like a positive gain. The same man or woman who is at first ashamed to discuss telephone technique will be more or less at ease with the subject later on and consider that ease a sign of maturity and sophistication.

As discomfort decreases, the ability to conceive of new and more daring solutions increases; the lovers freely borrow or invent techniques for talking to each other even at risky hours and in the presence of others. If a neighbor has dropped in unbidden for morning coffee and the phone rings just then, the conversation may go like this:

She: Hello?

He: Hello, honey, it's me.

She: Oh, thank you for returning my call. Look, I think it's the choke
      again. I keep stalling when I start up.
He: Damn. Somebody there?
She: Yes, and there's a smell of gasoline, too.
He: How about an hour from now? I can phone then.
She: That would be fine. An hour from now. Thank you.

Some grow so bold and so comfortable about using their code as to
dare to phone each other in the evening. Usually they have thought
things through so far as to recognize that if the spouse answers, it
would be unwise to hang up, for this arouses suspicions in the
unsuspecting, and confirms them in the suspicious. Instead, they
are more likely to be ready with a protective device such as the
wrong-number dodge: "Harry? Isn't this Harry? I'm trying to reach
Harry Dombrowski. What number *is* this? Oh, sorry." If the caller's
voice is known, particularly where the deceived spouse is a good
friend, this obviously will not do. A vocal disguise would be the
logical answer, but few people have the skill to get away with it. If
the caller has thought things out ahead of time, he may be prepared
to identify himself and pretend that it was the deceived spouse he
was calling. But unless he then has something to talk about, he may
flounder about dangerously, although one of my interviewees, in
such a fix, had the wit and the nerve to extricate himself as follows:
"Hi, Arthur, it's George. How's everything? Listen, Arthur . . . say,
would you believe it?—it's slipped my mind already why I dialed
you. God, what the busy season does to me!"

For those who live some distance from each other, or for those
whose spouses are at home much of the time, letters may seem safer
than the phone. But even the beginner recognizes certain obvious
risks: An unfamiliar return address (even with no name) is bound
to raise questions, and the absence of a return address is even more
likely to do so. Trusting the mail to arrive after one's husband has
left for work seems feasible—until he stays home with a cold and
gets to the mailbox first. Some people therefore ask a trusted friend
to serve as a mail drop—but if even one friend is privy to the secret,
many others may be.

A solution independently arrived at by many people is to rent
a post-office box to which all such private correspondence can be
addressed. Yet in smaller cities and suburbs this has its hazards.

One woman, in a city of 20,000, says that whenever she goes downtown she sees people she knows; if she rented a box, sooner or later someone would see her getting mail from it, and since almost all householders in her city have delivery service, this would look very strange.

Letters sent to one's office and marked "personal" are fairly safe, although secretaries often rightly guess what they are about; this is not necessarily risky, but it may prove uncomfortable. ("Good morning, Mr. Almquist. Your mail is on your desk." Sweet smile. He looks: one large pile, businesslike, all opened and laid out; one small pile of two blue envelopes addressed in a feminine hand, marked "personal," and unopened. He glances out the door; another sweet smile, all innocence.)

Burning love-letters, or tearing them up and flushing them down the toilet, is painful—but keeping them is sheer folly. The freezer, the "SARS to SORC" volume of the *Britannica,* the lingerie drawer, the box containing last year's paid bills, have all seemed ideal hiding-places—and have all proved vulnerable. Even the writing of letters is liable to be risky, for on occasion a spouse may unexpectedly walk in on the writer and ask questions. Only the brazen can handle the situation as well as one woman who, caught in the act, tore up the letter she was writing, enraged at being doubted; later that day she wrote a second letter, quite innocuous, then tore it up, pasted the pieces together, and contritely presented it to her husband, saying that she had been wrong to get so angry and wanted him to see what it had all been about.

A second group of practical problems of the extended affair concerns a meeting-place suitable for sex. One of the simplest and cheapest is the automobile, but most people find that what served them well enough in their youth seems thoroughly inadequate in their adulthood. The lack of space, the fugitive atmosphere, even the nubby or leathery texture of the seats, make sex in the automobile seem tawdry and degrading. Nor is the car entirely safe; not only does it involve the risk of being come upon by others, including the police, but it has neither plumbing nor hot water to help one get rid of the evidence before going home. The car itself, moreover, is a clue-collector: Bobby-pins, match-box covers, crumpled tissues or cigarette butts with the wrong shade of lipstick on them, have a remarkable way of appearing from under the seats days or weeks later.

The rented room offers more space, a proper bed, relative safety, a shower, towels. But motels and hotels are difficult for the novice to face, particularly the female. There is a dreadful deliberateness about going to a hired bedroom, and even in a clean, modern motel, with all the comforts of television, air-conditioning, wall-to-wall carpeting, and instant coffee, both man and woman may feel dirty or ashamed.

Even getting into the motel or hotel room is enough to kill the mood of love. What if someone they know sees them in the lobby? What if someone recognizes the car? Should they register under a false name (which is illegal in some places), under the right name (in which case forgotten articles may pursue them home), singly (which constitutes a fraud against the landlord), or as "Mr. and Mrs." (which is psychologically difficult)?

To register without luggage is tantamount to announcing what one is up to; almost every beginner remembers to bring at least a dispatch case to forestall the desk clerk's faint, knowing smile. As with telephone technique, beginners may feel squeamish about discussing this subject with each other, but if the affair endures and flourishes, they come to take a certain pride in discussing how foresighted they have become: He has learned to equip his dispatch case with a toothbrush, whisky, and a clean shirt (in case the one he is wearing gets eyebrow pencil or lipstick on it); she has learned to outfit her tote bag with hair curlers, setting spray, and even a second diaphragm so that she can leave one at home for her suspicious husband to find.

If one partner in the affair is single and has his or her own place, many of the problems connected with renting rooms can be avoided; the chief remaining one is that of the married partner's safe arrival and departure. The smaller the community, the greater the risk of being recognized by someone; even one's car is practically an advertisement of his presence. If both partners are married but one of them has a spouse who is safely out of the way all day, it may be possible to use the very bed of marriage for illicit lovemaking, although, curiously enough, many people feel queasier about this than about the use of their own bodies. Sometimes the lovers meet in the morning, as soon as the husband and children have left the house; more often they prefer the lunchtime period, when the man can be away from his office without raising questions. But whatever time they choose, all daytime meetings have the same hazards: The visitor's coming and going are visible to the neighbors, and the mood of the lovers is likely to be shattered at any time by the phone or doorbell. A young woman who lives in a suburb of San Francisco offered the following caveats, based on her own experience and that of two friends:

Lock the doors but don't pull down the shades except in the bedroom, and then not all the way; it looks too suspicious.

Put your car in the garage and close and lock the door; they'll think you went downtown with somebody else.

Don't answer the doorbell; it couldn't be that important. Even if it was a detective, what good would it do to answer it?

Take the phone off the hook; you shouldn't answer it at such a time, but letting it ring might kill the whole thing for that day.

Keep plenty of liquor in the house, and try to have more than one bottle opened at a time; some husbands have a sharp eye for the level.

Change the bed as soon as he leaves, and bounce around a little on the fresh sheets to muss them up. Some husbands notice everything.

Some people have places of business that serve the purpose. Photographers and artists have studios, doctors and dentists have offices, writers, mail-order entrepreneurs, and small businessmen of many sorts have private offices or other quarters away from home. But all these have certain drawbacks. Their locations are known to the spouse, they are vulnerable to interruptions except during limited and often inconvenient times, and most important, they are rarely aesthetically suitable: The examining table, the studio floor, the plastic-covered couch in the waiting room, are discouraging to the act of love.

The most secure and generally acceptable meeting-place is a small apartment, secretly rented expressly for the use of the lovers. But the "pad," as it is often called, is an expensive solution to the problem; moreover, it is apt to produce a feeling of emotional as well as financial entrapment. To overcome these disadvantages, groups of men sometimes rent a pad cooperatively, but this makes for multiple problems of scheduling and housekeeping; even worse, it gives the apartment the tainted atmosphere of a house of assignation.

A third problem is that of finding time. The "matinee" (the mid-day meeting) is difficult or impossible for most people with jobs, if there is any distance to travel, and for most women with children, except those still in the crib and playpen. Late afternoon, on the way home from work, is the time the French favor—they refer to such a rendezvous as a *cinq-à-sept* (5 P.M.-to-7 P.M.)—but the American, lacking the excuse of the Frenchman's traditional stopover for a leisurely apéritif at a café, may find it hard to explain his late homecoming.

For the occasional or irregular rendezvous, the once-in-a-while excuse seems favored: for men, the all-evening business conference, the reunion with war buddies, the fishing or camping trip; for women, the fund-raising meeting, the lecture at the woman's club, the hen party. But in a steady affair people seek a standing excuse —an activity which provides a reason to be away from home regularly and without special or repeated explanations. The lawyer or sales representative may begin having evening meetings with clients and buyers; the man who has not played poker in years develops a renewed taste for it; the housewife may sign up for a course in interior decorating; married students and faculty members ostensibly are immured in library stacks, where they cannot be checked up on; and so on.

By one method or another, the lovers manage to see each other fairly often, even if only for short periods of time. And they will even meet in the presence of their own spouses at parties, sacrificing the chance for intimacy and even finding a perverse pleasure in being near without being free. The fleeting look, the whispered word while dancing, the spoken allusion to something that has a special meaning for the other, the almost palpable feeling of an invisible bond between them—all these make such meetings bittersweet. If one of the lovers is single, the other may have to use a "beard" on such occasions, this being a helpful friend who serves as the escort and date of the single one. Several of my interviewees had beards bring their lovers to their own homes; one man even took special pains to draw his mistress and wife together in conversation, a situation he found incomparably exciting.

In recognizing the existence of these various problems and seeking solutions to them, the extra-marital partners are motivated by a keen awareness of the need to keep the affair secret. But as they acquire expertise and refined perception of the situation, they realize that there are many ways of giving themselves away which they had not even considered. One man begins to exercise, take off weight, dress in mod clothing, grow a handlebar moustache; not until it is dangerously late does he realize that his wife has become suspicious, and with good reason. An ordinarily cheerful woman falls into contemplative moods and often sighs deeply without knowing it; her husband asks her what is bothering her and she recognizes that she has not been monitoring herself carefully enough.

Even more difficult to control is the effect of the affair on one's sexual behavior at home. Only the unthinking person, or one who wants the spouse to know, deliberately and abruptly cuts down on marital sex; most try to continue as usual. But often it is not easy. Some, as we saw earlier, may become impotent or frigid with their mates because of guilt. Others, though they make a special effort to "keep everybody happy," find it wearing. A man who has just given his all to his mistress may be in trouble if he comes home to find that this is the night his wife is in the mood; a woman, in the same situation, may find the problem physiologically simpler, but psychologically just as difficult.

And there is the opposite danger that, having become newly active and aware in the extra-marital sex relationship, one may reveal unwonted enthusiasm or new knowledge in the marital bed. It can be as obvious as an incautious comment that implies a comparison with someone else ("You're such a lady—you never make a sound"), or as subtle as an increased interest in playful variations ("*Albert!* What on earth. . . ?").

*   *   *

Despite the risks all extra-marital partners must take and the clues they cannot help leaving, an affair may go on a long while without coming into open conflict with the marriage. This avoidance of conflict often owes much to the cooperation of the deceived spouse, who refuses to notice or to believe the signs and portents. In my two samples, only about one out of six spouses definitely knew, while it was going on, that their mates were having an affair, but many people say in retrospect that they should have known but refused to see what was before them. Even where there were accidental slips of the tongue, odd phone calls, or other clues, deceived spouses often refused to notice them, felt suspicions but rejected them, harbored them but avoided any confrontation, confronted the unfaithful mate but gratefully accepted his bold denials.

For the facade of fidelity is immensely important to the ego and to the public image of the deceived spouse: The same wife who will quietly live with suspicions for years may be either crushed or enraged if her husband openly admits his infidelities, and the wife who does know about and tolerate discreet infidelity may sue for all she can get if her husband grows careless. Which is why one veteran adulterer said, concerning the confrontation scene, "Deny! Lie! Say anything. She'll believe you because she wants to!" and another said, "Never admit a thing, but if you have to, tell him the least you possibly can. Resist the temptation to make a clean breast of it." Even a high-ranking clergyman agrees: Bishop Pike feels that where two lovers have decided an affair is justifiable, they may have an obligation to lie about it for the good of others. "Once a primary ethical decision has been made a particular way," he writes, "more often than not secondary ethical responsibilities [i.e., secrecy and deception] are entailed."

But many an unfaithful spouse who keeps quiet about his affair yearns to confess it. Filled with warring feelings of love and loyalty, he wishes he could end his conflicts without hurting anyone or giving anything up; he longs to explain to his spouse that one person can love two people, and to be granted understanding and forgiveness—and the right to continue. Dr. Louis Ormont points out that this is much like the child's wish to have the loving parent forgive his naughty deeds while letting him continue doing what he wants to do. But it is rare for the child to have such an ideal parent, and even rarer for the adult to have so ideally parental a spouse; adult commonsense prevails and the urge to confess is controlled, for the time being.

---

ii keep it light

Some extra-marital affairs do not grow after consummation, but remain arrested in an early stage of development. Repeated meetings scarcely add to or deepen the relationship; the lovers increase their total number of shared conversations, meals, and coitions without growing closer or knitting their lives together. The game-playing, the intrigue, the flirtatiousness and sexual excitement that preceded the first sexual experience, remain the sum and substance of their affair. If you see them meeting in a hotel lobby, or whispering close in a corner of some restaurant, you might assume things about their feelings that are not so, for theirs is only a miming of love, a counterfeit intimacy. Though they link their bodies, most of what is within each person remains enclosed, private, unrevealed. Yet this is no drawback; indeed, for most of those people it is the very limitation of involvement that makes the affair comfortable and gratifying to them. Here is how two such people speak about relationships of this kind:

—"The only thing he and I had in common were bad marriages and Sunday puzzles, which we used to do when both families were together—we were neighbors and very chummy, although neither his wife nor my husband knew what was going on. He wasn't the right man for me, from a long-range point of view, but for the time being he was fine—sympathetic and good-looking and very convenient. The affair was a kind of aspirin for my aching marriage; it eased the pain without curing anything. And that was just what I wanted—that and no more."

—"When I'm on the road, I'm in the sack with a different girl three nights a week, but I keep seeing the same ones again and again over a period of two or three years, and a lot of them have come to think of me as a Rock of Gibraltar—a man they can confide in and really talk to. But I was never in love with any of them and almost none of them has ever been in love with me. I guess I must do something that makes it turn out that way, but I don't know what it is. Jesus, if one girl has said this, twenty-five have—'Baby, as a lover you're a technical marvel, you're tremendous, but you don't get through to me emotionally.' After we've made love and we're having a cigarette, they say, 'Honey, it was great but there's something missing. You don't really give a damn about me, and I know it.' But it doesn't bother me; in fact, I prefer it that way."

A few behavioral scientists have begun to suggest that extra-marital affairs can be not only harmless but actually helpful to certain marriages. Virginia Satir, family therapist and *doyenne* of the avant-garde Esalen Institute at Big Sur, regards affairs as "inevitable and necessary" for many contemporary marriages, if they are to avoid becoming stale and destructive. Dr. Ernest van den Haag says he has seen a number of cases in which the marital relationships would suffer if the unfaithful partners deprived themselves of the benefits they got from their affairs. Cuber and Harroff report that some of their interviewees claimed their lives and those of their spouses had been benefitted rather than harmed by their affairs. The anthropologist Bronislaw Malinowski, speaking of preliterate cultures, said that extra-marital activity was not the antagonist of marriage but its complement, and other anthropologists have pointed out that in many societies the function of ritualized or sanctioned extra-marital sex has been to prevent hurtful liaisons and to preserve marriages by making a limited amount of variety available.

Some of the narratives I collected seem to bear out this viewpoint, particularly those that concern low-involvement affairs of the kinds just illustrated. (High-involvement affairs are another matter, as we will see later.) Apart from the relief of boredom, low-involvement affairs can be beneficial in two important ways: First, a person who is insecure or deficient in self-esteem may gain temporary reassurance and contentment from each new conquest; second, a person getting insufficient satisfactions from a marriage that is seriously defective can find his outside relationships supplemental and ameliorative. A case which illustrates both benefits:

—A research physicist, a tall, diffident, soft-spoken man, found his second wife becoming alcoholic and asexual early in their marriage. Unable to get her into treatment, but ashamed to be divorced again, he suffered frustration for years until he met a waitress he describes as "very pretty, very warm, very passionate—and very dumb." Overcoming his reserve, he asked her to dinner, and on their second date became her lover. By their sixth or seventh evening together, he found it almost impossible for them to carry on an extended conversation: They had used up the easy questions and answers, and his interests were over her head while hers were acutely boring to him. "Nevertheless, for a year and a half we spent every Thursday night and every Sunday afternoon together because we had a perfect physical union. But since we couldn't stay in bed all that time, we had to find things to do—like exploring the city or going to the beach—so as not to feel ill at ease with each other. Just the same, it was wonderful. Sexually, I had done very poorly as a youngster and in both my marriages, and the fact that I could have a relationship based on nothing but sex, and not only get great satisfaction myself but give a woman satisfaction every time, was a continuing joy. It kept me cheerful and contented for a year and a half, until she broke it off."

Far from regarding the shallowness and lack of emotion of the light affair as a flaw, people who like such relationships see this as a positive asset and even as a sign of maturity and health. "No entanglement at all!" exulted one man, recalling an affair with "one of those new California girls to whom such things are natural—she could divorce the whole thing from emotion. What freedom, to be with such a woman!" Says another man about a similarly unemotional woman: "There was no hang-up about 'What do I mean to you?' or 'What are we going to do about all this?' or any of that neurotic jazz. That's what made it so great." And a forty-year-old homemaker, recalling a series of affairs she had in her twenties and early thirties, is almost rhapsodic about it:

—"It was never the physical part that mattered the most to me; in that department, my husband was and still is the best. What I liked was the interplay of personalities in the game of love. You meet, you give out little signals, you start to build up some tension, you try to create the right mood in the right place, you play at love and believe in the game for a while even though you really know better. It goes on a few months, during which you have sex a few times, and then it fades away and you become just friends, and go on to another. Each time, it's flattering and challenging and mysterious—all the things marriage can't be."

The shallowness of these relationships is not imposed upon the lovers by circumstances; rather, one and sometimes both of them take deliberate steps to keep the affair light. Traditionally, it is supposed to be the man who tries to hold back or remain partly free in a love affair, while the woman wants the relationship to be deep and binding. But unfaithful wives prefer an emotion-free relationship more often than has been generally recognized. Perhaps this is because, being married, they already have security and status, and can afford to let themselves enjoy trivial relationships, while unmarried women cannot, or are afraid to.

Practitioners of the casual affair try to establish the premises at the outset:

—"I always make it plain to a woman at the start, that I'm interested—but that I don't want her soul and I'm not offering mine."

—"Men can tell from my attitude that I might be interested in friendship and sex, but that if they want more, they'd better forget it and look elsewhere."

But they also continue to manipulate and control the relationship as it progresses, in order to keep it within the desired bounds. Sometimes they are primarily concerned with controlling their own emotions:

—"I try never to let my feelings get out of hand; I hold on to them."

—"If it starts to feel important to me, I cut out; I date a few other men to break it up and to distract myself."

More often, they exercise control over the other partner, limiting the degree of feeling and involvement they will allow. One woman, whenever her lover was becoming too intense, would tell him she was overwhelmed by business appointments and family obligations for the next two or three weeks; the lay-off would anger and alienate him just enough to reduce his intensity to a level she could tolerate. A New York businessman, having an affair with a young woman while his family was in Maine for the summer, always found some excuse, after they had made love, to get dressed and go home for the night although he could easily have stayed; this seemed to him to keep his involvement within manageable limits. A career woman in Los Angeles, ordinarily warm and affectionate to her lover, would abruptly become chilly and even angry whenever he became serious about his feelings; two or three times, after sex, he used words of love or alluded to his wish to marry her, whereupon she flew into a tantrum-like rage, accused him of trying to "corner" her, and did not calm down until he promised to avoid such subjects in the future.

When such a person is taken unawares and blunders into more involvement than he or she intended, it rarely lasts long; neither the situation nor the individual's emotional make-up permits it. The affair comes to an early end and leaves the person ruefully vowing never to care that much again. A perennially philandering businessman who got carried away only once speaks to the point:

—"She was the only one I ever got that involved with, and I knew it was trouble all along. When we broke up, I cried, I really sobbed. I don't remember ever having an experience like that before, and I don't want anything like it again. Ever since then, I take greater care to hold down my feelings. At a party or on a date I can lose myself again for a few hours, but in the morning I wake up and remind myself that I have a wife and five kids and a big house, and I turn it off. I refuse to let it happen."

PEGGY FARRELL, ET AL.

Something of the sort happened to Peggy Farrell after she had had more than two dozen casual affairs; for a brief moment she opened the doors to feeling, then slammed them shut again and returned to her regular ways. But that was four years after her first affair with the Eastman School professor had started her on her way. Although the first evening they spent in the motel had made her feel greatly pleased with herself, it proved to have been practically the high point of the relationship; from that night on the professor was far less energetic in pursuit of her than she wanted him to be. Stricken by guilt, he failed to telephone her for nearly a week—she had expected him to call several times a day and to be inconsolable until they could meet again—and when at last he did call, she had to prod him into making the next date. Thereafter, he would meet her about once a week for lunch, or drinks at night, plus a brief visit to the motel, but for a number of reasons he found even those occasional meetings somewhat onerous. As Peggy puts it: "He was a real doll, and very fond of me, but a lot of things kept him from being attentive enough for my taste. For one thing, he had a heavy teaching load. For another, he was a devoted family man, and taking time away always made him feel dreadfully guilty. And not being too strong, physically, he just couldn't do everything he had to do and still manage the explosive kind of romance I craved. I don't just mean sexually, although that was sometimes a bit of a problem. I mean he didn't have time or energy for the *activity* I wanted—lots of phone calls, meetings in the middle of the day, drinking and staying up late, fighting and making up, all that. I must be some kind of nut; a peaceful love affair doesn't do much for me. My husband, when I first knew him, was a wild one—he was still boozing it up a lot and living like a hippie, and we would always clown around, or do crazy things in public, or flirt with other people and have terrible fights and then bang on each other's doors at three A.M. and make up. It was *great.* Then we got married, and Andy went AA and became so square and dull that I could scream. Sometimes I did.

"But my professor wasn't any swinger, either. For a little while I found our affair exciting, but it was really just a quiet tryout, a rehearsal for bigger and better things. When he'd phone me, he'd be courtly and flattering, but there wasn't any great passion in him. He didn't *have* to have me—in fact, I generally had to push him into the next date. And when we'd meet, sometimes he'd take me to a bar and we'd have a couple of drinks and hold hands, but he'd say he was too tired for sex. Other times we'd go to a motel and it would be okay, but it was never terrific—and of course there never was any orgasm for me, nothing even close to it. So after a few months, we just quietly drifted apart."

In much the same way, Peggy's subsequent affairs were always launched with excitement and drama, and thrust aloft toward the consummation by the powerful mixture of flirtation, make-believe, secrecy, and sex—but all too soon the magical propellant would lose its thrust and the affair would fall back to earth; something was missing from the mixture. Yet she was content, or thought herself so, and recalls her most active years as a period of continual challenge and excitement.

"I always had something going on—and if I didn't, or if I was bored with the current thing, I'd always find myself turned on by the sight of a new crop of men, wherever they were—in a bar, in a bus, in one of my night classes. I'd mentally rub my hands in glee and think, 'Okay, let's see, which one should I work on?' I particularly loved that part of it—the business of starting things off with a new one. There's nothing like it—the thrill of making him notice me, the little hints, the kidding and the byplay, the phone calls and messages, the first arrangements to meet secretly, the waiting to see what kind of pass he makes, the first time we take our clothes off and see and touch each other. But for all that, I never really fell in love with any of them except one.

"From time to time, I did wonder whether I might not be tramping around a little too much, but for a long while I told myself I was still trying to find a man who could make me feel like a complete woman. I don't believe that any longer. I think I was looking for just what I found—the fun and the challenge of it all, the suspense and the intrigue, the hunting around for something newer and better. Oh, I was a busy one, I tell you! Three or four nights a week, after tucking Petey in bed and clearing away dinner dishes, off I'd go to meet some guy, or to attend my college classes, or to hang around in some bar for a while. Andy would have his nose glued to the TV, and he'd just grunt at me when I was leaving and tell me not to be too late." She giggles, and adds, "He didn't give a damn, as long as I got back in time for him to have a quick piece before he went to sleep." Then she grows thoughtful, her bright sauciness giving way to seriousness. "I don't know—looking back on it all, now, I find it suddenly makes me weary. It gives me the shivers—all that time and energy, and all for what?" But as if hearing herself in this unusual mood, she laughs again and shrugs it off: "Just the same, I really did have a ball for years and years. I was the original go-go kid."

Astonishingly enough, Peggy managed all this without arousing her husband's suspicions; he always believed she was with woman friends, or at college. They had drifted into a semi-independent way of life: He spent his leisure with Petey, watched television, or drove into town with the boys for an evening of pool or bowling; Peggy had her own evenings out for her classes and, ostensibly, for bridge games or doorbell-ringing for the Republican Club. Their social life as a couple consisted of one night of cards per week with neighbors. Peggy, an energetic and efficient person, kept the house in order, took care of their son, shopped, cooked, studied, and still had time and energy for her affairs.

But she was grateful when circumstances relieved her of one of her obligations for a while. "The best period of my life was four years ago, when Andy's firm had a special project going in Brazil and he had to go down there, supposedly for two or three months. Once he was there, it stretched on and on—he was away nearly nine months in all—and because we didn't have much money, and Petey was anemic, we agreed that Petey and I wouldn't join him. Probably I ought to say I missed him—and sometimes I did, especially on holidays, when Petey should have had his Dad around—but mostly it was great for me. Every weekend I went to some bar where there was a friendly atmosphere, and I'd meet all sorts of men. I was Queen of the May. I looked great—I had lost still more weight—and I was on the Pill and didn't have to worry about anything. It was one long lovely daisy-chain. Sometimes I'd go out even during the week, or have some fellow stop by for a while after Petey was asleep. I wasn't lonely one minute, and I hadn't ever had a better time in my life.

"Then one Friday night, in the Sheraton Bar, I met a career soldier, a lieutenant-colonel who was on a special assignment, visiting various contractors around the country; he had come to Rochester to see Bausch & Lomb about lasers. He was a good-looking, soft-spoken man of about forty-five, but looked much younger. He was married and had been away from home seven weeks, and he was horny as hell, but I didn't know that at first, because he didn't come on like that. He was a gentleman—pleasant and friendly, and he seemed to enjoy my company without having anything else in mind. Toward the end of the evening, he told me that he was a happily married man but was terribly lonely and would enjoy more of my companionship. He said he hoped I'd be back the next night.

"I said I would be, and I was. And that time I never bothered with anyone but him the whole evening long. When we said good-night, I invited him to come out the next day for Sunday dinner. He came at around three. He changed into a sport shirt and made himself at home, and played with Petey. I had roast beef with all the trimmings, and he carved. It seemed great to have a man around the house, especially one who was manly but warm and easy to talk to, not hostile and screwed-up like so many of the men I had known.

"I wasn't sure what he had in mind for later, but I knew what *I* had in mind. As soon as Petey was asleep, I got out the gin and tonic, turned the lights down low, and put some soft music on the record-player. Well, naturally it worked out fine; in less than an hour we were in a very interesting condition on the couch and decided we'd better move on into the bedroom. Once we got there, he never got up again until morning; it seemed perfectly natural for him to stay. But I threw a pillow and blanket on the couch so Petey would think he'd slept out there. After breakfast, I lent him my car, and he drove downtown, worked all day, came back at dinner-time, and stayed overnight again. We lived like that four days—well, really, only three nights—and all of it was perfect. It wasn't mainly a matter of sex—our sex wasn't the greatest, and we didn't have time enough to work out the adjustments. It was just that he was warm and good, he cared. He was a wonderful man. I started out just having fun, but after two days of it I woke up to the fact that I was crazy about him.

"But he never said anything to mislead me. I knew that he loved his wife and would be going home to Texas on Wednesday, and that I'd never see him again. He never lied to me about it. He did say he 'cared a lot' about me, but he was too honorable to go further than that or give me any false hopes. Wednesday afternoon I drove him to the airport. I waved goodbye when he went through the gate, and turned and walked away as fast as I could, crying over a man for the first time in my life.

"I never heard from him again. I knew I wouldn't because he's too fine a person to play games, but I was annihilated. I couldn't think about anything but him and our few days together. It seemed as though it had been a dream, yet it also seemed like the most real relationship I'd ever had. I couldn't make my mind work, I couldn't pay attention to Petey or the house, I couldn't study, I couldn't eat or sleep. So after five or six days I took the cure—I leaped into a crazy affair with some jerk of a salesman who was married but who thought he was hopelessly in love with me and who didn't miss one night. I wasn't in the least in love with him, but having him around made me all right again."

* * *

None of Peggy's earlier affairs had grown, or developed any content, after they were under way, and even the four-day idyll with the lieutenant-colonel owed much of its perfection to their awareness that they had time only to play out a make-believe love for a few days. The kind of person who has brief, low-involvement affairs outside of marriage either flees from one that threatens to become deeper or mismanages it until it breaks up. This pattern may endure for life, or may yield to changes in the personality which bring about a search for relationships of another sort. But if there are no such changes, people of this kind may have casual liaisons for many years without disturbing their marriages. Peggy's various imbroglios, for instance, do not seem to have done her marriage, such as it was, any harm. To be sure, most marriage counselors hold that if a person like Peggy did not expend her sexual and psychic energies outside and find solace there for her dissatisfactions, she might work on her marriage and make it a "good" one: that is, intimate, involved, and monogamous. But what is good for one man or woman may not be for another; a person who lacks the emotional apparatus for intimate marriage would find such a relationship galling and oppressive. For such a person, a "poor" marriage may be preferable, and casual discreet adulteries may supplement it without creating difficulty. Although some unfaithful people with such marriages do get divorced, they do so not because their casual affairs blocked the growth of intimacy in the marriage, but for other reasons: The marriage may have been abrasive and contentious; the mates may have been sexually incompatible; one of them may have needed the intimacy and warmth the other could not give.

But what effect does the casual affair have on the intimate and involved marriage? While I agree with those authorities on marriage and sex who believe that an occasional minor affair may benefit marriage, I feel this is true only of marriages that need benefitting: the distant, the boring, the conflict-ridden. I have heard of marriages said to be loving, satisfying, and close, in which one partner or both have casual affairs that benefit the marriage or at least do it no harm, but each time I have been able to investigate such a case, it has seemed to me that the marriage is amiable rather than loving, tolerable rather than satisfying, and comfortable rather than close. This is not to rate it as inferior to any other; if it best meets the needs of both partners, then for them it is superior to any other. But I have not yet seen any evidence that the loving, satisfying, and close marriage can be improved—or even that it can remain unthreatened—by casual affairs.

---

iii love with limits

If the briefest extra-marital affairs are usually the least involved, the longest-lasting ought to be the deepest and most intensely felt. But this is not necessarily the case; some of the most durable affairs are those with only a moderate degree of involvement. Very often, the marriages of one or both partners in such affairs are also only semi-involved; the marriage and the affair do not so much compete as collaborate. They tend to specialize in function, each providing a different but limited set of satisfactions. The people who achieve a long-lasting combination of this sort like and need somewhat more involvement in their relationships, both marital and extra-marital, than people like Peggy Farrell and the others we have just been looking at. Nevertheless, they can go only part way in revealing themselves or identifying with any one person, and find it reassuring to divide their emotional requirements between two partners, giving a different part of themselves to each while holding back the rest.

Novelty, variety, and conquest are not the goals of affairs of this kind; generally speaking, their purpose is to be supplemental or adjunctive to marriage. The affair may, for instance, provide companionship and understanding missing in the marriage, or affection, or flattering attention; yet the marriage remains valuable and rewarding because it offers an established social role, a home base, parenthood, the gratification of living up to one's responsibilities. If the marriage is particularly stormy and painful, the primary purpose of the adjunctive affair may be to provide consolation; the outside partner may not be one's ideal, nor a potential marital partner, but an excellent part-time comforter and restorative. A newspaper feature-writer in a large eastern city describes such a relationship:

—"Things had been bad in my marriage for a long time, especially for the two years before this all started. My wife was very dissatisfied with my degree of success and was forever belittling me for not trying to move on to bigger things. I was feeling beaten down by the running battle until I met Sheila while doing a feature on young actresses. She was twenty-six and unmarried, and not very successful as an actress, but I interviewed her because she seemed a typical struggling young hopeful. Something clicked between us. She thought I was great, and she made me *feel* great. She was so much what I needed that we fell into a regular pattern very quickly. I'd turn in my weekend piece by Monday noon and rush off to her place. We'd be in bed minutes after I walked in; then she'd make lunch for me, and afterwards we'd take a walk or see a movie or go shopping. If the weather was bad we'd stay in and read a scene that she was preparing for acting class, or I'd bring along a carbon of the piece I had just written and let her read it; I got a great deal of pleasure out of her admiration. Late in the afternoon, I'd go home; I always told my wife I'd been out interviewing someone for the next piece.

"I saw Sheila once a week, and occasionally more often, for nearly three years. There were times when I found it a drag, as any regular arrangement is when you're not really in love, but I couldn't break it off. My wife and I would get into a long, miserable quarrel, and she'd criticize me and berate me, and when we'd go to bed I would feel no desire whatever; it would seem as if my parts were dead. But then I'd visit Sheila and everything would come to life. Our sex life was fine for both of us—but for me it was more than a good lay: It put me back together, it restored my self-respect. Yet I was never actually in love with Sheila; she wasn't all that attractive or mentally well-rounded. Unfortunately, she was more or less in love with me, and after a while the situation got to be bad for her. I told her I wasn't the kind of man who could ever desert his children, and as for my wife, I had gone with her since we were kids and I couldn't dump her despite the way she was now. Sheila would cry, and say that she could make me truly happy, if I'd give her the chance—but she was already making me as happy as I wanted her to. She had a pretty good idea how things were with me, but I guess she kept kidding herself that something might happen to make it go her way."

Sometimes the adjunctive affair is more socially than emotionally supportive: In certain wealthy and jet-set circles, an extramarital affair of some durability is a status activity, and virtually *de rigueur* for anyone of prestige and significance. In such circles, marriage is based on property and family in the classic pagan-courtly fashion, while the affair, whatever its emotional value, gives one his or her sexual identity in the group and supplies an aura of accomplishment and attractiveness. This kind of affair is common in New York and all the fashionable places to which New York's "beautiful people" fly, whenever some season starts. But it is also seen in other large cities, wherever a sufficiently wealthy, bored, and sophisticated group exists. In the upper-class society of San Francisco, for instance, the status affair is quite openly accepted, and the social news-notes in San Francisco papers customarily list the names of extra-marital couples who have been seen arriving together at some resort or major social event. Since everyone already knows who is what to whom, the appearance of the linked names in the paper is a source not of embarrassment but of pride. Writes Frances Moffat, society columnist of the *San Francisco Chronicle:*

On the whole, society marriages tend to be stable. It's too good
a business arrangement for divorce. . . . [but] either the husband or wife
has an affair with a member of their own set, and while it is in progress,
they go everywhere together. They don't live under the same roof, but
they go to the same parties, dance and dine together, and are on the
same lists when hostesses plan weekend parties. . . . The marriage
remains intact, the education of the children continues. Husband and
wife appear as a devoted couple at Parents' Day at their children's
school or stand together receiving guests at their daughter's wedding.

The status affair of the jet-setters is a special case; far more
often, as with the newspaper feature-writer and the actress, the
value of the adjunctive affair is emotional. But it need not be
primarily comforting; it can be romantic, sexual, playful, understanding, in various combinations, according to the needs of both
partners—or, more often, of one partner. For the adjunctive affair
is frequently one of emotional inequality: One partner is seeking
limited satisfactions and pleasures outside of marriage and merely
supplemental to it, while the other partner is seeking a total relationship, and hoping that the affair grows into one. This situation
would be unstable except that the former partner—quite often the
man—has so much to offer that he can dominate or control the
situation; the subordinate partner—usually the woman—hopes
against hope that time will change him and make possible a fuller
relationship, culminating in marriage.

The most clear-cut form of this, though relatively rare in
America, is the long-term affair between a well-to-do married man
and his kept woman. Lover and mistress are bound to each other
by ties of sex, affection, even genuine understanding—all contingent upon, and limited by, the partial or total financial support he
provides. There is an ever-present tacit recognition on both parts
that he is paying for her various services; the underlying emotional
interaction is therefore largely that of master and servant. This is
why the arrangement is not usually a major threat to his marriage;
the mistress accepts her special and limited role, and for years may
make no effort to attack the existing marriage. An example:

—A pretty, fragile little woman of forty, about to be divorced from her husband, was seated at a business convention banquet next to an Oklahoma oil millionaire in his late fifties, well-known as a bon vivant and philanderer (his excuse being that his wife was a scold and an alcoholic). She knew of his reputation, but found him immensely engaging and warm; halfway through dinner they were launched upon a devil-may-care flirtation, and halfway through the night they became lovers. She spent two idyllic days with him; then the convention ended and they went their separate ways to homes five hundred miles apart. Every two or three months he would ask her to come visit him for a week or two, sending her an airline ticket and installing her in a suite at the best hotel in town. In between visits, she—being now divorced—went out with other men and he with other women; they considered themselves in love, but neither expected or spoke of exclusivity.

After several years, during which they slowly grew closer, he suggested that she give up her job and move to his city; he said he would find her a house and "take care of things." She thought it over for a while, asked him some specific questions about finances, and then accepted. Four years ago she moved herself and her two teen-age daughters into the house he had bought for her, began receiving a monthly check from him covering all her needs, and started being exclusively his. In the soft, honeyed tones of a Southern lady, she tells how she views their arrangement:

"I never asked him whether he would try to get out of his marriage for my sake. He's a very self-willed man and he's been pressured too much all along by his wife, so I just wasn't going to pressure him any more. Besides, his wife had nagged him until he started staying away from home and amusing himself with other women, and I was bound and determined to be different.

"Anyway, his wife hardly seemed to matter. He would try to stay away from her, or go places without her whenever he could. She didn't even care, so long as he gave her enough money to buy furs and go on cruises by herself or take trips to New York. He went home a couple of nights a week, but he had an apartment downtown and would stay there most of the time; he told her he had too much to do to come home—the house was a long way out from the city—and he took good care of the building employees to make sure she couldn't ever spy on him. That's where I go to be with him; he never stays over at my house. He takes me to company parties, and the symphony, and good restaurants, and I move into his place for a few days at a time (my girls are nearly grown-up, and can take care of themselves) but after a while he always finds some way to suggest that it's time for me to get on back home. He says it's for appearance's sake, but it isn't; it's because he needs to be alone. Or more likely because he wants to play around with some other woman who doesn't mean a thing to him. I *hate* that part, but what can I do? I just don't believe it's something I can discuss with him."

Aside from the time she spends with him, she leads a quite domestic suburban life with her daughters; they understand the situation and seem to accept it, and the neighbors, knowing nothing of her private life, assume she is living on alimony. Her present and future, though not assured by any kind of contract, seem fairly secure to her: The house is in her name and mostly paid for, and he has set aside for her a sizable chunk of stock in his own company. Occasionally, when she is angry at him, she sleeps with some other man, but she carefully limits herself to one-nighters. "I don't want any man getting interested enough in me to take a chance on spoiling things for me. Because if we ever do break up I'm sure he'll leave me financially well off—unless it's my fault. But I don't think we ever will break up. He needs me; he just doesn't know how much he does. I guess I wish he would divorce his wife—they're separated now—and marry me, but he seems to feel that that might spoil a beautiful relationship. I can't do anything about it. If he ever does marry me, it will be because he wants to, not just because I do."

Most American men, however, cannot afford a kept woman, and in any case would find such a relationship uncomfortably close to mere concubinage. What is far more common as a durable medium-involvement affair is a subtler form of the same thing: an affair of emotional inequality in which not money, but the hope of the future, is the controlling factor. Most typically, the man is married, fairly well off, and has no desire to see the affair become a marriage, since it is already giving him just those extra satisfactions he wants; the woman is either single or divorced, not very well off, and has a very great desire to see the affair become a marriage in which all her needs can be met. The man may assist her financially, but the money is a gift—a by-product of the relationship and not its central or motivating force. The stability of the relationship depends on the woman's willingness to adapt herself to his requirements and to overtly accept the limits of the exploitive relationship, while covertly hoping and even laboring to expand them. But the stability of such an affair also often owes much to the cooperation—whether conscious or unconscious—of the wife. The continuity of the affair makes it very likely that, over a period of time, there will have been numerous clues—not just physical objects or slips of the tongue, but the man's continual absences, excuses, and lack of interest or sexual appetite. But a fair number of middle-class and upper-middle-class wives are so dependent upon their husbands for their social and creature comforts—the house, car, furs, jewels, maid, trips, country-club membership—that they consciously refuse to see anything that would require them to disrupt the arrangement; even if they do see such things, they may choose to overlook them, feigning ignorance in preference to open complaisance.

LEWIS AMORY AND THERESA SCHROEDER

Dr. Lewis Amory's marriage and his affair with Terry Schroeder follow this pattern. Lewis has eaten six or seven thousand dinners with his handsome, cool, blonde wife, and slept as many nights in the same bed with her, but he and she have always dealt with each other in the amiable, cooperative, and rather impersonal manner of relative strangers crewing together on a sailboat. They have built and furnished a handsome house, raised two attractive daughters, gone to the right places and had the right people to their home, but never told each other their innermost thoughts and feelings. Arlene seems content enough with church and club, friends and children, the carefully tended home and carefully arranged social life; if she is not fulfilled by all this, or is disturbed at Lewis's frequent absences, she gives no sign of it. Lewis, for his part, is comfortable and contented with their arrangement; he wants no more of the marriage than it gives him, and has cheerfully sought the rest of what he needs in a series of relationships with steady girl friends.

In these affairs he has always functioned so well that the sexual weakness he experienced the first night with Terry Schroeder, his tachycardia patient, was a severe shock to him. He had been greatly taken by her bright, mobile, not-quite-pretty face, her sturdy well-fleshed little body, her enthusiasm and intensity, but he was genuinely fearful of putting himself to the test with her again. Yet he could not get her out of his mind—nor could she get him out of hers. They had long, warm telephone conversations from time to time, but he put off seeing her for over a month; finally he felt ready to take another chance and invited her to dinner. He was delighted and reassured at how spontaneous and close their relationship was in the restaurant—only to be dismayed, once again, at how difficult and disappointing his sexual response to her was in bed. A third and a fourth time the same thing happened; he and she privately searched for answers, wondered why on earth they were persisting in the relationship, and yet found themselves compelled to do so.

Lewis: "I think the trouble, or at least one trouble, was that I resented her having had all these affairs before me. By my standards, she had had more sexual experience than a girl her age should. Also, since I was still stuck in one thing I was trying to get out of, maybe I wasn't eager to get into another, especially with someone as intense as Terry. But I kept on seeing her because I never had a better time with any woman. No matter where we were, she kept things going; I didn't have to entertain her or try to stir things up. She always wanted to do things, but she didn't care what they were or where we went so long as we were together.

"When we're together, the conversation never stops; I'm never at a loss for words with her, although I don't talk half as much as she does. Terry's interested in all sorts of things that interest me— rock music, pop art, and even sports, which is my main interest outside of my practice. At home, Arlene and I haven't talked much about anything for years; she's quiet and rather lethargic, and doesn't care a great deal about anything except the children, the house, and social activities. She doesn't even know much about my work, while Terry does and is always fascinated whenever I tell her about some of my current cases.

"About half a year after I met Terry, I finally got rid of the waitress. The physical part of it with Terry had been improving slowly and was getting fairly good by then; I was almost like my old self. And by the end of the first year, our sex life had become the best I'd ever had with any woman. That's very odd, when you consider how we started."

Terry was aware of the limitations and disadvantages of the relationship from the start, but forced herself to accept them. "I found him a terrific guy, just a great guy. Strong and wise, and lots of fun but very polished and well-bred. Genuinely interested in his work and his patients; underneath the cool, he *cares*. He's a man with a sense of right and wrong; that's why I could understand his saying that he would never leave his wife. But on the other hand, he's a man who insists on a man's privileges and won't let himself be pushed around. I had a pretty good idea he was still seeing some other girl and I told him I didn't want to be one of a string, but he said he would do what he had to do when he was ready to, and not before. I was wild about the guy, and I had to let it go at that. And one time, early in the affair, I tried to make him jealous, but I found he wouldn't play my game. It was like this: A fellow I knew invited me to spend a weekend with him in Miami Beach and I told Lewis about it and asked him if I should accept or not. He refused to tell me because he said he was married and didn't have any right to. So I said, 'It seems to me that you just don't care,' and he was very calm about it and said he did care but wasn't going to tell me what to do because he didn't own me and couldn't own me.

"I never did go to Miami Beach, and after a while he did get rid of the other girl. From then on, things between us got better and better. The sexual problem slowly disappeared and after a while it got so he could keep up with me, and more; I could hardly believe it. He has told me that if I ever fall in love with any other man, I should never tell him all the things I told Lewis about my sex life at the outset. He seems to think that that was part of our trouble. But I don't know—he had fooled around with lots of wilder ones than me without having any trouble. There must have been more to it. I think for a long while he just wasn't sure he wanted to get seriously mixed up with me because I wasn't a come-easy-go-easy type."

As their relationship grew better, they fell into the habit of meeting every Thursday, unless he had an emergency case. They would have cocktails at any one of half a dozen quiet little bars, go to dinner at some out-of-the-way place, and then proceed to a motel. Lewis also spent a second night in town every week and had long done so, but he kept it to himself for the time being, not wanting to commit it to Terry irrevocably. He did, however, talk to her on the phone two or three times each week either from the club or from the study in his home, where he had a private line. He traded news and daily experiences with her, listened patiently to her problems, and offered her firm, sensible advice. Before the end of the year, he had lost interest in prospecting for other women and began seeing Terry on his second night in town. Moreover, he grew somewhat bolder and began to take her to better restaurants in Chicago, avoiding only the Red Carpet and La Chaumière, at both of which his wife was known. "I used to be careful about going to the good places with a woman other than my wife," he says, "but with Terry I got tired of skulking around in dives, and I decided we might as well go to the top places. It felt right. Besides, if I ever ran into anyone I knew at a nice place, I could get away with any story I made up—but if I got caught with her in a dive, there wouldn't be anything I could say."

Besides their evenings together, he began taking her to football games (Arlene hated the game), a few small parties given by bachelor friends, and even to a party given by a somewhat bohemian married couple in Evanston; more ambitiously, he took her along on an overnight cruise on a yawl owned by a divorced friend, and on a weekend trip to a medical meeting in New York. But he drew the line at certain things: Although he sometimes called for her at her apartment and had even met her sons, he would never stay there overnight even though she said she could make it seem as if he had been in the living room. And while he neither refused to answer her questions about his marriage nor forbade her to discuss it, he was laconic and close-mouthed about himself and Arlene; even when he did speak about his marriage, he never did so in such a way as to justify his infidelity or to manipulate Terry by giving her false hopes.

Terry: "I admire him for that—he's an ethical guy. I gather that he has a real affection for Arlene—sort of like the feeling he has for his daughters—and that they get along quite nicely, but that there isn't very much going on between them; nothing like what he has with me. But he doesn't claim he's unhappy with her, or anything like that. In a way, he's taking a chance by being so honest with me, but that's the kind of guy he is. The best thing about his marriage, I would guess, is that he and Arlene get along without any friction —maybe because they don't have a great deal to do with each other, but also because she's content as long as things look good on the surface. Lewis often says to me, 'Don't rock the boat'—I *hate* it, and sometimes I get sore as hell—but he never has to say it to her. He likes her calmness, and he says he likes the opposite in me, but if anything ever happened to her I don't know that he could actually live with me full-time."

Lewis never seems to wish, as a puritan-romantic might, that he could have the best of each in one person and one complete love; he is quite well pleased with the limited love he feels for his two very dissimilar women. His explanation: "With two such different women it's as though I have two separate lives. And I enjoy each, and I'm a different man in each situation. A friend of mine likes to kid me about my 'Captain's Paradise' and remind me how everything turned out for the worst in the movie, but I'm not about to give it up. I don't know how long it can go on, but it's hard for me to imagine the future in any other form."

A major step toward greater closeness to Terry was his taking a place they could call their own—a modest enough thing, compared to the home he shared with Arlene, but nonetheless a considerable commitment in psychological terms. Terry had become so concerned, after a year and a half, about the money he was spending on motel rooms that she suggested it might be cheaper to have a furnished sublet; perhaps, too, she also hoped for the closer tie it would create. "I told her to go ahead and find one for us, and she did. It was a little studio apartment in Old Town, close enough to everything to be convenient for both of us. I paid for it out of the office account, which Arlene never sees. We had our own phone there; it was unlisted, but my answering service knew where to get me in an emergency. It wasn't the greatest place in the world—it was small, and the furniture was nothing special—but it was clean and private and ours; we kept a few clothes and personal things there, and it was a lot nicer than going to motels. Three or four times a week we'd meet each other there at the end of the day and have a drink and sit around and talk awhile, with our favorite records on a portable record-player. Then we'd go out to dinner, or occasionally she'd bring something in. Sometimes we'd go to bed together before dinner, sometimes after, and by eleven o'clock or so I'd generally head home. I had kept all my old excuses alive with Arlene, and added a few new ones. The few times I stayed over, I told Arlene I'd be at the club. If she had ever phoned there late at night, I'd have been in big trouble, but I don't think it would occur to her to check up on me. Terry says that Arlene must know and doesn't want to catch me because then she'd have to do something about it. That's possible, but I doubt it. . . . Well, I suppose I'm not sure one way or the other; at any rate, she doesn't say or do anything that sounds as though she were suspicious."

Besides renting the apartment, Lewis began helping Terry out financially now and then in the form of gifts for special causes: a lump sum to make a vacation trip possible, a check to cover some major repairs to her car. But he never undertook to regularize this help: "I didn't want to support her—it would have been tough for me to do, anyway—and I made sure she didn't count on it. But I did and still do like to help her. It makes me feel good; I do care for her."

It is not clear to him, however, whether his caring is the same as loving; in talking about it, he is hesitant and patently unsure of his own feelings. "I suppose the term love applies. . . . I *think* I'm in love with Terry, as far as my understanding of love goes. . . . But I'm also in love with Arlene in another way, and I guess that would seem incomprehensible to most people. . . . The fact is, I'm not sure that I've ever known what love is supposed to mean or be. . . . No wonder it's hard for Terry to understand the way I feel; it's hard for me to understand it myself. She asked me once whether, if I had it to do over, I'd marry her or Arlene, and I wriggled out of it somehow, but the truth is that I'd probably marry Arlene. Arlene has the kind of background and family and character I want in my children's mother. I haven't been the most devoted father, I suppose, in terms of the time I've spent with my daughters, but I want the best for them—the best upbringing, the best education, the best moral standards. And that means a mother like Arlene, and a solid home-life such as the one we've had all along. I've tried to be honest about it with Terry; I've told her that what she and I have is something wonderful, but that there are real values in my marriage and that I won't give them up.

"Sometimes, though, I *have* told Terry things she wanted to hear, such as how my wife and I have very little to say to each other, or how we have almost no sex life (I told her I pay a 'courtesy call' on Arlene now and then). And once or twice I've said that if Arlene were killed in an accident tomorrow, things between us might be . . . well, different. But barring that, she knows I'm never going to do anything to get out of that marriage, and I think she actually respects me for that, even though she wishes it weren't so."

Despite the limits of his feelings, Lewis grew so accustomed to seeing Terry all the time that he even began to use a "beard" in order to have her close by on certain important occasions. His lawyer and good friend, Allen Carson, was a bachelor, and Lewis cajoled him into bringing Terry to a dinner dance at the country club, and even to a large Christmas party at the Amorys' home. Terry was so flattered that she went, but on these and similar occasions she felt the situation to be "spooky" and dangerous. At the Christmas party, for instance, she and Lewis talked together until Allen whispered fiercely to them to break it up, but when Lewis then danced with Arlene, who was a little high and unusually affectionate that night, Terry found herself violently jealous. Later Terry wondered whether Arlene's performance hadn't been for her benefit: "She must know, or at least suspect. How could she miss it? He's away three or four nights a week, and even if she didn't have any idea who it was, when I started showing up at a few of these things she had to have a good idea.

"If she doesn't know, she's the only one who doesn't. Lewis's office assistant and his nurse both know, and so do those of his friends who are doing the same kind of thing. Bill, my older boy, knows—he kept asking me questions and I finally decided to explain it all to him. Even my father and mother know. I told them Lewis was separated from his wife, and they kept asking me what was going to happen, but one time I slipped up and they realized I hadn't told them the truth. They were shocked and depressed for a while, but they had met Lewis a few times and could see what kind of person he is, and I think they've come around to accepting it and secretly hoping something will work out for me some day. But Dad seems to feel that it shows real character in Lewis that he hasn't ditched his family, as so many other men might have done.

"What worries my folks most is the question of my future. Well, me too—only, I found I had to learn to live from day to day, and not think about the future, because every time I did, I would get in trouble. I would think, for instance, how when Arlene's girls finally went off to college, she would start coming into town a lot and would try to corner Lewis for herself. Or I'd think about what would happen to me if I let so much time go by that I got too old to find somebody else, and then Lewis and I broke up. Thoughts like that would terrify me, so I just forced myself not to think them. And for a while, at least, I succeeded."

                                *   *   *

In Lewis's judgment, neither his earlier affairs nor his present one have had any significant effect on his marital relationship; he feels, however, that they have made him a happier and more easy-going person than he would otherwise have been. I asked all my interviewees a number of questions on both these points. About half the men and half the women indicated, like Lewis, that their affairs had changed their marriages very little, either for better or for worse; but even without any important changes, about half the men and a third of the women felt that their affairs had made their marriages more tolerable. Significantly, the extra-marital relationships of most of those who answered in this fashion were of the two types we have just been looking at—the short-lived and shallow, like Peggy Farrell's, or the enduring but emotionally limited, like that of Lewis Amory and Terry Schroeder; most of these people, moreover, seem to have had marriages which were low, or at best middling, in their degree of involvement and emotional inter-dependence. Such marriages may not be ideal, according to cultural tradition, but they may be the most suitable for most of these individuals. If they have judged rightly that their affairs have made them more content but done no harm to their marriages, their infidelities, when judged according to situation ethics, would seem, more often than not, to be defensible.

iv the affair of rebellion

For conscience-controlled people, particularly puritan-romantics who once had (or wanted to have) a totally committed and involved marriage, it is rare for the extra-marital affair to remain casual or emotionally limited. Instead, it tends to be a dynamic and disruptive process that either grows by invading and claiming parts of the marriage, or is counterattacked by it and driven off. For such persons, an extra-marital affair is neither an innocuous amusement nor a durable comfort, but a crisis that must be resolved one way or the other.

Which way depends in part on which type of affair it is, for these people seem to have two rather different types. In the first, the individual's marriage is basically good but has always failed to satisfy certain lesser needs or has ceased satisfying them because of the wear and tear of time. The unfaithful person seeks, in the affair, to experience romantic courtship, playfulness, the intensity of new sexual experience, the excitement of mutual disclosures and unveiling; meanwhile, his deeper needs—for emotional security, understanding, reliable sexual gratification, parenthood, position in the community—are quite adequately met by the marriage. The affair therefore rests on a narrow and insecure base of rebellion against adulthood and married life, the grievance being that they force one to give up the dreams and pleasures of youth in return for special fulfillments only they can provide.

In the second type, the individual's marriage is seriously defective and fails to meet most of his deeper needs, either because it was an unsuitable mateship from the very first or because it has deteriorated badly. In going outside his marriage, the individual is seeking not only the stimulus of romance and sexual novelty, but the fundamental gratifications that he has long missed. Such an affair rests on a broad and relatively secure base, since it is not a rebellion against adulthood and married life but a quest for adult fulfillment in an enduring love-relationship.

Affairs of rebellion exhibit certain telltale characteristics, perhaps the most common and obvious of which is the lover's poor choice of love object. If he—"he," of course, meaning "he or she" —were seeking only sexual variety and fun, he would not need an emotionally, intellectually, or socially compatible partner. But he has a thoroughgoing commitment to deep involvement, and implicit in his thinking is the possibility that the outside lover may prove a better mate than his present one. Whether or not he thinks in terms of divorce and remarriage, he yearns to have the affair become a total, and totally satisfying, relationship. Unfortunately, in the affair of rebellion it is not his mature self that is directing his actions, but a young and unrealistic self within his unconscious mind; he is therefore very apt to choose someone with whom a satisfying adult relationship is impossible, and with whom at first he finds intense gratification and, later, intense frustration. An example:

—In her mid-thirties, the wife of a Cleveland furniture dealer fell in love with a bearded, beatnik playwright-cabdriver whom she met while visiting her family in New York. She herself was somewhat unconventional—girlishly longhaired, interested in avantgarde books, outspokenly left-wing in her politics—but she knew that her own eccentricities were no match for his. "He's way out; he's been using pot and speed and acid for years, and he's someplace else, in his head, most of the time. But he had an effect on me like nothing I could have imagined. When he talked, I was fascinated. When he looked directly at me, I went all weak. And when he put his hands on me, I went wild. I loved him as I had never loved before or ever expected to, even though I never was able to communicate with him very well. He has a brilliant mind, but it works very strangely—in jumps or leaps, or it goes off on some other level where you can't follow him. He lived in a filthy walk-up apartment in the East Village, and would drive a cab when he needed money but as soon as he had some he'd quit and bum around or write a little until he was dead broke. I couldn't get him to see the point of any other way of life, and he got furious at me when I tried; once or twice I thought he was going to do something violent. And I had three children, and a middle-class way of life, and a husband I liked, so there was no possible future for our love, no outcome, no hope at all. I knew all that, but I kept beating myself against it like a bird caught indoors, beating against the windows. For a couple of years I would get to New York every three or four months, and each time, for a few days, I'd live another life, lost in him. Then I would come home to my big well-furnished house and my clean, wholesome family and my nice Saturday-night dinner parties, and afterward, lying in bed next to my husband in the dark, I'd have to put my fist in my mouth to keep from screaming. There was far more misery than happiness in the whole affair, but for a long while I couldn't make myself stop. I wanted to, but I couldn't give him up. Finally I got a rude assist: For a couple months no letters came and the operator said his phone was disconnected, and then I got a letter from a nurse's aide, saying he was in a mental hospital because he'd freaked out altogether on drugs. When he got out, he wrote me that he had moved in with some woman because he needed to have somebody take care of him, but he said she was way out too, and wouldn't mind my sleeping with him next time I came to town. Like the fellow who amputates his own leg with a penknife, I wrote him a Dear John letter. But I was in such a terrible state for a long while that my husband, who knew nothing about the cause of it, made me start seeing a psychologist."

This narrative not only illustrates the wrong choice of partner, but highlights a second frequent characteristic of the affair of rebellion: the considerable ambivalence the lover feels toward the partner and the affair. He wishes to love but would like to stop; he defies his own superego yet would prefer to obey it; he loves but also dislikes or disapproves of his beloved; he enjoys staying up all night, talking, drinking, and making love, but also wants to get some sleep, carry out his duties properly the next day, and hold on to his marriage, home, business, and friendships.

Even in the flourishing phase, therefore, such love affairs are rarely even-going and continuous, but turbulent and intermittent, being riven by inner and outer struggles, fights and flights, reunions and rejoicings, alternations between starchy self-control and surrender to impulse. Time and again the lover struggles to deny his own desires and then abandons himself to them and to the clouded future they portend—yet often he is oddly pleased with himself for giving in. A case in point:

—A thirty-five-year-old city planner in a western state had drifted into an extra-marital affair—his first—with the wife of a colleague. After three consecutive trysts with her, he was overcome by guilt; he got drunk, drove home recklessly on a rainy night, and skidded into a tree, escaping unhurt but shocked at his own self-destructive impulse. He phoned her the next day and told her about it; they agreed that they should break off the affair immediately and force themselves to revert to being, once again, merely friends. Saddened but relieved, and filled with a desire to expiate through work, he labored all day and most of the night revising a presentation he was to make to the mayor and his staff the next morning; when he gave it, he spoke brilliantly and had the entire group spellbound. "Afterwards I hurried back to my office and phoned her; I wanted her to know how good I felt as a result of our difficult decision. I told her that I was completely under control again and that I had never spoken better; she said she was very relieved, and had never wanted my love at the cost of my well-being. She was content—even though miserable—to give me up if it meant that all was well with me again. Then, because I still wanted to feel just a little of the forbidden thrill, I told her that all the same, the cure was excruciating, I longed for her terribly, and it was hard to believe that I would never hold her in my arms again. At that point I heard her crying and whispering 'Darling,' and love and desire welled up in me. I said, 'I'm wrong about having things under control—I'm losing it right now. This conversation is getting too much for me. We'd better hang up before I'm in trouble again.' We did, and I went to lunch, but I couldn't eat. I picked at my food for a while, and cursed myself for having made the call. Then, like a conversion, I had a blinding flash of illumination—I suddenly thought, 'But it *was* magnificent to feel my own feelings for her just then. . . . Anything *that* good has to be right.' Allowing myself to think such thoughts and to feel my feelings was like suddenly coming back to life after being inert and dead. In a minute or two, I was happy and hungry; I wolfed down my lunch, rushed to the office, and called her again and said, 'To hell with everything I said before lunch. I don't give a damn—I love you, and that's that. I don't know how it will ever work out, but I can't bottle it up. I have to love you.' She cried, and whispered that she adored me, and we made a date to meet in a couple of days. After I hung up, I felt bursting with life and full of juice instead of shrivelled and withered. I knew that what I had just done was foolish and could come to no good, but strangely enough I felt proud of myself for having done it."

But one episode does not settle the matter; the battle continues through skirmish after skirmish. A man may firmly resolve to see his mistress no more than once a week, and then find himself writing her daily notes, calling her often, driving past her house and impulsively telephoning from a nearby booth to see if he can drop in. A woman may promise herself to keep the affair light and joyous, yet hear herself using words of love, crying after sex, trying to get him to tell her how much it all means. Time and again the affair gains the upper hand; step by step the lover yields ground to the new feelings, moods, and intimacies shared with his beloved.

And yet the intimacy and depth of involvement are partly fictitious. It is not with the real person that the lover is involved so much as someone he imagines her to be, for he projects upon her the old unrealized wishes of childhood or adolescence, persuading himself that he sees in her the qualities and virtues he wanted the ideal woman to have; she is a screen upon which he throws the image long stored in memory. Dr. Sandor S. Feldman of the Department of Psychiatry of the University of Rochester Medical Center, who studied a number of cases of this type, summarized their psychological mechanisms in a paper entitled "The Attraction of 'The Other Woman'," although much of what he says would apply equally well to the attraction of "the other man." In this type of extra-marital affair, the man feels that he has found the woman for whom he has been secretly waiting all his life; he sees her as beautiful, subtle, refined, intelligent, exciting, and sexually ideal. Yet he loves his wife, has no intention of divorcing her, "could not do such a thing to her," and feels that the other woman will simply have to understand that this is so.

"The psychological background in such cases," writes Dr.

Feldman, "is monotonously the same: the mother was beautiful, sensitive, cultured, romantically minded and unhappy with her simple-minded husband, who was interested mainly in being successful in his profession. The boy pictured himself as understanding his mother's feelings and needs; he made silent vows to make up to her for her frustrations when he grew up." Both the wife and the other woman are idealized aspects of mother: The wife is that aspect of mother interested in the happiness of her family, and selfless in working to achieve it; the mistress is that aspect of mother hungry for romance and for the complete love of a "real man." The fantasies the little boy had of taking father's place, or of someday perfectly loving a woman like his mother, seem to be coming true; the rebellious, regressive self, denying reality and time, acts out the old impossible daydreams in the flesh. No such lover, of course, thinks of it this way: The love he feels seems to him a response to the real person herself and to his need for her—but curiously enough he does little or nothing to make their relationship permanent and acts as if, at some level of awareness, he knew that she was not ideal for him and, indeed, not even halfway suitable.

The affair of rebellion nevertheless brings about a number of important changes in the lover. In yielding to old, long-ignored wishes and acting them out, he feels himself liberated and seems to be discovering important truths about his real nature. A man who could never be romantic or poetic with a woman discovers that he is able to speak and act romantically and poetically; a woman who was never foolish and impetuous in love discovers that folly and impetuosity are an important part of her. A man may find that he has a far greater capacity for repeated sexual intercourse than he had ever realized; a woman who fastidiously avoided certain sexual words and acts that she thought vulgar now is fascinated by her own appetite and finds those same words and acts earthy and wholesome.

Sometimes the capacity for creative work is greatly increased. A writer told me that for several months, during the first flowering of such an affair, he wrote more easily and imaginatively than ever before, completing assignments ahead of schedule even though working only half the usual amount of time; he likened this unleashing of power to his new-found sexual capacity. A person in a non-creative field may, on the other hand, suddenly find his daily work mundane, drab, and boring compared to the love experience: In him, the imaginative but self-gratifying child has temporarily over-powered the plodding but responsible adult. Such a lover ignores his work not because he cannot concentrate or function, but be-cause he sees things differently, and regards work, achievements, and family life as trivial and mundane goals.

But at the same time, being in an emotionally expressive mood, he may be more openly and easily affectionate than usual to his children and his mate, even though spending less time with them than formerly. He means not to let his mate be hurt by the affair, yet is almost childishly unaware that the changes in his mood, schedule, and work habits are far from unnoticeable. Men and women who have been through such affairs often are astonished to see, in retrospect, how blindly they obeyed impulse and desire, trusting to luck to avoid detection and living day by day like chil-dren in adult clothing.

EDWIN GOTTESMAN AND JENNIFER SCOTT

Edwin's love for Jennifer is virtually a paradigmatic case of the affair of rebellion. His marriage was intimate, emotionally secure, and the very center of his life and work; Betsy, however, was so controlled, well-bred, and sensible that with her Edwin had never been able to see himself in the role of impetuous, gallant, passionate lover. He believed that his own behavior reflected the whole man, and was convinced that he was a dull fellow; he felt aggrieved that fate had made him so. Jennifer triggered off a rebellion of self-discovery. "I hadn't ever had much fun in my life. I hadn't ever felt young, romantic, or sexy. Actually, my sex life with Betsy was fine, so I suppose I mean 'sexy' in a special sense; maybe I mean 'success-ful with women.' Until I met Jennifer, the most important thing in life to me was money, the second most important was self-develop-ment, and the third was the welfare of my family. After I met her, money and self-development and my family all were put aside. She became the most important thing—because I liked the way I acted and felt when I was with her."

The first sign of this revolution in his values appeared only a few hours after his abrupt return from Puerto Rico. Betsy, pale and nervous, wisps of dark hair escaping from her usually faultless bun, met him at the airport; she had left Buddy and Sue playing at a neighbor's in order to be alone with him for a little while. Edwin kissed her, reminding himself not to be unduly warm or enthusiastic. He asked solicitously if she was feeling better, and then began telling her about the Puerto Rican property, the people he had dealt with, the sights he had seen; he was pleased to find himself skillfully acting like a husband so innocent as to be quite unaware of her suspicions, even to the extent of speaking admiringly of the number of beautiful women he had seen in one hotel. By the time they were halfway home, she was looking relieved and a little ashamed of herself for having made a fuss.

It was a Sunday, and the pale January light was fading when they arrived home. Buddy and Sue came home from the neighbor's house, uttering squeals of delight, and flung themselves upon him. Edwin built a fire and sat in front of it with them, reading the Sunday comics aloud (they'd heard them already, but wanted to hear them again from him). Betsy made Bloody Marys for herself and him, and in due course produced some excellent goulash and a salad. Through all this, Edwin felt the inner warmth of a man doing the Right Thing. Then he looked out at the black wintry landscape and thought for a moment of the afterdeck of the yacht, the warm silken night air on his face, the laughter and tinkling glasses, the languorous heavy-lidded looks Jennifer cast upon him —and was crushed by a leaden weight of melancholy. He struggled to get his breath, hoping that neither Betsy nor the children would notice his distress.

At 5 A.M. that morning he rolled over in bed, woke halfway, thought of Jennifer, and at once was wide awake and unable to get back to sleep. After half an hour he quietly arose, put on his robe and slippers, and went into the living-room, where the embers of last night's fire were still glowing. He took some papers out of his bag in case Betsy awoke and came to see what he was doing; with them by his side, he settled down in a deep chair before the fireplace to think. "I tried drawing up a balance sheet in my mind of the assets and liabilities of the two women in my life. Looks, education, social poise, skills around the house, skills with children, moral values, and so on. There was no comparison. On most counts, Betsy was much superior. Jennifer could never have run my home properly, brought up my children decently, or even handled a dinner party for my friends and associates. Yet I wanted her, I ached for her. I couldn't understand at that time what it was; I only knew there was something immensely *important* about the way I felt about her. Was it the age thing? I found it very flattering that a girl of twenty-two wanted me—but I told myself that that shouldn't matter so much. Was it the fact that my folks still talk with an accent and keep kosher, and I had never even had a date with a *shiksa*, let alone have one admire me and make love to me? Not a very good reason to feel turned all upside-down. Was it her looks? To me she was beautiful, but I knew that others might not think so. Her brains? To me she seemed very bright and understanding, but I could see that other people might not agree. Her personality? To me she was free and natural, but I was certain that a lot of people would call her lazy and sloppy. But when I got all through trying to score her off and get rid of her, I said to myself, '*Schmuck*, stop trying to be so sensible! The truth is, with that girl you *lived* a little —and that's worth everything'."

And so that same day, knowing that Jennifer would be arriving home, he sent flowers, and, timed to arrive the next day, perfume, and the day after that, a little volume of love-lyrics. After all these had arrived, he telephoned her at work (she had no telephone at her place); at first she was a trifle cool, but when he told her he had been up every morning at 4 or 5 A.M., thinking about her, she grew warmer. They agreed to meet on Saturday; he would arrive in time to take her to lunch and spend the afternoon with her. He told Betsy he had business in Philadelphia but would be back in time for a dinner party to which they had been invited. It was his first trip to Philadelphia without any actual business to transact; he sat in a parlor car, feeling guilty, excited, and very worldly. Jennifer met him at a large Polynesian restaurant on Walnut Street, dark enough for hand-holding; by the time they had finished one round of drinks, his flight from Puerto Rico was erased, and after the second round they were closer and more nearly loving than ever.

After lunch they headed for her apartment. It was a bleak,

chilly day; Edwin asked if her fireplace worked, and she said it did but she had no wood, whereupon he stopped, phoned a dealer, pleaded emergency, and had an order of logs delivered less than half an hour after they got back. "She had almost no furniture up there—a narrow old bed, a couple of folding chairs and a card table, and a trunk for her clothes—not even a bureau! But I had bought a bottle of red wine on the way back, and we sat on the one little throw-rug, in front of a roaring fire, drinking wine, and it was marvelous. I was completely happy. It was an escape from everything that weighed down on me; it was another world. We talked and sipped wine and necked, and then we went to bed and made love; afterwards, I was feeling so overflowing that I told her she meant more to me than I would have believed anyone could. She said that I meant a great deal to her, which was why she had felt terrible when she thought I was gone for good, and she had been overjoyed when the gifts started arriving and she knew I would be back.

"I dragged myself out of there to catch a plane—the train would have brought me back too late—and I got home just in time to change and rush off to the dinner-party with Betsy. All through the evening in that expensive house, I would smile and nod while people talked to me, but I was thinking how much happier I would be sitting on a ten-dollar scrap of used throw-rug, in front of a fire, in that bare little room with that nobody of a girl, than standing here on a six-thousand-dollar Kerman, in this hundred-thousand-dollar house, with these successful men and their expensive, perfectly turned-out women. And I felt immensely superior to them—what did any of them know about life and love?"

For the next two months or so, Edwin visited her about once a week. Saturdays would have been too hard to explain, on a regular basis, so he went up on weekday afternoons, telling his secretary he would be driving around prospecting for new land and couldn't be reached. He and Jennifer would have only a few hours together for dinner and part of the evening; then he would leave by 9 or 10 P.M., and even at that would not get in until well after midnight. (Betsy, long used to his strange work habits, had no further twinges of suspicion.) To supplement the brief visits, Edwin talked to Jennifer by phone three or four times a week; he had had a phone put in her apartment and took care of her bill. "I liked doing things like that for her. The next one was when I noticed she had only a thin, worn-out suede coat, and for her birthday in February I bought her a dark-red woolen coat with a mink collar. She was beside herself with joy, and I was happy to see her that way."

The next piece of largesse was bigger. Jennifer's boss, the realtor, recognized that she was involved with Edwin; as soon as his transactions on Edwin's behalf were completed, he felt it safe to let her go, as he had long wanted to do. She phoned Edwin, in tears, but he calmed her down by telling her that he wouldn't let her starve or be dispossessed for lack of rent money. When she failed to find another job in the next month, he suggested that she move to Washington, where he could help her find a job and she would be near him. Jennifer had no family ties in Philadelphia—her divorced parents and her brother and sisters had all moved elsewhere—and her friendships were almost all expendable; after a day's reflection, she agreed to the suggestion. A week later she was installed, with her few meager possessions, in a cheerful little apartment not far from Rock Creek Park, and had a new job as secretary to a building contractor who owed Edwin a favor; she could hardly afford the rent at her salary, but Edwin said he'd pay half of it plus her phone bill.

From then on, they saw each other three or four times a week. Sometimes, as the spring days grew long, they would drive into the country for dinner; other times they would either go to a fine restaurant or order something sent over to her apartment. On these evenings, he rarely got home before midnight, but Betsy was used to his working long hours and made no comment. The time he spent with Jennifer, however, soon made a difference in his income. "Before, I would put in many an evening in meetings, or going over plans and figures, or studying the market, but at this point I didn't bother doing half what I used to. It didn't seem important. I could see my income dropping down, down, down—and I couldn't have cared less. What I was doing with my time seemed much more valuable."

In late May Jennifer was fired by the contractor, who apologized to Edwin but said she wasn't cut out for secretarial work. Jennifer desultorily looked for modeling jobs and did get two or

three bits of work, but Edwin and she began spending a good deal
more time together than ever. He took care of her rent and began
giving her money to live on, although both of them said this was
only a temporary arrangement. They wandered around town by
day, shopping or going to places of interest, and in June they started
going out of town for sailing and tennis lessons. To explain his long
absences from the office, Edwin told Betsy he was scouting around
for new properties; he did do some, with Jennifer along, in order
to have something to tell Betsy about when she asked.

"All this was costing me plenty—what I wasn't earning, plus
what I was spending on her. Boating, tennis, rent, living money,
extra money for clothes to get her dressed decently, a watch that
I gave her because she was so often late meeting me, regular visits
to a beauty parlor, a good bed that I bought her, and a few sticks
of furniture. All these things gave me very mixed feelings. I did
them because I wanted to, and because it made me feel wonderful
to do things for her—but at the same time I felt annoyed and uneasy
at doing them. It was a violation of my upbringing. I had always
been very conservative and frugal until I met her. I spent money
on my house and furniture, but that was different, that was permanent and my own home; but with Jennifer I became a big spender
outside of my home, and it made me feel very good and very
disturbed, both at the same time.

"But I couldn't stop myself, and I didn't even want to. This
wasn't just a roll in the hay, it was a very important thing to me;
it seemed like the biggest thing that had ever happened to me. Our
sexual relationship had gotten quite good, but it was never the most
important thing; the most important was the whole way I felt about
being with her and doing all these crazy marvelous things with her.
If we got a nutty idea in our heads to rent a little plane and have
a pilot fly us up to Connecticut to have lunch with an old girl friend
of hers, we'd do it—and if I had to cancel a business meeting
because of it, I'd tell myself I was having an experience to remember, and that was worth more than money. That's the way it was.

"And because she was so important to me, I wanted her to be
part of my life. I introduced her to those of my friends and business
associates who had similar arrangements, and once in a while half
a dozen couples of us would have a party at one fellow's hotel suite.

I even took her to my own doctor when she was having some female problem, and I told him to take good care of her and to keep it quiet. But no matter how much I saw of her or did for her, it wasn't enough for me. The nights I stayed at home, I would tell Betsy I was out of cigarettes and drive to an all-night coffee shop and phone her from the booth and talk for half an hour. If Betsy said something, I would tell her I had been chatting with the guy behind the counter.

"For a man like me, the whole thing was crazy, absolutely crazy. I had the best wife you could want, and a good life, and I had been making a hundred thousand a year, and here I was letting my business fall apart and making only a half or a third that much, and ignoring my kids and my wife, and taking more and more chances, and letting more and more people in on what I was doing. And what did I think would come of it all? I didn't think. I couldn't imagine myself ever asking Betsy for a divorce, but I couldn't see things going on like this indefinitely either. Jennifer said she loved me—we used that word, by this time—and she'd be happy just to see me a few times a week; she'd settle for that, she didn't have any future plans. I half believed her, because I wanted to, and said it was fine with me.

"Which was nonsense, but you can convince yourself of anything, for a little while. Something had to give, and soon. A man like me couldn't be so much in love with a girl like Jennifer without wrecking his home and destroying his career. But I wouldn't look at the facts; I felt I was living the best and most exciting life possible, and I didn't ask myself any questions because I didn't have any answers."

---

v the affair of fulfillment

In the poetry and drama of the last several hundred years, one kind of extra-marital love—the affair of fulfillment—has often been presented with sympathy and approbation. Although illicit and contrary to the traditional code, such an affair embodies the same values held in greatest esteem by puritan-romantic tradition. For it is an all-encompassing, totally involving love: a synthesis of passion and tenderness, of romance and emotional security, of playfulness and serious purpose; a simultaneous giving and getting, a dovetailing of opposite but complementary needs; a love that grows not by absence, longing, and imagination but by nearness, satisfaction, and the sharing of experience. In the Western value-system, such love is the pinnacle of human relationships, and although it is supposed to exist only as an ideal marriage, even when it occurs extra-maritally it is viewed with admiration and considered noble.

But all noble things, Spinoza ruefully remarked, are as difficult as they are rare. As to difficulty: Margaret Mead has said that totally involving and monogamous love between man and woman is probably the most complicated and demanding human relationship that has ever existed. As to rarity: Out of eighty unfaithful people and seven unmarried partners of unfaithful people whom I interviewed, only ten had been involved in affairs of fulfillment, and at that four of those were borderline cases. But if the affair of fulfillment is both rare and difficult, it is also potentially the most rewarding. For some it can mean emotional survival; for others it can bring about major personal growth; for all it is both disruptive and reconstructive, destroying what stands in its way and remolding the lives of the lovers closer, hopefully, to the heart's desire.

In contrast to the affair of rebellion, the affair of fulfillment generally involves a right choice of partner. This does not mean that the partner necessarily becomes a spouse—circumstances or unpredictable emotional conflicts may prevent that—but that the lovers are sexually, emotionally, intellectually, and culturally a good fit. They meet each other's needs on many levels; aside from their existing commitments, there is no apparent reason why they could not become a happy and deeply loving married couple.

In the very beginning, however, they may not realize how well and thoroughly they suit each other; the initial attraction may be a circumscribed one. In some cases it is sex that first draws the lovers together; in others, intellectual or emotional values precede sexual attraction; and in still others, the lovers interact at all levels from the beginning. Those whose interaction begins in a limited way may be hiding the potential completeness of the relationship from themselves so as not to feel endangered by it. They reassure themselves that what they feel is only a physical desire, or a mere infatuation, or a species of friendship; they try to see the affair as something limited and supplemental to their marriages rather than admit to themselves that it is potentially a total and exclusive relationship. But once they do admit this, they know there will be no peace and no stability in their lives until they resolve the conflict between the affair and marriage one way or the other. Here is how two such people describe their unwilling recognition of the real nature of their relationships:

—"Louise and I began seeing each other on the basis of 'friendly sex.' I made it clear I wanted no emotional complications because I was married and had children; if we went to bed, it would be because we desired each other and because it was fun, not for any larger reasons. We started sleeping together about once a week, but I enjoyed being with her so much that it built up gradually until it was three or four times a week. I'd go to her place in the late afternoon, or sometimes right after dinner, and stay for hours; I told my wife I was trying to make a break-through in my research project, and would be in the laboratory or the animal operating room, where she knew she was not supposed to bother me. Louise and I would make love, and then lie side by side and talk for two or three hours and then make love again. We discussed the books we were reading, the shape the world was in, my work, her work. We told each other about our childhood, our parents, our friends. Each of us came to know almost everything the other was thinking and doing every day. We were funny and we were serious, silly and sober—we were everything. And that's how it became love, against my intentions and my wishes. It escalated and escalated until it was emotionally intense, intellectually tremendous, and sexually the best thing I had ever known. It was everything my marriage wasn't. And we realized that something would have to give—we couldn't go any further without actually living together."

—A married woman who went back to college felt an intense attraction to her history professor and, as we have heard, swiftly and unhesitatingly began an affair with him. "Two weeks after I sat in his class the first time, we went to lunch and he kissed me; two days later we became lovers; the week after that he asked me to go to work for him as a part-time editorial assistant on a textbook he was writing. In less than a month, we were seeing each other in class three days a week, working many afternoons and evenings together, having dinner fairly often, making love in motels or a borrowed apartment two or three times a week. For a while I didn't let myself look at the implications of it all; I turned everything off, and just refused to think about what it was bound to mean for both our marriages. Then after about three months, one night at dinner it suddenly hit me what we were up to, and how complete it was or could be if we weren't married to other people. It frightened me, it scared the hell out of me, and I told him so. I said I thought we should try to love each other a little more lightly, and he understood and agreed—but of course that didn't work at all. It was an all-involving thing; there was no holding back for either of us."

As even these brief accounts indicate, in the affair of fulfillment the lovers strive to achieve complete interaction instead of the limited interaction other kinds of lovers have. Even those who are limited to clandestine hours in bedrooms and restaurants range in their dialogue far beyond the narrowly personal; they want to know and vicariously experience each other's lives from breakfast to bedtime, from kindergarten to the present.

All of which takes time. But it is difficult for most married people, especially housewives with small children, to steal away for more than a few hours a week. Affairs of fulfillment are therefore rare not only for psychological reasons, but because some people who are capable of such a relationship, and who are not content with less, simply cannot find the time required. A number of my interviewees had had affairs that bade fair to become total relationships but were choked off and ended abortively because of the limited time available to one or both lovers. In other cases, a partner who saw the possibilities of having such a relationship deliberately held back until after his own separation or divorce, rather than struggle against all the mundane impediments and frustrations he perceived.

The affair of fulfillment is not only rare and difficult but highly unstable because, almost from the beginning, it tends to reach throughout the personality and to be in direct competition with the marriage. All unfaithful people are likely to make comparisons between the lover and the spouse, and the ways of life connected with each; in many such comparisons the spouse is seen as possessing certain valuable traits and the lover certain others. Both, therefore, seem worth holding on to. But in the affair of fulfillment this rapidly becomes impossible. The lovers soon come to interact and to identify throughout their beings, and the old love suffers by comparison at every point. The period in which it seemed possible and desirable to have both loves has given way to a period of struggle within the soul of the unfaithful person.

For a while, as this internal conflict rages, the unfaithful spouse makes desperate efforts to save his marriage from disintegration; he seriously dicusses with his mate the differences that have arisen between them, he makes special efforts to adjust and to get along peacefully, he observes undeclared truces or even avoids his mate much of the time in order to minimize conflict.

Usually these endeavors neither adjust nor repair the marriage but only hasten its disintegration, for since this is what the unfaithful person actually wants, the ways in which he seeks to salvage the marriage damage it even further. He believes that he is thinking things through in hopes of finding the reasons for his marital discontent; actually, he is juggling the books of married life in order to find his new love superior at every point. He means to talk things out with his spouse in order to clear up their misunderstandings and differences; actually the discussions give him the chance to be openly angry and hostile, and to find any similar anger or hostility on his mate's part a proof of the hopelessness of the situation. He tries to damp down conflict between them by truces or avoidance, but only succeeds in starving the relationship to death. By these and other methods, he provokes his mate into behavior that offends and alienates him—and, by thus justifying his dark wishes, gratifies him. The overt confrontation and fight to the finish between the affair and the marriage is now imminent.

NEAL GORHAM AND MARY BUCHANAN

Monday was a wasted day: Neal sat at the typewriter for hours, trying to concoct a humorous ad for a comic novel and crumpling up each new effort in disgust. Not only was his left-over Presbyterian conscience tormenting him for imagining Laurie dead in a turnpike crash—her safe arrival with the children had only partly relieved him—but he had at last admitted to himself that the affair with Mary was making serious inroads upon his ostensibly happy and indestructible marriage. Mary phoned him late in the day and immediately sensed that something was amiss, but Neal said that he had a headache; the next day, however, he met her at lunch and blurted out the story of his nightmare, his fantasy of Laurie's death, and his feelings of guilt and alarm. Mary grew pale and silent; after what seemed a long while, she said that it was plain enough that their happiness was bound to bring immense grief to both of them, and particularly to him. Hesitantly, almost inaudibly, she added that perhaps they ought to end the affair at once, before it did irreparable damage or became uncontrollable. *Had almost wanted her to say so and to make the decision that would relieve me, but as soon as she said it I knew it to be impossible. How could I repudiate the person I had finally become? Give up the love I had only begun to know? Turn away from the new life I had scarcely tasted? A retreat back into the torpor, the flatness, the dessication of my former ways, would be accepting an imprisonment for life, with only my few recollections as a tiny window through which to look out upon the dear lost world.* The two of them alternated, one renouncing and the other pleading, then vice versa, all during lunch; when it ended, they found temporary relief in a decision not to make any decision for a few days. But the next morning, at his office, he received a special delivery letter from her which read:

Dearest:
    Your Calvinist conscience was right, after all. I spent all afternoon staring out the window and thinking about the things that are happening to you and to me. I cannot delude myself: I am already bringing you more pain than joy, and I have no right to help you destroy your marriage just because I need your love so much. We must give each other up, and at once. For me it will be a partial death, but I prefer that to seeing you grow to hate me for wrecking your home.
    We have to continue working together in the office, but because we care about each other and respect each other, we will manage that.

                                        Formerly your
                                        Mary

Neal phoned her instantly, and raged at her with angry words of love; he told her that he could not possibly do without her, that he needed her love more than she needed his, that his marriage might or might not be wrecked in the process, but if it were, it would be because it had long been moribund. Almost fiercely, he said that he must see her after work and would accept no excuses; she meekly, gratefully acquiesced. They met at a favorite place of theirs, the Palm Court of the Plaza Hotel, *where we held hands, devoured each other with our eyes, and by turns were loving, witty, passionate, sad, reassuring. And even businesslike: spent ten or fifteen minutes working out the advertising program for two upcoming novels, delighting as always in the give-and-take, the interlacing, of our two minds. Business done, we got back to ourselves, whereupon the violinist, playing schmaltzy melodies, came over, beamed upon us, and played as if to declare us lovers; we were embarrassed, delighted, amused. . . . Mary said, finally, that she had made her big effort at renunciation and was through with it; she would try no more. I: "Thank God that's over with and we can get on with our tragedy," both of us laughing a little uneasily at my hubris and wondering if we would be punished for it.*

Mary: "I felt as if we were displaced persons, with nowhere to go, nothing to belong to, except each other; it was going to be lonely and isolated for the two of us. But it was also going to be the greatest adventure of our lives. And if Neal couldn't give it up and settle for what he had, neither could I, though I had just tried. In Neal I had found that combination of traits I had always dreamed about but thought didn't exist. He was masculine but he was sensitive, fearfully bright without being arrogant, concerned about my welfare but reasonably and healthfully selfish, very sexual with me but rather proper and reserved elsewhere. Loving him, I was like someone who has just had a religious experience; how could I not believe?"

From then on they saw each other as often as they could. They met fairly often at lunchtime, and on a mild day might settle for a milkshake and spend their time wandering in and out of stores, or visiting an art gallery or a museum. She helped him choose fabrics and collar styles when he ordered some custom-made shirts; he accompanied her to Bonwit Teller's to help her pick out a spring coat. They reversed their own policy about avoiding business meetings and saw each other often in the office, sometimes in front of Cal; the surer they felt about each other, the easier it was to work together without feeling the urgent but dangerous desire to give each other private signals.

For some weeks, they had little opportunity to make love. A few times they met at the end of the afternoon for a couple of hours at the Wellington, a hotel which was a little out of the way and moderate in price. He told Laurie that because of a new account, he would have to work one or two nights a week for a while, and would be home rather late; she was annoyed but not suspicious. Mary found excuses of her own, and was able to spend those evenings with him. And once, when Cal went out of town, they were even able to spend the whole night together at her apartment, he telling Laurie that he'd be at the Yale Club (where he carefully checked in, but ordered the switchboard to put no calls through to his room until 8 A.M.). *A bit of real life, at last: night-talk after love-making, voices growing thick and sleepy; tangle of arms and legs, murmured goodnights; her sleeping body, weary and content, instinctively curling up into the curve of my own when I turn over; matinal sounds—yawning, scratching, washing; the wholesome, toothpaste-perfumed kiss of morning; scrambled eggs, fresh coffee, and Thou beside me in the Wilderness. . . . I make fun, but it was rich and important to experience each other like this.*

Mary: "It seemed to get better all the time. We reached a point quite soon where we weren't hungrily trying to find out all about each other, but enjoying each other no matter what we were doing or saying. Once or twice, after love-making, he fell asleep, and I loved just lying on his shoulder and listening to him breathe. Our time together was a patchwork of hours here and there, and yet because we were so complete with each other, I felt almost more a wife to him than to Cal. Neal and I were together in our thoughts, we understood each other completely, we shared everything with each other, even the innermost things. The trouble was that it wasn't enough—we wanted each other all the time, and Cal and Laurie were in the way. They were in our thoughts almost all the time. At first we talked about them with sympathy, later on with exasperation, and finally with desperation."

No longer had that early foolish hope that I could love both women, no longer the conviction that I could accept Laurie as she was, if I also had my Mary. Everything Laurie and I discussed led to quarrels and misunderstandings. The children's eating habits, when to repaint the shutters, whom to have over at the next dinner party, all grew instantly into causes. Our sex life dwindled away almost to nothing: after an evening of bickering, we would get in bed, turn out the light, omit even our old habit of a moment or two of snuggling. One night, feeling sad about it all, I drew her close to me in bed, was instantly ready—and got nothing but passive, patient waiting; I collapsed like a stuck balloon. Accused her of coldness; she said that I expect sex but never take time to arouse her. (Take time?—but I have discovered that my very being arouses a real woman at once, and without any patient, deliberate preparation.) I: "Well, what would you like me to do?" Pause; then she: "Nothing in particular." Bitter taste in my mouth, pressure in my head. In a level, icy voice: "Then let's not do anything, any more, until you want to. I wouldn't want to impose on you." Felt good, thrusting this blade into her guts; an evil deed, and I knew it but relished it. . . . Grouchy and cool to Mary on the phone next morning; twice as grouchy when she pointed it out. Had lunch with her; we avoided each other's eyes and had little to say; finally we talked about it, and after a while I realized I had been angry at her and myself for the way I was acting to Laurie. Both of us felt relieved that we had found what it was, but troubled by it, too.

Mary: "Every time Neal told me about his growing troubles at home, I felt terribly ambivalent. I wanted to encourage and comfort him, because I knew already that the one thing I wanted was for both of us to get divorced and to marry each other. But he was much more closely bound to his marriage than I was to mine—he'd been married thirteen years, and had two children whose home-life he felt a great sense of duty to keep intact, and whom he loved even though he wasn't a man to spend much time playing with them. It all made me feel responsible and guilty. I'd be a home-breaker, I'd make two innocent children lose their father—and what if, after all, he should feel so wretched that our relationship itself were blighted? But by this time I had no such mixed feelings about my own situation; I was practically ready to give up Cal without a twitch. In fact, I was beginning to see how far I could go to provoke him: I'd come home late for dinner a couple of times a week, I'd make excuses for being out of the office and working late to make up for it, I'd pay little attention to him at home—not that I was nasty, but I treated him like the grocer's delivery boy or the maid. He even seemed afraid to approach me sexually except when we'd both had a lot to drink; we weren't having sex more than once every few weeks. All the signs were up for him to see, but he was acting like a frightened child, not like a man. I disliked myself for treating him the way I did, but I was contemptuous of him for taking it. I thought, 'You're a fool or a weakling, or both.' I would have liked it if he'd raised hell, I would have felt better if he'd belted me one and walked out. A little punishment, and then freedom: It would have been a perfect solution to my problem."

April Fool's Day, 1966. Last night Laurie and I had an argument that went on until four in the morning and ended not in truce but exhaustion. It was a stale bitter rehash of every major complaint and disagreement of thirteen years. How can I be what I seem in her eyes and also what I seem in Mary's? I think I could live with Mary and never display the traits Laurie detests in me, and I cannot imagine ever being, with Laurie, the other man I am with Mary. There is but one life for each of us (O rare Neal Gorham, to have made such a discovery!), and too late I have discovered much about myself that I had not known. Too late because I have a daughter and a son who need me at home for another decade, a fading, too-plump, semi-frigid wife who will probably not let go, and a damned Presbyterian conscience that will never give me peace. I both utterly regret and am totally grateful that I have known what could have been, although—April Fool!—it will not be.

chapter 6: DECAYING

i running down

Sooner or later, the vigorous flourishing phase of the affair gives way to a decline that ends in death, sometimes violently, sometimes as if in sleep. The simplest kind of decay takes place with little conflict or struggle; it is a premature aging, a withering-away that occurs in its very infancy. Casual, uninvolved affairs that undergo no development after the consummation are the ones that most often exhibit this early senescence; they offer little continuing reward beyond sexual pleasure, and this, powerful as it is, generally is not enough to keep them going. For with consummation, the principal values of the casual affair disappear: The excitement of the new situation, the sense of adventure, the challenge of the first physical intimacy, the pride of conquest, all inevitably are lost. If nothing but sex remains, the relationship soon fades away, but painlessly; the extra-marital partner was more a useful object than a person, and little emotion was invested in him or her. The decline of the affair is virtually devoid of stress or even of memorable episodes, and the statements people make about this process are characteristically brief, flat, and colorless:

—"Things went very well for some months, but I wasn't in love with her and I had no long-range plans about her. Then I learned she was telling the girls at work about us, and I didn't go for that. The whole thing was getting to be somewhat of a drag, and I started to think it was pretty nearly time to get out of it."

—"The first time I went to bed with each of them I'd think, 'Hah! I showed you, you bastard!'—meaning my husband, of course—and it felt great. But after the first few times, I'd have very little interest in continuing. The good feeling of revenge didn't last; besides, I'd begin to worry about getting caught."

PEGGY FARRELL, ET AL.

Peggy Farrell too, like these people, has generally been untroubled by the decay of her affairs. Except for her brief encounter with the lieutenant-colonel, she has never been "really in love" with any of her lovers or considered breaking up her dull, loveless, comfortable marriage to Andy for any of them. She has been infatuated and excited by each of them in the beginning, briefly gratified by each new conquest, and then bored all too soon. But boredom is hardly memorable, and though most of her affairs took place only a few years ago, she can recall little of what happened as they decayed.

"It's the beginning of an affair that sticks in my mind. It usually starts off great—we spot each other, we talk a bit, we both know; in a little while we feel we just have to get together, we can't wait. That's the best part. Then for a while there are the phone calls, the long talks, the jealous quarrels, the secret meetings, the screwing. But even in the middle of all that, I know it's only a game; there's never anything real to it. I guess the trouble is that I find most men boring after a little while. . . . Well, that's not quite fair: they haven't all been boring. . . . The real trouble was that nothing happened between us, I didn't ever really care about them or them about me. Sometimes I'd be lying next to some man, both of us all unwound and feeling good after sex, and I'd wonder, 'How come I don't feel anything for him? Where did it go?' Or I might be at a bar with the man I was seeing and I'd feel restless and itchy; I'd spot someone new who looked interesting and I'd think, *'That* one could really turn me on!'—and the poor guy I was with would suddenly look awfully dull and I'd wonder why I had ever found him exciting. As soon as I began thinking thoughts like that about a man, I'd know it was just about all over. Sometimes I *would* get so wrapped up in a man that I'd think about him day and night, for a while, and believe that I actually loved him. But it's hard to remember now which ones I felt that way about; besides, I must have had thirty or forty men, all told, in less than seven years, and they sort of blur together."

Peggy does not remember that there were any outstanding events in the decline of these relationships except an occasional sharp quarrel and angry goodbye; more often, there was merely a tacit disengagement. "Sometimes, when I stalled some guy about making another date and gave him all sorts of excuses, he'd sound hurt or angry, but I think that was more talk than anything real. Nobody ever killed himself on my account, and nobody even tried to break up my marriage by getting through to my husband. Mostly it was quite painless."

*   *   *

The longer-lasting affair which provides comfort, companion-ship, and other benefits, but within well-managed emotional limits, also sometimes subsides fairly quietly. Because it is more involved and complex than the casual affair, its waning phase is marked by a certain amount of stress; nevertheless, where there has been a limited interdependence, and where the more involved partner accepts the fact that the affair cannot long continue, the decline may be more a matter of quiet atrophy than of violent disintegra-tion.

—The newspaper feature-writer who had a long comfortable affair with a young actress—we heard him describe it, in the previ-ous chapter—finally revealed to her that his future plans did not include her. "My affair with Sheila could have gone on indefinitely, but I began to think I was heading for divorce, and as much as she had done for me, I didn't see her as my next wife. In fact, I found myself wanting to be free of her so I could look around for somebody who was really right. I felt I ought to level with her about my long-range plans and finally I did. She was hurt, she cried, she said it was rotten of me not to have told her sooner—but she got over it in a little while and continued to see me almost as before. But I kept urging her to see other guys, and finally she started to. I was pleased by that, because I didn't want the burden any longer, but still my pride was always wounded when she told me some guy had taken her out and given her a great time. On the surface, everything looked the same between us, but we both knew it was different now. Then, instead of going ahead with plans for a divorce, my wife and I had a reconciliation. That did it; Sheila accepted a job in a summer theater that took her far away for three months, and toward the end of summer she called me from out there to say that she had just been married and was very happy. So was I, for her sake, although I felt depressed and regretful for weeks afterwards."

The burden this man so wanted to be rid of was no heavier in the declining stage of the affair than it had been earlier, but it seemed to be because the rewards were fewer. With affairs that fail to develop and deepen, the effort and cost of maintaining them look larger as the original delights lose their early intensity. The experience of a reasonably well-married St. Louis businessman is typical:

—"Each time, in the beginning, I don't give a damn about the effort or time or money. But later on I invariably find myself wondering, as I drag home exhausted, 'Why am I bothering? Why go to all this trouble?' Because my wife is just as good a piece, and I like her better than this broad, and the affair has turned out to be so arduous and time-consuming and expensive, and generally such a pain in the ass, that it really isn't worth it. So I get out. It always takes me about a year to forget all the problems and remember only the fun; then I'm ready to get involved in another one."

The affair of rebellion, too, may waste away due to inherent weaknesses. But a love of this type involves a prodigious investment of emotion and hope, and dies hard. Though much of what the rebellious one loves about his partner is of his own imagining, he is deeply and passionately involved with that idealized image. Sooner or later he begins to see things more clearly and recognize the extent of his error; then he is outraged and inconsolable—and still ready to grasp frantically at any straw of hope.

Because the affair has meant so much to him, reality seems a shocking affront, a barbaric cruelty visited upon him by his beloved. Horrified and enraged that she is not at all what he supposed, he fights with her about it, demands that she be what he thought she was; she, in turn, is first wounded, then infuriated, at being found less than marvelous and ordered to improve. But as their clashes increase in intensity and frequency, so do their efforts to recapture the earlier illusions and satisfactions; they thrust each other away time and again, only to rush back into each other's arms. The mortal illness of their affair, as of any major love, is no quiet wasting-away, but a series of fevers and convulsions interspersed with moments of blessed remission—each of which is followed by still worse seizures.

EDWIN GOTTESMAN AND JENNIFER SCOTT

Such was the case with Edwin Gottesman and Jennifer Scott. Although their affair began to decay for more than one reason, the intrusion of reality and Edwin's slow recognition of the special and unworkable nature of his love for her played a major part in the process.

Even before Edwin got Jennifer to move to Washington, he was aware that he had very mixed feelings about the things he had begun doing for her. He took great pleasure in playing benefactor, but at the same time felt disturbed at being a spendthrift on her account. In Washington, this conflict grew sharper as the scale of his benefactions increased and as he began to perceive her real character through the enveloping make-believe. In the fall, for instance, Jennifer got a couple of modeling jobs for a department store; she at once spent everything she had earned from them, and more, on two extravagant birthday gifts for Edwin—an imported brocade smoking jacket for $165 and a Dunhill pipe for $90. Edwin, momentarily shy, was deeply touched until Jennifer, with childlike glee, told him what they had cost; then he was shocked and disapproving, and rather pointedly hinted that if she had spent less, she could have paid some of her own bills instead of relying wholly on him. Jennifer stared at him for a moment, then snatched the jacket and pipe from his hands and threw them on the floor in the corner. She accused him of not really loving her, of reckoning the cost of their relationship in dollars, and, worst of all, of being stingy. Edwin, who considered that he had been extremely openhanded with her, was stung. He snapped back—astonished at his own words— that she was either a vicious bitch or a stupid child; this felt so good that he began pacing the floor and enumerating his acts of generosity, counting them off on his pudgy fingers. After a while, Jennifer put her hands over her ears, and Edwin stormed out, slamming the door, and walked the streets in a fury for half an hour. But then he envisioned her crying and repentant, the lovingly extravagant gifts lying unwanted on the floor, and he grew contrite and sad. He called her from a phone booth and was back at her apartment ten minutes later. They got somewhat drunk and went to bed; curiously, he felt both great relief and a sudden sense of entrapment. "I heaved a big sigh, I felt at ease inside; everything was all right again, my world was back in place. And I was pleased with myself that I hadn't been able to stay away. But then she went to the bathroom, and I looked at her as the light from inside caught her going through the door: she was wearing heavy false eyelashes, her hair was flaming red at that time, and even stark naked and wet with sweat, she walked with an affected, sexy waggle. I asked myself, 'Is this what you want? For this piece of *dreck* you make yourself miserable, you knock yourself out, you rob from your wife and children?' But the answer was yes."

This episode was hardly over when her next-door neighbor, an affable middle-aged homosexual, phoned Edwin at home one Thursday evening and told him that Jennifer's place had been broken into and robbed, and that she was hysterical and wanted Edwin to come at once. Edwin hesitated, then said all right. He told Betsy that he had completely forgotten he had an evening conference at the Mayflower with two principals of the Puerto Rican venture; with that, he rushed off. There was little actual loss or damage at Jennifer's—the only missing items were a clock-radio and a fur stole, both of which he had given her, and the only thing broken was the lock on the front door—but she sobbed uncontrollably and told him in hiccupy bursts of words that she hated the apartment. It was too far from the center of town, the street was dark and scary at night, the tenants above her were noisy, the apartment had no fireplace like her lovely little place in Philadelphia, where they had been so happy. As she went on, thinking up new grievances, she worked herself into a veritable tantrum: She was all alone, she missed her mother, she never saw her girl friends or her ex-boy friends, all of whom lived in or near Philadelphia, she had given up everything for Edwin, and what did she get out of it but a little of his time every day—just enough for him to get laid? "She was so wound up that I could hardly get a word in. After listening for a while, I began to feel sick; I didn't have the heart to even answer her. I got up while she was still raging at me, and walked out the door, thinking, *'This* time it's for real. This closes the books, this ends the most foolish chapter of my life.' And I felt sure I would never go back, and was relieved; I had found out what kind of person I was mixed up with, and I knew I would be better off without her.

"Even in the morning I still felt the same. But when I got to the office, there was a message that the superintendent of her building had called. I phoned him back, and he asked me to authorize him to repair the front door of Miss Scott's apartment at my expense; Miss Scott had told him to call me about it because she had to catch a train and would be out of town for an indefinite period. When I heard that, I could hardly talk for minutes. I realized I'd been kidding myself: I'd really been expecting to go back to her as soon as she got around to apologizing. I rushed over to the apartment in a panic, talked to the super about the door, and then hurried upstairs and ran around the apartment, looking for clues. Half her clothing and cosmetics were gone, and so was her one and only suitcase. On the window sill, by the phone, there were some scraps of paper with numbers scribbled on them and a little address book. I collected the papers and the address book, and went back to my office; I told my secretary I wasn't in to anyone, and closed my door and started calling New Jersey and New York numbers from the pieces of paper and from her book. I said I was 'Detective Simpson of the felony squad,' and I was looking for Miss Scott in connection with the burglary of her apartment. I'm amazed when I think of it now; I had never done anything like that before in my life.

"I must have made fifteen calls without finding her; finally I decided to call her mother, in Red Bank, New Jersey. I gave her my right name, and said I was the man Jennifer had been seeing so much of for the past year, and I was terribly worried about her sudden disappearance from the city without leaving even a note. Her mother sounded vague and fishy for a little while; then she admitted that Jennifer was on her way there, and said she'd have her call me when she arrived. I nearly went out of my mind, waiting all afternoon; I didn't want to call again, but finally I couldn't stand it, and called, and she was there. She was crying, and I was crying, and we said we loved each other and it was ridiculous of us to fight; we agreed to wipe the record clean. But she said she wanted to spend a week with her mother, and then a few days with her father and stepmother in Maspeth, Long Island, while she got things straight in her own mind. I said, 'Please don't. I beg you, I'm asking you as a favor, come back. Stay a day or two with your mother, but come back on Monday. I'll meet you at the apartment in the afternoon and we'll spend the evening talking everything over. I *need* you.' She promised she would come back, and I said I'd call her again during the weekend.

"Sunday afternoon I phoned her again. Her mother said she had bad news for me: Jennifer had taken a Saturday night flight to Rome and left no forwarding address. I stammered like an idiot, trying to ask questions, but either she didn't know anything more, or wasn't saying. I hung up, and sat there with my head in my hands for a long while."

Edwin couldn't imagine her reasons for doing this to him; he also couldn't imagine where she had gotten the money, why she had put in for a passport without telling him, or what she meant to do in Rome. It seemed evident that she must have been planning this for some time, but the betrayal this signified was incomprehensible. "For two days I was immobilized, and didn't do anything except call her mother every few hours to see if she had heard from Jennifer. She hadn't. I couldn't take care of my business at all, I couldn't eat, I couldn't sleep. Betsy knew something was wrong, and I told her I had some complicated business problems that I didn't feel like talking about. She looked very puzzled; I used to tell her nearly everything. The third day, I started making long-distance calls. For days I played the detective, telephoning people and asking questions—I began with her sisters and her brother, I went on to her father, her former boy friends, her former employers. I told a hundred lies—I had no shame about anything. No shame, did I say? Sometimes I even told the *truth!*

"I learned that she had had the passport for three months; that was a body blow, because I had trusted her. I learned from TWA that she had bought only a one-way ticket to Rome, using the last check I had given her plus some cash; her mother admitted she had given Jennifer the cash. But I still hadn't located her. Finally, I thought to call the consulate in Rome, and said I was her lawyer and had to reach her on a matter of great urgency. They told me she had just gone to Spain. I lost heart; I quit trying. I was half dead, a zombie.

"A week or so later, I was on the long-distance phone with a major investor who was going to back a deal I had on the fire when I saw in my morning mail a letter from Madrid, and practically hung up on him. I read and reread that letter ten times. It was very short. She said she was sorry she had run away, but she couldn't stand it any more—but she didn't say what it was she couldn't stand. She said she loved me very much and would be coming back to me as soon as she got things straightened out in her own mind. That was all. There was a six-hour delay on calls to Madrid, so I got the chief operator and told her it was a life-and-death matter, a question of a wrong drug handed out by a pharmacist. It's amazing what a man will do under those circumstances. In about an hour I had her on the phone. I told her she was destroying me, I had to have her back at once. She cried and said she'd come home in three or four days. I was so happy that I was blubbering like a child. Then she said the only difficulty was that she was in debt to the hotel and to a friend of hers, and had no return ticket. If I'd cable her four hundred dollars and a ticket, she could come back. It was like a cloud coming over the sun, but finally I said I'd send it, and I did. Then I waited and waited—and five days later I got a cable from Casablanca saying she'd been delayed, but would be in touch with me soon.

"That's the way it went for well over a month. She told me one story after another: She had a chance to try out for a bit part in a movie, her luggage was missing at the airport, she had a brief bout of fever—and always she was sorry, was coming home, would make it all up to me. I accused her of shacking up with some guy, but she swore it wasn't so and said she couldn't stand that kind of sick jealousy, and I wanted so badly to believe her that I did, and even apologized.

"After a month, I told her I had found a new apartment for her in Georgetown near everything interesting—a partly furnished place on the first floor of an early nineteenth-century house. It had a big living-room, a fireplace, a few lovely pieces of furniture, a nice little kitchen, and a bit of a garden. She cried again, and said she would have come home long ago but she was in debt once more and had been ashamed to tell me. So I sent her more money and three days later met her at the airport with my heart in my throat. It was all tears and forgiveness, and old times again. I made myself believe everything she told me, despite all the evidence to the contrary. I drove her to her new apartment, and when she saw it, she was out of her mind with joy and kissed me a hundred times. Then I had to leave because we were having a dinner party at our house that night. The physician I had taken her to was there, and I told him all about it, expecting understanding, but he looked around at my wife, my children, my friends, my home, and said, 'With all this, why do you do such a thing? What do you want with such a person?' It made me sick. I knew he was right—and I knew I wasn't going to pay any attention to him."

In the ensuing months, other troubles kept cropping up; Jennifer seemed to have an endless supply of them. Her teeth were bad and needed work at once. He sent her to a dentist whom she told, in confidence, to give her the best available job of mouth rehabilitation, no matter what the cost, because her "rich boy friend was paying for everything." The dentist, a friend of Edwin's, called him and repeated Jennifer's exact words. Jennifer, when confronted with this, said that the dentist was a liar, and grew hysterical; Edwin apologized and sent her to another. A girl Jennifer had become friendly with while modeling became pregnant; Edwin located an abortionist in Baltimore who took care of her. Jennifer wanted a parakeet, and he gave her one; when it died after a month, she got the notion of giving it a funeral, and nothing would do but that

Edwin use his influence with a local undertaker to carry it out in style.

"The whole thing sickened me. I could see that I was involved with someone who was a liar, a spendthrift, unfaithful, greedy, lazy —but when she hung around my neck and clung to me, or when we went out someplace together and I had that big showy girl on my arm, I didn't care. I'd talk to her on the phone ten times a day, I'd see her almost every afternoon or evening. I hardly saw my wife or children, I was ignoring my business shamefully, I was spending eight hundred, a thousand, twelve hundred a month on her. I was like a man in a poker game who's been losing and losing, and insists on playing for higher stakes because he has to win it all back.

"She was no damned good, and I tried not to admit it, but little by little it was forced on me. Like the business of the boutique. I wanted her to work at something useful, but she couldn't seem to find anything on her own, so when I heard that a boutique on Connecticut Avenue was for sale, I told her I'd buy it for her and she'd run it. She loved the idea. The owner was a lady in her sixties, a woman of real class, who had created the place and built up a regular clientele over twenty years. We had the papers all drawn up, but the morning after the owner first met Jennifer, her lawyer called me to say that the deal was off. He weaseled around until I pressed him; then he told me that the owner said she didn't want her beloved boutique to be in the hands of someone she described as looking and acting like a French whore. My reaction was very peculiar: I should have been furious, but instead I was deeply ashamed, because I knew it was the truth. I said to myself, 'I've got to get out of this. I've got to save myself before it's too late.' "

---

ii conflict of interest

Some affairs neither wither away prematurely nor sicken from disillusionment and disappointment, but fall ill of a conflict of emotional interest between the partners—a basic disparity between

their degrees of need for involvement. Long-term, emotionally limited affairs display this disorder fairly often because in many of
them one partner exploits and controls the other, getting comfort
or pleasure from the relationship but keeping it within specified
bounds.

Sometimes, as in the case of the feature-writer and the actress,
the affair may merely atrophy; more often, the conflict of interest
pursues a stormier downward course. Although such an affair may
start well and grow vigorously, after a while it reaches a degree of
closeness and commitment beyond which one partner would feel
uncomfortable or even endangered. Here he holds fast, and the
development of the affair levels off. But the other partner, whose
appetite grows by what it feeds on—and whose life situation may
make greater involvement desirable—feels frustrated, hungers for
completeness, and begins to wage a fight for the larger goal. The
conflict gradually pervades the affair, afflicting it with a mortal
fever. Yet because the struggle is one for greater closeness versus
the status quo, neither partner realizes that the relationship is becoming more and more unstable; one or both may suppose they are
closer than ever when, in fact, they are poised on the brink of a
complete break.

Conflict of this sort arises not only between the exploitive
married man and the exploited unmarried woman, but between
lovers both of whom are married and, initially, think themselves
reasonably content. At the outset, both may regard the affair as an
exciting but superficial adventure; as it develops, however, for one
of them it promises—and for the other threatens—to become more
than that. The former becomes aware of needs that have gone
unmet in marriage and begins to see the affair as a possible new
marriage, the latter sees it as a supplement to his existing marriage
and wants it to remain just that. A department-store manager in his
thirties describes the kind of clash that may result:

—"One night, right in the middle of making love, she whispered, 'It's happening—I'm beginning to love you more than my
husband. More than I've ever loved anyone.' But that was exactly
what we had agreed in the beginning not to let happen. We had told
each other we both had kids, we both had positions to maintain in
the community, we would never let this thing get so deep that it

could break up our marriages. It certainly hadn't become that deep for me. When she said that, I got so angry that I pulled out at once, got up and put on my bathrobe, and walked around, giving her hell. First she cried, then she turned vicious. She called me a Don Juan who could conquer but couldn't love, an emotional fraud, a spiritual cripple. She asked what kind of monster I was to let her get so involved while I was just playing, and why I hadn't had the decency to break it off long ago. Finally I told her to tone it down or I would walk out and never come back; I said we'd either continue on a light and cheerful basis, as we had agreed to, or we'd have to break clean right now. Many tears and words later, she agreed to take what she could get and not demand any more, while I promised not to abandon her. We sealed the bargain with a walloping big sex scene. But I should have known: The truce wasn't a couple of weeks old before the shooting started again."

His is only one of a number of ways in which the less-involved partner, pressured by the demands, reproaches, and sufferings of the more-involved one, defends his position. He could, of course, break off the affair, but usually it is too rewarding and meaningful for him to do so until he has tried everything he can to keep it under control. He may redouble his use of techniques we heard of earlier, such as the deliberate withholding of inner thoughts and feelings, a general coolness of manner, and a careful spacing-out of meetings. Or he may go further, doing bizarre and unpleasant things by way of counterattack: One man refused for three weeks to read a love-letter his mistress had written him on his birthday, and when at last he did, he tore it to bits and raged at her that he did not love her, never had loved her, and would see her no more if she continued to do such things. Another would laughingly tell his mistress in detail about his occasional one-night sexual escapades because his narrations inevitably outraged her and chilled her feelings for him to a level he could tolerate. One woman, as we saw in the last chapter, flew into a rage and ordered her lover out of the house when, right after sex, he expressed his love for her and spoke of wanting to divorce his wife for her sake.

But the sturdiest bulwark against greater involvement, the most unimpeachable apologia for incomplete loving, is the existence of one's present family: The defensive partner can always talk of his love for his children, his loyalty to his good but uninteresting mate, his obligations and moral principles. The classic situation in which this drama is played out is not the affair between two married lovers, but the lopsided relationship we have already seen in which an unmarried or divorced woman falls deeply in love with a married, somewhat exploitive man who gives only a part of himself to the relationship and has no desire to divorce and remarry. Usually the woman tries to convince herself that she is getting enough out of the arrangement to make it worthwhile, but her emotional needs may be less troublesome to her when completely suppressed and ignored than when fully aroused and only partly satisfied. She swings back and forth in her feelings, sometimes thinking she would be better off to give up the affair completely, sometimes telling herself that half a love is better than none.

LEWIS AMORY AND THERESA SCHROEDER

This was the case with Terry Schroeder, the one-time tachycardia case who had become the mistress of her cardiologist. Even though she had understood from the beginning that Lewis was satisfied with his marriage and had no thought of divorce, each new step toward deeper involvement—particularly the renting of the studio apartment—led her to daydream and to consciously hope that somehow, some day, she and he might marry. But after the rental of the studio, their relationship reached a plateau; the amount of time they spent together, the kinds of things they did, the extent and intensity of his feelings about her, were stabilized. To him their affair seemed ideal, but to her it slowly came to seem tantalizingly and frustratingly incomplete. For a while she avoided looking at the central issue, and focussed her attention upon the peripheral ones: She thought her dissatisfaction stemmed from the need to get up, dress, and leave Lewis in the middle of the night to go home to her children, and from her continual struggle to pay her bills and take care of her small apartment. But gradually she had to admit to herself that what troubled her far more was the fact that so much of Lewis's private life was shared with Arlene. She frequently asked him whether he and Arlene were sleeping together,

was morbidly fascinated by his allusions to discussions he and
Arlene had about the children or household matters, and was dejected and jealous whenever he mentioned that he and Arlene had
gone to a party or were making vacation plans. She tried to hide
her growing discontent but could not; perhaps she did not really
want to. But her unhappiness, rather than winning sympathy from
Lewis, only alienated him.

LEWIS: "Things were very good for a long while, especially in
the first few months after we took that little place for ourselves. But
then more and more often she'd meet me for dinner and be glum
from the word go. I'd try to jolly her out of it, but nothing would
work; it would be just one of those evenings. I'd think, 'Boy, I'd like
to get up and get out of here and go home.' But I never did. I'd be
cheerful and friendly, and avoid asking what was bothering her,
because I knew damned well what it was. She'd drop little clues
anyway, and after a while, she would come right out and talk about
it openly. She'd say that she had known what she was getting into
with me, and had been willing—and still was—to continue this way,
but that sometimes it just got her down and she couldn't help it. I
don't think she was consciously being insincere but the message
was that she needed a man full-time, one who could give her all the
love and attention she needed, and be glad to have all of hers in
return—and what was I going to do about it? I would tell her that
she was crazy to waste these years on me in which she should be
finding herself a husband. I'd tell her that I loved her, but that I was
a selfish s.o.b. and that things were going to remain the way they
were. And I wasn't knocking myself just for show; I really do think
I am rather selfish, because I want a lot from her but I don't want
to give any more than a part of myself. I have never made any secret
of this, though she would like not to believe it."

Terry has a slightly different interpretation of these discussions: She feels that he, not she, initiated most of them, although
she admits that she was growing more troubled by the situation and
that her distress showed. "Sometimes I could put up with all this
without any quibbling or bad humor. Other times my dissatisfaction
would rise up in my throat like bile. Sometimes I'd feel very nervous, and I even had a couple of brief attacks of tachycardia again.
I would wonder what I was doing, what would become of me in

another twenty years, what kind of a mess I was making of my life. At first I was able to fight off such thoughts, but after we'd been going together two or three years and nothing was changing, I couldn't fight them off any longer. I've got two kids to consider, I've got myself to consider, I've got the years ahead to worry about— I was thirty-six when I met him, but that was a while ago, and the Big Year was coming up mighty soon. Also, I felt terribly lonely a lot of the time; I *was* alone at home without him half the nights of the week, but also I felt he kept me shut out of a large part of his life, and kept himself out of a large part of mine. Even if I didn't say anything about all this, he could tell from my manner what was going on, and he'd feel awful about it and start telling me to quit wasting myself on him."

Discussions of this sort grew particularly heated at each holiday season. "When there's going to be so much time that we can't be together, and I know he's going to be with Arlene and his friends, I get very upset and depressed. He knows it, but he doesn't do anything about it. So last year, before the holidays, I started going to a few meetings of Parents Without Partners, and began to date a couple of fellows I met there. I told him about it, of course. I don't know what I expected him to say—probably something that would make me drop them—but he didn't. He approved. Well, for the next couple of months, everything he said seemed to nettle me. We argued more and more, and it was getting uglier and uglier. It hit a low point late last winter, three years after we'd met. One night we were sitting in my car and arguing, and all at once we looked at each other and said it was a damned shame. We said we shouldn't wreck things and break up in bitterness and anger; it would be better to keep all the happy memories unspoiled. So we decided, as lovers and friends, to break clean and not to see each other any more. It was dreadful—but both of us felt noble about it. He kissed me, just once, and got out and walked away."

LEWIS: "The way I remember it, she'd been telling me she had a good prospect in some other guy, and I said, 'Fine, then this is the right time for us to let go of each other and save our beautiful memories from being ruined. I'm suggesting that I leave you alone for your own good.' But she was quiet, so I said, 'Look, if you won't say it, I'll have to: We aren't going to see each other any more. I

Conflict of Interest   209

won't bother you unless you want me back and need me.' She said,
'Okay, fine,' and I kissed her on the cheek and got out and walked
away. I felt good, in a way, and terrible, in another way. I got to
my car and had to drive past hers because of the one-way streets,
and she was still sitting in it and crying. It went right through me.
I couldn't stand seeing her like that, little and helpless. I wanted her
to feel okay about it, and although I had nothing new to say, I
parked my car and got in with her, and went through it again for
a couple more hours, trying to make her see it was all for the best.
I was really wrung out by it. The next morning I called Thorne's
office to see how she was, and she wasn't there. I called her at home,
and she answered in a sick little whisper and told me she couldn't
face the world. It tore me up to hear her. I canceled appointments
right and left and was able to be at her place by one o'clock. We
were in each other's arms instantly, and it was better than ever;
everything was back on. Probably I was just being selfish again; I'd
been high-minded for twelve hours, and maybe that was all I could
stand. But she was out of her mind with happiness to have me back
on the same old basis, and it made me feel good to see her happy,
even though there wasn't any more future for her in it than the day
before. I was giving her something precious by coming back, but I
knew that I was depriving her of a lot, too. I'm not trying to sound
noble when I say that; I did feel that way—and I couldn't do
anything about it."

But the problems, once brought out in the open, never disappeared from view again. Terry continued shopping around for other
men and frequently talked to Lewis about her future, and from time
to time she or he raised the question of another try at breaking up.
Toward summer, during a rather tense evening he mentioned that
the two-year lease on the studio was up for renewal, and she tartly
suggested that perhaps he ought not renew the lease, since they
weren't sure just how long they might need the place. Lewis, with
a show of reluctance, agreed. "It was what I wanted. I thought it
would be better for her, and better for me, too. The studio had
become a symbol, a heavy obligation; it was so convenient that it
was a trap for both of us. It was keeping me away from my home
and my children too much, it was keeping Terry too tied to me to
cultivate anybody else. All in all, it was a relief to back off somewhat

by giving it up. But I must say that taking our things out of it and closing the door for the last time, after two years, was rough. It was a real struggle not to let her see how strong my feelings were."

TERRY: "There we were, back on the motel kick again, a big step backwards. The whole relationship seemed to be going sour. There were a heck of a lot of heartaches for me then, and an awful lot of things that hurt. I began to think that the whole thing was bad for me, and I'd better get out. I told myself even if he had a sudden change of heart, even if he wanted me for his wife, I wouldn't want to be the cause of the break-up of his marriage; I couldn't live with that on my conscience. I told myself he and I probably wouldn't have been able to make a good marriage anyway. For one thing, I would never be able to relax and trust him if he stayed in town at night; I knew too much. And I probably could never be all the things that Arlene is because I don't have her background. I'd always be afraid he'd be looking for someone else like her who could play the part better than I. . . . But all this was just sour grapes, because I knew by now that we could never be married unless something happened to Arlene. The ideal thing would be if she'd run off with some other man, but she's the last woman in the world to do that. So the only real answer is that she'd have to—well, die in an accident, or have a fatal heart attack, or something. Isn't that a *lovely* thing for me to say and to wish? But that's what happens to a woman in a situation like mine."

---

iii   force majeure

Unlike all the foregoing, some affairs decline and fall in response to inimical forces outside themselves. Occasionally, employers, ministers, friends or relatives learning about the affair can exert enough direct pressure on one or both lovers to break up the relationship. Usually, however, the power of such persons is small compared to that of the deceived spouses; these are the people who, if confronted by the evidence, can often exert such force as to bring about an unwilling renunciation.

How often does an unfaithful person's spouse know about an ongoing affair? Most Freudian-oriented psychotherapists feel that the wronged spouse *always* knows, in some degree, although very often the knowledge is so threatening that it is thrust out of awareness into the unconscious. But it is conscious rather than unconscious knowing that leads to the direct countermeasures we are considering here. And such knowing is considerably more common than the unfaithful would like to believe. Among my interviewees, one out of six said that their spouses knew with certainty, while the first affair was going on; in later affairs, one in three spouses knew. Beyond this, about one in three spouses lacked certainty but were clearly suspicious, during both first and subsequent affairs.

Obviously, keeping extra-marital activity a total secret from one's mate is extraordinarily difficult. Modern life offers few times and places for extra-marital lovers to be together in perfect safety, and modern marriage allows so little privacy to either partner that complete security is all but impossible. Besides the various possibilities of accidental disclosure that we saw earlier, there are innumerable others: the chance encounter in a restaurant, parking lot, or even on a street corner with a wife, mother-in-law, or teen-age son who was supposed to be elsewhere but changed plans unexpectedly; the unpredictable attack of trichomonas, cystitis, non-specific urethritis, or even gonorrhea, all of which are hard to conceal from one's spouse, especially if sexual relations at home are normally frequent; the accident or injury to a child that sends a frantic wife in search of her husband—who proves not to be where he said he would be; the well-meant remark of the headwaiter or bellboy who mistakes one's mate for the partner last seen.

Also accidental, in a sense, are such give-aways as the stigmata of extra-marital sexual enthusiasm—bites or bruises on the arms or shoulders, scratches on the back or arms. One man, much scratched up by a hyperactive partner, got by for a week by wearing only long-sleeved shirts, though it was summer, and by contriving to undress and dress only when his wife was not looking. His scratches healed by the week's end, but left white marks against his suntan; his wife finally saw them, asked what they were, and found his story that he had been "roughhousing with the kids" at the beach not at all convincing.

Sometimes the stigmata are deliberately planted by an extra-marital partner in order to make trouble at home: A woman may, for instance, purposely smudge her lover's collar with lipstick, hoping to provoke quarreling in his marriage and possibly a separation. Other wronged spouses find out about their mates' infidelities through anonymous tip-offs or even directly from concerned friends. The latter way, however, is rare; a conspiracy of silence surrounds the deceived spouse—probably because wronged wives and cuckolded men bitterly resent being told the demeaning truth.

Some suspicious spouses use detectives to gather definite evidence, but this, too, is relatively rare and for much the same reason: One can only detest dealing with persons who gather information one hates to hear. In fact, detectives are usually used with great reluctance, and only in response to the urging of a lawyer, mother, or someone else with a special interest in exposing the unfaithful person and breaking up the marriage. The suspicious spouse is right to be reluctant; the process proves as debasing to him or her as it does humiliating to the unfaithful one. It is hard to know, for instance, which of the two following speakers—an unfaithful husband and his wife—suffered more from the incident in question:

—The husband: "We were nearly asleep in our hotel room when the door burst open—I guess the chambermaid had been bribed to fix it. Flashbulbs were popping in our faces and five people were standing there staring. I rushed, naked, into the bathroom to get away from the cameras, but they broke the door open. I grabbed the only thing at hand to attack them with—a can of spray deodorant—and blasted away at them, but I had it backwards and got it straight in my own face. That was the final blow. Then somebody said, 'That's enough,' and they rushed out. We were both quivering, speechless, in total shock. We felt violated and disgraced, and couldn't even look each other in the face for hours."

—The wife: "My lawyer and my best friend both told me that I had to do it. I held out for a long while, and then finally I hired the detective and gave him the go-ahead. But when he called on me and told me the details of the raid, I ran out of the room and threw up. I kept on doing it again and again, until I had to go to bed; I stayed there for days. I've never felt so vile and dirty in my life."

Perhaps more common, and certainly more emotionally significant, than any of the preceding is the phenomenon of unconscious self-incrimination. Quite often, seemingly accidental slips that reveal the truth to the deceived spouse are the kind of thing a sensible person could easily have avoided. They are the expression, as I indicated earlier, of an unconscious desire to inform the spouse, sometimes by way of revenge, sometimes to provoke divorce, sometimes to enlist the spouse's aid in breaking up the affair. It is quite possible to harbor one of these wishes while being unwilling to deliberately implement it; the unconsciously contrived slip or accident is the outcome—and sometimes they are blunders of so obvious a nature that even those who make them are astonished. Some people accidentally leave letters or notes from their lovers lying around where they are bound to be seen; some forget the story concocted to cover an absence and contradict themselves about it; some bring home gifts or memorabilia and hide them without reckoning on reasons the other mate might look for something in that very place. One woman, a part-time painter, did a portrait of her lover and hung it in her home; when her husband seemed upset and suspicious, she realized that her feelings about the man she had painted were bound to be obvious to anyone who was familiar with her work.

Voluntary and deliberate confessions are also fairly common. Among my interviewees and questionnaire respondents, roughly a third of those whose spouses knew about their affairs said that they themselves had told them. The motives behind voluntary confessions are many and varied: guilt and the need to be forgiven, the wish to be stopped, the wish to be given permission to continue, the desire for divorce, the desire for revenge. Such confessions may be planned in advance; more often, they come about spontaneously, in the course of a marital quarrel. One man, for instance, who neither wished nor intended to tell his wife about his infidelities, did so spontaneously when provoked beyond his limits:

—"When she said for the fifth time or sixth time that night that it was no wonder she had always been cool about sex with me because I had never been good as a lover, I finally said, 'I've got reason to think otherwise. I've been *told* otherwise. I've been assured that I'm great, that I'm *fantastic.*' My wife looked as stunned as if I had belted her with a two-by-four, and never said another word that night."

One would suppose that virtually all spouses who find out that their mates are unfaithful would have violent negative reactions, but a surprisingly large minority do not. Of the interviewees and questionnaire respondents who said their spouses knew about their affairs, somewhere over one quarter characterized their spouses' primary reactions as tolerant, understanding, or even happy. (The latter reaction may well be limited to mate-swappers or those with sexual difficulties who feel that the affair relieves them of conjugal obligations.)

But nearly three quarters of the spouses who find out do react in traditional fashions, experiencing emotions ranging from para-lyzing fright to fulminating rage, and including jealousy, humilia-tion, and overwhelming depression. Their resulting behavior runs the gamut from total passivity to violent action, depending on how easy or difficult it is for them to express anger, how much they blame themselves for the affair, and how alarming the thought of divorce may seem. Some men smash furniture, beat their faithless wives, and threaten to kill their lovers; women sometimes do simi-lar things, though rather more often they throw tantrums, weep hysterically, or threaten to kill themselves. Other men and women grow pale, silent, and withdrawn; still others, though quivering with rage or on the brink of hysterics, control themselves by heroic efforts and masochistically insist on knowing all the details of how, when, where, and especially why. ("Just tell me one thing: Where did I fail you? What has she got that I haven't got? I have to know.")

The counterattack upon the affair may be delayed days—or even months—by the shock of the discovery or the fearfulness of the deceived spouse. Whether it comes soon or late, it takes forms almost all of which are already familiar from literature. Initially, women may use the appeal to sympathy (tears, outcries, visible suffering), the resort to violence (tantrums, smashing of chinaware, assaults with fists or fingernails), the reduction of services (the cold dinner of left-overs, the unmended socks), sexual and emotional rejection (the bed made up on the sofa, the cheek turned to the morning and evening kiss), financial retaliation (expensive redeco-rating or shopping, visits to specialists, trips for the health), and physical separation (the changed front-door lock, the abrupt flight to parents or friends). Men who discover the faithlessness of their wives take certain analogous steps, but their preferred methods include stony silence, raging vituperation, the withholding of money and sex, drunkenness and gambling, temporary desertion, and threats or actual assaults upon the mate or the lover. Either sex will sometimes use the children as a particularly effective weapon of counterattack: Pointed or allusive remarks made in their presence about the unfaithful person's behavior is unbearably shaming and guilt-producing. (It is also probably seriously damaging to the children, a fact the vengeful mate manages to ignore.)

Many of these measures are applied discomforts rather than appeals to conscience; they constitute punishments for misbehavior, and, by implication, will be rescinded when the misbehavior ends. This kind of counterattack is most effective when the affair is only casual or limited in involvement, and when the unfaithful mate wants to remain comfortably married. A young assistant district attorney recalls the scene of his own enforced reversion to fidelity:

—"I came home one night about midnight, and this girl, who had become much too serious about me, was sitting there with my wife, waiting. It was shattering. I hardly said a word; I had nothing to say. My wife pointed to a chair, and I sat down, and the abuse started from both of them. I just sat still and listened, and hung my head. They wouldn't even let me have a drink—and I needed one. I can't remember any time in my life as bad as that. The hell those two gave me! The threats they made to expose me and ruin my career! I could never have imagined such a scene. It went on until about four in the morning. Then the two of them went upstairs to sleep, and my wife threw my pajamas and one blanket down the stairs and told me to use the sofa. What a night! . . . In a couple of days I struck a truce with my wife. The heat was on—I had to go straight. I cut all my extra-marital connections and began coming straight home from the office. I was scared, and determined to stay out of trouble, and I did, for four months. Then, when the heat was off, I started backsliding."

A wronged spouse who is too passive or timid to strike out at the offender may instead turn his or her anger inward. This can take the form of accidents, the neglect of health, suicide attempts, or other self-destructive behavior. Such a counterattack can be very effective, even if the unfaithful spouse is a low-guilt type; it turns the screw not so much upon his conscience as upon his dislike of disruption in his home life and his fear of public disgrace. A young business executive tells how it felt:

—"I came home late. The lights were on, and she was lying in the middle of the living-room floor, out cold and snoring, with a whisky decanter and a half-empty bottle of sleeping pills nearby where I couldn't miss them. 'Good God,' I thought, 'couldn't she have tried something less drastic?' I pulled her to her feet, got her to the bathroom, and shoved some ipecac into her to make her throw up. I walked her around outside in the cold air for a while, and then sat her down in the kitchen and made her eat buttered toast and drink a lot of coffee. She was crying and blubbering that she felt like a total failure. I kept telling her I had merely been acting like a typical restless male and it didn't amount to anything. But that didn't comfort her at all. Finally I had an idea: I said I would go into psychotherapy to find out why I had been unfaithful. The implication was that I was deeply neurotic. I didn't believe that, but I had to do something. Suppose she tried again and succeeded, or suppose somebody else found her before I did? How could one live with that kind of thing on the record for everyone to see? How could I face my son and daughter the rest of my life if they ever found out—as they'd be bound to—why their mother killed herself?"

Now and then a spouse whose mate is unfaithful will try to compete in a positive fashion with the outside beloved. Sometimes a wife, in the fashion long advocated by writers for women's magazines, will buy new lingerie, get her hair restyled, and attempt to be more amusing, attentive, or seductive than the Other Woman. Occasionally a husband will get rid of some weight, have his clothes retailored, take his wife to a show or two, pay her more attention. But anger, hurt, and low self-esteem are hardly conducive to such behavior, and aggrieved spouses apply pressures and penalties far more often than seductive or appealing measures.

The strongest penalty available, in most cases, is divorce, but it is so hard upon the punisher as well as the punished that it is used more in threat than actuality—and even then, usually not until other methods have failed. Only about a third of those who learn of their mates' infidelities threaten to divorce them if they do not desist. They may make the threat spontaneously, in the middle of an argument; they may do so by design, after having had a secret preliminary conference with a lawyer; or for maximum shock value they may go so far as to have the threat come in the form of a letter from the lawyer to the unfaithful spouse which arrives unheralded in the mail one day while they are still living together and even sleeping in the same bedroom. (But not sleeping together; in most states, the lawyer is duty-bound to inform his client that sexual relations with an unfaithful spouse constitutes "condonation," wiping out as grounds for divorce all unfaithful actions up to that point.)

If the verbal threat or initial visit to the lawyer are not enough, the written notice that suit has been filed will often bring about capitulation and a promise to be faithful. Even the stubborn hold-out, unmoved by tears, rages, and assorted punishments, may find the actuality of divorce based on his or her infidelity a much more serious matter. Over and above the break-up of the family, the shame and embarrassment of having one's friends and acquaintances know, and the thousand logistical problems of separation, there is the dual specter of finanical ruin and the loss of one's children. For the aggrieved spouse's lawyer makes it plain at once that he is going to drive a hard bargain in out-of-court negotiations, since he could certainly do so in court, judges being notoriously harsh on adulterers in divorce proceedings. It becomes clear to the straying husband that he will be saddled with crippling alimony and that his wife means to make it hard or almost impossible for him to see his children; it becomes clear to the straying wife that she will get little or no money at all, and that her husband means to fight her for partial or even total custody of the children.

The decay of an affair under external pressures and penalties can thus take any one of several courses. Sometimes the very first counterattack is enough to disrupt the affair; sometimes the unfaithful spouse promises to end it but continues it secretly, though with more difficulty, for weeks or months; sometimes, in a stalemate or even a show of open defiance, he or she flagrantly continues the affair while living at home. But sooner or later the counterattack causes the unfaithful spouse to see the affair in a different light. If it were a deeply involved and richly gratifying love, it might now look like the Promised Land; the counterattack would not only fail, but would advance the cause of the affair. But in the case of casual affairs or those of partial involvement and limited gratification, the hundred discomforts of hostility at home, plus the ominous warnings of dissolution of the family and of an embittered divorce, begin to create in the unfaithful person an involuntary resentment of his extra-marital partner. The cost is too high for the rewards, and though this is hardly the other one's fault, he feels and acts as though it were. He makes barbed half-humorous remarks or is briefly testy about the difficulties of continuing and about the stresses and the expense of their meetings; their love-making may still be passionate, but there is a desperation about the way they hold each other; time and again, minor differences lead to arguments or awkward silences.

Yet most of these couples, sensing what is happening and knowing they never meant to love completely or to marry, try at this point to play out the ending graciously, falling back on certain standardized clichés that forecast the end of the affair:

—"I can't stand seeing you so unhappy. You need to make your peace with her. Go, with my blessing."

—"When the time comes, let's make it a clean break. No phone calls, no letters, no turning back. Promise?"

—"I'll never regret any of this. I'll only regret that it had to end."

—"Of course I'll cry. But I wouldn't have missed you for anything."

And with these soothing and mutually forgiving words, they assure each other that neither is to blame for the dying of the affair. They feel ennobled by tragedy, grieved by their mutual loss, and relieved at the approaching end of tension and strain—and being relieved, may find their passion briefly redoubled, their last meetings virtually orgiastic. The children have been called home from play, but will take one last wild hop-skip-and-jump before obeying.

Sometimes, even when an affair is neither deep nor richly rewarding and does not have marriage as an implicit goal, the counterattack by the aggrieved spouse may fail to break it up: He or she may be too timid to press hard or far enough, or the unfaithful mate may be so thick-skinned as to ignore the harassment, or so tricky as to placate the aggrieved one just enough to keep things under control. An extreme example:

—A timid and dependent woman, married to a well-to-do exporter, suspected him of infidelity because of his sudden interest in physical fitness, his lack of sexual appetite, and his many evening appointments, but she feared to challenge him about any of this. When a "Mr. and Mrs." hotel bill came in the mail one day after he had been on a so-called business trip, she hunted through his papers and found similar bills. She confronted her husband with all this one night, but without a trace of discomfort he explained them away as a tax gimmick; his roommate, he said, had actually been one of his associates. Unconvinced, she spent months sleuthing on her own, and finally found out who his mistress was and where they spent time together. But when she faced him with her findings, weeping uncontrollably and begging him to explain why, he told her he loved only her and had already given the girl up because she meant nothing to him. For the next few months, his wife, crying and scolding, would confront him time and again with new pieces of evidence—lipstick marks, a hotel key in his pocket, a late-night phone call from his drunken and angry mistress—but he claimed again and again that he had to keep seeing the girl in order to forestall a suicide attempt, and that he was cooling the affair off as fast as possible. His wife lost weight, became seriously anemic, and developed a dependency on sleeping pills; she made sure he knew about her poor health, but he merely ordered her to see a doctor. She finally informed him that she had an appointment scheduled with a divorce lawyer; he laughed and told her she was a silly girl —he had ended the relationship weeks ago. She cancelled the appointment, but of course he had not broken off with the girl, and when this became clear to her, she finally met the divorce lawyer and told her husband about their conference. He grew very agitated, and asked her to pay the lawyer for the meeting but to tell him she had no further need of his services; the relationship would be ended that very night. She concludes:

"That was four weeks ago. Last night he went to one of his

many 'poker games' and came home with pancake makeup on his undershirt again—the third time since he promised to end the affair. I don't know what to do; I'm not in a position to make a move. I am really too frightened. I guess the trouble is that I don't think enough of myself to believe I'm capable of living without him, no matter how much money I might get from him. I've never had a life of my own; ever since high school, my home, my children, and my husband were everything. Sometimes I feel I'm not even a *person* but only a shadow of my husband—and he knows it. No matter what I may threaten him with, he knows I'm too frightened to do anything real, so he keeps on doing what he wants. I don't know how to cope with it."

Even if pressed with vigor and determination, a counterattack against a casual or limited-involvement affair may fail if the marriage itself is so unrewarding as to offer little more than housing. The thundering and pounding of the counteroffensive do no great harm to the affair, but only weaken the already crumbling marriage. This is particularly true of people like Peggy and Andy Farrell who, for social and psychological reasons, were relatively unconcerned about what their peers and relatives would think of their marital failure.

Peggy Farrell, et al.

Ironically enough, it was not Peggy's infidelities, but her husband's, that caused the unsuccessful counterattack which hastened the collapse of their marriage. During Andy's nine-month stay in Brazil, when her extra-marital activity reached its peak, she began to be plagued by suspicions that Andy, too, must be carrying on, and probably had been all along. She had never thought he was the type, but now she was harassed by the notion that his nights of bowling and pool with the boys had been filled with adulterous revelry. "The more I fooled around, the more jealous and suspicious I got. In my letters, I finally accused him of running around, but he passed it off as if I were kidding. When he got back from Brazil, I pestered him about it even more, but he just ignored me or made jokes. Then he was assigned to a new job where he was in and out of the office a lot, and would have to work at night a couple of times every week. It nearly drove me nuts. I was still running around myself, even though I had lots to do—I was in social-work training at that point—and I had no right to complain, but I couldn't stop myself. I nagged him all the time. I said things like, 'I kept calling you today and you were out of the office all afternoon—balling, right?' or 'Night work—what a laugh! I know you're screwing around. I can tell.' It was absolutely crazy of me, particularly since I'd never felt there was anything wrong about my own affairs.

"He finally began to get fed up with it and told me to go fuck myself; he even smacked me around a couple of times. But he didn't admit a thing. So I started to go through his pockets at night and look through the car with a fine-tooth comb. Finally I found a cigarette butt with lipstick on it—he smokes but I don't—and then I was in business. I came into the house screaming like a banshee, I threw dishes at him, I called him all kinds of names and carried on for hours. I was a real terror—and that time he didn't lay a finger on me. Eventually I wore him down: He admitted he'd had a couple of things cooking in Brazil, and a few even before that—and he'd had something going ever since his return. He said that none of them were big deals, but after he told me all this, I felt as if someone had let all the air out of me. I folded up, I collapsed. I cried like a baby for hours, and beat my head with my fists. For days, I carried on. I spent whole evenings curled up on the couch in the fetal position—I wanted him to see me suffering. I bit my fingernails until they were a bloody mess, and showed them to him. One evening we had hardly anything for dinner, and I explained it was because I had had an attack of hysterics in the supermarket and had run out without buying anything. I phoned him at work ten times a day, I told him I had a detective trailing him (which wasn't so), and a few times, when he came home late from work, I made him let me look at his penis to see if I could tell anything from it.

"It was all just childish and idiotic, and the more I bore down, the worse things got between us. Our marriage hadn't been worth a damn, and all this fuss didn't make it any better. And it wasn't doing Petey anything but harm—he was nearly seven, and he picked up all the vibrations and started bedwetting again and even stammering. And me a social worker in training!

"Maybe that woke me up—woke both of us up. Because even dull, plodding Andy began to see how empty our marriage was, and what a nothing kind of home-life we were making for Petey. As for myself, somewhere along the line I did some hard thinking—I even spent a few hours talking things over with a senior social worker —and came to the conclusion that I wanted more than I'd been getting out of my life, too. But not with him. For the first time I wanted to find someone I could love for real, and with whom I could have an important and long-lasting relationship. Partly, I think, I wanted such a love in order to revenge myself on Andy, but partly I could now see that there wasn't any real or lasting satisfaction for me in the kind of affairs I'd been having, and that I had to find something much more adult and complete.

"But I didn't know where to find it, so for a while I went back on the old trail. I kept on living with Andy, but with more distance between us than ever. The closer I got to finishing my social-work training, the more I thought about breaking out—Andy didn't make a lot, and I knew I would have to work—but the key thing was meeting Peter. We met in a bar, the way I'd met so many other men, but I felt different about him almost from the first. Peter is good-looking in a mean sort of way—rough, rugged, bulldog-faced, stout —and he attracted me physically right away, but what made the difference was that he really needed me. As big and tough as he was —he was a detective on the police force—he's very insecure and always having to prove himself sexually. With my problem, I could really understand, I could help. I was the best thing that had ever happened to him. . . . Well, that's all another story; the point I wanted to make was that after I had known Peter only a month, I was ready to give Andy the final shove. I came home one night, supposedly from a PTA meeting. Andy had been drinking and he started acting horny, even though he hadn't been interested in me for weeks and weeks. He grabbed me, but I pushed him away and said, 'Sorry about that, but my boy friend says you can't have any more.' He looked at me as if I had run a truck into his stomach. It got pretty rough for a while, what with the yelling and cursing, breaking things, my locking him out and his breaking in, the cops coming around, all that and more—but it was only wounded pride on his part, and in a couple of weeks he packed up and got out, which was just what I wanted."

With this, Peggy's concentrated period of marital infidelity ended. She was now launched on a wholly new quest and faced by a wholly new problem: She was now the unattached Other Woman, trying to pry her married lover away from his wife.

---

iv soul-struggles: the victory of the old love

The decay of the deep-involvement affair is usually a very different process. As much as anything else, it is caused by a conflict, within the heart of the unfaithful person, between desire and duty, rebellion and acceptance, fulfillment and obligation. The kind of person who has such an affair—usually puritan-romantic and basically monogamous—finds the exhilarating and expansive period when it seems possible to have both loves all too short. He —or, of course, she—soon learns that the more he opens himself up to the new love, the more he has to shut himself off from the old; the more he seeks to preserve the old, the more he blights or seems to repudiate the new.

Pulled in both directions and racked by opposing feelings, he recognizes that he can end his distress only by choosing one relationship and abandoning the other. He makes one resolution after another to do so, but abandons each as being unworkable; he vacillates between the alternatives, and despises himself as much for not choosing the one as for not choosing the other. But what choice could satisfy him? The new love is romance, passion, emotional intensity, youth; to give it up is to throw away his chance of realizing a lifelong dream of happiness. The old love is home, family, security, shared experiences; to give it up is to throw away the reality of his life and his personal history.

The internal struggle manifests itself in physical and emotional symptoms like those we saw earlier during the struggle with temptation, and again after the first actual physical infidelity. Some conscience-directed people, torn between the old love and the new, cannot sleep, or sleep only to find themselves tormented by nightmares; others cannot eat, or eat but are plagued by digestive disorders. Some develop rashes, migraine headaches, or difficulty drawing breath. Men may be unable to concentrate on their work, women on their household and child-rearing duties; men may easily burst into rages, women into tears. Both forget birthdays, errands, and bills that must be paid; get speeding tickets, quarrel bitterly with old friends, and have trouble with their employers; talk of quitting their jobs, of moving, of finding something new. Most often of all, the need to make a Procrustean choice causes them to suffer from depression: They become withdrawn, languid, and unable to interest themselves in anything, some requiring medication, others psychotherapy, and a few even having to be hospitalized.

This ambivalence and internal conflict soon begin to contaminate the affair. If the man is moody and dejected one night, the woman may do her best to cheer and comfort him, but she herself becomes anxious, doubts his love, is resentful that he is so torn between her and his wife. Or perhaps it is she who is worried one night about her eventual confrontation with her husband; her lover may sympathize and reassure her, but he himself begins to wonder whether she will ever really make the move, and to question whether she loves him as much as she says. One may speak of wanting to see the other more often, even though it is clear the other cannot presently manage it; as a result, both are unhappy, the former for being refused, the latter for being pressed. For by now they want more of each other than it is possible to give while still married to their present mates, and their desire for each other, though flattering, nettles the one who cannot give more as well as the one whose demands cannot be met. They hear themselves uttering clichés they might once have laughed at but which now seem deeply meaningful:

—"What's going to become of us?"

—"I only want to do what's right."

—"We have a right to be happy, don't we?"

—"I have to live with myself the rest of my life."

—"Can't we go on just as we are?"

And in answer to the last question, the ultimate cliché:

—"We can't go on like this."

And indeed, they cannot, for the situation is insupportable. The affair cannot endure as it is; it must swiftly triumph over the marriage or it will sicken and die like a plant that has outgrown the pot it is in, or a business that has expanded beyond its capacity.

Yet even now, one (or both) may remain immobilized: He—or she—cannot give up the new love but cannot take any step toward freeing himself from the old. He may think—in part, correctly—that he is held back by duty, loyalty, love of his children, a sense of right and wrong, but much of the time these factors are secondary to the more fundamental fulfillments, the broader spectrum of satisfactions, the marriage offers. For even if the marriage has become, or has always been, placid and unexciting, it may be built around an adult love that meets most of the individual's deep emotional needs; in contrast, the affair may be built around an immature love, based on illusion and projection, that meets few of them.

His inability to choose is not necessarily weakness, but an indication that he mistrusts the new love or unconsciously senses it to be defective or unsound. He may not clearly recognize that his extra-marital beloved is a poor choice and that their relationship would prove unworkable in the long run, but he does know that even though it is absolutely necessary for him to make a decision and to act upon it, he cannot; something stays his hand. In this quandary, he may turn to outside sources for advice and for a decisive push—but he is likely to seek out those who will tell him what he unconsciously wants to hear. If the affair is not basically sound, or if the marriage has important and enduring values, he will probably talk to conservative friends, a minister, or a marriage counselor, whose primary commitment is to saving marriage. But just as often he may tell his own spouse—deliberately or otherwise—in order to have her help him end the affair. But not necessarily by using threats: With an unfaithful spouse of this type, the deceived spouse's instinctive reaction may be to play the martyr, greatly exacerbating the unfaithful one's guilt and thus tipping the balance against the affair. A small-town banker in his mid-thirties tells about his own unplanned confession and its consequences:

—"The affair was infinitely exciting and romantic—everything that I dreamed of. But I had this damned nagging guilt, which gradually spoiled all my enjoyment. I would think about her all the time and imagine being married to her, yet I couldn't conceive of splitting up two families to gratify myself. Meanwhile, my wife was puzzled and unhappy because of my remoteness. I could see this and it hurt me, but I couldn't seem to do anything about it. After a while, being too damned honest and conscientious for my own good, I simply couldn't keep things secret from her.

"It happened like this: We went to play tennis one day and the only open court was one next to the Simpsons, who were playing already, and I said to my wife, 'I can't play.' She said, 'Why not?' and I said, 'I just can't.' She asked what was wrong, and I said, 'Get in the car and I'll tell you,' and as we drove home I told her that Phyllis Simpson and I had been seeing each other secretly, and that Phyllis was in love with me and I was trying to avoid her. It was cowardly and dishonest of me to put it that way, not admitting that I loved Phyllis too, but I couldn't go that far. Even so, my wife was dumfounded and crushed by the news. But she didn't make any scene, she just asked a lot of questions and then sort of curled up within herself and suffered in silence. . . . Looking back on it now, I think I must have told her in order to find some way out of the affair. I must have had some idea that Phyllis and I would have made a bad marriage, and by telling my wife, I made it very difficult for myself to continue seeing her. And being confronted with my wife's suffering, I myself suffered; in fact, I couldn't stand it. She never threatened me—instead, she kept telling me that if Phyllis was what I wanted, she wouldn't try to hold me, she'd let go of me. She and the kids would manage somehow, and she wouldn't even turn them against me. If she had fought me, it might have turned me against her, but she was so decent and so deeply unhappy that I couldn't possibly bring myself to leave her."

More often, however, the person immobilized by conflict takes no such steps to resolve the deadlock of his feelings. This, however, is a form of choice—a choice against the affair. For immobility is fatal to it: His inability to take action against his marriage is interpreted by the extra-marital partner as a rejection of her, a preference for the spouse. And so the lovers' discussions give way to quarrels, tears are replaced by anger, understanding and compassion are supplanted by ultimatums and threats of abandonment. Yet even when it is clear that the situation has become critical and he is about to lose her unless he acts, he does nothing; that is, he chooses to lose her. A research scientist in his early forties tells just such a story:

—"I was sexually and mentally bored with my wife. I was weary of the whole stale relationship. Diane was vastly more alive, imaginative, sensual, and beautiful—in fact, it seemed to me that she was everything I wanted in a woman. But she must not have been, because all I had to do was say to my wife, 'We've both known for a long while that things are hopeless; maybe we should talk to a lawyer'—but I couldn't do it. The words wouldn't come out. The moment was never right, or else it *was* right but I'd break out in a sweat and get knots in my stomach, and be unable to say a word. I'd go back and tell Diane I hadn't done it yet, I hadn't been able to, and she'd get that look—at first baffled but later on desperate —and she'd ask, 'What *is* it? Do you still love her? Don't you love me?' I'd hang my head and tell her that I didn't love my wife the way I loved her, and that I *had* made up my mind to do it but I just couldn't, not yet, I needed more time. The longer this went on, the more everything turned sour. Finally, she began warning me that she was going to have to get out of the situation unless I made a move—and still I didn't.

"One day she told me, very matter-of-factly, that she had quit her job and was going to New York, where there were lots of fresh opportunities. I begged her not to, and she said I could call her that night if I talked things over with my wife, but otherwise she'd be on the plane the next day. I told her I was going home at once to straighten things out, and she cried and kissed me as I left. But all the way home, my resolution was fading, and before I got there I knew I didn't *want* to do it, and wasn't *going* to do it. I wanted to stay married to my nice dull wife, and live with my kids, and find a little love on the outside whenever I could. I sent her a telegram, telling her I would always adore her, but that I couldn't do what I had promised, and this was the real goodbye. I felt unbelievable pain—but at the very same time, to my own surprise, I felt a great sense of liberation from my own emotions."

This man, and men and women like him, unconsciously recognize that their affairs are unrealistic and would prove less rewarding, as marriages, than their present ones. But if they end their affairs with their illusions still intact at the conscious level, they may be tormented for years by regrets and longing, and come to resent the spouses for whom they gave up so much. The more fortunate ones are those who come to grips with the matter, consciously compare the new love to the old, and eventually make a decision based on realistic values. Where the extra-marital partner is a poor choice and the marriage is basically rewarding, disillusionment with the former and new appreciation of the latter go hand in hand; self-interest cooperates with the urgings of conscience, and the affair decays and dies without destroying the marriage.

EDWIN GOTTESMAN AND JENNIFER SCOTT

Edwin's growing disillusionment with Jennifer might of itself have led to the end of the affair except for the strength of his need —which it so well gratified—to see himself as romantic, virile, free-spending, and beneficent. Alarmed about the relationship but unable to relinquish it, he was much like an addict who hates his own need for the drug, knows its comforts to be ephemeral and ultimately destructive, but whose craving makes him say and do anything to obtain his temporary quietus. But there was a countervailing force at work in the form of his love for Betsy and for the children. For a while, he had suppressed and ignored the conflict in his feelings, but as the affair grew into an obsession with him and made ever more serious inroads upon his marital relationship and his home life, he could no longer keep the conflict hidden from himself.

"As time went on, I could see myself becoming less and less a husband and a father. I tried not to think about it because I was having so exciting a time with Jennifer, but somewhere inside me I felt it was very wrong. Not that there was any trouble at home. Except for that time in Puerto Rico, Betsy never acted suspicious. She knew something was wrong but she thought I had business troubles. She was so sympathetic and trusting that I felt sad for her; it didn't seem right. As for our sex life, I always had enough left over for once or twice a week at home—and not just as a duty, either. Sometimes, when Jennifer and I had a fight and weren't seeing each other, I'd come home after the kids were in bed, and Betsy would fix me a drink and sit and chat with me awhile before dinner, and I'd feel like smacking my forehead and saying to myself, '*Putz!* For a slut like that, you take chances of ruining your marriage to this wonderful woman?' I *knew* better—but knowing didn't matter."

Indeed, after Jennifer's return from Europe, a year after he had met her, Edwin began to have fantasies about marrying her. The more demanding she became and the more he quarreled with her about money or about her not working or about other men—she sometimes dated others on nights when Edwin was at home—the more he wanted to own her, and felt that if they were married she would become less flighty and demanding, and the frictions between them would disappear. "I knew she was trouble, I knew she was a mess—but I wanted her, and when things were going well between us, I made myself believe that it could be like that all the time."

Finally, Jennifer herself brought up the subject. Right after the boutique deal fell through, they had another serious fight about money and didn't speak to each other for days; then there was another tearful, erotic reconciliation, during which Jennifer said that there was only one solution: Edwin would have to divorce Betsy and marry her. "I was feeling so good at the moment that I admitted to her I'd had the same thing on my mind for weeks. Her face was something to see—she looked overcome by happiness. I knew how crazy the idea of marrying her would seem to any of my friends, but I wanted to do it. I was living in some kind of dream. Yet I was also half awake to the truth. I made a dinner appointment with a divorce lawyer, but the day I was supposed to meet him I took a long look at a picture on my desk of Betsy and the children, when they were little, and I called the lawyer and broke the appointment. I never did go see him. I just played with the idea in my mind after that, like a man who daydreams about selling his business and moving to Tahiti and living in the sun. Yet sometimes I would say to myself, 'What is a wife and children, property, a good business, compared to what I have with Jennifer? Does any of that make me as happy as I am with this girl?' I would try to find faults in Betsy and magnify them in my mind to make it seem right. But it wasn't easy. Sometimes I did find a few silly little things to be angry at, like the way she kept pestering me to take her to concerts of the National Symphony that winter and spring. I didn't want to go because symphonic music bores me, and we actually had a quarrel about it. I liked having something to be annoyed at, but a few days later I realized what I was doing, and I was ashamed of myself."

All spring and summer, his relationship with Jennifer oscillated wildly: Either they were closer and more loving than ever, or so quarrelsome that they avoided each other for days at a time. Her phone was out of order several different times when Edwin, out of town on business, tried to call her; he accused her of leaving the phone off the hook while she was in bed with another man and told her that he was through with her, but each time his resolve lasted only a few days. Three times that spring Jennifer vanished without a word for a few days, going off to New Jersey to see her mother, or to New York, where she looked for modeling jobs. "It didn't work on me the way it did when she ran away to Europe. I'd think, 'Let her go—this is my way out,' and I'd spend more time at home, and feel good about it. Then Jennifer would call me, crying and in some kind of trouble, or telling me she loved me and needed me —and pow!—I'd be back again."

Edwin cannot pinpoint the end of the decaying affair since there was not one end, but many. He began cutting down on the money he gave her, she disappeared again and again without warning, they had more "final" partings followed by reconciliations. One evening in June during one of Jennifer's disappearances, Edwin played nurse to Betsy, who had hurt her back in a fall and was strapped up. Sitting up next to her in bed, he began to reminisce with her about their college days, and felt overcome with love and regret; he silently vowed to make it all up to her from then on. "A few days later the doctor unstrapped her. She told me with a little smile that she was all right, and whispered that it was a pity it was so long until nighttime. This was on a Saturday, a perfect summer day, and we were having brunch on the patio with my parents and our nearest neighbors. Our two kids and the neighbors' three were running in and out of the woods, the sun was bright and the grass very green. I looked all around and asked myself, 'How lucky can a man be? Who needs more than this?' And I felt that the other thing was definitely over, once and for all."

With that idyllic scene the story should conclude, but people often lack good aesthetic judgment about their own lives, and the affair limped along for almost two months. By this time Edwin was putting much more effort into his work again and this, plus a certain amount of deliberate attention to his home life, made the gaps in the affair convenient and almost welcome. Only one more time, during a passionate interlude in August, did the question of marriage come up again; it was Jennifer who mentioned it, but this time Edwin felt both uncomfortable and irritated. He changed the subject rather abruptly and obviously, and the evening ended on a distinctly sour note.

He phoned her the next morning, but her line was busy for two hours and the rest of the day rang unanswered. The following day, when he called, an unfamiliar homosexual voice answered and explained that he and a friend had sublet the apartment from Miss Scott for two weeks while she was out of town, and that she might be giving them a long-term sublet after the two-week period. Edwin felt almost relieved. For several days he scarcely missed her, but toward the end of the two-week period he kept expecting her to call him, and grew edgy and impatient. When she finally did, he rushed off and met her at a restaurant in mid-afternoon. She said she'd been in New York, where she made a couple of good contacts for modeling and agreed to share an apartment with two other girls. Edwin was astounded and angered. He told her so, but Jennifer replied that he obviously wasn't going to marry her, so why should she waste her best years on him? He said he still cared about her and wanted her, but it wasn't *his* fault if they were so different they could never make a go of it; if she had thought otherwise, she had been kidding herself.

Jennifer called him a bastard, got up violently, knocking over her coffee, and fled from the restaurant; Edwin threw money on the table and rushed out after her. He ran half a block in the choking September heat, caught up with her, and, panting and sweating, begged her not to end it this way after they had loved each other so dearly. She relented and they went into a bar, drank, held hands, cried a little, and came to the same conclusion, this time calmly and

232 DECAYING

sorrowfully. Then she asked him if, as a favor, he could lend her two thousand dollars to get started in New York. Edwin was disgusted, and said so plainly. Again she rushed out. This time he paid the check at his leisure, and took a cab back to the office, telling himself for perhaps the tenth or twelfth time in as many months that this was the end. And this time it was.

Two days later, the homosexuals told Edwin that Jennifer had sublet the apartment to them for the remaining two years of her tenancy, and had sold them her linens, silver, dishes, a Duncan Phyfe table, an antique chiming banjo clock, the draperies, and the color television set. Edwin was all but apoplectic with anger and for an hour or two thought about suing her, since he considered the property at least half his; then he realized the absurdity of any such action, and amused himself by counseling himself like a kindly old Jewish uncle. "Eddie, *mein kind,*" he said, "don't go looking for trouble—it can find us without any help. Grab the bargain. She's letting you out very cheap. Instead of being upset, you should drink to celebrate. Have a *bissel schnapps* on me." He poured a stiff drink from a bottle he kept in the desk drawer, downed it with an unuttered *Mazeltov!*, and called Betsy to say that he would be coming home in time for dinner that night.

v soul-struggles:
the victory of the new love

Finally, there is the soul-struggle which turns out the other way: An affair of deep involvement grows and becomes competitive with the marriage, the inner conflict of the unfaithful person mounts to a crisis, and the situation is resolved by an emotional breakthrough that leads to the dismantling of the marriage in favor of the affair. This outcome is most likely where the new love, unlike the kind we have just been looking at, offers much more than romantic and sexual intensity or a temporary realization of adolescent fantasies; where, in fact, it seems to promise broad and thorough emotional satisfaction in an adult context. At the height of the internal conflict even such an affair may languish, seem to be decaying, suffer a brief hiatus or two. But if the marriage is seriously defective, the chances are that the unfaithful person will sooner or later make the decision to break away from it, and start to take action. As soon as he does so, the affair springs back to life and renewed growth, and even shows preliminary signs of turning into a marriage.

It does not always do so, for many imponderables may stand in the way, but to the puritan-romantic personality, this is its one acceptable outcome and its principal justification. The kind of individual who desires deep and thoroughgoing identification with a love-partner does not, even at the outset, become unfaithful primarily for fun or for comfort. His real aim and hope, whether he is aware of it or not, is to find a total, and totally satisfying, monogamous relationship. If he does find an extra-marital love which seems to have this potential, it is this love to which, at the turning point, he becomes faithful, while the marriage comes to be the unfaithful act that must be forsworn as soon as possible.

The breakthrough that ends the inner struggle may come soon, if the marriage is severely flawed and the new love is particularly rewarding and free from uncertainties. To the astonishment of the unfaithful spouse as well as the deceived one, a marriage of ten years' standing can be shattered by an affair that has existed only months or weeks. An extreme case, which we saw earlier, was that of the hardware dealer from Philadelphia whose first extra-marital affair, after twenty years of fidelity, so galvanized his emotions that after one week he tearfully told his wife all, packed a bag, and left the same night. Rather more typical is the following experience, narrated by a thirty-six-year-old woman who had been married fourteen years at the time of which she is speaking:

—"Who could ever imagine anything like that happening to my marriage? My husband was the squarest, straightest of men— a deacon in the church, a Little League Dad, a Cub Scoutmaster, a non-drinking, crew-cut, junior executive. But I let it happen. Our marriage had become nothing but a kind of corporate enterprise without my ever taking time to wonder about it. How it got that way I don't know. It seemed as if we were so busy with children, the house, and local activities, that we never paid any attention to each other, we never said anything real to each other. As for sex, I was bored by it. I felt I could nicely live forever without it, and tried to avoid it as much as possible. I hardly ever thought about any of this, but when I did, I told myself that every marriage goes through phases of this sort and there was nothing to worry about. I was living in never-never land, refusing to see the truth or do anything about it.

"A year ago, we took a place at the shore for the summer. I stayed there with the children, and my husband came out every weekend, like all the other men. But while the others were having a good time, he always seemed depressed. He never did anything all weekend but sit apart from us and stare out at the ocean. He wouldn't talk to anyone, not even old friends. Once or twice he said, 'Nobody understands my problems,' but that was all. . . . In early September, when we were back in the city, he sat down with me in the living-room one evening after the children had gone to bed and said, without any preliminaries, 'Did it ever occur to you to wonder why I've been acting the way I have?' I said I had supposed his new position in the company was proving more than he could handle. He said, 'Didn't it ever occur to you I could be in love with another woman?' I just laughed. *'You?'* I said. 'Oh no! You must be kidding.' 'I'm not kidding at all,' he said, and I stopped laughing. I felt stunned. I thought, 'This can't be real. This happens to other people, not me.' Then he told me all about her, and it became too real. She was a night-club dancer, quite young, but already divorced and with a little girl. She was long-haired, hippie-looking, very free in her manner and in her way of life. He said they had a marvelous physical relationship, but that was only part of it; she really loved him, fussed over him, understood him. I listened very quietly and made no outcry, because I felt I deserved it. I knew how I had been behaving all along toward him, I knew I had never tried to do anything about it, hadn't even cared. So I told him I was glad for him. But I felt destroyed. It was as though the whole world had caved in under me.

"We didn't come to any conclusions that night, but we talked about it again and again for several weeks. I kept trying to get it through my head that our whole marriage could all collapse, just like that. Sometimes it made me feel I was losing my mind. But finally, one night, I faced up to it. I said, 'You and she and I are all miserable this way, and there's no sense in three of us being miserable. One's enough. Why don't you just get the hell out of here and go to her?' That's what he'd been waiting to hear. He shot out of the house without even stopping to take any clothing. That was the last night he and I ever spent under the same roof."

The kind of person who is guided by conscience and a strong sense of reponsibility to his mate and children does not easily or quickly cut the ties, particularly if the marriage was once very close. Much as one grieving for the dead disconnects himself bit by bit from the feelings that give pain, so the unfaithful person with a dead marriage usually has to disconnect himself from it step by step over a long period. Every minor quarrel, every silence, every mood of discontent enables him to care a little less, to feel less guilt about the act of violence he is thinking of committing upon the relationship. This process, however, is neither continuous nor consistent, and during the process the affair, too, suffers. When things are at a standstill, the lovers are gloomy and irascible; when the marriage seems to have deteriorated a little further, they are cheerful and loving toward each other. They are unduly optimistic over trifles, and just as unduly pessimistic over other trifles; they easily feel alarmed or dejected, and on the one hand cannot help feeling angry with each other for delaying, on the other for urging greater speed.

But generally the standstills are only external; internally, changes are taking place in both the marriage and the affair. With perspective, one can see that in most such situations the marriage steadily declines, the affair steadily gains, but the lovers, in the midst of the daily and weekly vacillations, are hard put to recognize this and often feel that the moment of decisive action will never come. They may even judge the situation hopeless at a time when they are nearer than ever to the breakthrough. A divorcee in her early thirties speaks:

—"After two years, I feel as though I'm his real wife. I'm the one he talks to about everything, the one he asks for understanding and help in his work, the one he shares everything with. We're closer than ever. Even the physical side of things is better than ever, and that's saying a lot. Yet time and again I feel like giving up, and I start making plans to move away from here, back to my home town, because he doesn't seem to be getting any nearer to making a break with his wife. He looks so *tortured* when we talk about it. He feels sick at the thought of leaving his children behind, he thinks his wife would try to ruin him financially, he's afraid she might even attempt suicide. But he also says he can't work or eat or sleep without me. So I stay. . . . But what the future will bring I no longer try to imagine. I have no hopes left, and hardly even any dreams. Maybe I'm neurotic to remain stuck in such a relationship—or maybe *he's* neurotic to be so unable to do anything about it."

But her assessment of the situation was quite wrong: A month after she made this statement, her lover and his wife began to discuss the possibility of divorce, and three months later they were separated.

The breakthrough is often triggered by some trifling incident which gives the individual a flash of insight, a clear vision of his marital relationship, as contrasted with his affair, that frees him from conflict and allows him to use his blocked energies to achieve his goal. It is rarely a major incident, but often it is a particularly revealing one. A man overhears his wife talking on the phone about vacation plans as though he does not exist or has nothing to say about it; the contrast with his mistress is so clear that at last he is able to act decisively about the situation. A woman unable to choose between her husband and her lover tries to get the former to go into marriage counseling with her but he refuses, saying that there is no point to his going, since none of their marital troubles are of his making; she hesitates no longer to start pressing for divorce.

Sometimes, of course, the first talk of divorce comes from the deceived spouse—but even so, it is usually because the unfaithful one, having made a decision, has been behaving in such a way as to bring this about. Whichever one first mentions the matter, the discussions often, though not always, include the revelation of the love affair. People who are generally conscience-directed are deeply uncomfortable with secrets and half-truths, and even in an embattled marriage they prefer to be open; they feel relieved when they can finally tell the truth. And if the marriage had once been very close, there is still a powerful wish to be understood and forgiven by the spouse, and allowed freedom to seek happiness.

Sometimes, as we have seen, the deceived spouse does prove to be understanding and accepting, freeing the unfaithful one almost at once. But even when the deceived spouse is furious and vindictive, the revelation of the love affair may occasionally bring about immediate separation. Far more often, however, it produces a frantic last-ditch effort to hold on. Women may weep, plead their helplessness, beg for time; men may rage, lapse into frozen silence, state their absolute refusal to let go. Deceived spouses of either sex may profess great love, blame themselves for their own shortcomings, demand that the errant mate try therapy before divorce, offer to try it themselves, develop unusually strong sexual desires, play upon the unfaithful mate's guilt feelings. Often these tactics delay matters and sometimes even wreck the affair, but more often, if the marriage had become only marginally satisfactory, the victory of the affair of fulfillment is only a matter of time.

And all these discomforts seem worth it, for now the unfaithful person no longer dislikes himself. Up to this point, he has been disloyal to each love; now he is at last loyal to the new one. Up to now, he has been a deceiver; now he is a truth-teller. He feels sorry, sad, and guilty for inflicting pain—but he no longer detests himself for behaving in ways that are repugnant to his basic values. A host of practical problems still lie ahead, but he feels confident that he can handle them, for once again he has integrity; the greatest of his problems is solved.

NEAL GORHAM AND MARY BUCHANAN

After Mary's short-lived effort to renounce Neal, he and she enjoyed a few idyllic weeks during which each luxuriated in their love for each other and all but ignored its import. But soon enough, both became painfully aware of their own impatience and exasperation at being tied to their spouses, and of the disloyalty and deceitfulness required. To Mary, Cal seemed more lumpish and petulant than before, and to Neal, Laurie seemed more quarrelsome, belittling, and cold than he had ever noticed. The lovers, in an effort to reduce their feelings of guilt, talked to each other at great length about their mates and their marital problems, harping upon their complaints and remarking time and again how totally different their own relationship was from either of their marriages. After these sessions, each felt strengthened to say and do scores of little things at home that only touched off new quarrels and made for new grievances; but each felt gratified at every new grievance and more justified in thinking about divorce.

Over this stony path each drew closer to the goal. Mary did so faster than Neal: By April, three months after they had met, she was ready to act, while he, as we saw from the diary entry for April 1st, had not been able to make an emotional breakthrough and was mired in feelings of hopelessness and defeat. The situation was so painful that although he had never been more than a moderate user of alcohol he began to numb himself with drink. *Had too much again, night before last. Why? To obtain relief? Or to convey my misery to Laurie, hoping for some unexpected understanding? Or to provoke a fight so severe that she would ask me to move out? Don't really know—but it did none of these. It simply made things worse. Laurie looked pained when I went to the bar after the children were in bed. By 10:30, three or four drinks later, she suggested that we go to bed early. And I, drunk and foolish, gladly went, thinking perhaps she suddenly desired me. Into bed in minutes; pulled her close, felt her stiffen in surprise. She asked if I had forgotten that I'd said there wouldn't be any more love-making until she wanted it. Bounded out of bed, cursing; pulled on bathrobe, went down to the library, got even drunker, watched idiotic old movies on TV until 2:30 A.M. She never came after me, nor did we speak of it in the morning. Was hung over, exhausted, wretched in body and spirit, almost unable to go to the office, where I have fallen far behind in my work. Recovered somewhat by mid-afternoon. Felt grimly determined to fight my way through; had my secretary phone Laurie to say I was tied up, would be working late and staying at the Yale Club. Spent evening with Mary at the Howard Johnson Motel. Told her I needed her desperately, realized I had to get out of the marriage before I was damaged, unmanned, or made into a lush. Added that it was clear enough what I wanted most in life at this point—to be married to her. At the time, she was lying on my chest, looking down in the semi-darkness at me; as I said all these things, her warm, salty, happy tears began to fall onto my face. Said I'd better call the front desk and complain that it was leaky in my room; she dissolved into a fit of giggles.*

Mary: "Neal seemed quite clear and resolute about it that wonderful night, and I believed the path ahead lay straight and open. But then, dear God, the awakening! For two whole months he agonized, changed his mind back and forth, said he could and he couldn't. He'd want to talk to me about it all, I'd listen and discuss it with him, and he'd slowly come around to saying he knew what he had to do, and even though it would be grisly and dreadful, the sooner he did it the better. But the next time we'd talk, he'd be ashamed or defensive and say he had been thinking about Robin and Billy and what it would do to them. Or maybe he'd realized he ought not spring all this suddenly on Laurie, but ease into it gradually. Or else he thought that through marriage counseling she'd see it was hopeless, and *she'd* make the break instead of his having to do it. For a while, I was patient and logical, but then I began to feel depressed and weepy, and sometimes I got good and mad. Finally I got so fed up that I said, 'Oh, Christ, Neal, cut it out! You've been having a nice little affair and enjoying it, and you never meant it to be more than that. Don't bother lying to yourself about it anymore—or to me.' I was a real bitch that time—but I was sick of it all, and I felt lost and betrayed. At times like that, we both drank a lot, and when we were good and stoned we'd go to bed and fuck —I mean just that—we wouldn't make love, we'd *fuck*. Once or twice, after that happened, I had a crying jag. I thought I might have to call the affair quits; I didn't think I could take it much longer."

Neal also behaved in impulsive and erratic ways. Once, at lunchtime, he spent an hour sitting alone in the Fifth Avenue Presbyterian Church, hoping in vain for some kind of enlightenment, although he had been an agnostic since his late teens. Another time, he made an appointment with his former psychotherapist, cancelled it, made another, and cancelled that one too. He met his close friend, Everett Gamble, for lunch, told him the whole story without identifying Mary, and asked his advice, but rebutted every one of Gamble's sensible suggestions and almost lost his temper several times.

He and Laurie, for the first time in thirteen years, began to quarrel in front of others. They disagreed strenuously with each other in company about Vietnam, New Left politics, a current novel, the Darien school system—always in bitter tones thinly candy-coated with "dears" and "darlings." At home they were frostily and distantly proper with each other, their conversation ever more impersonal and perfunctory, their silences longer and more deliberate. But when, occasionally, they did have an open quarrel, it was savage and unrelenting, and usually ended without resolution.

One such quarrel began in a restaurant, on a night in late June when they had theater tickets and were dining in town. They resumed it during the intermission, in a bar next to the theater, and never went back for the second act because Neal, suddenly overcome with fury at Laurie's reiteration of all her old complaints, handed her the parking check, told her he was staying in town, and walked away. By II P.M., quite drunk, he phoned Mary from a motel room.

Mary: "We were in bed, reading. I answered the phone and nearly dropped it when I heard Neal's voice. He said, 'I just walked out on Laurie. I'm at the Howard Johnson Motel, room six-twelve, and I need you.' Cal was pretending to read, in the next bed, but he was all ears, though he couldn't hear Neal's voice. I said, 'It's very difficult. . . . You're tearing the seam.' Neal said, 'So let it tear.' I hung up and said to Cal, "I have to do something. I'm going out for a while.' If ever Cal was going to play the man, that was the time for it. He should have said, 'Like hell you are,' or 'Over my dead body,' but all he said was, 'All right.' And he turned off his bed light and pretended to go to sleep. I got dressed and turned back at the door and said, 'Cal, I may not even be back tonight,' and he said, 'Do what you have to do.' Who the hell was he trying to be—Jesus Christ Himself?

"So I hurried off to Neal, and found him drunk and maudlin and very sorry for himself. I asked him to tell me just what had happened, and I very slowly got it through my head that he hadn't *left* Laurie, he'd merely had a god-awful fight with her and walked out on her. He was so drunk and so absorbed with himself that it hadn't even occurred to him what he had just made me do. I flew into an absolute rage. I screamed at him, 'You goddam sonofabitch, do you know what the scene was on the other end of the wire? Do

you realize that now Cal knows and *you* made me spill it to him
—while you, you bastard, you pisswilly, you haven't even done it
yet?' We went round and round for a while until I slapped him, and
he slapped me back so hard that I fell down. He picked me up, and
then he slumped down on the foot of the bed, with his head in his
hands, and said he had been a selfish, thoughtless, self-pitying ass.
And then he fell back on the bed and passed right out. I was still
so mad that I slammed out, leaving the lights on, and went home.
It was nearly two o'clock. The bedroom door was closed and the
lights were out, so I went into the second bedroom—Freddy had
already left for the summer, to be a camp counselor—and I went
to bed in there. But as mad as I was at Neal, I was also oddly pleased
about what had happened, because now the fat was in the fire and
I felt sure that Neal would have to get off his duff and make the
break with Laurie. I actually fell asleep in a little while and slept
soundly.

"In the morning, as soon as I opened the bedroom door, Cal
came out of the other bedroom half-dressed, his face the color of
skimmed milk. 'All right,' he said, and his voice was all shaky, 'I
have to know. Where did you go?' I took the leap. I said, 'I saw a
man.' Just four words, but I felt a tremendous relief when I said it,
and I didn't care what hell there'd be to pay. I *was* brought up a
Catholic, and still am one, more or less. Cal just said, 'Okay,' and
went back in the bedroom to finish dressing. When I came out of
the bathroom a few minutes later, he said, 'Have you been having
an affair?' and all I said was, 'Yes, I have.' He didn't say a word but
went off into the kitchen this time and got himself some breakfast.
Then he came into the bedroom, where I was getting dressed, and
asked, 'Are you going to continue it?' and I said, 'I think so, but I
don't know.' He thought for a moment and then said, 'I guess I can
live with it, but I don't want to know anything about it.' Christ! the
let-down I felt! Here I'd thought I'd taken the big step, and was
about to be free of him, but I was still locked in. He left, and I went
in the kitchen and poured a cup of coffee, at which point I heard
him coming back in. He came to the kitchen door and said, 'No,
I can't take it, I absolutely can't take it. I'm going to leave you. I
want a divorce.' I said, 'I don't blame you.' He said he'd come pick
up some clothes after work, and asked if I'd be coming to the office.

I said I would, a little later, and he said okay, and left. By this point, with all the ups and downs, it all seemed completely unreal. I was totally numb."

Neal called a few minutes later, badly hung over, deeply re- morseful, and hideously ashamed. When he heard what had hap- pened, he soberly told her not to worry; he would go home that evening and talk it all out with Laurie, and put an end to all the uncertainties. *Which resolve lasted until 11 A.M., when Laurie phoned, begged me to forgive her, and burst into tears. She said many things: she had been dreadful last night but it was just before her period; she realized she had been difficult recently, but wanted to be forgiven and make a fresh start; finally, she had started mari- nating a shish kebab, and would I please come home for dinner? Told her I'd be there. Stared at the skyline for an hour, juggling my life, and then wrote that infamous note to Mary, the very thought of which fills me with shame. I abdicated, I ran out on her, pleading the pull of old loyalty and the children—and even tried to sound noble about it. Some indication of how distraught I was: I failed to make a copy for this diary, forgetting my usual narcissism in my disgust with self.*

Mary: "I tore it up, but I remember it perfectly. He said he loved me more than he had ever loved anyone, but he realized he wasn't able to leave Laurie and the children at this point, and might never be. And since going on this way was excruciatingly painful for both of us, he was doing the most decent thing he had done in half a year—he was giving me up. Oh, I tell you it was a *flaky* goddam letter, a stinking cop-out. My man had a real Achilles heel. Had one?—he *was* one! 'You lousy rat,' I thought, 'you rotten bastard, it's one thing to be madly in love when the lady is married and you're safe, but quite another thing when she's available— especially if you made her that way.' I tore up the letter and I didn't even answer it. I just thought, 'Well, I'm starting all over, and I suppose I'll survive.' "

But she didn't have to start all over; Neal called her a day later to give her important news and to revoke his abdication. *Shish kebab flavored with rue, salt tears, sweet love remember'd. After Robin and Billy were asleep we talked—earnestly, fair-mindedly, intently—trying to sort it all out (but I always holding back the quintessential fact of Mary). No luck. Exhausted, shaking from weariness, we both finally took sleeping pills, agreeing to talk more the next night. All through that first evening of talk, felt the simultaneous existence of both wishes—the wish to succeed in repairing it, the wish to fail and be set free. The second night we seemed unable to agree about anything, yet were calm and resigned. Finally, I hesitantly said: "Since it is like this, why don't we let go of each other peacefully and affectionately?" She (looking at me with sudden non-sequitur intuition): "Neal, are you having an affair with someone?" I (caught short and unable to lie): "Yes, since January." She (with instant divination): "With Mary Buchanan!" I: "Yes, with Mary. How do you know that?" She (looking like the Madonna in Michelangelo's* Pietà): *"Oh, you poor man—you must feel so guilty." And she gazed upon me with such kindness and pity that I was helpless. Brilliant of her. Total martyrdom was the one defense I could not breach, the one attack against which I was defenseless. She, the very soul of kindness, suffering, loving, understanding, wearing a* mater dolorosa *face, bade me tell her all about it—what it meant to me, what I wanted from it, how I had been tormented by it. I, voice aquiver and hands trembling, played her game, responding as she wanted me to in order to earn my freedom, getting my own way through self-abasement, washing myself clean in the martyr's tears—when I should have told her plainly and honestly that she had been a lousy wife for years and that it was her shortcomings that made me want another and better woman.*

Mary: "When he called with all this news, I was still so mad that the things he was telling me didn't sink in at once. But he was so contrite about that letter, and so proud and relieved that he had finally told Laurie about us, that eventually I became absolutely euphoric. We met for dinner, celebrated our great leap forward, and then, because Cal had already taken most of his clothes away, we went back to the apartment. And then it was just like a script for a bad movie: We were undressing at ten or ten-thirty when the key turned in the front door. It was Cal; I guess he wanted to talk to me. Neal rushed into the bathroom to hide, but Cal came into the bedroom and saw his clothes on the chair. He went over and tried the bathroom door. The lock never did work right; it opened, and there was Neal, caught dead to rights and looking ridiculous in his shorts. Cal said, 'You s.o.b. I should have known it was you.' Neal was wonderful—he stood up straight and said, 'Cal, if it would make you feel any better, go ahead and hit me. I won't hit back. But first I want you to know one thing—I *love* Mary and I want to marry her.' Cal turned away and looked at me. Then he said to Neal, '*This* is the woman you love? This bitch? This sweet loving creature with bile instead of blood, with a block of ice where her heart should be? This ball-breaker, this man-eater, this frigid cunt who can't screw her own husband unless she's stinking drunk? I pity you.' I didn't know he had it in him to talk like that. Then he left, slamming the door as if to break the walls down. We sat there shaking. We filled two tall glasses with Scotch, and tried to wash away our humiliation. Both of us were almost glad for Cal that he had let loose like that, but it left us so turned off that we never even made love that night—the first night we were in the clear."

Neal took a room on a monthly basis at the Yale Club and, on his lawyer's advice, rarely stayed overnight at Mary's, though he and she were together most evenings. The other one or two evenings and nearly every Sunday afternoon, he went to Darien to visit the children, usually returning on the 8:50 but occasionally sleeping over on the library sofa; Robin wept inconsolably the first time she saw it made up for him. For the first month or so, Laurie always stayed around when he was with the children and treated him with maddening gentleness; as a result, he found himself drinking far too much during and after these visits. Eventually he went to see his psychotherapist a few times, and was able to feel angry about Laurie's punitive use of kindness and her carefully exhibited suffering. He got back onto a fighting basis with her, which was healthier for them both, and thereafter insisted on taking the children out or having her go out while he was visiting them.

The divorce negotiations dragged on for half a year, with Laurie becoming tough-minded and almost vindictive in her demands. Eventually, however, they reached an agreement and in January, 1967, she flew to Mexico for an overnight divorce. The hostility between them decreased thereafter, and a year later each of them could say they had become "friends."

Cal, on the other hand, had no stomach for anger or the combative side of divorce proceedings. A week after his brief outburst at Mary, he met her for a drink and asked to be forgiven for his show of anger; he could not live comfortably with the thought of bad blood between them. She begged him, in return, to forgive her for the hurt she had caused him. They assured each other that each was a decent and good person but that they had been ill-matched as husband and wife, and ended by agreeing to be friends and striking a quick bargain: Mary kept the apartment, half the furniture, and several thousand dollars she had brought with her into the marriage. "I have to be nice to you," Cal concluded with heavy-handed bonhomie, "I couldn't get along without you as my advertising manager." Mary, knowing it to be more truth than jest, said that the only way he could get rid of her would be to fire her. Cal felt so relieved that he even asked if she and Neal would have a drink with him some evening. Neal detested the idea, but did it for Mary's sake and found it less uncomfortable than he had expected. He realized that Cal had an immense need to feel accepted and befriended, rather than excluded, even by the two who had deceived him.

Neal's diary, after late July, consists only of half a dozen scattered brief entries, the need for it apparently having subsided once the affair was out in the open and his inner conflicts resolved. Mary summarizes their relationship from July until the following April. "We were together every evening and all weekend except for the time he spent in Darien. We became very domestic and comfortable with each other. It was actually a much happier and more contented time than any we had known, even though there weren't those moments of incredible excitement. We had some ups and downs, though: When things were going badly in Darien, he would be grouchy, and I myself have a nasty bit of Irish temper now and then. But mostly it was something like a prolonged honeymoon. We loved being together all the time, and the fact that we weren't married and he had to leave at night only added a little spice to it, for the time being.

"But he got awfully edgy, once we were both free. Cal and I were divorced in September, he and Laurie in January—and then he began to stall. By that time, he had moved everything over from the Yale Club and we were living just like a married couple, but he said there was no need to be in a hurry to make it legal. We were two adults, nobody minded in the big city, and he still felt too newly divorced to be tied down again. I let it go for a while, and then I blew my stack. I was a real wildcat. We had several Donnybrooks about it—once he even went to the Club and slept overnight there —but then he talked to his shrink some more, and in April we got married—with a minister and all. The Gambles were there, and Neal's folks flew up from Florida, and my mother came in from Chicago. In the pictures Everett Gamble took, I look better and happier than I ever did in my life. You'd never know, looking at them, what we had gone through to reach that point."

chapter 7: **AFTERMATH**

i transition

Societies cushion the impact of transitions in the life of the individual by providing him with standardized or ritualized ways to behave. People know, in general, what to expect, how to feel, and how to act at a graduation, leave-taking, wedding, funeral—or at the end of a love affair. But not an extra-marital love affair. For since society does not accept the latter, it has developed no code of expected and appropriate behavior for the situation. One might suppose that, without such a code, people would be inclined to feel and to act much as unmarried lovers do at the end of a love affair, but this is far from true, for there is a very great difference. Since the newly ended extra-marital affair had been kept wholly or largely secret from society, the lovers are under no social obligation to show grief at its ending, if they feel none. Conversely, however, if they do feel grief, the secrecy of the affair isolates them and deprives them of the sympathy and emotional support they need.

The casual extra-marital affair, as we have already seen, generally decays almost painlessly, and the final goodbye (if there is anything definitive enough to be regarded as one) need not be followed by a period of simulated unhappiness. The lovers are not concerned that anyone will think them callous, but can obey their real feelings, accepting the ending with a philosophic shrug and a brief spell of mild regret or equally mild relief. A woman who has had dozens of casual affairs puts it this way:

—"Most of the time I'm the one who wants out, so usually I'm relieved to be free of something that's run its course. But even when the end leaves me a little blue and sorry for myself, the feeling doesn't last. Anyway, I know something else will always come along, sooner or later."

Even a long-term relationship, if it has little emotional content or involvement, may end with virtually no sense of loss and no display of grief. Had it been an affair between two unmarried people, each would very likely have felt obliged to evince at least some regret or suffering to his friends and perhaps even to himself, but in the case of a wholly secret extra-marital affair the lovers are free to omit the show of something they do not feel. The research physicist who, for a year and a half, had spent every Thursday night and every Sunday afternoon with a waitress he could hardly talk to, but with whom he had an excellent physical relationship, describes the ending of the affair and his own reaction:

—"We had one of our best evenings ever—it was really marvelous—and afterwards, as we lay there having a cigarette and feeling very affectionate, she said she had something to tell me. She was going to get married next week, and this was the last time for us. Just like that. . . . Well, maybe she was a little uncomfortable, but nothing more, because she knew I didn't love her. I was surprised as could be—I had no idea she was serious about someone —and for a moment I felt put down at being dumped. But also I felt relieved, because I too had been thinking it was time to get out of this thing. On my way home that night, all I felt was, 'Well, that's over, but it was good for me while it lasted.' And although we had spent so much time together for so long, I never missed her for a minute, never once felt like calling her or felt any emptiness or nostalgia. I didn't even miss her physically, and by the time I might have, I was into a new relationship. I wouldn't have believed all this possible. It sounds almost subhuman. Yet I know I have the capacity for real feeling, so it didn't worry me. And since I was the only one who knew about the whole thing, except for one old friend, I didn't care."

Many would label such a reaction abnormal or even psychopathic. How could two people use the gestures of love toward each other for so long and yet have no feeling of distress after the parting? But such a judgment assumes that sex and love always are, or should be, conjoined—a puritan-bourgeois assumption that most of our European ancestors would not have shared, and most of the peoples of the world would have found incomprehensible. In our own society, people who can and do enjoy sex with little or no emotional involvement are not necessarily abnormal or psychopathic; they are merely social deviants, following the underground tradition—and because of the isolation of the unfaithful, they are freer than single people to be honest with themselves about these loveless relationships and their neutral, emotionless aftermath.

With the somewhat more involved affair—the durable, but limited-involvement kind that is not competitive with marriage, but supplemental to it—there is likely to be more of an emotional reaction to the end of the relationship. But it is often a specialized feeling—not the grief and deprivation we ordinarily think of as the result of losing love, but a sense of the loss of youth or of one's flattering self-image. A forty-six-year-old man explains:

—"There was nothing wrong with my marriage, but after twenty years I was bored. I had laid the same woman a couple of thousand times, I'd heard every word she had to say. This girl, who works for one of my clients, was something new and different, something exciting. She made me feel completely awake again and aware of everything. I wasn't in love with her, but I enjoyed the whole feeling of being in such a relationship. It lasted five months. Then my wife found out by going through my pockets, and blew sky-high. The yelling and screaming!—I never saw her like that in all those years. She made me move out, filed suit, and wouldn't even let me see the children. It took a couple weeks for all this to sink in, but finally it did. I was losing everything—my family, my house, my social life, my swimming pool, my savings. It was just too much. I called her and said I had come to my senses. Learned my lesson. Seen the light. Given up the other woman. I crawled, and she took me back. But it wasn't easy, afterwards. I missed the phone calls, the excitement of sneaking off for a secret get-together, the romantic moods, the sex. I missed feeling like a man having a love affair. I felt as if it was all over for me."

Other affairs of this genre often break up because of a conflict of interest between the lovers, and when this happens, relief and grief are intermingled in each lover—but not necessarily in the same proportions. Where one had been more exploitive, he or she is likely to be the more relieved, while the more exploited and involved partner is the one more grieved. A Chicago socialite, generalizing on her reactions to the end of her several affairs, illustrates the point:

—"I've loved eight men besides my husband, and all eight were artists or writers—all of them struggling, all of them needing me for a while, and all of them terribly important to me. Almost all of my affairs ended when the men were ready to move on to New York or the Coast. I always felt lost and abandoned, but each man who left me told me I would be all right, and although I never believed it at the time, after a few weeks I always *was* all right. The hardest part of it, actually, was that I had to bear it almost alone —I have only one woman friend to turn to, and most of the time when I was feeling awful I had to hold the tears back and go about my business. As for the men, they always seemed relieved. Some of them said they felt deeply unhappy at leaving me, but who can tell about such statements? They're such a simple way to be generous."

As one would expect, it is the most deeply involved and emotionally powerful extra-marital affair, wrecked by conflict with the marriage, that has the most distressing aftermath. The symptoms and sufferings of the broken-hearted lover are familiar to us all, but those of the extra-marital lover who had cared very deeply are particularly complex and vexing. Such a person cannot show his sorrows or even speak freely to friends to relieve his suffering. And while the decision to give up the affair in favor of the marriage relieves some part of the conflict, it does not end the yearning, the hunger, the sense of loss. These may be excruciating for a long while, and damaging to the very relationship for which the unfaithful person gave up the affair. Resentment and the feeling of self-sacrifice may create a chronic discontent with one's lot and one's mate, expressed in complaints, criticisms, or sexual coldness. One woman, having given up her lover, insisted that her husband woo her carefully and patiently every time he wanted intercourse, and even then often found fault with his performance. One man, unable to use loving words when in bed with his wife after giving up an affair, began to use words she considered filthy. Other people suffer from depression and its various somatic expressions. Some dull their pain with alcohol or drugs; others have to turn to psychotherapy, even though they may have been able to avoid it during the conflict period itself. But this is not surprising: The secrecy of their suffering greatly exacerbates it, and the opportunity to talk to someone about it becomes more precious than ever.

Without some such source of relief, and without some way of finding new satisfaction in the marriage, such persons are long subject to attacks of regret and yearning during which, breaking their promises to themselves, they telephone their ex-lovers or write them notes, telling of their wretchedness and asking for pity and some continued contact. Often they add self-insult to the injury they have sustained, berating themselves in such phone calls or letters for having lacked the courage, steadfastness, or personal worth to have won the love they now have lost.

Even if this masochistic appeal to the ex-lover succeeds, it is likely to lead only to a new failure. For in the attempted revival of their love, the conflicts are almost sure to be as strong as ever, but the fabric of love more frail. The reunions are tense, explosive, and disillusioning. The lovers meet only to break apart, break apart only to meet again, finding joy in neither. Peace comes only when one or both partners make a genuine effort to find real satisfaction, not merely a sense of rectitude, within the old marriage. There are many variations on this kind of finale to the affair, but one example will serve; a divorcee, a pale and somewhat ethereal blonde of thirty, describes the multiple endings of her affair with a married physician:

—"I don't know how many farewells we had—I lost count. He

was the one who felt he had to break off, but he could never stay away when I phoned him, and I couldn't keep myself from phoning. After many of these reconciliations and break-ups, we agreed to swear off, and he came to my place one night for what was to be a hands-off farewell. Instead, he got drunk and literally ripped my clothes off. Then, looking at me as I stood there in tatters, he put his head in his hands and wept like a child. And naturally we went to bed and forgot the farewell. But in the morning he phoned from his office in a fury and accused me of rigging the whole thing to trap him again. I got mad and said that people who want to say goodbye don't go about it the way he did, and that obviously he didn't really want to. I hung up on him, so he wrote me a poison-pen letter, telling me how I'd castrated my ex-husband and my little boy, and saying *he* wasn't going to have it happen to him. I sent back a scorching reply, and that was the end of that.

"Only it wasn't, because a month later I called him, in a weak moment, and we ended up going out of town together for one last crazy fling. After one day, he was so much in love with me again that we were necking in restaurants, like a couple of kids. But then, of course, he got alarmed and turned nasty, drank too much, and got so angry at me that he crushed a drinking glass in his hand and cut himself—and cursed me, saying it was my fault. I packed my bag without saying a word, while he stormed around the room giving me hell, and left for home without him. The end? No, not the end. A month later he phoned and begged me to have dinner with him, and was so sweet and remorseful and warm that I couldn't resist. But that wound up in a hideous fight, too. . . . Three months later he told me on the phone that he had rebuilt his marriage to the point where he could see me in a new light—loving but platonic. He came to my place, and we kissed a few times, and talked for hours about our affair as a beautiful memory. We were both glad that we had loved each other, and glad that his marriage hadn't been destroyed by it, because he would have been impossibly guilt-ridden. But we were also glad it was all far behind us, because we couldn't live with it any more."

ii never again

Some people, after experiencing extra-marital love, give it up and mean to be faithful from then on. One out of every five unfaithful men and one out of every three unfaithful women I interviewed had had only one affair, and most of these people did not intend to have others. In addition, nearly as many more of each sex revert to fidelity after having had a number of affairs. Some of my interviewees resumed fidelity (in the same, or in a later, marriage) after having had dozens of outside liaisons, and one man who estimates that he had over a hundred and fifty during the fifteen years of his first marriage has had none during the eight years of his second. Still others decide in favor of renewed fidelity only to relapse after a while, try fidelity again, and relapse yet again, repeating the cycle many times during their lives.

Those whose return to fidelity is short-lived have most often done so under pressure exerted from outside. Some have been discouraged by the difficulties and costs of maintaining an affair, or alarmed by the prospect of scandal or marital conflict, or coerced by their mates. The mood of these people, being based on practical considerations and not on internalized values or a revitalized marriage, ranges from the gently stoical to the fiercely embittered. The former say things like this:

—"It was fun for a while, but finally I found it more trouble —and more expensive—than it was worth. I'd proved my point, anyway. So I quit."

—"After that last close call, I decided the whole thing was too risky. I did the sensible thing and gave it all up. I miss it, but I breathe easier."

But those who have been forced back into the fold by their mates often speak with a sharper, harsher tongue, like that of the man who said that he "crawled" in order to be taken back by his wife but felt afterwards "as if it was all over for me," or that of the young district attorney who, after a confrontation by one of his girl friends and his wife, concluded that "the heat was on—I had to go straight"—and struck a truce with his wife. Not surprisingly, these are the people who are relatively likely to be unfaithful again at some time in the future—when the "heat" is off, or their dissatisfactions become intolerable, or some combination of opportunity and temptation proves too much for their resolve.

It is quite otherwise with those who return to fidelity primarily for internal reasons—because conscience and guilt finally win out, or because the changes the affair produced in the unfaithful person enable him to work out certain problems in his relationship with his mate, or because he recognizes that his marriage is more precious than it had seemed. These people, upon giving up their affairs, speak very differently from the previous group:

—"It was the first secret I'd had from my wife in eighteen years. It was the first thing I'd ever done that would have really hurt her, if she'd known of it. I couldn't seem to stay away from that girl —but I couldn't take the guilt, either. If my wife was ten minutes late coming home, I'd be in a sweat, wondering if she'd found out and done something awful, like trying to kill herself. So I gave it up, and made up my mind to be contented with her and not even think about anyone else."

—"I still have no idea why I drifted into that affair—I love my husband, and always have. I must have needed something, but what? Excitement? Proof that I wasn't getting old and unattractive? A stronger, more successful man? Well, I had all that in the affair —and it nearly destroyed me. I couldn't stand wanting both men, hurting two good marriages, being selfish and deceitful. I could even see it affecting my husband's emotional balance, though he didn't know what was happening. I broke clean, but I was depressed for months afterwards. Even now, three years later, I wish I didn't have it forever on my conscience."

Whether the decision to be faithful again is motivated primarily by convenience or primarily by conscience, and whether it comes after one affair or many, the most important questions to ask are what the marriage is like afterwards and how fidelity feels to the one who has returned to the fold. For if the marriage has been badly damaged, or if renewed fidelity proves galling, he is likely either to become unfaithful again in the future or to break away from the marriage altogether. But if neither of these is the case, he may never feel compelled to do either thing.

The firmest hold on renewed fidelity would, of course, be obtained by those who found their marriages actually improved. But can this ever really be the outcome of infidelity? An older generation of experts did not think so. The late Dr. Abraham Stone, a distinguished pioneer in family planning and marriage counseling, categorically stated in a national magazine in 1954, "From my quarter century of counseling on marital problems, I cannot recall a single case where infidelity has strengthened the marital bond." Perhaps he, like many others with a similar view, came to this conclusion because he saw only troubled clients; perhaps infidelity was more deeply disturbing to many people a generation or so ago than it is today.

Whatever the case, a number of recent and contemporary investigators claim to see evidence of another sort. Kinsey, in his volume on the American female, reports that sometimes there is "an actual improvement of the marital relationship following extramarital experience," and cites three studies other than his own that have indicated the same thing. Many psychotherapists and marriage counselors to whom I spoke said, in guarded terms, that stagnant marriages are sometimes stirred into life by the sharp new awareness the unfaithful person has gained of his or her needs, which leads him to make subtle new demands of his spouse and to respond positively when the other meets them. In other cases, when an affair comes out into the open, the marital partners may decide to repair and reconstruct their relationship together; some couples try it on their own, others with professional help, but in either case, they might never have done so without the stimulus of the affair.

And sometimes the improvement comes about much more simply: The outside experience, a concrete test of one's fantasy, may yield a new and realistic appreciation of one's mate. Dr. Hyman Spotnitz and Lucy Freeman express the conservative view, in *The Wandering Husband*, that almost all infidelity is psychologically unhealthy, but add, "We can make no ironclad rules, for there are instances where it may have saved a marriage. It may have convinced a husband that the other woman, far from being more desirable, is much less attractive than his wife."

Among the people I sampled, a small minority of the unfaithful did claim to have better marital relationships as a result of their affairs. About one out of every ten interviewees said their first or some later affair had increased their sexual satisfaction within marriage; roughly the same number said it had brought them emotionally closer to their spouses; and one out of eight said it had strengthened the marriage by turning the partners back toward each other. (The questionnaire figures are similar but larger.) The improvement seems more likely to be minor, or peripheral, in those cases where the deceived spouse never finds out, more likely to be major and central where the affair has been made known and produced a searching re-evaluation of the whole marital interaction. An example of minor improvement:

—"I feel closer to my husband than ever. Not that anything has changed between us, but after so many years of marriage I had forgotten how important he is to me. The affair was like living through an accident or an operation—you see things clearly once again, you make a special effort afterwards to enjoy what you have."

And one of more substantial improvement:

—"My wife felt pretty shaky about us for a long while after she learned about it, but I think she has come to see me in a different light as a result of it—maybe because I saw myself in a different light. She even said one time, 'In a way, I'm almost proud of you,' as though she had discovered that I wasn't a boy, but a real man. . . . Interestingly enough, nowadays she has orgasm nearly all the time, although before the affair she rarely did. I wouldn't claim that we're completely happy now, but I would say that things are definitely better than before it all started."

The great majority of those who give up their affairs do not have so positive an outcome. Although most of them deny that the affair caused any major loss of sexual satisfaction or emotional rapport, they do seem, upon first resuming fidelity, to be keenly aware of the confinement and self-denial involved in it, and of the faults and shortcomings of their mates. This is particularly true of those whose return to fidelity has been forced upon them by threats or pressures, or by their fear of the consequences of disclosure. Yet even those who have given up infidelity out of guilt, loyalty, or love, often feel much the same, as witness this comment:

—"The guilt nearly wrecked me, and yet I never felt as alive as I did during the affair. Now I'm slumping back into the old familiar pattern and it oppresses me with its routine, its neutralness. I feel cut off from real feelings. My wife and I are active in the community, we both read a lot, we see friends, but—well—I just don't find life exciting any more."

This kind of discontent, however, is not so much the result of forsaking extra-marital experience as of returning to a marriage with shortcomings. Those who have such feelings on resuming fidelity had them beforehand, though they may have denied or repressed them—but after the affair they find it far harder to do so. Happily, the mind takes steps to protect itself, and for many of these people, especially the conscience-directed, the sharp awareness of discontent gradually grows dull, the marriage eventually coming to seem only marginally less satisfactory than it had before infidelity.

But for the rest the outcome is different. The feeling of constriction or deprivation does not fade but remains strong, and grows stronger with the passage of time. And for good reasons. Some of these people, who want and are capable of a single and faithful relationship, may have learned so much from their affairs about their own sexual, emotional, and intellectual needs that they see for the first time how badly matched they and their mates are. Others, having found the best answer to their emotional needs in undercover polygamy, feel frustrated and deprived without it.

In both cases, the effort to resume a life of fidelity is likely to fail. It may do so in either of two ways—divorce or the resumption of infidelity. Those who gave up their affairs primarily because of internal conflict are more likely to respond to severe discontent by eventually seeking divorce, in order to licitly pursue and possess what they had illicitly tasted. Over a third of my interviewees were eventually divorced as a direct result of their extra-marital experiences—not necessarily to marry an extra-marital partner, but to seek a marriage that more nearly comes up to their expectations.

In contrast, those who gave up their affairs primarily because of fear, inconvenience, threats, or penalties are more likely to steal cautiously back into the forbidden territory of infidelity. They, too, learned something about their marriages and themselves: They learned that their marriages are imperfect but about as good as they are likely to find, and that they can apparently best gratify their wants by remaining married and solacing themselves with extra-marital affairs.

---

iii a way of life

A majority of the men and a minority of the women who once experience extra-marital love make a way of life of it thereafter. The needs they satisfy in this fashion have a broad range, their extra-marital affairs constituting anything from self-indulgence to self-preservation; but from one extreme to the other, these converts to infidelity consider it a legitimate activity for themselves, and a good many of them neither hope nor expect to be faithful again until they are too old not to be. (Few of them, however, consider such conduct legitimate for most other people; the majority of the unfaithful uphold the norm of fidelity, while making exception for themselves.)

There are several distinguishable patterns of chronic infidelity which these people adopt, according to their emotional needs and the state of their marriages. Some people drift into a kind of undercover polygamy in the form of a series of casual and usually brief affairs. One may succeed another without interruption, or they may be intermittent and irregular, depending on the individual's appetite and freedom of movement.

For some, the unbroken series of casual affairs is merely a continuation of their premarital sexual behavior. The first infidelity worked no change of heart, for none was needed. Before marriage, an almost complete dissociation of sex from love made casual premarital affairs easy and guilt-free; after marriage, the same dissociation made casual extra-marital affairs just as easy and just as guilt-free. The travelling salesman who was proud of having "twenty-five to thirty other wives" on the road had been routinely and guiltlessly unfaithful to his fiancée before marriage, and felt no inclination to be faithful after:

—"I never stopped chiselling on her before we were married or after, and it never bothered me. Honest to God, I don't think I ever consciously dug into it to see what I should or shouldn't be doing. Of course, I knew I wasn't *supposed* to be doing it, but a conscience is one thing I'm afraid I don't have."

So strong a predilection to infidelity is, however, rare among middle-class men and almost non-existent among middle-class women. Most of those who fall into a pattern of chronic casual infidelity are at least briefly faithful at the beginning of marriage, and some are faithful for years. Yet their fidelity is fragile; the first exposure to extra-marital experience may shatter it completely. It is as though such people had been living a lie and denying their true natures; the illuminating experience seems to teach them that in reality they are easy-going hedonists, cheerfully and wholesomely amoral. Here is how they speak about their self-discovery:

—"Once I started, I realized how much it meant to me to chase different women and to succeed with them. I read once that men who do that are latent fags, but I don't feel that's my trouble. I feel I'm collecting wonderful experiences, doing all the beautiful things I can while I'm young enough."

—"When I was unfaithful to my husband the first time, I had to be 'in love.' But that's a mistake—it can wreck your marriage by making you think the other man is better for you. After a while I came to see that going to bed with someone other than my husband is no worse than sharing a good steak with someone other than him. It gives me pleasure, and that's all it has to do."

Others make such self-discoveries only in the course of trying to do without affairs after having had a number of them:

—"She forgave me when I promised to cut out all the nonsense, and I did for a year and a half. But by then I was ready to blow a gasket. I needed an adventure, the feel of some other skin, a shot in the arm. I realized I could never be a hundred per cent faithful again—but I could be faithful enough, by keeping things short and sweet. Now, whenever I get that urge, I go bar-cruising, find some agreeable girl, bang her in a motel—and goodbye. I get as much kick out of a one-night stand as I need—but when I need it, I don't hang back."

The combination of shallow extra-marital affairs and a relatively uninvolved but practical marriage can be quite stable. Many unfaithful people find this a satisfactory combination: They suffer no conflicts, feel nothing lacking, crave no closer relationship. They view the combination of workaday marriage and casual affairs as a liberation from outmoded inhibitions, a feasible solution to the conflict between the demands of society and those of the flesh.

The pattern can remain unchanged for many years, unless external forces disrupt it: The deceived spouse may find out; the couple may have to move to a community where casual affairs are difficult or impossible to arrange; increasing financial responsibilities may stand in the way. And sometimes internal forces cause the pattern to change: Some people, after years of chronic casual infidelity, develop new needs or emotional capabilities, and begin to seek a more involving and intimate kind of relationship. This was the case with Peggy Farrell.

PEGGY FARRELL

For over half a dozen years, a combination of an uninvolved marriage and an unbroken series of casual affairs had provided Peggy with a steady, and seemingly satisfactory, way of life. Then, Andy's admission that he had been unfaithful to her not only during his long stay in Brazil, but back home in Rochester before the trip as well as after it, broke the pattern: She, the chronically unfaithful wife, no longer felt secure in her marriage. But this was far from the only new factor affecting her. At the time of the disclosure, she had completed her B.A., was halfway toward finishing her social-work training, and could begin to envision herself as a human being of value, her self-esteem no longer resting solely on new sexual conquests. Perhaps, too, her counseling with a senior social worker gave her some significant insights that helped free her from compulsive promiscuity.

Thanks to these several influences, her affair with Peter, though it began like almost all her others, rapidly grew into a relationship of quite another order. "It started in a bar, when I saw him looking at me. He came over and asked if he could buy me a drink. I liked his looks, so I said yes. At first, it was all fun and banter on both sides. He told me that he and his wife, who is years and years older than he and something of a lush, had just had a hellish fight and she had gone off to New York for a week, which left him free to prowl. I told him I wasn't sure I liked prowlers, and anyway he looked more like a cop. He broke up, he howled, because he *was* one—a detective. But he's a real prowler, too; if he notched his gun for every woman he's laid, he wouldn't have much of a gun left. Yet I can understand him. He's terribly insecure about his own sexuality. As rugged as he is, and as many women as he's laid, he's always having to prove himself again, and I could sympathize with somebody who felt like that.

"Of course, I didn't know all this the first evening—we were playing games with each other, feeling each other out, finding out what things we had in common. Before the evening was over, he was swearing on his mother's grave that he was in love with me, but of course he was loaded at the time. To test him, I refused to tell him my last name or phone number. He followed me out when I was leaving, made a big point of copying down my license number, and then traced it. The next night, there I was in the living-room with Andy when the phone rang. I answered, and it was him. Yuk! I damn near gave it away. But I covered up at once by calling him 'Elaine,' and saying, 'Oh, that's awful, honey—okay, I'll get there fast as I can.' I told Andy that Elaine was running a fever and I was going to do a few things for her. He had never heard of any Elaine, but he had his nose glued to the boob tube and didn't even ask questions. I met Peter in a parking lot. He was cold sober, but still said he loved me. We made it in his car that same night, and were off on a big romance.

"We saw each other almost every single day after that. Either he'd meet me after my classes, or I'd tell Andy some story and run out for a while. We met in bars, we sat in the car in parking lots, we even went to Peter's house and made love on the sofa while his wife was upstairs, knocked out on booze and sleeping pills. It took me about three days to become infatuated with him, which is par for the course. But it went on from there, and after two or three months of seeing him all the time, it began to seem to me that my life wouldn't be anything without him and that I wanted him for my husband. It wasn't enough just to be in love with him. I wanted to be a part of him, I wanted to take care of him. As for him, he adored me, he'd do anything I asked him to do, he'd take wild chances at home or on duty just to talk to me.

"Finally, we agreed we'd both get divorces and get married. I hit Andy with the news a couple days after the time I told him that my boy friend said he couldn't have any more. We were divorced about half a year later, which is rather fast. I didn't get much alimony under our agreement, but I didn't want to drag things out, and I knew that in a few more months I'd be able to take a job as a social worker. Peter, on the other hand, couldn't seem to get going on his own divorce. Whenever he tried to talk about it, his wife got hysterical or stalled him off by playing sick, and he couldn't get up the nerve to simply walk out on her. She was much more in control than he. In fact, I often had the impression that she acted like a sickly mother, and he was the naughty boy who stops misbehaving when he sees what it does to her.

"It became a kind of running gun-fight—he'd pester her, she'd raise hell, he would storm out and meet me and stay out all hours or maybe even not go home until the next day. She kept threatening to tell his departmental chief, and finally he got so mad that he quit the force and took a plant security job, where it wouldn't matter. Every time he got ready to leave her she'd threaten suicide. Finally he did walk out and move in with me. And what did he do then, that lousy Mick? He got stinking drunk the next day, called her up and had a big tearful talk, thumped the hell out of me for having broken up his home, and went roaring back to Mama."

Peter shuttled back and forth for months, alternately leaving his wife to stay with Peggy, then abandoning her, usually in a rage, to go back home. Part of his anger, she came to think, was due to great insecurity on his part. He was absurdly jealous and always accused Peggy of being unfaithful to him, but he had no such problem at home, his wife being much older than Peggy and not very attractive. Eventually he did leave home and take a furnished room, although he stayed with Peggy much of the time. But a year after Peggy had her divorce, he still had taken no legal steps toward obtaining his own.

For a while Peggy was content, finding him an affable and devoted companion apart from his recurrent fits of jealousy—but not someone she could marry. For she now saw him as weak, immature, and selfish. "I enjoy his company immensely, and that's what keeps me in this relationship. That, and the fact that I'm a social worker and I like to help—and he needs it, let me tell you!" Someday, she adds, she hopes to find someone who could be much more to her than a companion and an overgrown child, someone to whom she would want to be faithful. And despite her previous history, she now believes that if she found the right man, she could be faithful. "I still think monogamy isn't natural, but it's what we're brought up to believe in, and so, in a way, it's what we want. Would you believe it, I've come back to some real square ideas about love and marriage? If I found the right man—he wouldn't have to be handsome or a sexual marvel, but he'd have to be strong, intelligent, and very warm—if I found one I could really belong to and who wanted to belong absolutely to me, I'd never let myself go back to the games I used to play."

That was half a year ago; since then Peggy has travelled still further in this new direction. At the moment, however, the road is lonely, and she is deeply unhappy. A recent letter from her, couched in language quite unlike her former breezy, coarse way of talking, reads in part as follows:

> Well, Peter is gone. We had a serious disagreement, and he went off to New York or wherever his wife had moved to. Living has a certain peacefulness it hadn't had for a long while—but the unutterable loneliness, the unbearable halfness of it! No, I don't miss him—but I do miss having *someone*. And there is no one. Where does one look, at my age, for intelligence, humor, and compassion? Not where I used to look. And I don't know where else to go instead. I believe I have grown immensely, I feel capable of a loving, loyal, dependable relationship—and yet I have not even dated in months! There *must* be someone. I can only wait and hope.

* * *

Some people, after their initiation into infidelity, fall into a pattern one might call serial bigamy: It consists of a very durable, but not particularly close, marriage, and a series of those relatively long-lasting but emotionally limited affairs I have called "supplemental." In this pattern, the unfaithful person does not roam freely in search of quick conquests but is content with one extra-marital relationship at a time, each lasting months or even years and considerably more developed than the casual affair.

These people are not grossly dissatisfied with their marriages. Sometimes they have a few complaints, sometimes many, but they are content to have their marriages continue, imperfect though they may be. Experimenting with infidelity, they discover fairly soon, perhaps even with the first experience, that the best mode, for them, is to have a reliable second love-relationship outside of marriage, which supplies whatever the marriage does not. The incomplete marriage and the affair together provide them with everything they want, without either relationship requiring more than they can give. A novelist, a man in his upper thirties, clearly articulates the compartmentalized and specialized nature of his relationships:

—"The first affair taught me why I'd been restless and unhappy for seven years. My marriage, I could see, was a going concern, a practical enterprise. Fine—that's worth keeping. But my first affair was a thing of high intensity, of maximum emotion. Fine—that's worth a hell of a lot, too. I recognized that my wife is a woman with many good traits, but simply not everything I need. The half dozen women I've had extra-marital affairs with all have their own good traits, but none of them has everything I need. No two people are wholly congruent, no two people completely fit each other. There are always parts of us that go ignored and frustrated unless they can be dealt with in a second relationship. I learned all this during my first affair. It committed me to a style of living, and when that affair began to break up, I knew I was going to have to seek something else of the same kind. But I also knew I needed the solid underpinning of marriage and home life."

Persons of this type seem to treat their mates and extra-marital partners somewhat like useful objects, not parts of themselves. This neither troubles them nor strikes them as wrong; they often acknowledge their own selfishness, or claim that in gratifying themselves they not only give pleasure to the extra-marital partner but keep their marriages healthy and free from strain. A forty-four-year-old housewife and dabbler in the arts takes the latter view:

—"My husband is a good man, a *nice* man, but not very exciting. He has his mind on his research projects all the time, and he's not with me even when he's in the same room. Even in bed he's not very open or expressive. So a need seems to build up slowly in me, and every two or three years I have to fall in love and have an affair with someone dynamic and exciting. I need it, my marriage needs it. It lasts for maybe a year, runs its course, and gradually dies. I may not feel like starting another for a long while—but when I find things beginning to happen between me and someone new, I know it's time." Such self-administered therapy, she feels, has not only made her a happy person, but as we earlier heard her say, has made her marriage a better one than those of almost all her more conventional friends.

There are, of course, many variations on this theme. Some people, like the last speaker, have affairs intermittently, while others are almost never without one. Most are faithful to their extra-marital partners, but some occasionally have a fling elsewhere at the same time. In many cases the marriages are tranquil and the affairs turbulent, but in some cases the pattern is reversed. Some keep their infidelities secret from their mates for a lifetime, while others gain tacit or even overt permission to maintain outside relationships. All, however, seem basically pleased with the system they have worked out; for them, serial bigamy is not a temporary or imperfect solution to a problem but a way of life, not a means to some other end but an end in itself.

LEWIS AMORY AND THERESA SCHROEDER

This is precisely what his extra-marital affairs have meant to Dr. Lewis Amory. Except at the very outset of his marriage, he has been involved almost continually with one woman or another outside it. Nearly all of his affairs have been carefully confined but relatively durable. None of them has competed with his marriage, but each has offered him something the marriage did not. Whether the marriage was potentially capable of offering more is beside the point: He did not want it to encroach upon him, and did not let it do so. Nor did he want more from his affairs than he got from them. In his affair with Terry, however, he slowly allowed himself to enter into the relationship more deeply than he ever had with another woman—for a while, indeed, too deeply for his own comfort; yet never did he consider it a possible future marriage or feel any serious conflict between it and his marriage to Arlene.

When dealing with his patients, Lewis is sensitive and perceptive; when dealing with the women in his life, he seems to maintain his own comfort by turning his gaze away from how they feel. Here, for example, is the way he speaks of the woman to whom he has been married for over nineteen years:

Lewis: "Sometimes after I've stayed in town with Terry a couple nights in a row, I feel bad that I haven't seen my kids. Not that I don't think of Arlene too, but I think of the children first and take Arlene for granted. That may sound cold, but I don't think it really is. She and I have a pretty good relationship, even though it's not close. She doesn't *seem* unhappy, and I hope she's not. Maybe she's just afraid to make trouble. By now she probably suspects what I'm up to, but she's careful not to bring it up."

He is somewhat more sharply aware of Terry's problems, but the affair, as it is now constituted, suits him so well that he cannot make himself give her up. "Some time ago I did try to get her back into the rat-race for her sake, as well as to take some of the responsibility off me. But I've quit trying. The relationship is much too good, much too important to me. I worry about her being so tied to me and I know how she feels about her situation, but I don't want to give her up. I've even been thinking about having her become my office assistant—she'd be perfect in the job, and I'd like having her around. But that would tie her even closer to me, and me to her, which would probably be a mistake for us both.

"This affair has lasted the longest and is the most important I've had, but if Terry ever got interested in someone else and was thinking of marrying him, I'd bow out. Or so I tell myself. But it's an academic question as long as we see so much of each other and she's so hooked on me. There's no lack of other women, of course;

one would come along. But I want Terry, not another one—even though I won't ever divorce my wife for her."

Terry accepts the status quo, although doing so costs her more than it does Lewis. She seems to have subjugated her own wishes to his and accepted a good deal of chronic frustration, to keep their conflict of interest from breaking them apart. To achieve this, she has had to do a lot of rationalizing about her situation.

Terry: "The more men I meet, the more I realize there's no one for me but Lewis. Even if the situation has its drawbacks, it would be stupid to lose everything by asking for too much. It took me a while to see things the way I now do. Even after we gave up the apartment, I kept on telling him my worries, complaining about the unfairness of the situation for me, generally making a lot of fuss. But one time, after I picked a fight with Lewis about half a year ago, it dawned on me that I was ruining the good things we had together. So I took a new tack. I decided to enjoy us just as we are, because I'm not sure I could ever find anything as good with anyone else. Since then things have been a lot smoother and more settled between us. I still have my same old financial problems, but I manage, and Lewis helps me out when he can. We both know that our relationship isn't the best thing for either of us, but we can't seem to get along without each other. The Lord alone knows what will happen tomorrow, but today we're still going strong.

"I've come to the conclusion that every man needs more than one woman. Lewis isn't different from anybody else. I could have married a man who has someone else on the outside, or I could be what I am—the someone on the outside who has him as her lover. I don't have the financial security and the social position Arlene has, but I have the better part of Lewis, and I wouldn't settle for the part she has. . . . Of course, if one day I found out I couldn't see him ever again, I'd remarry quick enough. I'd probably fall for the first halfway decent guy who came along. As for Lewis, if I ever did meet someone else and break off with him, I know he'd miss me terribly—and he'd find someone to take my place."

* * *

The intensely emotional but essentially ill-founded relationship I call an affair of rebellion has quite different after-effects. Some people end an affair of this kind with their illusions largely intact, or having learned only that the particular person they chose was wrong for them. Even if they are badly hurt, they gamely struggle to their feet and go on with the search, falling in love with the same ideal time and again—an ideal they project upon one prospect after another. Each time they experience intense joy and equally intense despair, never giving up until age compels them to leave the arena or until other influences modify their needs.

—An intense young woman, starved for emotional contact in her marriage, had her first affair (as we have seen) with a flamboyant but unsuccessful artist. For a while, it transformed her life, filling it with meaning and glowing emotion; the artist, however, always needing a new conquest, soon lost interest and eased out of it, leaving her desolate and bereft. From then on she hunted for other imaginative, unconventional, but unsuccessful men, and had affairs with a series of them. Looking back on fifteen years of this, she writes as follows:

> I believe they were all manifestations of my father. I was looking for someone like him to run away with—away from the safe, well-to-do, colorless life I had. My marriage was a sanctuary, a complete contrast to life with my father, who had been a dashing, one-time actor, a failure who died of despair. I have been falling in love with despairing people all my life. Each time it brings me joy for a while —and ends in misery. But I won't give up my fairy tales because I can't live without them.

Others, who were more clearly disillusioned and badly hurt, grow cautious and try to avoid further affairs of this type, limiting themselves to trivial encounters. This seems particularly apt to happen where the unfaithful person has come to see the depth of his own need for his marriage, yet continues to want something it fails to offer. He may miss the feeling of youth and freedom he knew in the affair, but not want to risk the emotional turmoil it entailed. He therefore acts worldly and cynical, looking for casual encounters, choosing partners he cannot love. But while each episode briefly puffs him up, he never feels transfigured or reborn as he did during his *grand amour*, and he looks back on that love affair with mixed feelings, seeing it as both his darkest and his finest hour. In the words of La Rochefoucauld: "Those who have known great passions remain all through their lives both glad and sorry they have recovered."

EDWIN GOTTESMAN

Much of this is exemplified by the case of Edwin Gottesman. It is well over a year since he saw the last of Jennifer and considered himself well rid of her, but he is not the person he was before they met. He praises his wife but feels something important lacking in his marriage, has adopted a libertine attitude toward extra-marital sex, is chronically restless and dissatisfied with his life. With his round stomach, his pale fleshy face, his thinning hair, he is hardly the stereotype of a romantic male, but the soul of one lives within him and mourns the past.

"There has been a big improvement in my home life in the year since Jennifer's been gone. I appreciate Betsy much more than I used to, I'm home a lot, I do many more things with her and the kids. I realize how important she is to me and what a fine and loving woman she is. But all the same, there is something missing. Betsy herself is much happier these days, but I'm not. I'm contented—but I'm never *happy*, the way I used to be when I was seeing Jennifer. Yet I know that it's impossible to have a good marriage and an affair like that at the same time. The affair eats up your time, it destroys your mind with crazy emotions you can't control, it leads you to make rotten decisions, it ruins your business, it wrecks your family life.

"The things I used to do! Rushing around playing tennis, taking sailing lessons, hiring airplanes. The fighting, the drinking, the love-making. The lies, the chances I took, the loving things I did that I never knew I had in me. I would have done anything for her, and yet she was no good—a total mess, a complete misfit, not even a great lay. But she made my heart beat fast, she made something happen in me, she made me feel like somebody very different from the president of Edwin Gottesman Enterprises, Inc. . . . I brought the smoking jacket home and told Betsy that an investor I had done a favor for had given it to me. That's a year ago, and still, when I see it in my closet, it sometimes gives me such a pang that my eyes fill up with tears. Actual tears! Once in a while I even put it on. It gives me a peculiar bitter pleasure to sit in my living-room in that jacket, knowing where it came from and how I used to love that girl.

"She was nothing and nobody, but she changed my outlook on life. Today I wouldn't do for any woman except Betsy the kind of things I used to do for Jennifer—but on the other hand, these days I sleep around and lie to Betsy about where I've been, and I don't even feel guilty. Right now I have seven different women I occasionally sleep with, and none of them means a damn to me. Last week I took out three different women and laid two of them. Me, Edwin Gottesman.

"What do I get out of it? Not what I got with Jennifer, not at all. So why do I do it? To make myself feel young, I suppose. To get away with something. Maybe just to relieve boredom. I don't know. . . . But if my wife is so marvelous, why isn't she enough for me? I wish I knew. She loves me and I love her, and it's very nice, very comforting. But it leaves me feeling middle-aged and settled, and I'm not willing to accept that. Yet I don't want anything like the Jennifer business again, so I run after women I don't care about. I play the game, I chase them, I get laid, I go home feeling good for a little while. . . . But the truth is, I'm not as happy as a man should be who has everything I have. Go figure it out."

iv la vita nuova

The most romantic outcome of the extra-marital affair is divorce followed by the marriage of the lovers. And it is not only romantic, but seems to justify the affair in the eyes of others; all but the most conservative will forgive them their trespasses if, unhappily married, they found happiness with each other and transformed their illicit love into an acknowledged union. Thus is the dilemma solved, the forbidden but idealized love made acceptable to society, the *Liebestod* transformed into the *Domestic Symphony.*

Divorce and remarriage therefore are the model many of the

unfaithful follow—in their intentions. In actual fact, it is a rarity. Only about one out of ten unfaithful people I interviewed had married, or were about to marry, the person with whom they were having extra-marital affairs. It is true that over a third of the interviewees had been divorced as a direct result of their affairs, but only part of these divorces were sought in order to marry the partner outside; even when they were, the planned remarriages took place only about half the time.

There were many reasons for the high proportion of failures to marry. For one thing, divorce alters many of the conditions under which the love affair thrived. It introduces new strains even while eliminating the old ones, and exposes even the most intimate couple to each other more completely than ever before. One man came to know a woman's children for the first time after she and her husband separated, and found them exasperating and bratty. Although he had felt quite certain for months that he wanted to marry her, this caused him to have serious misgivings, and she, perceiving them, felt frightened and betrayed. Conflict appeared for the first time in their relationship, and both began to wonder if they might not have chosen better than this. The new marriage died unborn.

A couple with a seemingly ideal relationship hoped to marry, but circumstances prevented the woman from obtaining a divorce for nearly two years, although the man was quickly able to arrange his own. Finally she was free; her lover, a lawyer, then met her parents for the first time—and found himself hopelessly at odds with her father, an authoritarian patriarch and judge. The lawyer discovered, unhappily, that his mistress idolized her father and sided with him; she, for her part, saw her lover for the first time as passive and insufficiently manly. Their love affair, stalemated, continued for a while, but eventually she met another and far more dynamic man who swept her off into marriage.

Even without such complications, an affair headed for marriage may falter and come to grief when freedom, after a hard-won divorce, alters the emotional balance that had existed. A suddenly reluctant man tells how he feels:

—"I've been more or less living with her since my divorce. It's been convenient and comfortable, and I find her just as desirable as before. But something's different. It took me years to fight my

way out of my marriage, and now that I'm free, I'm jumpy as a cat
about tying myself down again. I feel much too tied down as it is.
Like she expects me to meet her for dinner every evening, and that
bothers me. It isn't so much that I want to chase other women,
although that's part of it, but just that sometimes I'd like to be
quietly by myself, or sit in a bar all evening talking to friends. She's
getting impatient with me, and nervous—and mad. And that's making me mad, too."

Yet even when an affair that vanquished an existing marriage
fails to turn into one itself, the lovers are likely to have learned a
great deal, and to seek other relationships of the same type but free
of the defects they discovered in their affairs after divorce. The
lawyer whose prospective marriage was blighted by his conflict with
the authoritarian judge is now happily married to someone else. But
his marriage and that of the judge's daughter are founded in large
part on the growth experiences each one had in their affair. Her
testimony:

—"My husband and I were like business partners. Until I had
the affair with Roy, I had no idea what it meant to love and be
loved, or to respond to a man sexually. Roy taught me the meaning
of my own womanhood. It was tragic the way he and my father
interacted. It damaged my feeling for him, yet I can't deny that it
was Roy who made me ready for my present marriage."

His testimony:

—"My first marriage had been hopeless. My wife was beautiful
and very well-bred, but rigid and sexually cold. My affair with Fran
was completely different. I had never been as emotionally involved.
It opened up things in me that had always been closed off. To tell
you the truth, I'm not sure I could stand being opened up like that
twenty-four hours a day, but I'm very lucky I had the experience.
It left me permanently changed. The girl I met and married doesn't
share absolutely everything with me, the way Fran did, and our
relationship is not as intense—but it is warm and thoroughly compatible, and I owe much of that to Fran."

But what of those extra-marital affairs that do go on to become
marriages? Do they confirm the romantic myth that lovers who
have struggled long to possess each other live happily ever after, or
do they belie it?

They do both. Although the available evidence is scanty, it would appear that about half work out well, while about half fail—a failure rate little higher than that of second marriages in general. Still, one might consider this rate high in view of the depth of involvement and the long period of testing that preceded marriage.

Perhaps, then, there is something about the illicit origin of such marriages that dooms them: The puritan conscience would find such an answer intellectually and morally satisfying. Indeed, in a fair number of cases there does seem to be a special kind of marital problem or cluster of problems that relates to the way the relationship began. But when one looks more closely, it seems clear that for these difficulties to prove hurtful, there must be pre-existing psychological pathology in one or both persons, or in their relationship to each other.

Either or both may, for instance, feel considerable guilt for having deserted their mates; this, however, is not likely to become crucial and destructive of their love unless, to begin with, they were chronically and harshly self-punitive, or were unduly plagued by a sense of obligation, or the like. Where there are such pre-existing conditions, however, the intensity of the guilt the individual feels may create in him a corrosive resentment of the person for love of whom he is suffering. Again, some marriages mysteriously lose a purity and sweetness they had as affairs, and become contaminated by the kind of conflict and cruelty that had existed in the old marriage; it may be that an unhealthy need in one partner to be cruel to someone of the opposite sex had been met in the old marriage as long as it existed, and when it ended the individual had to begin meeting his need in the new one. Sometimes, too, a joyous and passionate affair is comfortable even for an inhibited or puritanical person as long as he or she is paying the penalties of secrecy, worry, or harassment by an angry spouse; liberation from all these, however, upsets the psychological balance, and the unpunished joys of the new relationship begin to afflict him with pervasive and intolerable anxiety.

These are but a few of the ways in which problems that remain concealed or at least seem controllable during an affair can assume lethal power after its metamorphosis into marriage. With hindsight, one can see that it was such problems, inherent in the personalities and the relationship of Neal Gorham and Mary Buchanan, that determined the eventual fate of their marriage. The short and unhappy history of that marriage is candidly told by Mary to an old friend, in a letter postmarked London, September 28, 1968:

> My conscience troubled me for not writing or calling you before I left New York to tell you what had happened, and why things turned out as they did. Your letter saying you'd finally heard, and sounding so genuinely concerned for me, finally reached me here by a roundabout route. I've wanted to answer your many questions, but it has been terribly difficult; I've begun and laid aside this reply a dozen times, and taken weeks to finish it. Here it is—the product of many hours of scribbling and many sleepless nights. I thank you for getting me to do it. It has been helpful. . . .
>
> Where shall I start? I find myself without any good answers to your queries. Never before in my life have I been left with so many questions unanswered. But never before have I engaged with anyone who has Neal's capacity to close himself off, to turn off his feelings. As open and emotional as he was when we were lovers, just so shut in and frozen did he seem in the final months of our marriage. Little by little he bottled up his feelings—both of love and hate—until, toward the end, he seemed to feel nothing at all except a desire to escape from me.
>
> Our marriage started out well enough, although, as you know, there had been plenty of prior commotion. The only trouble, in the beginning, concerned his children. He had arranged with Laurie to have them spend most weekends with us, and from Friday evening to Sunday evening he would play the perfect father, assuaging his guilt for having left them by giving them undivided love and attention. I was mere background; he hardly seemed aware of me when he had the kids, and he wasn't interested either in bringing me into their thing, or having any kind of normal weekend social life. Whenever I said something about it, he seemed to feel that I was competing with his children and trying to come between them and him. We had two or three awful fights about it, and then I stopped fighting because I saw I couldn't win. I told no one; I was ashamed to.
>
> But my feelings leaked over into other areas of our life, and I took out my anger where I could. For the first time, we couldn't agree how to handle some of the big books on the list—we'd have a conference, I'd make a few barbed remarks, he'd get testy, I'd become even sharper

of tongue, and finally he'd put on his frozen Calvinist face and become polite and monosyllabic. Christ! It drove me wild. I found myself beginning to wonder, for the first time, about his complaints that Laurie had withheld love from him in their marriage. Maybe, by withdrawing into hurt silence, he had shut her out more often than she had him.

But for the most part things were pretty good between us, and sometimes even wonderful in the old way. Then in June, Laurie began talking about moving to southern California to be near her parents— they'd left Virginia and moved there during the winter—and by August she had definitely decided to go. Neal was in a flap. He talked to her on the phone hour after hour, trying to persuade her to change her mind. He even took her to dinner a couple of times to discuss her situation. In a way, he was almost wooing her, in order not to lose his children. Maybe other things were going on in him, too. I've been seeing a psychoanalyst here in London, and he thinks it quite possible that Neal unconsciously longed for the homemaker, the mother, the sexually unresponsive wife—everything reassuring that I was not. He says that perhaps Neal's own sexuality and capacity for joy, which were so liberated during our affair, became alarming to him when he didn't have to endure punishments that balanced them out.

Which makes sense to me now. But at the time I couldn't understand the changes in our sex life; in fact, I could scarcely believe what was happening. It had been superb when we first fell in love, and it stayed that way for a year. It began to fade a bit after he got his divorce and moved in with me, but I thought that was just a normal levelling off. After we were married, however, it definitely became less frequent and less intense, and when the problems with the children and the matter of Laurie's moving to California came to a head, it got to be a once-a-week sort of thing. I don't mean he openly rejected me. But somehow he always seemed to be working late, or feel worn-out after playing all day with his children, or we'd be alone for the evening but he'd drink too much and fall asleep the minute he got into bed. He even brought home some marijuana, and said that it helped his writing but turned him off sexually. (I thought it was supposed to do the opposite, but he claimed it could work either way.) In short, he had a whole string of excuses for not making love. Mother of God! Couldn't he remember that's just what he said Laurie used to do to him? (Or was he fooling around with someone else? I despised myself for that thought, but he'd been unfaithful to Laurie for my sake—so how could I ever totally trust him?) And it got steadily worse. After

Laurie moved to California in September, he made love to me no more
than once every three weeks or so, and even at that I felt as if he were
only servicing me to keep the peace.

We had always been great talkers with each other, but our talk
dried up just like our sex life. If we disagreed about anything, he'd get
that tight, closed-up look, while I'd get loud and heated. The icier he
became, the hotter I became, and the more I tried to get through to
him, the more he closed off. Anything could do it—book advertising,
vacation plans, even something as minor as choosing a movie to go to.
It would wind up with his telling me I was contentious and castrating,
and my telling him that he only pretended to want a woman who was
truly alive and responsive, that what he really wanted was a nice,
passive, bread-baking neo-Victorian housewife right out of a ladies'
magazine.

Then one night he casually mentioned that he was thinking about
looking for a job in southern California so he could be near the children. I was dumfounded. New York was where I worked, where I'd
spent my adult life. Southern California meant nothing to me. And he
hadn't even asked me how I'd feel about living there. But when I
started asking questions and raising some of the issues, he said it was
just an idea he was exploring, and he'd let me know more about it
when he had thought it through. He'd gone back once or twice to see
his psychotherapist, just about that time, and I thought maybe he was
discussing it with him, and I let it go at that.

So I wasn't braced for it when he offhandedly broke the news to
me over cocktails, about a month later, that he'd been offered a job
as head of public relations and publications for a foundation in southern California, in a town less than an hour by car from where Laurie
and the children lived. I gasped. "What about *me, my* job, *my* wishes?"
I said. It developed into a real rhubarb in about three minutes—at
which point he said, in his best thin-lipped manner, "I may as well tell
you that I've made up my mind. I'm going to give the agency a
month's notice. The foundation people want me out there by the
beginning of February. I'm sure you'd find work of some sort, the
climate's marvelous, and you might even *like* the life out there. In any
case, I'm going. You can tag along or not, as you like."

If he'd gone about it some other way . . . but that's idle specula-
tion. He didn't. I was furious. I asked him how in hell he had dared
go this far without consulting me. Didn't I mean a goddamned thing
to him any more? He was quiet, thinking it out, and then he said, "You
do mean something to me, but not everything. My own peace of mind

means more, and so does the welfare of my children." I said a lot of things in reply to that, he said as little as possible, and the scene went on and on, ending in a truce of exhaustion. We never ate dinner that night; neither of us had any appetite. We had a few more talks in the next several weeks, but for the most part we avoided each other. I did tell him, at one point, that I didn't want to go to California under these circumstances—he didn't want me or need me and there wasn't even anything for me to do out there. I suppose I was testing, looking for some kind of positive sign—but all he said was that he didn't blame me, and I ought not blame him for doing what he had to do.

He also said, more than once, that he wondered if we hadn't married less out of love than out of a need to justify having broken up two marriages. Maybe our troubles were the inevitable pay-off for what we had done. I worried about that many a night, but my analyst thinks that much of our drive toward marriage had been healthy. Sound impulses were there, we *almost* made it work, and we might have succeeded if both of us had been in treatment, he tackling his tendency to withdraw from contention with any woman and to punish himself for imagined guilt, me tackling my compulsion to see any man as a challenge and to cut him down, one way or another, out of a fear of being subjugated.

We had one more fight two weeks before he was supposed to go. It was so awful that he moved into the Yale Club and came back only once to pack his things and to talk about money and other practical matters. I wanted to talk about the two of us, to see whether there was any hope at all, anything we could do, but he never let the discussion get around to that. So I choked back my tears and acted very calm, and when he was leaving I said *"Ciao!"* very brightly—feeling like a fool, because I never ordinarily say that—and offered him my cheek to kiss. And then he was gone, and I was one of the walking dead. That was early February. We exchanged a few letters and phone calls in the next month—even Neal had some agonized moments, when he couldn't deny his misery and longing, and wanted to find some way back—but nothing came of them.

Dear old Cal tried to help me. I think he even imagined I might want him back. But I decided to get out of there and away from it all. I had a few good contacts in London and wrote them, looking for work; I finally got one modest offer from an ad agency, and took it instantly. In April, I came here, found a flat (chilly, too small, but a beachhead), and started work. I learned that fees for private psychoanalytic treatment are only about a third what they are in New

York, so I decided to give it a real try, to see if I could find what I'd been doing wrong. I've been here less than six months, and in analysis only four, but I'm learning a lot and coming out of the doldrums. So much so that I started dating a couple months ago, and recently even felt up to spending the night with one man.

I hear from the Gambles that Neal has settled into his job, spends a lot of time with the children and Laurie, but still drinks too much when he gets depressed, which is fairly often. I don't know if he's back in therapy or not. We once had a great love in the making, but it was undone by old unsolved problems that each of us brought along. I often daydream of trying it with him again some day, if he irons out his kinks as I'm ironing out mine. Or is this just one more neurotic fantasy that I have to give up?

* * *

Neal and Mary's story notwithstanding, about half of the extra-marital affairs that finally become new marriages are successful, some of them extraordinarily so. An illicit love that is strong enough and enduring enough to conquer so many obstacles may, in the absence of serious neurotic problems, fulfill virtually all the hopes and expectations of the lovers and even improve upon them. Some part of the intensity and sharpness of their love is lost, but they knew it would be; what they did not know was that the deeper, sustaining, completing aspects of it would prove far greater than they had anticipated. Freed of constraint and conflict, secure in each other, socially acceptable, at peace within themselves, they are finally able to experience to the full those feelings which they had only sampled thus far. A case in point:

—The wife of a young Detroit banker, a Madonna-like blonde, went to visit friends in Buffalo in order to escape briefly from her dying marriage. At a dinner party, her partner was a dark, sardonic, somewhat older man, an art dealer and occasional lecturer who was in town to give a talk the next day. Each knew the other was married, each knew this was a night when they were far away from mates they no longer loved. A spontaneous and largely animal attraction sprang up between them (she, indeed, was almost entirely ignorant of his field and hardly his intellectual equal at that time); obeying it without question, they made love fiercely, almost savagely, in his hotel room later that very night, and at 5 A.M. said farewell without promises or tears. A few weeks later, however, he sought her out when he was travelling near to Detroit, and they met again. After the fourth such meeting, they were infatuated with each other and she, at least, thought herself in love. A little later, after she had separated from her husband, the art dealer daringly took her with him on a ten-day business trip, and it was in what she calls "the quiet times"—travelling, shopping, dining, bathing—that they got to know something of each other's backgrounds, tastes, and habits, and actually began to realize the depth of their feelings about each other.

To be near him, she moved to New York and they began to see each other several times a week, always briefly and surreptitiously, at her apartment. Soon, despite the limitations of their meetings, it was she, rather than his actual wife, who was privy to all his thoughts and feelings, who gave him the love and encouragement he required, who delighted in his stories of new purchases and exciting sales. It was she to whom he read the drafts of new lectures on the phone at midnight when his wife was asleep; it was she who went with him on overnight speaking trips because he felt he did so much better if she were in the audience. By this time, she felt sure it was as deep a love as she was capable of, or would ever know —and yet it seemed doomed by his paralyzing fear of his wife's reactions to a demand for divorce.

Although the affair nearly came to grief over this, he did finally manage to broach the subject of divorce to his wife, and after some difficult weeks he moved out and took up residence in a furnished room. For the next half year, while he was engaged in a running battle over divorce terms, the lovers saw little more of each other than formerly. He was afraid to have her up in his room or to remain long in her apartment, and he never stayed overnight with her for fear detectives might be watching them. But because at last he had taken the great step, there was a new peace on her part; uncertainty had been replaced by impatience, a far more tolerable kind of discomfort.

The day he received his copy of the Mexican divorce in the mail, he packed his bags and carried them to her small, neatly furnished apartment. "As much as he and I had grown to love each other during the previous three years, it got still better when he moved in. I would wake up in the morning and he was always there next to me—and it was a new kind of feeling, and far better than I had hoped. When he left to go to the gallery, I always knew he'd be coming home to me—and that feeling, too, was stronger and even better than I had expected. We could be together all evening, all night, and never wonder whether a detective was keeping track of us. He took me to parties and introduced me to his friends, and for the first time I felt he acknowledged me—and that seemed amazingly important too.

"But though I wasn't very clearly aware of it then, there was still a certain amount of holding back, a guardedness between us, because he was free to marry me and wasn't doing so. Whenever the subject came up he would only say he wasn't ready and mustn't be pushed. I didn't think I cared—I had got more than I had ever hoped for—but again I was wrong, because we did get married half a year later, and since then it has changed again and become still better. Before, it was always 'he and I,' emotionally speaking, but now it's 'we.' When he introduces me to people, it's not as a girl he's proud to have on his arm but as his other self. There's no more testing, no watching, no measuring. If he talks to some other woman at a party, I never wonder whether he prefers her to me, and when I meet some man who's attractive I never wonder if maybe he mightn't have been a better choice.

"We're so interwoven now that what went before looks very incomplete. We see each other all the time, but I always love to hear his voice when he phones me during the day, and if I go downtown and drop in at the gallery, his face always lights up. We often start to talk about the same subject at the same time, as if our minds were keeping time with each other. Whatever he experiences during the day, he wants to share with me at night, and it's the same with me. At home, if I'm cooking, he likes to come sit in the kitchen to do his reading, and if I'm soaking in the tub, he likes to use that time for shaving, so he can be in the bathroom with me. I don't think he knew, beforehand, that it would be like this for him, and I certainly didn't know it would be like this for me.

"For a while, though, there was one flaw—his boys seemed resentful of me, probably because their mother brainwashed them.

But they've spent a lot of time with us this past year and by now they're quite at ease and fond of me. Maybe more than fond. The little one, who's only seven, said last month that he thinks of me as a 'second mother' rather than a stepmother. The older one, who's ten, asked us last week whether we're going to have any children because he'd like a baby sister and when we said we didn't know, he said very seriously, 'Well you ought to, because you're so happy together it would be fun to be your child.' We hugged him, and couldn't speak."

epilogue

i

Nearly everyone feels the temptation to be unfaithful during married life, whether occasionally and only in the form of fantasies, or continuously and in the flesh. Lifelong sexual fidelity is neither biologically nor psychologically natural to the human being; it is imposed on him by his societies—and not even by most of them at that. In our own, the traditional code justifies the imposition of fidelity not only on religious and moral grounds, but on the ground that it is a *sine qua non* of successful marriage and the happy life. For people of certain psychological types this does seem to be true —yet to some degree even for them, and to a greater degree for nearly everyone else, fidelity constitutes one of the basic discontents of civilization.

ii

Resisting the extra-marital urge brings satisfactions at the cost of deprivation; yielding to it brings other satisfactions at the cost of personal and social penalties. If, in the past, the choice has never been easy, today it is more difficult than ever. Marriage has become increasingly fragile, and infidelity, accordingly, has become an even greater threat than before—and yet harder to avoid. For it seems less sinful and more tempting than formerly: less sinful because in modern eyes the greater sins are inhibition, frustration, self-denial, and joylessness; more tempting because extra-marital love is a panacea, or at least a placebo, for many of the ills of modern marriage and of contemporary life.

We marry earlier, live longer, are healthy and youthful at a time of life when our grandfathers were weary and middle-aging; marriage becomes boring long before the organism is safely beyond desire, before fantasies and temptations have become empty threats. But apart from boredom, marriage disappoints us more often and more keenly than it did our ancestors because, in some ways, we expect so much more from it—unflagging sexual joy, unfading love, emotional security, companionship, thoroughgoing compatibility. The remedy that lies closest to hand, for boredom and disappointment alike, is extra-marital love.

But it is also Everyman's answer to the impersonality, the disconnectedness, the gigantism of modern society. We have lost our names and become numbers, lost touch with our friends and replaced them with people who merely live nearby, lost control of our destinies to governments, industries, and machines that ravish our earth and control our lives. If the individual feels powerless to remake or even salvage this world, he can at least comfort himself by making a world of his own through love. In each of its many forms, ranging from casual sexual encounters to the deepest emotional relationships, it gives him a sense of his own uniqueness, a vital connection with some other human being, an area of freedom within which he can manage a part of his destiny. Those who love construct a microcosm of their own, a world in which they are at once Creator and created.

iii

Love is a way to remain human in an inhuman society; it is therefore more prized, in every form, than ever. A higher percentage of American adults are married now than was the case even in the familistic nineteenth century—but because marriage so often fails or cannot continuously manage to meet the special needs of modern men and women, a much higher percentage of husbands and wives are also unfaithful.

But even if both marital and extra-marital love derive much of their present appeal from the same social sources, they remain hopelessly antithetical in the minds of many people and in the social code. Marital love, for many people, signifies maturity, commitment, stability; extra-marital love signifies youth, freedom, change. Few are able to fill all these needs within a single relationship; generally, they must do without one set of satisfactions or the other. A type of polygamy consisting of marriage plus extra-marital relationships might solve the problem, but our society's traditional code will neither legally countenance it nor admit its emotional validity; according to that code, he who loves his mate cannot love another, he who loves another cannot love his mate.

Some people do find this true: One love always competes with the other in their feelings, and they cannot successfully practice any form of infidelity without intolerable inner conflict, which they resolve by giving up either the marriage or the affair. Many others —probably a majority—do not find this true: They are not only capable of maintaining several partial or limited love relationships, but seem to need them. Even so, infidelity remains a grave threat to their marriages for practical reasons: The code makes it such an unacceptable affront to their spouses that, if discovered, it produces retaliatory measures up to and including divorce.

---

iv

Such is the dilemma. Americans resolve it variously, each way having its own advantages and disadvantages, each seeming to some people the only right or sensible choice.

Those who elect to remain faithful pay varying penalties and obtain varying benefits. Some, even though very unsatisfactorily married, resign themselves to total monogamy, foregoing both divorce and infidelity. For religious, social, or ethical reasons, or even because of severe self-doubt, they accept frustration and unhappiness as their lot, choking back their desires or satisfying them vicariously through fantasy and fiction. Yet there are rewards of a sort for these people: This choice meets the requirements of their consciences and allays their insecurities.

Others, though equally plagued by unmet needs and dissatisfactions, take a more positive approach and sublimate their drives, expending their unused erotic energy in compulsive work or political activity, over-zealous homemaking, and the like. This choice, too, has its rewards: The fruits of such labors are socially and personally acceptable to these people, whereas illicit love and sexual pleasure are not.

A smaller number, fortunate enough to achieve a happy and satisfying marriage, have few unmet needs and thus remain faithful with little effort. Even when the passage of time makes them yearn for variety and freshness, the desire remains relatively weak; some of them, moreover, manage to redirect the extra-marital urge aroused in them by outside persons back toward their mates.

A large and growing number of people choose the other horn

of the dilemma, defying the monogamous code in order to meet needs ranging from the trivial to the profound, to achieve goals ranging from momentary physical delight to lifelong emotional fulfillment. The one socially sanctioned form of violating the monogamous code is divorce and remarriage—a special adaptation sociologists sometimes jocularly refer to as *sequential polygamy,* although it could as well be called *sequential infidelity.*

But it is the other significant alternative—the search for extra-marital love outside, but concurrent with, marriage—that we have been examining throughout this book. We have seen several major patterns of extra-marital relationships, from casual shallow sex-conquests to long-lasting, marriage-oriented love affairs; we have seen the intricate interplay of these different kinds of affairs with various kinds of marital relationships; we have seen their widely varying effects on different personalities. It is clear that extra-marital experience has not one but many different kinds of impact and effect, ranging from the disastrous to the highly beneficial. Code ethics admits of no alternatives, but situation ethics measures each act of infidelity according to the circumstances that created the need for it, the kind of extra-marital relationship engaged in, and the effects upon all concerned.

V

None of the various resolutions of the dilemma is ideal for all Americans, none is the "best" answer for everyone. We are a diverse and conglomerate people, and no single sexual-marital norm could be ideal for all the ethnic and cultural strains among us. America is, moreover, an extremely fluid and mobile society, and the norm that makes sense to one generation may make none to the generation succeeding it. Again, our family system produces a wide range of personality structures; unlike the people of smaller, closer-knit, more homogeneous societies, we are not psychologically cut from the same cloth.

Diversity is our condition, the monolithic code our misfortune.

Many of us, therefore, secretly live by deviant codes of conduct that fit our needs better than lifelong fidelity to a single mate. The first Kinsey Report astounded the nation in 1948 by revealing the extent to which hidden deviancy and diversity existed. But while recent studies such as Vance Packard's 1968 survey, *The Sexual Wilderness,* indicate that diversity has increased still further, they no longer shock us, for in the intervening twenty years the monolithic code has begun to crack; many of the forms of sexual and emotional behavior that depart from the traditionally acceptable have become less deviant, less secret, and less dangerous as choices.

I find this trend reassuring. The most wholesome sexual ethic for our time would be an ethic of diversity, the best answer to the dilemma of infidelity a set of answers. The mature and emotionally healthy individual, taking into account his own needs, those of his mate and children, and the probable effects of his acts on all connected with him, can make a better choice for himself than can society. The most beneficial changes that could take place in our national sexual attitudes would include a still greater and more overt acknowledgment of the diversity of our emotional and sexual needs, and a far greater toleration of our varied ways of satisfying them.

---

vi

Whether this greater toleration of diversity will continue to develop, no one can be sure, but I think it rather likely. Forecasting the future in an area as complex as love and family life, and as intimately interwoven with a multitude of other unknowable changes, may seem folly to some, but this prediction is an extrapolation of present trends, not a plea for any one favorite adaptation or utopian scheme, as are many so-called forecasts.

We hear every day, for instance, that marriage is obsolete, dying, virtually extinct; that it will soon give way to common-law unions or to five-year renewable marriage contracts; that love is archaic, irrelevant, and a "hang-up"; that American sexual behavior will come to be built around freely tolerated infidelity, mate-swapping, the "group sexual turn-on," the free expression of all our innate "polymorphous perverse" desires—predictions offered not with scientific dispassion but with the moral fervor of the prophet or the evangelist.

But the facts we have at hand warrant neither publishing the funeral notice of marriage nor heralding the coming of total sexual permissiveness. The content and style of marriage are changing, but marriage itself is more popular than in the past; even the high divorce rate, still growing toward an unknown limit, is no sign of disaffection with marriage but only with unsatisfying marriage, for nearly six sevenths of the divorced remarry. The manner and mood of expressing love have changed much, but every survey of marriage and of young adults indicates that love is no less important than before; only the sexual radicals, a tiny minority, find it archaic —and there is no proof they are any more trend-setting than sexual extremists ever have been. Writers from Bertrand Russell to Albert Ellis have argued in favor of permissiveness by marital partners, but relatively few have tried it, and very few of those have succeeded; in our society and with our emotional equipment, such arrangements prove too threatening, too productive of jealousy and conflict. They might, of course, work in some other age and among some other people, but this hardly helps those who are living here and now.

The adults of the next generation are the college students of today. Despite sensational journalistic accounts of their behavior, what reliable knowledge we have of their practices and attitudes indicates that the sexual future is hardly likely to be apocalyptic. Recent studies by competent behavioral scientists agree that while distinct changes in sexual behavior have occurred on campus in the past twenty years, there has actually been no bona fide sexual revolution. Premarital sex, though much more widespread and open than formerly, takes place primarily within serious, not casual, relationships; promiscuity is no more common than it ever was. Even the young campus couples who boldly live together are almost all conventionally monogamous and engage neither in partner-swapping nor in open infidelity. The one truly notable change, however, is in their attitudes. Today's students are much more unashamed and easy-going about sex than the previous generation or two, and do not consider it the major problem or focus of anxiety that it was for their parents. (The major problem they see is to find meaning in their lives, their society, and their personal relationships.) They have a considerable degree of tolerance for the sexual behavior of others, and many of them are far more permissive about the actions of others than about their own.

It seems likely, therefore, that in the next twenty years or so Americans will become increasingly tolerant of a diversity of sexual styles and standards. People will feel increasingly comfortable with their own choices, and unthreatened by the differing choices of those around them.

I suspect that for both psychological and social reasons, a considerable number of men and women will continue to seek the intimacy and comfort of a faithful monogamous relationship—yet will feel freer, if it fails, to end it by divorce or to look for love extra-maritally, hoping to turn it into a marriage.

At the same time, a large number of persons who have little cultural or emotional allegiance to fidelity will continue to marry largely for comfort, social status, and parenthood, and will feel even less hesitant than their predecessors to seek affairs for pleasure and variety. Some of these people—more, probably, than is the case today—may gain tacit permission from their spouses to do so, and a tiny contingent will even obtain and grant in return complete sexual freedom, or will practice communal sex among groups of married friends and acquaintances.

It seems to me most unlikely that Americans will develop any single new sexual ethic, any generally applicable or ideal solution to the dilemma of infidelity. Many solutions will continue to exist, each better for some people than the others, each with its own drawbacks and rewards. The denial of polygamous desires will nearly always be somewhat galling, even when practiced in the name of love, while the indulgence of polygamous desires will nearly always incur some risks and costs.

Yet how could it be otherwise? Any number of zealots, revolutionaries, poets, and philosophers have offered mankind utopian solutions to its many dilemmas, but over the centuries not one of them, if put to the test, has proven ideal after all. For ideal solutions exist only in men's dreams; in their real lives, the best they can find are compromises among their warring desires.

notes on sources

The research for this book began with an examination of recent published surveys, case studies, and other non-fiction writing about extra-marital experience in America. A selected Bibliography of the most useful items follows these notes.

In various parts of the country, I visited and spoke to nearly forty professional persons who are particularly well-informed concerning extra-marital behavior; they included psychiatrists and psychologists, marriage counselors, sociologists, sex-behavior researchers, ministers, and lawyers. Those to whom I am most deeply indebted are named in the Acknowledgments. Though few of these people had any data, most of them contributed valuable insights and provocative hypotheses concerning the causes, meanings, and effects of various kinds of infidelity.

My own original research consisted of two parts. First, I designed a questionnaire with the help of Dr. Frank Furstenberg, a

sociologist at the University of Pennsylvania, and staff members of
the Russell B. Stearns Study, a social science research group at
Northeastern University. The questionnaire was administered by
the Stearns Study, and went to a sample of middle-class Americans
taken at random from the subscription list of a large, now-defunct
national magazine. That subscription list was largely white and
middle-class: Median income was $8,850, median age thirty-seven,
geographical distribution national, male-female distribution nearly
fifty-fifty. About thirty per cent of the list were college graduates,
and the proportions of those adhering to, or having been reared in,
each major religion were roughly the same as those of the nation
at large. The Stearns Study received 360 replies, and encoded up
to two hundred items of information from each one on IBM cards.
From them, a computer produced three massive sheaves of cross-
tabulated statistics, the most significant of which I have used from
time to time, in brief form, in this book. The Stearns Study and Dr.
Furstenberg, as contractors to me, offered me guidelines to inter-
preting the statistical print-out, but the interpretations and conclusions I have reached are my own and I assume full responsibility
for them.

Because my sample is modest in size and all responses were
voluntary, I have used the data with caution, regarding my findings
as suggestive rather than definitive. Nonetheless, the demographic
characteristics of the respondent group do not differ measurably
from those of the total subscription list; it therefore seems likely
that the respondents are an unbiased subsample, and reasonably
representative of the American middle class.

The most important part of my research consists of depth
interviews with eighty unfaithful men and women, four aggrieved
spouses, and seven unmarried people who had had or were having
affairs with married men or women. As a group, the ninety-one
interviewees were similar to the questionnaire sample in age and
sex distribution, religious background, and geographical location,
but were, on the average, somewhat better educated and more
affluent. All the interviews were tape-recorded with the knowledge
and permission of the subjects. Most of the interviews lasted two
to three hours, but some extended over several sessions and totalled
as many as fifteen hours. In all, the interview transcripts include
nearly three quarters of a million words.

Some of my friends, astonished that people would speak to me freely about their infidelities, have suggested that my interviewees are an exhibitionistic, peculiar, and unrepresentative lot. I do not think so. I solicited the interviews by means of a far-flung network of professional persons I have come to know in the course of many years of writing about the psychology of love, sex, and marriage—sociologists, psychoanalysts and psychotherapists, marriage counselors, sex researchers, ministers and lawyers—who have special access to confidential material and are trusted and highly regarded by their confidants and friends. On my behalf, these people asked various persons who had confided in them, or whose stories they knew, to permit me to interview them, assuring them that I would disguise identifying external details in anything I wrote. Not exhibitionism, but quite other motives, led my interviewees to agree: One was a feeling of duty or obligation, another the desire to play a part in a serious and potentially helpful study, the third a deep need to speak freely about their experiences to someone accepting and understanding, the fourth a hope that in discussing their experiences with me they might learn something of value to themselves. With regard to the latter two points, I should add that I resisted the temptation to play therapist, although I did sometimes tell them something of what I had been learning; but the very act of telling me their stories and answering my questions was both relieving to many of them and a source of insights they had not previously had.

But did they tell me the truth? Those who were displeased or shocked by the Kinsey material comforted themselves by deciding that the informants were liars and the interviewers gulls. Some may say so about my own research. But any skilled veteran interviewer doubles back, asks verifying questions from many different angles, looks for internal consistency. More than that, he is aware of body movements, facial expressions, and changes in vocal manner that indicate evasion or concealment; he appraises the general credibility of his informant in the course of the interview, and—at least in a loosely structured interview—modifies his questions accordingly. The loosely structured interview yields credible information for still another reason: Through the flow of free association, truth comes out and evasions or lies are unmasked, even as in analytic psychotherapy. But not always: I discarded a handful of interviews over and above the ninety-one, where I felt my informants had been unusually evasive or untruthful and where my interview technique failed to penetrate their defenses. The rest of my interviewees did not systematically lie or evade, and most of their unwitting distortions were, I believe, corrected by their equally unwitting revelations. In a number of the most important cases I was able to verify, correct, and enrich given accounts by interviewing lovers or friends of my interviewees, or obtaining letters (and in two instances diaries) the latter had written.

Whatever the faults of the interview method, its virtues far outweigh them. Surveys, statistics, and psychosocial analyses of infidelity all yielded valuable information—yet any one individual's story taught me more than all of them about why one becomes unfaithful, how it feels, and what it does to one's life. The two kinds of knowledge are complementary, not antithetical, but statistics and explanations are artifacts, while experiences and feelings are reality.

The sources of data and observations other than my own are as follows, all references being to the editions listed in the Bibliography:

[pp. xii–xiii]:The very considerable differences between middle-class and lower-class behavior in this area have often been pointed out. See Komarovsky, *passim*, and Levinger, pp. 806–807. E. E. LeMasters, *The Blue Collar Aristocracy* (a work in progress), has similar relevant findings; my thanks are due to Professor LeMasters of the School of Social Work, University of Wisconsin, for an advance look.

[p. 9]: Varying professional opinions about the length and degree of involvement of "typical" affairs exist through the literature. Two examples: Kinsey (1948), p. 588, and (1953), pp. 419–420, believes the casual encounter the most common type, while Cuber and Harroff, pp. 146–171, seem to feel that deeper and longer-lasting involvements predominate.

[p. 10]: . . . *instead, they have solicited the respondent's attitude:* Terman's classic study, for example, asked only about fantasies and attitudes, but not about actual extra-marital activity, and a number of major polls summarized and excerpted by Erskine were purely attitude surveys and did not even ask about fantasies.

[p. 10]: The Family Service Association of America kindly lent me the original questionnaires, but the survey is summarized by Callwood, q.v.

[pp. 10–11]: Kinsey (1948), p. 585, Table 64, and Fig. 73; Kinsey (1953), p. 416, Tables 144 and 115, and Figs. 74 and 75.

[p. 11]: Dr. Gebhard's remarks were part of a personal communication.

[p. 12]: Cuber and Harroff, pp. 41–42; Satir, p. 9.

[p. 12]: The penalties for adultery are those specified in the criminal codes of the named states as of late 1968. For a tabular summary of the laws and penalties regarding adultery in all fifty states, see Hefner, p. 131; this, however, is as of 1964.

[pp. 12–13]: For numbers of divorces in New York prior to the 1967 revision, see *Statistical Abstract* (1968), p. 62; on lack of enforcement of criminal code in New York, see *Columbia Law Review*, 1964: 1469 and 1539, footnote 489; on the vote against revision of that part of the New York penal code dealing with adultery, see *The New York Times*, June 9, 1965, p. 1.

[p. 13]: On the law in Illinois, Ill. Rev. Stat. 1967, ch. 38, sec. 11–7. See also Hefner, p. 134; also letter in *Playboy*, September, 1964, p. 67, from Chas. H. Bowman, chairman of the drafting subcommittee of the Joint Committee to Revise the Illinois Criminal Code.

[p. 13]: Christensen, p. 130. *McCall's* survey: see Blum, pp. 135–136 and 139.

[p. 17]: The not very revolutionary nature of the so-called sexual revolution is attested by Reiss, and by Simon and Gagnon (1969). For popular summaries of evidence on the same point, see Rosenfeld, and Karlen. See also note to pp. 288–289.

[p. 18]: The data on societies permitting or forbidding extra-marital relations are from Ford and Beach, pp. 107–108 and 113–114; the figures cited from Kinsey were drawn by him from Ford and Beach, Murdock, and Kinsey's own studies; on all this see Kinsey (1953), p. 414 and esp. footnote to same page.

[p. 19]: The points made about Ovid, *l'amour courtois*, and puritan marriage are dealt with in detail, and documented, in my own book, *The Natural History of Love* (Hunt, 1959), chaps. V, VI, and VII.

[p. 20]: The data from the *McCall's* survey: Blum, p. 138.

[pp. 20–21 and footnote]: On the attitude of French women towards non-serious infidelity in their husbands, see Christensen, p. 127. Italian attitudes are sketched by Barzini (1965), p. 205, and Barzini (1968), *passim*. The Italian, and especially the Sicilian, attitude of husbands toward unfaithful wives is described by Barzini (1968) and Wise; the similar attitude of lower-class Greek men is described by Safilios-Rothschild.

[p. 21]: For a resumé of the history of American laws dealing with adultery, see Ohlson, *passim.*

[pp. 21–22]: The conflict between the approved model of marriage and the limited intimacy needs of many people is mentioned by Cavan, pp. 112–113, Comfort, pp. 106–109, and others.

[p. 23]: Franklin's letter can be found in Schuster, pp. 160–162, and elsewhere.

[pp. 24–25]: A brief review of earlier psychoanalytic thinking concerning fantasies and some of the current research on the subject can be found in Singer. The assertion that fantasies may lead to actions is not stated by Singer, but is my own conclusion from interview material and from discussions with numerous psychoanalysts and other psychotherapists. Singer does, nevertheless, seem to support this view to the extent that he considers the classic Freudian view incomplete, and offers evidence that fantasy achieves not only drive-reduction but mood-change.

[pp. 27–28]: The main evidence for the prevalence of extra-marital desires and fantasies is in Terman, p. 336. Kinsey's evidence is in Kinsey (1948), p. 584, and (1953), p. 431.

[p. 32]: Socio-economic differences in fantasy content are from Singer, *loc. cit.,* p. 20.

[p. 32]: The need to dream was suggested by Freud in *The Interpretation of Dreams,* and recently given clinical proof by experiments in dream deprivation: see Luce and Segal, p. 229, Dement, p. 1705, and Diamond. As for the ability of fantasy to perform somewhat the same tension-relieving function, see Singer, *loc. cit.;* he considers this one (but only one) of its important functions.

[pp. 36–37]: The sexually stimulating effect of novelty on rats is described by Bermant, and on other animals by Kinsey (1948), p. 589, and (1953), pp. 409 and 411. The assertion that the monogamous behavior of the human female is learned rather than innate is made by Kinsey (1953), p. 409, and Ford and Beach, p. 118.

[p. 41]: The division of controls over behavior into internal and external follows Ruth Benedict's classic differentiation between guilt cultures and shame cultures; see note to p. 127 below.

[pp. 41–42]: The use of mental defense mechanisms for the specific control of extra-marital desires is mentioned by many sources; see, for instance, Fried, pp. 255–257.

[p. 42]: Ellis and Harper, p. 189.

[p. 43]: People ready for an affair but unable to find anyone suitable are mentioned by Cuber and Harroff, pp. 188–189.

[p. 44]: Dr. van den Haag's comment was part of a personal communication.

[pp. 44–45]: Neubeck and Schletzer's study appeared in *Marriage and Family Living*, August, 1962, and will reappear in Neubeck (1970), q.v. Religion as a factor in the control of infidelity is from Kinsey (1953), p. 424 and Table 121, and (1948), Table 129.

[p. 45]: On the weakening of internal controls, see Kinsey (1953), pp. 298 and 427, Cuber and Harroff, chap. 10, Bell, p. 323, and Neubeck and Schletzer.

[pp. 45–46]: For the penalties exerted by the spouse through divorce, see Hunt (1966 b), chaps. 2 and 7. One of many sources referring to weakening of external controls other than the spouse is Farber, p. 118 f.

[p. 46]: On the differences in infidelity rates between large cities and small ones (or rural villages), see also Kinsey (1948), p. 456.

[pp. 47–48]: Page references for the three quotations are: Caprio, p. 7, Saul, pp. 91–92, Spotnitz and Freeman, p. 28. For further documentation of the conventional Freudian view, see Astley, Blum, Callwood, and Weisberg. Neubeck and Schletzer, and Whitehurst (1966) give numerous other examples of this view.

[pp. 49–50]: Bernard (1956), pp. 86 and 272. Other sociologists who see most of unhappy marriage and divorce as the product of normal malfunctions and not neurosis include Goode (1956), and Blood. Cuber and Harroff's comments are on pp. 62 and 117–118. . . . *Such complaints come closest to being acceptable*, etc. : see Blum, pp. 135–136 and 139.

[p. 52]: Dr. Ormont's comments were part of a personal communication.

[pp. 53–54]: Whitehurst (1966) and (1967); the quotation is from (1967), p. 7.

[p. 54]: The increase in the incidence of infidelity among middle-class men and women as they grow older is dealt with by Kinsey in (1948), Table 85 and p. 587, and (1953), Tables 114 and 115. But he found quite a different pattern for the lower-class male; see (1948), pp. 585 f.

[p. 69]: Flirtation as an end in itself is discussed by Lobsenz, Fried, pp. 281–287, and Astley, pp. 48–49.

[p. 69]: Fried, pp. 281, 283, and 285. Dr. Gebhard's remarks were part of a personal communication. See also Ellis (1967).

[p. 75]: For the cocktail lounge study, see Roebuck and Spray.

[p. 79]: For one brief report on the custom of the "conjugal vacation," see Hartman.

[p. 80]: Men and women who virtually force affairs upon their spouses are discussed by Family Service Association of Cleveland, *passim;* Weisberg, pp. 200–202; and Spotnitz and Freeman, p. 175. For a more benign view of the motives of highly permissive spouses, see Kinsey (1953), pp. 434–435. The related phenomenon of mate-swapping is portrayed by Avery and Avery, in Grunwald, ed., pp. 248–254. This and other permissive and coercive arrangements are breathlessly portrayed by Lipton, chaps. 1 to 5.

[p. 82]: The data on extra-marital petting by women are in Kinsey (1953), p. 427. While giving no data for extra-marital petting by men, he asserted that there is "an increasing tendency to accept petting as an extra-marital relationship among persons who would not think of having extra-marital intercourse": see Kinsey (1948), p. 532.

[p. 92]: On subjective reality, see McLean in Arieti, ed., pp. 1762–1763, and Hunt (1964), pp. 154–155.

[pp. 104–105]: The connection between demanding parents and low self-esteem is well-established in the clinical literature. For a popular summary, see Hunt (1966 a).

[pp. 117–118]: The relative lack of guilt or fear in mate-swappers, at least initially, is implied by both Avery and Avery, and Lipton (see note to p. 80 above). Virginia Satir, a leading family therapist and co-founder of the Esalen Institute, tells me (in a personal communication) that mate-swapping seems to be almost the only type of extra-marital involvement free from pain for the married couple.

[p. 120]: Plutarch: "Coniugalia Praecepta," *Moralia* . . . . *happier, younger, or more self-confident:* the questionnaire did not ask about self-confidence per se, but it is implicit in other answers. Noteworthy percentages of the respondents said they felt proud, happy, youthful, or carefree anywhere from sometimes to all the time, as a result of their affairs.

[p. 125]: Normal (non-neurotic) infidelity is discussed by Cuber and Harroff, pp. 62 and 117–118, Whitehurst (1966) and (1967), and Kinsey (1948), pp. 590, 592–593, and (1953), pp. 433–435.

[p. 127]: Ruth Benedict's distinction between guilt cultures and shame cultures appears throughout her book, *The Chrysanthemum and the Sword;* her comment about the change in our own society appears on pp. 223–224. The distinction has been adopted by most social scientists; see esp. Piers and Singer, *passim.*

[p. 128]: . . . *findings of behaviorist psychology:* see, for instance, Wolpe, pp. 21–31.

[p. 130]: All the symptoms of guilt named here were mentioned by my interviewees, but see also Coleman, pp. 82–113 and 353–361.

[p. 138]: See Kinsey (1948), p. 588, and (1953), pp. 419–420; Cuber and Harroff, pp. 146–171.

[p. 145]: Cuber and Harroff, p. 193, and Kinsey (1948), pp. 594–598, both stress that infidelity often has no ill effects if thoroughly concealed from the spouse and the outside world.

[p. 146]: . . . *cooperation of the deceived spouse:* in addition to the stories told me by my interviewees, this point was made by almost every psychotherapist I spoke to. . . . Bishop Pike's quote is from p. 131 of his book. . . . Dr. Ormont's comment was part of a personal communication.

[p. 148]: *A few behavioral scientists:* Virginia Satir's comments were part of a personal communication, as were Dr. van den Haag's; Cuber and Harroff, p. 181; Malinowski and various others are cited in Kinsey (1953), pp. 413–414. See also Henriques, pp. 398–400 and 430–431.

[p. 156]: . . . *most marriage counselors hold:* quite apart from the published literature and my interviews, I found this view prevalent among the answers supplied by staff members of family agencies, in response to the Family Service Association of America's questionnaire survey (see note to p. 10 above), the originals of which the Association kindly lent me.

[p. 157]: Evidence that good marriages can be improved, or at least unhurt, by infidelity is offered by Kronhausen and Kronhausen (1964 b), p. 131, and Ellis (1967); see also Kinsey (1948), p. 593, and (1953), p. 433. . . . *each providing a different but limited set of satisfactions:* the point is also made by Cuber and Harroff, pp. 169–170.

[pp. 159–160]: Miss Moffat's column appeared in April, 1966.

[p. 175]: Dr. Feldman's paper appeared in *Journal of the Hillside Hospital*, January, 1964, vol. XIII, no. 1. A number of psychoanalysts have made the same points to me in discussions.

[p. 184]: Dr. Mead's discussion is in her *Male and Female*, pp. 253 f.

[pp. 196–197]: The essential unreality of the affair of rebellion is discussed by Bergler, pp. x, 45–46, 121, and 165, and by Family Service Association of Cleveland, pp. 190–191.

[p. 214]: Tolerant, understanding, or even happy spouses also seem to be implied by Kinsey (1948), p. 592, and (1953), p. 435; see also Cuber and Harroff, pp. 62 and 159–161.

[p. 217]: On condonation, see Pilpel, pp. 280–281.

[p. 223]: The symptomatology of internal conflict is compiled from my interviews, but see also Coleman, pp. 88–108.

[p. 235]: The process of disconnection from a flawed marriage is portrayed in somewhat more detail in my own book, *The World of the Formerly Married*, pp. 34–39.

[p. 236]: The question of who first mentions the subject of divorce, and who first decided to provoke such discussions, is dealt with by Goode, pp. 135–137.

[p. 247]: On the use of conventional and ritualized ways to meet life crises, see Honigman, chaps. 30 and 31.

[p. 253]: Besides my own data on the percentage of unfaithful spouses who have only one affair, Kinsey indicates in (1953), p. 425 and Table 122, that 40 per cent of unfaithful women have had only one affair.

[p. 255]: Stone, "The Case Against Marital Infidelity," *Reader's Digest*, May, 1964.

[p. 255]: The possibility that infidelity may improve a marriage is mentioned by Kinsey (1953), p. 433 and footnote citing other sources. Many psychologists and psychoanalysts who have seen this in their own patients told me the same thing. See also, Mudd et al., p. 194. The Spotnitz and Freeman quote is on p. 210 of their book.

[p. 257]: Less than two per cent of divorce suits are based on the complaint of adultery (*Divorce Statistics Analysis*, 1963, p. 49), but statements made in private to lawyers, marriage counselors, and sociologists show that infidelity plays a part in perhaps a third of all divorces, whether as cause or symptom. See Goode, pp. 117–118 and 123, Levinger, p. 805, Havemann, p. 137, and my own book, *The World of the Formerly Married*, pp. 22–23.

[pp. 270–271]: Infidelity and divorce: see previous note.

[p. 273]: . . . *it would appear that about half work out well, while about half fail:* the statement is based on the totality of my impressions from all verbal and written sources, plus my own sample, which is in this instance very small: six cases, in three of which the marriage has failed and in three of which it has been quite successful. (Two other pairs of extra-marital lovers, having divorced their mates are now living in common-law relationships, but one cannot count them successful marriages until they have undergone the actual psychodynamic experiences of the legal connection.)

[p. 282]: Although most of what Freud says in *Civilization and Its Discontents* has to do with the control of aggression, his main points apply equally well to the erotic life.

[p. 284]: *A higher percentage of American adults are married now:* see *Statistical Abstract*, 1968, p. 32.

[p. 285]: On redirection of the extra-marital urge toward one's mate, see Fried, pp. 283–287.

[p. 286]: The relative psychological homogeneity of people in smaller societies, especially with clanlike family arrangements, is attested by Kardiner, in chap. XIII.

[pp. 287–288]: *We hear every day:* for statements that marriage is obsolete, see Cadwalladar, Lear; on the five-year renewable marriage contract, Satir; on the two kinds of marriage, Margaret Mead, speaking at San Francisco State College in February, 1967; on the coming toleration of infidelity, Lipton, Satir; and on the future free expression of man's polymorphously perverse desires, Norman O. Brown.

[p. 288]: Russell, *Marriage and Morals;* Ellis (1966) and (1967). . . . *few have tried it, and very few of those have succeeded:* such is the impression I get from all sources consulted. My own book, *The Natural History of Love,* discusses this for the 1920s to 1940s; a study by Beltz of the failure of mate-swapping is worth looking at; Karlen gives some up-to-date estimates; and even Lipton, an advocate of sexual revolution, admits that many of the experiments work out badly. Dr. Paul Gebhard, director of the Institute for Sex Research, told me much the same thing in a personal communication.

[pp. 288–289]: Recent studies of student sexual behavior are by Reiss, Simon and Gagnon (1969), and one still unpublished by Dr. Joseph Katz of the Institute for the Study of Human Problems at Stanford University. For a popular summary, see Rosenfeld. Dr. William Masters and Virginia Johnson, informally gathering impressions on their extensive speaking tours, are in agreement. See also Karlen.

bibliography

ADAMS, IAN. "The Affair," *Maclean's,* April 1967.

AMERICAN ASSOCIATION OF MARRIAGE COUNSELORS. *See* Mudd, Emily, et al., eds.

ARIETI, SILVANO, ed. *American Handbook of Psychiatry.* New York: Basic Books, Inc., 1959.

ASTLEY, M. ROYDEN C. "Fidelity and Infidelity in Marriage," *Pastoral Psychology,* Jan. 1959. Also in Mudd and Krich, eds., q.v.

AVERY, PAUL, AND EMILY AVERY. "Some Notes on 'Wife Swapping'," in Grunwald, ed., q.v.

BABER, RAY E. *Marriage and the Family.* New York: McGraw-Hill Book Company, Inc., 1953.

BARUCH, DOROTHY. *Sex in Marriage: New Understandings.* New York: Harper & Row, 1962.

BARZINI (1965), LUIGI. *The Italians.* New York: Atheneum Publishers, 1965.

BARZINI (1968), LUIGI. "Divorce in Italy? Mamma Mia!" *The New York Times Magazine,* March 17, 1968.

BECK, DOROTHY FAHS. "Marital Conflict: Its Course and Treatment as Seen by Caseworkers," *Social Casework*, April 1966.

BECK, DOROTHY FAHS, AND ROBERT W. ROBERTS. "Marital Applicants and the Problems They Bring." Interim mimeographed report prepared by Family Service Association of America, New York, in connection with Public Health Service Grant MH-602 from the National Institute of Mental Health.

BELL, ROBERT R. *Marriage and Family Interaction.* Homewood, Ill.: The Dorsey Press, Inc., 1963.

BELTZ, STEPHEN E. "Five Couples," in Neubeck (1970), ed., q.v.

BENEDICT, RUTH. *The Chrysanthemum and the Sword.* Boston: Houghton-Mifflin Co., 1946.

BERGLER, EDMUND. *Unhappy Marriage and Divorce.* New York: International Universities Press, 1946.

BERMANT, GORDON. "Copulation in Rats," *Psychology Today,* July 1967.

BERNARD (1956), JESSIE. *Remarriage: A Study of Marriage.* New York: The Dryden Press, 1956.

BERNARD (1966), JESSIE. "The Fourth Revolution," *Journal of Social Issues,* April 1966.

BLOOD, ROBERT O. *Husbands and Wives: The Dynamics of Married Living.* Glencoe, Ill.: The Free Press, 1960.

BLUM, SAM. "When Can Adultery Be Justified or Forgiven?" *McCall's,* May 1966.

BOSSARD, JAMES, AND ELEANOR BALL. "Marital Unhappiness in the Life Cycle," *Marriage and Family Living,* 1955, vol. 17, pp. 10–14.

BROWN, NORMAN O. *Life Against Death.* New York: Random House, n.d. (orig. ed. 1959).

BURGESS, ERNEST W., AND HARVEY J. LOCKE. *The Family.* New York: American Book Co., 1953.

CADWALLADAR, MERVYN. "Marriage as a Wretched Institution," *The Atlantic Monthly,* Nov. 1966.

CALLWOOD, JUNE. "Infidelity: A Growing Problem in American Marriages," *Ladies Home Journal,* April 1965.

CAPRIO, FRANK SAMUEL. *Marital Infidelity.* New York: Citadel Press, 1953.

CAVAN, RUTH S. *The American Family.* New York: T. Y. Crowell Co., 1955.

CHRISTENSEN, HAROLD. "A Cross-Cultural Comparison of Attitudes Toward Marital Infidelity," *International Journal of Comparative Sociology,* Sept. 1962 (vol. 3, no. 1).

COLEMAN, JAMES C. *Abnormal Psychology and Modern Life.* Scott, Foresman & Co., 1964.

COMFORT, A. *Sexual Behavior in Society.* New York: Viking Press, 1950.

CUBER, JOHN F. "Adultery: Reality versus Stereotype," in Neubeck (1970), ed., q.v.

CUBER, JOHN F., AND PEGGY B. HARROFF. *The Significant Americans*. New York: Appleton-Century, 1965.

DEARBORN, LESTER W. "Extramarital Relations," in Morris Fishbein and Ernest W. Burgess, *Successful Marriage*. Garden City, N. Y.: Doubleday & Co., Inc., 1947.

DEMENT, WILLIAM. "Effects of Dream Deprivation," *Science*, June 10, 1960.

DE POITIERS, DIANE [pseud.]. "I'm Almost Ready for an Affair," *McCall's*, Feb. 1962.

DIAMOND, EDWIN. " 'The Interpretation of Dreams' Continued," *The New York Times Magazine*, Feb. 12, 1967.

DUVALL, SYLVANUS M. *Men, Women, and Morals*. New York: Association Press, 1952.

ELLIS (1965), ALBERT. *Sex Without Guilt*. New York: Grove Press, 1965.

ELLIS (1966), ALBERT. *If This Be Sexual Heresy*. New York: Tower Publications, 1966.

ELLIS (1970), ALBERT. "Extramarital Relations in Modern Society," in Neubeck (1970), ed., q.v.

ELLIS, ALBERT, AND ALBERT ABARBANEL. *The Encyclopedia of Sexual Behavior*. New York: Hawthorne, 1961.

ELLIS, ALBERT, AND ROBERT HARPER. *Creative Marriage*. New York: Lyle Stuart, Inc., 1961.

ELLIS, HAVELOCK. (Gawsworth, J., ed.). *Sex and Marriage*. New York: Random House, 1952.

ERSKINE, H. G. "The Polls: Morality," *Public Opinion Quarterly*, vol. XXX, 1966.

FAMILY SERVICE ASSOCIATION OF CLEVELAND (1962). "Infidelity in Woman as a Manifestation of a Character Disorder," *Smith College Studies in Social Work*, June 1962.

FAMILY SERVICE ASSOCIATION OF CLEVELAND (1963). "A Study of Husbands Whose Wives Are Unfaithful," mimeographed, delivered at the Jackson Memorial Institute of 1963.

FARBER, SEYMOUR M., et al., eds. *Man and Civilization: The Family's Search for Survival*. New York: McGraw-Hill Book Company, Inc., 1965.

FELDMAN, SANDOR. "The Attraction of 'The Other Woman,' " *Journal of the Hillside Hospital*, vol. XIII, no. 1, Jan. 1964.

FORD, CLELLAN S., AND FRANK A. BEACH. *Patterns of Sexual Behavior*. New York: Harper & Brothers, 1951.

FOREGGER, RICHARD. "The Love Triangle in Marriage and Divorce," *Mental Hygiene*, April 1966.

FREUD (1930), SIGMUND. *Civilization and Its Discontents.* New York: W. W. Norton & Co., Inc., 1962 (orig. ed. 1930).

FREUD (1938), SIGMUND. *The Interpretation of Dreams,* in *The Basic Writings of Sigmund Freud,* A. A. Brill, ed. New York: The Modern Library, 1938.

FRIED, EDRITA. *On Love and Sexuality* (originally published as *The Ego in Love and Sexuality*). New York: Grove Press, 1966.

FROMME, A. *The Psychologist Looks at Sex and Marriage.* New York: Prentice-Hall, Inc., 1950.

FROSCHER, WINGATE, AND HAZEL B. FROSCHER. "The Dynamics and Treatment of Sexual Problems," mimeographed report prepared in connection with Public Health Service Grant MH-602 from the National Institute of Mental Health.

GOODE (1956), WILLIAM J. *After Divorce.* Glencoe, Ill.: The Free Press, 1956.

GOODE (1961), WILLIAM J. "Family Disorganization," in Robert K. Merton and Robert A. Nisbet, eds., *Contemporary Social Problems.* New York: Harcourt, Brace & World, Inc., 1961.

GORDON, RICHARD E., KATHERINE K. GORDON, AND MAX GUNTHER. *The Split-Level Trap.* New York: Bernard Geis Associates, 1960, 1961.

GRUNWALD, H. A., ed. *Sex in America.* New York: Bantam Books, 1964.

GUYON, RENE *Sexual Freedom.* New York: Alfred A. Knopf, 1950.

HAIRE, NORMAN. *Everyday Sex Problems.* London: Frederick Muller, 1948.

HARPER, ROBERT A. "Extramarital Sex Relations," in Ellis and Abarbanel, q.v.

HARTMAN, FERRIS. "A 'Divorce' for the Summer," *San Francisco Chronicle,* July 18, 1965.

HAVEMANN, ERNEST. *Men, Women & Marriage.* Garden City, N. Y.: Doubleday & Co., Inc., 1962.

HEFNER, HUGH M. "The Playboy Philosophy, Part III." Chicago: HMH Publishing Co., 1963, 1964.

HENRIQUES, FERNANDO. *Love in Action: The Sociology of Sex.* New York: Dell Publishing Co., Inc., 1962.

HONIGMAN, JOHN J. *The World of Man.* New York: Harper & Row, 1959.

HUNT (1957), MORTON M. "Why Husbands Stay Faithful," *Redbook,* Aug. 1957.

HUNT (1959), MORTON M. *The Natural History of Love.* New York: Alfred A. Knopf, 1959.

HUNT (1962), MORTON M. *Her Infinite Variety.* New York: Harper & Row, 1962.

HUNT (1964), MORTON M. "Does Psychotherapy Really Work?" in Hunt, Morton M., *The Thinking Animal.* Boston: Little, Brown and Company, 1964. (Orig. publ. in *The New York Times Magazine*, Nov. 11, 1962.)

HUNT (1966 a), MORTON M. "Do You Underrate Yourself?" *Family Circle*, May 1966.

HUNT (1966 b), MORTON M. *The World of the Formerly Married.* New York: McGraw-Hill Book Company, Inc., 1966.

INGE, W. R. *Christian Ethics and Modern Problems.* New York: G. P. Putnam's Sons, 1930.

KARDINER, ABRAM. *The Psychological Frontiers of Society.* New York: Columbia University Press, 1945.

KARLEN, ARNO. "The Sexual Revolution Is a Myth," *The Saturday Evening Post,* Dec. 28, 1968–Jan. 11, 1969.

KINSEY (1948), ALFRED C., WARDELL B. POMEROY, AND CLYDE E. MARTIN. *Sexual Behavior in the Human Male.* Philadelphia: W. B. Saunders Company, 1948.

KINSEY (1953), ALFRED C., WARDELL B. POMEROY, CLYDE E. MARTIN, AND PAUL H. GEBHARD. *Sexual Behavior in the Human Female.* Philadelphia: W. B. Saunders Company, 1953.

KIRKPATRICK, CLIFFORD. *The Family as Process and Institution.* New York: The Ronald Press Company, 1955.

KNAKAL, JEANNE. "The Impact of Our Changing Sex Mores on the American Family," mimeographed, delivered at the Family Service Association of America Biennial, San Francisco, Nov. 1963.

KOMAROVSKY, MIRRA. *Blue-Collar Marriage.* New York: Random House, 1964.

KRONHAUSEN (1964 a), EBERHARD W., AND PHYLLIS C. KRONHAUSEN. "A Study of Wife-Swapping in California," *Fact,* May–June 1964.

KRONHAUSEN (1964 b), EBERHARD W., AND PHYLLIS C. KRONHAUSEN. *The Sexually Responsive Woman.* New York: Grove Press, 1964.

LEAR, MARTHA W. "The Second Feminist Wave," *The New York Times Magazine,* March 10, 1968.

LE MASTERS, E. E. *The Blue Collar Aristocracy, A Study of Tavern Life* (work in progress).

LERNER, MAX. *America as a Civilization.* New York: Simon and Schuster, 1957.

LEVINGER, GEORGE. "Sources of Marital Dissatisfaction Among Applicants for Divorce," *American Journal of Orthopsychiatry,* 1966, pp. 803–807.

LINDNER, ROBERT. "Adultery: Kinds and Consequences," in Ellis, Albert, ed., *Sex Life of the American Woman and the Kinsey Report.* New York: Greenberg, 1954.

LIPTON, LAWRENCE. *The Erotic Revolution.* New York: Pocket Books, 1966.

LOBSENZ, NORMAN M. "The Innocent Game That Disrupts Marriage," *Redbook,* April 1967.

LUCE, GAY GAER, AND JULIUS SEGAL. *Sleep.* New York: Coward-McCann, Inc., 1966.

MACE, DAVID. *Success in Marriage.* New York: Abingdon Press, 1958.

MASTERS, WILLIAM H., AND VIRGINIA E. JOHNSON. *Human Sexual Response.* Boston: Little, Brown and Company, 1966.

MAY, ROBERT. "Fantasy Differences in Men and Women," *Psychology Today,* April 1968.

MCLEAN, PRESTON G., "Psychiatry and Philosophy," in Arieti, ed., q.v.

MEAD (1955), MARGARET. *Male and Female.* New York: New American Library, 1955.

MEAD (1967), MARGARET. "Sexual Freedom and Cultural Change," paper delivered at forum, "The Pill and the Puritan Ethic," San Francisco State College, Feb. 10, 1967.

MORGAN, CLIFFORD T., AND RICHARD A. KING. *Introduction to Psychology* (3rd ed). New York: McGraw-Hill Book Company, Inc., 1966.

MORISON, ROBERT S. "Where Is Biology Taking Us?" *Science,* Jan. 27, 1967.

MUDD, EMILY, AND ARON KRICH, eds. *Man and Wife.* New York: W. W. Norton & Co., Inc., 1957.

MUDD, EMILY, et al., eds. *Marriage Counseling: A Casebook.* New York: Association Press, 1958.

MURDOCK, GEORGE PETER. "The Social Regulation of Sexual Behavior," in Paul H. Hoch and Joseph Zubin, *Psychosexual Development in Health and Disease.* New York: Grune & Stratton, 1949.

NEUBECK, GERHARD. "The Dimensions of the 'Extra' in Extramarital Relations," in Neubeck (1970), ed., q.v.

NEUBECK (1970), GERHARD, ed. *The Extramarital Sexual Relations.* (To be published in 1970 by Prentice-Hall, Inc., Englewood Cliffs, N. J.)

NEUBECK, GERHARD, AND VERA SCHLETZER. "A Study of Extramarital Relationships," in Neubeck (1970), ed., q.v.

NEUMANN, H. "Marriage and Morals," *Journal of Social Hygiene,* vol. 22, 1936.

OHLSON, WINFIELD E. "Adultery: A Review," *Boston University Law Review,* April and June 1937.

PACKARD, VANCE. *The Sexual Wilderness.* New York: David McKay Co., Inc., 1968.

PIERS, GERHART, AND M. B. SINGER. *Shame and Guilt.* Springfield, Ill.: C. C. Thomas, 1953.

PIKE, JAMES A. *You and the New Morality.* New York: Harper & Row, 1967.

PILPEL, HARRIET F., AND THEODORA ZAVIN. *Your Marriage and the Law.* New York: Collier Books, 1964.

Playboy "FORUM" (letters to editor): continuing series on extra-marital experience: July, Oct., Nov., 1967; Jan., Feb., Mar., May, July, Aug., Oct., Dec., 1968; Jan., 1969.

PLUTARCH. "Coniugalia Praecepta," *Moralia.*

RAINWATER, LEE. *Family Design.* Chicago: Aldine Publishing Co., 1965.

REISS, IRA L. *The Social Context of Premarital Permissiveness.* New York: Holt, Rinehart and Winston, Inc., 1967.

RIEMER, GEORGE. "A Frank Look at Marital Fidelity," *Good Housekeeping*, Jan. 1964.

ROEBUCK, JULIAN, AND S. LEE SPRAY. "The Cocktail Lounge: A Study of Heterosexual Relations in a Public Organization," *American Journal of Sociology*, Jan. 1967.

ROSENFELD, ALBERT. "Student Sexuality," *Life*, May 31, 1968.

RUSSELL, BERTRAND. *Marriage and Morals.* New York: Bantam Books, 1959 (orig. ed., 1929).

RUSSELL, BERTRAND, et al. *Divorce.* New York: John Day, 1930.

RYDER, ROBERT G. "Compatibility in Marriage," mimeographed, unpublished, National Institute of Mental Health, n.d.

SAFILIOS-ROTHSCHILD, CONSTANTINA. "Spousal Attitudes Towards Marital Infidelity," in Neubeck (1970), ed., q.v.

SATIR, VIRGINIA. "Marriage as a Statutory Five-Year Renewable Contract," mimeographed, delivered at the Amer. Psychol. Assoc. convention, Sept. 1, 1967, Washington, D.C.

SAUL, LEON J. *Fidelity and Infidelity.* Philadelphia: J. B. Lippincott Company, 1967.

SCHUSTER, M. LINCOLN, ed. *A Treasury of the World's Great Letters.* New York: Simon and Schuster, 1940.

SCOTT, LAEL. "Marriage on the Rocks," *New York Post*, June 26-30, 1967.

SHEEHY, GAIL. "Love-sounds of a Wife," *New York* (magazine of the *New York World-Journal-Tribune*), Nov. 20, 1966.

SIMON (1967), WILLIAM, AND JOHN H. GAGNON. "Pornography: The Social Sources of Sexual Scripts," mimeographed, delivered at Aug. 1967 meeting of the Society for the Study of Social Problems.

SIMON (1969), WILLIAM, AND JOHN H. GAGNON. *The End of Adolescence: The College Experience.* New York: Harper & Row, 1969.

SINGER, JEROME. "The Importance of Daydreaming," *Psychology Today*, April 1968.

SOCARIDES, CHARLES W. "On Vengeance: The Desire to 'Get Even,'"

Journal of the American Psychoanalytic Assoc., vol. 14, no. 2, April 1966.

SPOTNITZ, HYMAN, AND LUCY FREEMAN. *The Wandering Husband.* Englewood Cliffs, N. J.: Prentice-Hall, Inc., 1964.

Statistical Abstract, see United States Bureau of the Census.

STONE, ABRAHAM. "The Case Against Marital Infidelity," *Reader's Digest,* May 1954.

TARLOFF, FRANK. *A Guide for the Married Man.* Los Angeles: Price, Stern, Sloan, 1967.

TASHMAN, HARRY. *The Marriage Bed: An Analyst's Casebook.* New York: University Publishers, Inc., 1959.

TERMAN, LEWIS M. *Psychological Factors in Marital Happiness.* New York: McGraw-Hill Book Company, Inc., 1938.

Time. "Is Adultery Forgiveable?" Dec. 27, 1954.

TRACY, THOMAS H. *The Seventh Commandment: 13 Cases of Divorce and Adultery.* London, New York: Abelard-Schuman, 1963.

TRIMBOS, C. J. *Healthy Attitudes Towards Love and Sex.* New York: P. J. Kenedy & Sons, 1964.

UNITED STATES BUREAU OF THE CENSUS. *Statistical Abstract of the United States.* 1968.

VAN BUREN, ABBY. "When Your Husband Is Unfaithful," *McCall's,* Jan. 1963.

VAN DEN HAAG, ERNEST. "Love or Marriage?" *Harper's,* May 1962.

WEISBERG, MIRIAM. "Discussion: Role of the Spouse in Infidelity," *Smith College Studies in Social Work,* June 1962.

WHITEHURST (1966), ROBERT N. "Adultery as an Extension of Normal Behavior," delivered at 1966 meeting of National Council on Family Relations; also in Neubeck (1970), ed., q.v.

WHITEHURST (1967), ROBERT N. "Extra-Marital Sex, Alienation, and Marriage," mimeographed, delivered at Sept. 1967 meeting of the Amer. Psychol. Assoc., Washington, D.C.

WINCH, ROBERT. *The Modern Family.* New York: Holt, Rinehart and Winston, Inc., 1963.

WISE, BILL. "Coup de Grace for Honorable Homicide," *Life,* Oct. 14, 1966.

WOLPE, JOSEPH. *Psychotherapy by Reciprocal Inhibition.* Stanford, Calif.: Stanford University Press, 1958.

acknowledgments

A great many people deserve my thanks for their help in making this book possible. Unfortunately, those to whom I owe the most are the very ones I may not name here; they include 360 men and women who filled out and returned my questionnaires, 91 others who submitted to lengthy face-to-face interviews, and about a score of intermediaries who helped arrange for the interviews. I deeply regret that I may not publicly acknowledge my debt to them by name, but each of them knows the degree of my indebtedness and hence of my gratitude.

The technical expertise of Dr. Frank Furstenberg and of Dr. William J. Bowers and the staff of the Russell B. Stearns Study enabled me to obtain more and far better information from my questionnaire than I would have elicited on my own. Lenore Weitzman gave me valuable assistance with data preparation and, as a sociologist, offered technical comments about the manuscript. Dr.

Louis R. Ormont made a great many valuable comments about the manuscript from the viewpoint of a psychologist and psychoanalyst.

Among the organizations that provided me with information or helped me in other ways were the Family Service Association of America and about half a dozen of its member agencies in various cities, the Institute for Sex Research at Indiana University, the Minnesota Family Study Center of the University of Minnesota, the National Institute of Mental Health, half a dozen far-flung chapters of Parents Without Partners, and the Reproductive Biology Research Foundation of St. Louis.

Among the individuals who gave me valuable information were Dr. Stephen E. Beltz, Dr. Harold T. Christensen, Dr. John F. Cuber and Mrs. Cuber (Peggy B. Harroff), Dr. Edrita Fried, Dr. Paul Gebhard, Mrs. Virginia Johnson, Miss Jeanne Knakal, Mr. E. E. LeMasters, Dr. Abe Levitsky, Mrs. Shirley Gehrke Luthman, Dr. William H. Masters, Dr. Gerhard Neubeck, Mrs. Virginia Satir, Mr. Nicholas Suntzeff, Dr. Ernest van den Haag, Dr. Benjamin Weininger, Dr. Robert N. Whitehurst, the Rev. James P. Wilkes, and the Rev. Allan Zacher.

Robert Lescher has, again, been literary agent, painstaking critic, and long-suffering friend. My wife, Eveline, cheerfully relieved me of the burden of compiling the Bibliography. As always, Violet Serwin was the only typist to whom I would entrust my manuscript.

index

about the author

Morton Hunt was born in Philadelphia in 1920. He graduated from Temple University with honors and won a fellowship to the University of Pennsylvania, but his graduate studies in English literature were broken off by wartime military service. He spent four years in the U.S. Army Air Force, the latter two of them as a combat pilot in Europe.

After the war, Mr. Hunt was briefly a staff member of *Look* and later of *Science Illustrated*. Since 1949 he has been a free-lance writer, dealing most often with the behavioral sciences, and particularly with the psychology of love, sex, and marriage. Over two hundred articles by Mr. Hunt have appeared in major national magazines, and since 1959 he has published eight books, including *The Natural History of Love, Her Infinite Variety,* and *The World of the Formerly Married*. Mr. Hunt is married, has a son and a stepdaughter, and makes his home in New York and in Amagansett, Long Island.